DOWN THE ROAD

Nonda Chatterjee

First published in India in 2016 by:
Choitali Chatterjee

Copyright © 2016 Choitali Chatterjee

Print Book ISBN: 9789384439774

Typeset by Ram Das Lal, New Delhi (NCR)

Publishing facilitation: AuthorsUpFront

Cover design and illustration: Damini Sayeed
Cover layout: Neena Gupta

To Choi, my second born.
For so many reasons.

Introduction

My mother, Nonda Chatterjee, died shortly after completing her last novel, *Down the Road*. While writing the introduction, I was tempted to turn it into a eulogy, but Chatterjee's last novel, her finest and the most complex one in her oeuvre deserves more, much more than my inadequate pen can provide. In this deeply layered masterpiece, featuring a series of fine-grained psychological portraits, Chatterjee turns to her own past as a living historical source. Down the road of her own memories, she unearths a little known chapter from the history of Indian independence and reprises a new cast of characters. While framing the novel as a mystery about a prosperous joint family in the city of Allahabad, Chatterjee presents an unforgettable portrait about a class that fell silent after 1947. She writes with sensitivity and personal knowledge about an anglicized and anglophone class that had prospered greatly under British rule, but whose members became ambivalent about their imperial associations in independent India. Due to their reticence we know little about this transitional generation that came of age after 1947: of their hopes, anxieties and fears.

In *Down the Road* Chatterjee uncovers the complex cultural identities that grew out of the epic collision of the Indian sub-continent with that of imperial Europe. It would have been easy to satirize these personalities, to turn them into caricatures or stereotypes, as they remain

relatively unknown in contemporary India. Instead,
Chatterjee uses conversations and musings to untangle the
many skeins that fed the imagination of this generation.
We have very limited sources from this era as few wrote
about themselves, hesitant in an intellectual space that was
dominated by the discourses of nationalism, discussions
about what constituted an authentic Indian identity, and
postcolonial angst about modernization, gender, caste and
class. They spoke in coded languages within the tight circles
of the cognoscenti, and as a result the experiences of this
generation have been little represented in Indian history,
art, literature, or film. Perhaps they lacked the appropriate
languages of communication, or perhaps they felt a measure
of guilt about having prospered in the colonial era that
impoverished so many. Did they regret speaking English
with an idiomatic fluency and near native precision in the
Indian Tower of Babel? Did they simply lack the clarity
of vision necessary to evaluate their personal experiences
in historical perspective? I believe that my mother had
a premonition that her own end was near, and that it
prompted her to re-visit her childhood and youth with the
eyes of wisdom, and the critical distance of age. But I will
never know with certainty.

Nonda Chatterjee was born on 15 May 1938 in
Calcutta, at the house of her grandfather, B. C. Chatterjee,
the famous barrister at law who had successfully defended
the Bhawal Sanyasi case. An ardent nationalist and an
important member of the Hindu Mahasabha, B.C.
Chatterjee lived close to his British counterparts at 19,
Ballygunge Circular Road, and from all accounts, he
maintained a lavish and anglophile estate. Chatterjee's
great-grandfather, Surendranath Bannerjee, founding

member of the Indian National Congress, even as he fought tooth and nail against the British occupation of India, could write without any trace of irony, 'Our minds were steeped in the literature of the West. Our souls have been stirred by the great models of public virtue which the pages of English history so freely present.'[1] Chatterjee's legacy from her father's side was equally complex. While many members of her father's family served the British administration with distinction, some of her uncles were drawn to the more militant varieties of nationalism. Her paternal grandfather, Chief Justice of the Allahabad High Court, Sir Lal Gopal Mukherji, was knighted for his exemplary jurisprudence. And her father, Kalyan Kumar Mukherji, after graduating from London University, started his career as an officer in the British Indian Railway service.

While Chatterjee's summers were spent in her ancestral home in Allahabad, she also had the opportunity to travel as her father held many posts in the Indian Railway offices across northern and central India, before settling in Calcutta. She witnessed the terrible poverty of rural India as well as the opulence of the British and then Indian administrative residences in the Civil Lines of Indian cities. Chatterjee grew up in an anglophile household with her convent school educated mother, Boruna Chatterjee, and her father, who tempered his nationalism with a deep love for western literature, art, and history. Chatterjee's early education was at home where her father, a secular and imaginative educationist, taught her both Bengali and English. She was encouraged to read the Ramayana, the

---

1 *Speeches by Babu Surendranath Bannerjea, 1876-80*, vol. 6 (Calcutta: S. K. Lahiri and Co., 1908), 313

Mahabharata, the Bible and the Koran and ponder the
similarities and distinctions of various religious and literary
traditions. Kalyan Kumar was a man who was very much at
home in the world, and he imparted to Chatterjee a large
measure of his generous cosmopolitanism. He introduced
Chatterjee to the pleasures of late nineteenth century
Bengali literature as well as Victorian prose and poetry.
Chatterjee's intellectual world encompassed Milton and
Bankim Chandra Chatterjee, Browning and Tagore. At the
age of ten, Chatterjee began her formal education at St.
Mary's Convent, Allahabad. She graduated from Allahabad
University where she studied History and Economics. As
a college student, Chatterjee learnt to speak a chaste and
mellifluous Hindi, and she read the works of Munshi
Premchand, along with other notable North Indian writers.

I provide this digression about Chatterjee's early life
to provide a context for the central tension in the novel
between the Old Judge – ruthless, opportunistic and
materialistic, who won a great measure of success under the
British Raj – and his nationalist wife, who tried to instill
in their anglicized children a love of Indian languages,
landscapes, and culture. The progeny, Ronnie, Bobby,
Tony, Madonna and Small struggled to define themselves
against an overpowering father who used them shamelessly
to promote his own interests, and an equally overpowering
mother who ruthlessly decreed that the children find their
self-worth in self-denial, asceticism and selfless service for
the greater good. Chatterjee explores the fundamentalism
of both materialism and spirituality.

As the story unravels, each member of the family, including
a finely drawn cast of servitors, Lena and Robin, comes to
the realization that they had played an important part in the

family drama that was directed by the Judge. The Judge drew from both Machiavelli and the Kautilya in his understanding of the concept of power and wielded it with precision. He relied on the time-tested methods of fear, coercion, bribery, violence, and sowing discord among family members to preserve his omnipotence. The Judge's wife tried to offset her husband's terrible acts of selfishness with her epic acts of kindness, but she was reduced to the role of a wounded and silenced spectator. At the end of her life she begged her children to preserve the family peace at all costs even if it included whitewashing the reputation of the Judge.

The Judge's daughter, Madonna, inherited many of her father's proclivities and suffered the most from his arbitrary decisions. Like her father, she too desired to manipulate people in order to achieve her own ends. But Madonna's motivations were more complex than that of the Judge, who only desired power, money and sex. Chatterjee remarked several times while writing this book, 'poor, poor, Madonna.' All Madonna wanted was love and respect, to be the center of the family attention, to be praised by all and sundry for her many gifts, and admired for her undeniable beauty. As the novel progresses, Madonna's egotism grows immeasurably, and her self-absorption takes on tragic proportions. Her inability to see the world from the point of view of anybody else but herself, and her complete lack of imagination makes Madonna commit terrible acts against those she called her own. But to Madonna's great confusion, none of her well-planned actions ever results in the desired outcomes. At the end of the novel Madonna remains alone, cast on the stage of her own creation, but without the spotlight and the tumultuous applause that she so passionately believes is her due.

Leila, the strong sunlight to Madonna's world of shadows, proves to be equally inept and unimaginative in her understanding of human nature and family politics. Where Madonna aspires to rule by subtle insinuation and carefully planned attacks, Leila imagines that people will love her because she is unselfish, devoted to the family, and because she places the welfare of others above the demands of her own soul. Leila is disabused of her false assumptions at the end of the novel when she realizes that the conscious path of goodness and morality brings even fewer rewards than Madonna's more selfish path. Chatterjee shows that the path of righteous virtue is as egotistical a journey as the one in which we crave material rewards and success as compensation for our actions. The road of life is all that we can call our own, but we continue to believe, mistakenly in Chatterjee's opinion, that it is the destination that will bring us joy and happiness.

As the story unfolds, Chatterjee makes it abundantly clear that she believes neither in predestination nor in the undiluted categories of good and evil. We are the sum total of our many unique qualities, but we do exercise free will in selecting those that we choose to nurture, and those that we allow to wither on the vine. Chatterjee repudiates a theistic idea of religion and refuses to countenance a world where all our actions are pre-ordained by an omnipotent God. Instead, she suggests that we are the architects of our own destiny, and we determine the texture of our life by our every action, every thought, every feeling, and every prayer. We are the aggregate of our attitudes, our moral preferences, our proclivities, and our actions. But our actions are constantly mediated by contingency, interventions both human and natural, circumstances, and finally, by our own choices. Drawing on her interpretations of the Bhagavad Gita, Chatterjee offers a fine analysis of Karma Yoga, a path that she deems to be more important than that of knowledge (Jnana Yoga), or selfless devotion (Bhakti Yoga). As one of her characters says, 'Have you ever thought… that we create the road down which we travel every moment of our lives? Every action, every word, and every resolve builds constantly, brick by brick, to lay out the path we have to move on, yet certain choices are made almost without volition, against our better judgment and we are stuck with the consequences whether we like it or not? How formative a part does conscious will actually play in our lives?'

I invite you, dear reader, to start your own introspective journey as you open your copy of *Down the Road.*

Choi Chatterjee
Los Angeles, 2016

Down the Road

I too have been in arcadia
Where the land is paved with gold,
The trees bejeweled;
I too have walked with kings,
Shared a cup of nectar sweet at a road-side inn,
Dreamed their dreams
And again made and walked the road;
Only,
I did not know it was a dream
That would scatter into a thousand splinters,
When the serpent within
Reared its head…

Nonda Chatterjee, 2012

Cast of Characters

The Judge

Mother, his wife

Madonna and Small, his daughters

Bobby, Ronnie and Tony, his sons

Millie, Bobby's wife

Leila, Ronnie's wife

Rose, Tony's wife

Sunny, Madonna's husband

Dave, first cousin to Bobby and his siblings

Timmy and Sammy, Millie and Bobby's sons

Roma and Sheila, Ronnie and Leila's daughters

Two little girls, Tony and Rose's daughters

Josh and Bunny, Sunny's brother and his wife

Joy, Josh's son, adopted by Sunny and Madonna

Rob, Josh and Bunny's second son

'Old Man', Sunny and Josh's father, lawyer, politician and public figure

Mr. Wilson, Police Commissioner

Winnie Wilson, the Commissioner's wife

Willy, Timmy's friend

The Soothsayer

Robin, gateman

Gulab, gardener

Lena, Nanny to Madonna, Small and Tony, Robin's wife

Mukul, Madonna's friend

Justice Mehta, Presiding Judge

Mr. Purohit, Defense Lawyer

Mr. Narang, Public Prosecutor

Mr. Sen, family solicitor

Small's Friend

1. Ordeal of Innocence

SHEILA-SPEAK

Sitting on an old tree-stump, I, Sheila, looked down the sun-lit road, glad of the broad-brimmed straw hat that Lena had thrust into my hand as I was leaving the house, for it kept out some of the glare of the pitiless, end-of-May, three o'clock sun that beat down with magnificent disregard on plant, man and beast alike. But the trees that lined the road – the Gul Mohar, its dark branches unburdened with leaves but flaunting masses of golden-orange blossoms, the Indian Laburnum with its long strands of yellow flowers as bright as the sun-light it reflected, the Silk Cotton, its naked, twisted branches sprouting innumerable scarlet cups of pure blood – seemed to absorb the heat and throw it back in an orgy of color, passion and abandonment. How? Did pain and suffering alone elicit this kind of ecstasy? In that case, why had it brought only pallor and denial to Mamma? The road meandered away, past the old bungalows and mansions, past the field of the dancing, swaying Jhunjhunia, plants with prolific pods of tiny seeds that sounded a serenade of fairy bells in the breeze, past the muddy pond in which the black buffaloes had taken shelter from the sun, into the mysterious grove full of whispers and shadows. Hyenas snoozed there in the day but came out to forage at night and we could hear them laughing as they walked down the road and very soon after that, the yelp of a street dog they had caught unawares. Dog was their favorite food.

School was closed for the summer holidays. The men, India's new empire builders, were away at work, the boys still at summer-camp, and my sister who was away at summer school would only come home three weeks later. Most of the women were asleep in their darkened, fragrant, khus cooler conditioned rooms; my Aunt Millie in her studio, totally absorbed in the scene unraveling beneath the strokes of her brush, a demonic figure twisted into a gnarled tree, lurking in unholy glee for the unwary traveler. Everything as usual, except my mother, my beautiful, wonderful Mamma, once to us all the very picture of joy, goodness and virtue, the very foundation of our lives, now lay in her room, rigid and dry-eyed, catatonic, wanting nothing and no one but her own mother, knotted, completely out of tune. Only Small was wide awake, wandering around like a wraith keeping watch, observing endlessly as she had done ever since Mamma fell sick. Suddenly the claustrophobia had got to me and I had stumbled out of the house into the blinding sun, run a hundred yards, till I had arrived at the gate hot and sweating, but able to breathe again. Then I walked along the boundary hedge, came to the gap that refused to close and planted myself on my favorite perch on the old tree stump. I could see the road and the entrance to our house, but remained unseen myself.

If I turned my head in a hundred and eighty degree arc I could see our house, the only home I had ever known. Built in the colonial style, it was a very large bungalow, single storied, sprawling, spacious, boasting twenty-four rooms, a huge courtyard at the back where there was an additional eight rooms in a row: two kitchens, store-rooms, coal and fire-wood cellars, 'a utensil room' crammed with brass and copper utensils, a common room for servants and a room dedicated to Maharaj, who was the head of the domestic staff in our grandmother's department. A fastidious Brahmin and an imaginative cook, Maharaj had been her special servitor ever since he came into the household as a sixteen-year-old novice. Now an expert, he ran the kitchen and larder with an iron hand; he still managed breakfast, lunch and tea-time snacks with his own helpers, and allowed no interlopers! The second cook, not a Brahmin, but a very competent khansamah and an expert at Mughlai and western cuisine, a fine pastry cook, handled all social events, banquets, garden and tennis parties and the family evening meal with the help of two very experienced bearers and a fleet of masalchis (kitchen underlings), but though his name was Rajkumar (prince), he never acquired Maharaj's status due to his lowly caste! However, he was our favorite due to the endless stream of gingersnap cookies and stories that poured from his kitchen and came our way. Also, he was the only cook who could make a tennis cake where the lawn was made of green pistachio nougat, the net spun caramel sugar, and the players and their racquets were made out of white meringue. The court itself was marked out in castor sugar!

His favorite story was about Maji, our grandmother, who loved him like a son despite his lowly caste, and had saved his wife and only child's life on a day when no help was available. It was during the Quit India movement in 1942 when the country and the city was like the proverbial tinder box ready to ignite at the touch of a match. Draconian curfews had been imposed from six in the evening till six in the morning, and his wife had started labor pains at eight in the evening. There was no question of moving her to hospital or of getting a doctor when her water broke. The specter of a dry birth and breathless baby stalked everyone's mind excepting our grandmother. She told Maharaj to prepare cauldrons of hot water and armed with a sharp pair of scissors, some skeins of silk thread, a bottle of disinfectant, soap, clean towels and gauze, and with a cowering Lena in tow, marched to the woman's room where the expectant mother was writhing in agony. Two Herculean hours later the lusty cry of a healthy child had echoed through the night and people had rushed in to find the lady covered in blood and mucus, holding the bawling male child aloft triumphantly, a beatific smile on her face. The doctor who had come the next morning had admitted that he could not have done a better job, nor tied the umbilical cord more professionally.

The house itself was built on a corner plot with two frontages facing the two roads at right angles to each other; one looking back on a brick path edging a lawn bordered with flower beds merging into an orchard at one end, and the other a huge courtyard of flagged stones with a portico for parking cars at one end. The open part of the courtyard served as a play area for family children, especially during the rains when the rest of the garden became an ocean of mud. This was bordered by stone-lined beds protected by ornamental iron fencing and sported bonsai plants of every variety, almost fifty of them, from the exotic Chinese orange and ebony tree to the lowly guava and banana! The gardens and the tennis lawns at the back and second front were showpieces designed by our grandmother and almost legendary in their fame. She had planted bougainvillea creepers at intervals along the house and the entire edifice was framed by these woody creepers and their ecstatic bunches of blossoms in every color from rose pink to flaming orange and vivid magenta. The roof was bordered by a balustrade of stone, tawny and grained, giving the house − built of the same granite − the look of a semi-royal mansion. There was no doubt that a truly spectacular vision greeted the visitor when he walked through the massive gates flanked by a guard house where Robin held undisputed sway.

And all this had just been our regular life, this graceful and even tenor taken for granted, till the blow fell.

For instance, till six months ago I had always looked forward to the holidays with barely contained impatience, for holidays meant my sister coming home from college, holidays meant our father and uncles taking out time from their busy schedules to be with us, holidays meant fun with the extended family, holidays meant a trip to somewhere exciting, usually in the hills to beat the summer heat and 're-establish our bonds with nature' as our Father would put it. There to roll down hill-sides padded with brown pine needles like a thick mattress, Sammy and I racing each other, messing around banks of little, hidden, gurgling streams looking for wild watercress for sandwiches, stumbling upon raspberry canes, blackberry bushes, and little thickets of strawberry runners growing wild and loaded with fruit on which we gorged ourselves till we were sick! But despite our wild foraging we were famished upon our return to the Boarding House where we lodged with two old English ladies who owned and ran the place with a fleet of native helpers. There was no electricity, no running water, but the beds were comfortable, the service faultless, the food excellent and plentiful, the company most congenial. In the evenings we all sat around the fire and the Misses Blackburn told us stories about their early life in England, their arrival in India, falling in love with the country and never going back. It was they who taught us how to not hurt ourselves when we fell on the slippery pine needles by relaxing our muscles and to treat nettle stings with vinegar. One of the most elegant cameos of the Raj for all of us is still contained in these memories of easy and affectionate interchange, and in a strange way these memories still linger in the fragrance of the flowers and fruit they covered whole hill-sides with, and which grow wild today, still scattering incense as in the days of yore; as Daddy always said: 'the air here is exciting like wine...'

But most of all, I realized now, it meant Mamma's beautiful face irradiated with pleasure at having her family with her, taking care of all their needs with unobtrusive efficiency, smoothing over occasional ups and downs with unfailing tact, giving of herself with endless prodigality and yet with more to give. We had all taken her for granted, even our father who was still greatly in love with his wife of twenty-five years standing, but Mamma had taken it all in her stride and life had been quietly wonderful till six months ago, till six months ago...

That had been a quiet afternoon too, but in winter. Mamma had called me, willow basket in hand, and said:

'Come with me.'

'Where do you want me to go?'

'Never you mind, just come.'

'If it's into the garden, I'm not coming; I'm tired of admiring your stupid flowers.'

'You know very well that the flowers are not stupid, as

you so elegantly put it. By the way, have you any idea what a transferred epithet is?'

'Alright, alright, I'll come, but you have to let me go in fifteen minutes.'

'If you can complete the task I have in mind, I will let you go in ten.'

Mamma had taken me to the huge bed that the gardener had planted with peas, given me the basket and told me to fill it up with the luscious pods that were growing so abundantly on the creepers. She herself had taken a cloth bag and proceeded to pick and fill with characteristic dexterity. How we had got talking about poetry and music I had no idea, but I found myself reciting and singing along with my mother, trying to match her rich contralto with my still childish, sweet treble:

'Who is Sylvia, what is she,
That all our swains commend her…'

And in a sudden rush of affection I had dropped the basket and hugged Mamma fiercely, as though to ensure that she was real, would not sprout wings to fly away, and said:

'Well there is no mystery about that as far as you are concerned, we know very well why we love you to distraction, all of us including Daddy, because you are the greatest, wonderfullest, loveliest Mum ever born.'

And Mamma had placed her fingers, as soft as spun silk, on my lips and said:

'Hush child; don't you know that nothing good or bad happens but by the will of God? That not a leaf stirs or a sparrow falls without His will? Always remember that all that we are is by His grace, and that our only joy is to walk in his ways and fulfill the destiny he has chalked out for us. Not every day will be like today perhaps, but we must have the courage to face life, good or bad…'

And I had asked, truly curious:

'You really believe that, Mum? You don't believe that we have any personal will?'

And Mamma had answered without faltering:

'We do; but that personal will must be guided by complete faith that a "superior knowledge" directs our destiny, and that choices must be made in accordance with conscience, a gift from God.'

Too glib and well-rehearsed? It did not occur to me at that point but I did wonder later and do now whether she had any idea at that very moment how soon her faith would be put to the test and how seriously she would be found wanting?

'When the going is good, it is easy to be virtuous.'

These sardonic words spoken by my Aunt Madonna after Mamma fell sick, still echo ominously in my ears…

And then the spell had been broken. We had looked to the edge of the pea-patch to find Small hovering and looking at us with hungry eyes, and Mamma had immediately moved to her, put her arm around her shoulder and asked whether she wanted to help with the picking. But Small had pointed to the other end of the garden and said that one of the gardeners needed her advice about 'seed gourds', whatever that might mean, and they had moved away together, Mamma calling over her shoulder to tell me to take both bag and basket inside, adding that she would be back 'in a minute'.

I had given the peas to my Aunt Madonna and gone into my room to catch up with homework, and the music had been loud enough to cut me off from the world for the next two hours. It was only when Daddy returned from work and asked for Mamma did the household realize that Mamma was not in the house. Small piped up and said that she must have gone out, but as it had been drizzling lightly, and her car was in the garage, nobody thought this likely. Enquiries at the neighbors' drew a blank, and by eight o'clock panic had set in. When questioned, Small said that they had spoken to the gardener and then she had returned to the house while Mamma had tarried a little to pick some flowers. That had been the last time she had seen her. My Uncle Tony, competent and decisive as always, immediately called the men of the house together and organized a search party; all the compound lights were lit, and they set out in their rain-jackets and gumboots as much for the rain, as for the fear of snakes, for the unseasonable rain would bring the hibernating creatures out of their burrows. They did their work very carefully, methodically, fanning out radially from the house to the extreme edge of the three-acre garden, so that no corner was left unchecked.

It was my cousin Sammy who had found Mamma, sitting in a heap on a far-away garden bench under a weeping willow, whose trailing fronds had all but hidden her from view. He would never have seen her unless he had played the beam of his powerful torch in between the densely growing leaves, and he had done so only because he had known it was her favorite retreat on lazy winter afternoons with a book of poetry. Why had he thought of looking for her here, on a wet, winter night? But he only said later:

'...a hunch had driven me.'

She was soaking wet, not all of it from the rain for the willow would have kept out most of it, but apparently from the serpentine beyond the tree, where she had tried to …

drown herself? The thought when expressed aloud by the doctor took away the light from every concerned mask that stood around her bed where she lay unconscious, shivering violently despite the blankets piled on her, with a look of ineffable pain on her face.

That had been six months ago. It had taken the best part of two months to cure the pneumonia that had her in its grip, mainly because of her lack of will to recover, but after that the doctors had pronounced her physically fit. However, she had changed beyond recognition in every way. She was so emaciated that the perfect bones of her face protruded through her pale-as-parchment skin like a death-mask, her silken hands were like talons, she recognized nobody, wanted nobody but her mother who had rushed across half the country to be with her. That dignified old lady who had seen so much, suffered so much but seldom lost her equanimity, had almost broken down at the plight of her favorite child, and ever since she had sat day and night by her bed, hoping against hope that she would open her eyes and want not her, but someone else. But it had been a vain hope, and lately her daughter had indicated that she would like to go away to her childhood home where she would 'feel safe' with her parents, her brother's family. My father had fought this decision tooth and nail, but been compelled to give way when his wife and comrade of twenty-five years had threatened to go on hunger strike. When my sister and I had asked what was to become of us, Mamma had merely turned her face away and uttered one phrase:

'…it is God's will.'

The apparently simple faith that had irradiated our lives had suddenly taken on tones of the voice of doom. Was this the implacable God she had believed in with such certainty?

Very soon they were to leave, and then? Would she ever return? Would this nightmare ever end? How would I cope in a mother-less world? Who would bother with my whims and fancies? What was that line of poetry that our mother was so fond of quoting…?

'God's in his heaven, all's right with the world.'

Well, what had happened to that world now, I would like to know. Why was there this sudden scarcity of God? But Mamma, who had once seemed to have all the answers, now refused to look at me, leave alone bother with my queries.

For instance, a year ago, the whole family had been up in arms about my decision to adopt a squirrel. It had started with a lone individual who had fallen out of his nest, and almost died. It was Mamma who had helped save his life by putting him in a flannel nest and feeding him diluted milk with a pipette. He had soon recovered, grown with alarming speed, acquired a mate and proceeded to build a nest in the bamboo curtains in the verandah that were rolled down only in summer to keep the house cool. Since he began in early autumn, no one noticed or disturbed him till he had a flourishing family of six living in the rolled up curtain! Also, quite fearless, they felt that the entire house was their territory, since their mother, and now adoptive grandmother, lived there. The climax and the denouement of this drama took place when my Aunt Millie found eight squirrels happily feeding on a bowl of nuts that she had placed on the dining table for breakfast! Her timid attempts to shoo them away caused the patriarch to sit back on his haunches and chatter back angrily at her, whereupon she screamed the house down. The family had come running, full of apprehension, and then dissolved in helpless laughter at the cheeky squirrels, which had now begun to carry their supplies back to the nest. My aunt, furious with this frivolous response to her appeal, demanded that the squirrels be banished 'lock stock and barrel, immediately'! In any case, they had made so many holes in the curtain that it would have to be replaced. Mamma had poured oil so dexterously on troubled waters, she had agreed that 'the pests must go', but at the same time ordered the carpenter to build a proper house for them, which was hung up next to the ruined curtain which still hung awry. The squirrel family, who are well-known for their attachment to territory, had seen the obvious advantages of a transfer in this case and moved in happily. Then their 'house' had been moved to the greenhouse in the garden, about twenty yards away from the human house, and the family had followed automatically.

'An ingenious piece of social engineering…'

My youngest uncle, Tony had commented, and he was not given to paying gratuitous compliments.

However, the tie had not been broken; although they foraged outside in the garden, they regularly took flying leaps and landed on Mamma's and my shoulders when we took our evening walk, nibbled gently at our ears and kept up a continuous flow of conversation till it was time for both parties to go home. Till six months ago…for now she never went near the greenhouse, where the ferns and orchids were losing their luster and the squirrels were beginning to avoid us humans.

I remembered the time when, in the wee hours of a winter morning, I had been woken by a whispered conversation between my parents, for ever since my sister had left for college, Mamma had given up her 'boudoir' to me, and I had turned the elegant room into a typical 'would be' teenager's den with its clutter of posters, books, music system, trendy clothes that Mamma tried so hard to like, endless papers and sheer mess. I also slept on a cot in the same room rather than the one I had shared with my sister, for it was in another wing of this rambling old house. The door that separated me from my parents was never locked, and when I put my ear against it I could clearly hear Mamma pleading desperately about something and Daddy trying his best to put her off in his patient, 'most reasonable' voice. Phrases like:

'Yes, yes, I understand your concern perfectly, but it is hardly morning yet.'

Or,

'Don't you think they might find it slightly odd to be approached thus?' Or yet again,

'Would they have not got in touch with us if anything had been amiss?' filtered through till I could contain myself no longer; I had knocked and gone in to find Mamma practically in tears, and Daddy leaving his warm bed reluctantly. He had moved to the hall ostensibly to make a phone call, where he ran into my Uncle Bobby, his older brother, who was on the point of leaving for his morning walk, and through their whispered conversation it transpired that Mamma had dreamt that my sister had met with an accident and insisted that Daddy call the college to check. Daddy was looking thoroughly embarrassed at what he clearly considered excess; I myself tended to agree with him, but to my surprise, Uncle had reacted with unexpected vehemence:

'If Leila feels that way, you must call immediately; I have great faith in her powers of intuition, particularly where the children of the house are concerned. I sometimes think she understands my sons better than their own mother.'

And Daddy, muttering that this was 'a crazy household', had finally attempted to dial, when the phone had rung with shrill urgency, dispelling the peace of a near-perfect early spring morning. Daddy had picked up the receiver gingerly and listened without a word, his eyes widening and jaw dropping by the second... In the end, Mamma and Uncle Bobby had flown out to fetch my sister who had fallen off her bicycle and broken her knee, a multiple fracture. She had gone back six weeks later, completely healed, but Mamma had carried the vision that she had had of her elder daughter threshing about in agony on the school infirmary bed in her mind, and the consequent pain in her heart for a long time.

Sammy, Uncle Bobby and Aunt Millie's son, two years older to me, had always been Mamma's favorite nephew, closer to her than to his own mother with whom he was always feuding about something or the other. My Aunt Millie, an artist of some repute, escaped to her studio after household chores were done and always seemed more comfortable with people on canvas than people in real life. Her elder son Timmy, a scholar and budding philosopher, shared this remoteness from life and managed to steer a calm course between university, his 'political' friends and family. Not so the turbulent, riotous, rebellious, utterly charming Sammy, who was always in trouble with someone or the other, about something or the other. Tall, with promise of head-turning handsomeness despite his present pimples, creative in a disconcertingly unconventional fashion, bane of his teachers in school, frank to a fault, always ready to champion an underdog, with an endless retinue of 'lame ducks' in tow, he was utterly, impossibly, maddeningly 'different'. People commented on this 'difference' constantly; family members tried to draw genetic links, saying that Sammy was more like Daddy than Uncle, but were uncomfortably aware that this was not quite true, for my Dad, for all his charm and constant good humor, had built his life around a core of values that were solid, of the family, and therefore, pretty conservative in the long run, whereas Sammy seemed to view life from a perspective that was anything but 'taught', prescriptive, or familial. Everybody loved him with a kind of exasperation, particularly his 'immensely successful, formidably learned, head-of–the family' father, who sometimes seemed to think that he had got stuck with a changeling! Only my mother seemed perfectly tuned into his wavelength, and faced no problems of communication. As Sammy once said of his Aunt Leila:

'She actually tries to find out what I want, instead of trying to foist what she wants on me, like the rest of you!'

For instance, no one had noticed that Sammy was consistently using his left hand to wield his fork at meal times and keeping his right hand completely out of sight, except Mamma. So, after dinner she had followed him to his room and demanded an inspection. There had ensued a battle of wills, which had exhausted both of them, but ended with Sammy's capitulation. She had found that the brass ring he habitually wore had cut into the flesh of his finger and that the whole hand had turned septic. It was so swollen and full of pus, that the ring could hardly be seen. Minutes later, the family had heard Mamma start her car, and they trooped into the porch to find her driving away with Sammy. On enquiry, she had called back airily that they were going out for ice cream, but she had neither reduced speed nor offered to take any of the other kids with her. They had come back looking a lot happier and said they would 'do this' oftener. True to their word, they had gone out every day, but after a week their outings had ended as abruptly as they had begun. Much, much later had the family found out that Sammy would have lost his hand to gangrene if my mother had not rushed him to a doctor that night! He had got into a fight 'of honor' and deemed it dishonorable to 'tell'! Only one person as quixotically moral as himself had understood his reasons, offered help, maintained complete secrecy and along with it, his reputation, so vital to a boy of sixteen.

It suddenly dawns on me that all my thoughts are of the family, the family which we all took for granted, which we assumed would hold out against all attacks, a bulwark of comfort and strength for all individuals within it. But the family itself was under siege; someone who wished us ill had struck at the kingpin to destabilize us all. But how had they figured out what would throw Mamma off balance like this… after all, she was a pretty strong character? And what was it that had broken her so tragically and driven her to the point of no return?

Most importantly, who hated us enough to plan and execute a diabolical stratagem like this and why? Who within the family would take such a risk? It had to be an insider with the necessary knowledge and motivation, to succeed so completely, but also one who would gamble everything on one pitch and toss… who fitted the bill?

LOOKING BACK: SAMMY-SPEAK

I, Sammy, Bobby and Millie's second son, realize that I have been sitting on that bench behind the weeping willow a long time when I look at the palm tree to my left, for the rays of the sun have now mellowed the rough, brown, fibrous bark to a warm bronze, which contrasts dramatically with the rich green of the fan-shaped fronds that spread their arms in all directions. Behind the palm, the sun has climbed down and is now like a huge, brass salver hanging in a lavender sky; the shadows are getting longer and darker, but I am no closer to the solution of the problem that has brought me to this spot in the first place. Sitting in my aunt's favorite spot, trying to think like her, trying to re-create her mindset on that fateful evening, hence this unusual preoccupation with 'nature', which I normally ignore as a non-essential part of life. I had hoped to get an inkling, some kind of hint, some explanation of this inexplicable and uncharacteristic behavior on the part of a woman whose middle name is 'steadiness', but absolutely nothing has transpired. Meditation, atmosphere, vibrations, extra-terrestrial communication, astral influence, absolute rot! What is needed is the 'super sleuth' touch to be provided by the Great Sammy, for I do not believe for a moment that this is an 'act of God'. There is some very mundane reason behind this riddle, and a very wicked and clever person who wants to wreck our lives by striking at the very pivot of our existence.

Also, I have this uncomfortable feeling that this is only the beginning, and that worse is to follow…but who will help me to stem the flow of evil? The entire family is completely zapped and refuses to think pragmatically; even my 'ultra-rational' Uncle Ronnie is talking like a zombie about 'karma and original sin', and how it is all his fault, though 'unintentional'! My parents are too heart-broken to react sensibly; the servants at a total loss and still grieving; my widow aunt, Madonna is capable of intelligent speculation, but refuses to talk to me 'about serious matters' as I am a child. Child, my foot! I could tell her a thing or two about life that would leave her gasping. My third uncle, Tony, the youngest of the three brothers, appears immersed in his business and his own children, but it is a façade; he does care deeply, is thinking hard and I have great hopes of him. His wife, however, is not too unhappy at this turn of events. The least cultured, hailing from a home less illustrious than her sisters-in-law, she has always felt at a disadvantage. Now she hopes, with the main presence out of the way she will become the kingpin or queen-pin, only where and how she will acquire regality, is what I would like to know. That will certainly take some doing!

Small, now she could tell me a thing or two if she wanted to, I'm sure, but she wafts around, eyes hooded, muttering, listening at doors, jumping out at you taking you unawares, pretending to be simple as usual, and giving away nothing. However, she is never far from Aunt Leila and even at night checks on her several times, making it clear that she trusts no one. But if I push her too hard, she will cry and go and complain to my Dad or Uncle, who will berate me for my heartlessness in bothering their poor kid sister, 'not slow from birth but seriously disadvantaged' after her 'accident'. The details of this accident are never discussed, and we are all aware that the issue is sacrosanct. As a matter of fact, asking 'unacceptable' questions always causes the older generation to put up a barricade that we youngsters can never penetrate.

In the end it was Robin who suggested that I look behind the willows on the far bank of the serpentine for Aunt Leila's favorite get-away 'when the world was too much with her.' Robin is a smart guy and knows us all very well indeed, but it is very difficult to make him speak for the habit of 'discretion' is too deeply ingrained to be easily penetrated. But if he talks at all, he will talk to me and then the Super Sleuth Sammy with his forensic skills will triumph, never fear! He has to, or else that kid Sheila will die of a broken heart, or go mad or something…

MILLIE-SPEAK

Leila was everything that I, Millie, her sister-in-law by
marriage was not, though our names were somewhat
similar-sounding. Fair against my dark, flower-like against
my plain, the right caste against my non-conformity, flexible
against my angularity, out-going, anxious to please against
my self-contained personality, the contrast had struck
everyone except Leila herself. On the contrary, she had
been completely bowled over by what she, Leila referred to
as my many talents, and insisted that they be encouraged
by the family and displayed before wider audiences. To this
end, the large east-facing room that had been reserved for
guests had been turned into my studio with appropriate
lights, rolls of canvas, easels, paint-brushes and other
equipment. I had been spared many household chores
so I could devote the late morning and early afternoon
to my work, painting, batiks and embroidery. The first
exhibition of my art-work had been held in my studio, a
preview for eminent artists and critics, whose attendance
Leila had worked indefatigably to ensure. They had proved
kind, partly influenced I still think, by Leila's bewitching
beauty, and partly by my work, which they had agreed
was different thematically and perspective-wise though

traditional in technique. Quite a few paintings had sold at flattering prices and the next exhibition had been at one of the most prestigious galleries in town, again due to Leila's insistence and initiative. By this time, my position in the family, which had been tenuous for many years, had become much more secure and even my husband, who had married me against the wishes of his parents in a burst of uncharacteristic, young rebellion and suffered a great deal in consequence, was beginning to look at me with renewed respect because the other family members were taking me more seriously. I was almost able to put behind me the years of conflict, humiliation and indifference, all except one incident that I wished with all my heart had never happened, but had no way of retrieving...Only if Leila had appeared on the scene a year earlier, it may never have taken place... ah well, spilt milk.

It had also taken me many years to realize that as my artistic reputation had grown, so had Leila's – for virtue, love, generosity and kindness – and the uncharitable thought had crossed my mind once or twice that perhaps her spontaneous goodness was in fact well planned strategy? But I had thrust the thought away resolutely, immediately; such simple goodness could never be feigned so consistently.

My boys had taken to her from day one, and Leila's first efforts at needlework and knitting under my tutelage had adorned their little bodies, heads and feet in an endless array of colors and designs! My Sammy still keeps his blue, baby booties as a kind of talisman with him, and Timmy to date discusses all his crazy, revolutionary political ideas with her, and she with her acumen and endless patience is of course his safety-valve. Sheila, on the other hand, with her queer imagination and up-side-down way of looking at things, spends many an hour in the studio, trying her hand at various media. I think that child will create a stir someday…

But now, without her mother who had ensured that she would see what she was meant to see within the family, which way will she go? Heart-broken, she is looking for someone to blame, and will delve deep and range wide in her attempts to pin responsibility, very much like the terrier she loved so much. Will she actually succeed in penetrating the layers of hypocrisy and subterfuge; find her way in the twisting maze of appearances, pretty much like the forgotten, moss-grown and treacherous alleys of the oldest part of this old town? And what will she do when she finds that things are not what she had imagined or been made to imagine and turns up information that has nothing to do with Leila but is explosive for others? I am afraid… Particularly, as she looks to me, her Aunt Millie, as an ally, and fully believes that I will do my best to help her locate the culprit. Which way do I go, for all the alternatives available to me are fraught with danger: If I succeed, it might prove disastrous for the family, if I fail, I will lose Sheila's trust.

Who could have done this to Leila, strong and sensible as a rule, to turn her into an alien? What is it that she has taken to heart without questioning and is now suffering in silence?

Oh God, not something to do with Ronnie, surely…?

ROSE-SPEAK

They, my family, called me Rose, and rightly so. My high color and conscious voluptuousness had made a whole range of men, old and young, say rather stupidly how well suited I was physically, to my name as far back as I can remember, and my fragrance from the age of nine had brought them running to our alley, to the annoyance of my many, plainer cousins and the delight of my mother. Having produced three girls in succession, she was on the lowest rung of the family ladder, but some of the ill-fame had been dispelled on account of my good looks, and she had looked to me to make her upsides with the world. However, my talents in certain areas had been unmatched by desire for learning or school work and I had been at the bottom of my class with steady regularity and failed finally to clear high school. In any case, marriage had been the desired gateway to power and glory all along, and when this aristocratic family had actually deigned to consider me for their youngest, though least illustrious son Tony, it had seemed nothing short of a miracle.

A miracle, but not an unmixed blessing (I picked up the phrase from Madonna) for the atmosphere I stepped into was really weird… The house itself with its black and white marble floors, its vast rooms, long corridors, spacious verandahs, shining bathrooms with enameled baths on claws and gleaming silver taps, was a revelation. I did not know what morning rooms or smoking rooms or boudoirs or dressing rooms were, or what a 'powder closet' stood for, or why a gun hall was needed in the first place. The furniture too, a marble topped dining table for sixteen people, with mahogany chairs inlaid with ivory, beautifully carved and upholstered mahogany, teak, rosewood beds, sofas, chairs, settees, divans and desks. What on earth were occasional tables, an escritoire, roll top desk, deck chair or antimacassar? Why fill up a nice big room with books and call it a library, and put pianos, organs and violins in a music room? And why did these people read so much and listen to and play so much music, for heaven's sake rather than enjoy themselves?

If it had not been for Leila I would have been totally lost, but I did not love her for the help she gave so tactfully and ungrudgingly. No, I hated her for being who I could never be. Used to feeling good about myself due to my striking looks and domestic skills that my mother had assured me was what the husband's family always looked for in a daughter-in-law, I was horrified to find how inadequate I found myself in this strange household where reading, music and painting occupied people more than the realities of life such as money and food. Even though it appeared that my husband earned a fraction of what his elder brothers did, there was no discrimination, the household ran on oiled wheels and all my desires were met automatically. I was told to listen to good music, to read good books, to work at my spoken English with my governess and acquire a strange commodity called culture till I had it coming out of my ears! Fortunately my husband, twelve years my senior, was completely besotted by me, but he could not understand my secret worries or with what fear I faced each day. Worst of all was the conversation at family gatherings where no gossip was allowed, no juicy discussion of neighbors' follies and no lengthy account of servants' failings…only educated talk. The worst offender in this respect is Sheila's father, who seems to think that if you do not look at unpleasant things, they will disappear on their own. Very silly, it seems to me; I mean, how long can you hold down the lid of a pressure cooker without using the safety valve?

It was Leila who had taken off her own gold bangles, eight of them, and put them on my wrists before I entered the house, so that no one should comment on how inadequately I had been endowed by my parents. She taught me to pronounce difficult words, to refine my speech and do away with the crudities that had been quite acceptable at home; she gave me the confidence to take part in conversation and glossed over the mistakes which Sammy and Sheila were so quick to spot. She taught me to drive in secret and then gave the family a surprise by insisting that they buy me a car! My husband, always very fond of her, now worshipped her because of her kindness to me, and assured me that that if I tried hard enough, I would soon be like her! Poor man never had the sense he was born with and could not understand that I'd rather die than be like Leila. She was blind as a bat, could not see the gaping hole at her feet till she had fallen into it, and then made no effort to climb out and survive! I mean what is more precious than life? Why not cut your losses and make a fresh beginning?

For me this has been a bit of a windfall, but my husband cannot see that this turn of events has placed me exactly where I have wanted to be for the last ten years, near the head not the bottom of the ladder. He just mopes around wondering how he can help, appealing to me and the children to plead with Leila! I've tried once or twice for appearance's sake, but her eyes, dark pools of despair, strangle the false words of comfort that fall from my lips. My little girls who love her dearly just sit and cry, their tears mingling with hers, till I take them away almost forcibly. How long this charade will continue I have no idea, but pretend I must till she leaves, especially as I noticed Sammy looking at me rather oddly the other day; I had better watch my step.

ROBIN-SPEAK

Sitting on this chair in the gatehouse for the last forty years, how much of life have I, Robin, Head of Security for this illustrious household, seen flow by: people, events, conflict, reconciliation, accidents and happenings 'made to look like accidents'? You see, I have an advantage unavailable to anyone else, for I not only see and hear, but also have the time to think about what I perceive. Again, a gateman is not a person, but a figure as unchangeable as the gate itself, and people forget that behind the wooden face and the fixed smile, there is a sharp brain and deep knowledge of human nature at work.

'Yes sir, no sir, right away sir.'

Conditioned reflexes, no more, and people forget that you see farther than what you are meant to see. Only in times of emergency, the unforeseen, the unexpected, do they turn to you as a person, and appeal to you for help, like the other day when they could not find Madam Leila; it was I who told Sammy where to look, for I did not think that she would like to be found by me...too undignified, and she is one dignified person, a real lady, unlike some I could mention, even though they try so hard!

I was barely eighteen when my venerable father passed

away. It was a freezing cold night and he had dozed off for a bit, when the bell in the gatehouse had shrilled him to summons. His dedication to duty had proved greater than his wisdom and his foot had come down rather hard on his slippers, and the cobra coiled on it. Unable to distinguish principle from ill intention, the creature had reacted in his brute, unintelligent fashion and bitten him thoroughly before slithering away in swishing indignation. The head of the house, the Old Judge, father of the present head, Bobby, had put his mouth unhesitatingly to the wound and tried to suck out the poison and then rushed him by car to hospital, but he had died on the way. Not that anyone but his master had missed the old, foul-mouthed fornicator too much, but the incident had deprived me of my tree-climbing, bird-egg-stealing, guava-robbing boyhood and condemned me to this room for the rest of my life. In the days when there was a famine every year and poor people died like flies, one did not say no to a job, however unwanted or soul-destroying. Also it was not easy working for a family so determinedly pro-British, at a time when the whole country was turning nationalist with a vengeance. My loyalty never wavered, but sometimes it really went against the grain.

But time brings inevitable change and my personality, alas, proved no exception; as Lena said in her candid fashion:

'You are turning into a sahib, Robin and you even talk funny, very much like Ronnie; look at your jokes which are just like his, sort of twisted, meaning the opposite of what he says. Is this conscious imitation or pure hero worship?'

I told her to shut up and not talk nonsense, but she is pretty astute and has hit the nail on the head. Living with gentle folk one not only tries to imitate their patterns of speech but also their way of thinking. It is also more comfortable than running around imagining you are a freedom fighter, hungry and foot-sore! However, I did not let their preoccupation with morality cloud my judgment too much and as a consequence retained my common sense and ability to see a spade for a spade.

My relationship with Bobby and Ronnie, the eldest and the second brothers who are younger to me, has been very friendly, but also very unlike the easy camaraderie that had existed between our fathers, perhaps because we have never been partners in crime procuring, and later enjoying illicit country liquor and unwary village women. Women... very few people knew of this dark side to the old Judge's character, and those who did, including sons and family members, chose to ignore it, for he was a dangerous man to question or cross. In any case, no one had a quarrel with the enormous wealth he had inherited and managed to accumulate, for he was generous. His two elder sons, intellectuals and moral to a fault, were educated in Public Schools and picked up the Empire Culture on cricket fields, whereas the youngest, practical and grounded, went to a local Missionary School and was far more attuned to the Indian ways of life and thought that emerged in the post 1947 era. While the older boys went to university abroad and spent most of their time away from home, the youngest went to the local university, learned to keep his own counsel, and became the Mistress's unquestioned favorite. However, there was little love lost between him and his father; whereas Bobby and Ronnie were much more tolerant of their father's weaknesses of character, Tony harbored few illusions and was openly critical at times. All the boys were greatly influenced by their saintly mother, who in turn encouraged them into turning a blind eye to the more earthy side of their progenitor's nature and made the most of his virtues, teaching them to believe that the subterfuge was acceptable as a part of filial loyalty. Only the upper class with their endless questions about right and wrong has this capacity for self-deception! In the process, the older boys went to the other extreme, acquired a code of values that bordered on the puritanical, remote from life, and concepts like justice, righteousness, honesty, fair-play, mere concepts for most of us, came to be not only of primary importance to them but also dictated their way of life. Well, their survival up to this point has been more due to luck than anything else, for naturally, they fall into snares laid for them by the less idealistic with unfailing regularity. I mean look at the way they trust their youngest brother, believe all his hard-luck stories, when he has put away enough money to buy them up twice over! But it is also to Tony's credit that he loves them dearly and will move heaven and earth to help if they are in trouble. I sometimes feel the money he has saved is meant as a kind of insurance for the family to cover the absurd generosity of his bothers, for by nature, he is abstemious.

Look how seriously he is taking Madam Leila's case and given his tenacity I feel he will finally succeed in nailing the culprit. He is looking into all possibilities to narrow down the list of suspects including the immediate family, which is making some people very uncomfortable, even afraid, as it is very difficult to parry his blunt and direct questions. Besides, he never takes his eyes from your face, watching every expression like a hawk. While faced with this terrible happening, the first real tragedy, the older brothers still cannot see beyond their long, uninquisitive noses, and

Bobby a lawyer! They have examined their own consciences minutely for error on their own part as a causal factor, but they have not once asked themselves:

'Who will benefit most in this old house by putting Madam Leila safely and perhaps permanently out of the way?' Neither have they instituted any enquiries, for the family is sacrosanct, always beyond reproach.

Well, it is obvious to me who might have had the brains to engineer her possible departure, but why? I will have to keep my eyes peeled and talk to Sammy; that boy has some of the horse sense of his venerable grandfather and there is something else, of course, that sets him apart...

MADONNA-SPEAK

Today I am the widowed aunt in this family, a part, yet not a part of the household, the one who went away and returned; but in the old days my father always said that my face reminded him of Botticelli's Madonna, and that is how the name stuck, and finally became official. As I grew up, I came to realize that I was his favorite child, and always did my best to look and live up to the part he had chalked out for me, parting my hair in the middle and wearing it low over my ears, plucking my eyebrows and darkening my eyes to produce an ethereal, far-away look, subtly reddening my lips to look spiritual by reducing the natural 'cupid's bow', clothing myself discreetly to keep my bursting youth under control. Why did he choose this particular demure image for me? Was it a kind of vindication, that a man as earthy as he could produce a child who was strongly moral, entirely virtuous? If he had kept the genetic factor in mind, he would have concentrated on his sons, but I think it irked him that they were good anyway, due to their mother's powerful influence, so he concentrated on me and to a lesser extent, Small. Or was it a conscious experiment, one that would have tickled his quirky sense of humor, to see if the two of us, cast in his mold rather than our mother's, could be made into conventionally good people? Or did he hope that instinct would triumph, and that our appetite for life would win after all, and he would be vindicated in his own choices? Perhaps for the same reason, he took his youngest son's education in hand and kept him at home as a day-scholar, away from Public School?

I now think that my mother had a shadowy perception of what was going on, for she was intelligent as well as strong, but she played along to keep our illusions intact as far as possible to ensure that family relationships would endure. We had a nebulous idea of her early experiences, but as far back as I can remember her motto had always been: peace at any cost. As I grew older however, I began to sense what it had cost her to keep the peace. For example, though hailing from one of the most politically famous and patriotic families in the country, thoroughly imbued with the emotion and spirit of energetic nationalism and the love of the Motherland, when she had found herself in a completely alien atmosphere in this anglophile household at the age of twelve and was assiduously trained by English governesses and tutors to play the role of wife to her illustrious husband, she had buried her deepest feelings in her heart and done her best to conform. But in her leisure hours I would find her poring over the political news, keeping abreast of developments in the country, or humming the famous patriotic song of the moment under her breath. And although she played her part as hostess to perfection at banquets and parties, I could see that she was hard put at times to be civil with her British guests. But she never faltered seriously. How and why had she managed this compromise with her powerful conscience?

But then, I wound up doing the same thing, and I find

myself wondering very often even now whether I should have had the courage to speak out instead of allowing my heart to break steadily. He was everything my Father was not: idealistic, brave, straight as an arrow, completely convinced of his mission. To meet him was like watching the sun rise in a clear sky, bright and uncompromising. And he admired me, my intelligence, my individuality, my courage…said I should choose the right side before it was too late, run away with him…but it was unthinkable; my Father would kill him if he found out, and did he? For one day he stopped coming and I never saw him again. I thought I would die of sorrow, but I did not; does anybody really die of a broken heart?

That was it; our sins of omission were, I now think, more damaging than those of commission, and they had steadily paved the way for my Father's megalomania. Someone should have protested earlier. Perhaps our mother did not have an alternative, given her strongly religious background, her lack of formal, western education, the overwhelming personality of her husband, so she had considered it her mission in life to put herself last, to sublimate every personal factor to hold the family together, maintain the prestige of the house and keep all unpleasant facts of life from her progeny. Could she have looked into a crystal ball, would she have acted differently? Wouldn't we all? And in the end, would it have made any difference?

LENA-SPEAK

The sprawling servants' quarters at the back of the mansion have seen generations of servitors take birth, grow and die for the greater glory of the ruling house. These are like army barracks, a double row of rooms stretching in a long line, along the boundary wall, next to the road, housing several families. The rules too were as rigid as the army's and the bearer who failed to put the tea-tray on the Master's table at 5:30 a.m. on a winter morning, whether the tea was consumed or not, would be told to collect his pay and go. The women-folk had to be in by the same time, to prepare the morning meal, get the children ready for school, but since the mistress was very kind by nature, small lapses would be overlooked To her, servants were individuals, flesh and blood people, whereas The Master, except for his favorites, looked down on the entire lower classes and took their servitude for granted.

I, Lena, the official Nanny today, had run away from my home in the village when I had learned that my father was planning to marry me off to a man older than himself, because he would not only take me without dowry, but pay my father a suitable sum of money. I had hoped for something better, for though only twelve years old, my sultry, good looks attracted the young men of the village like honey draws flies, but they could not match the price that my father demanded. So I mixed some opium in his glass of bedtime milk, stole some money from his purse and left. The dose would not kill him but render him inactive for some time and prevent him from coming after me.

I traveled three days, on foot, by bus and finally train, slept in deserted hovels and under trees at night for our village was a good seventy miles from the nearest railway station. The itinerant singer who helped me escape was too old to be dangerous, and he very kindly brought me to the mistress of this house. She loved his songs, was very generous to him, and had requested him to look for a clean village girl who could play with her little daughter, Madonna, and teach her songs, rhymes and folk tales from the village, for she did not want her daughters to lose touch with their roots. Madonna had taken to me immediately, and we spent many pleasant hours of the day together. Her favorite story was the one about the clever fox and the stupid crocodile and the rhyme she liked best was:

> One Sun,
> Two Fortnights,
> Three Eyes
> Four Vedas,
> Five Arrows,
> Six Seasons,
> Seven Seas,
> Eight Vasus,
> Nine Planets,
> Ten Directions…because each line had a story attached to it.

Her teacher in school was very pleased and put the rhyme on the Display Board with matching pictures to teach the other children their numbers.

While Madonna learned her native language in my company, I picked up English from her; pidgin at first, but as time went my vocabulary and pronunciation improved apace and I learned to read fluently. I soon graduated to good books and my horizons suddenly seemed endless… The Mistress often called me into the sitting room when she had company to show off my language skills to her western friends, and I remember one of them remarking:

'You have a fetching piece there, Lady------, certainly not "the soul of a servant"! What plans do you have for her?'

And the Mistress in her calm and sweet way had replied:

'To ensure if God wills, that she never has to grow into the soul of a servant; she is too free a spirit and I will not allow her wings to be clipped.'

Fateful words, for God had other plans, but the Mistress never forgot her promise and kept her end of the bargain till the last.

Madonna was ten years old when my mistress decided to marry me to Robin, who had been gate-man ever since his father had passed away, and as he was very attractive with his muscular, lithe body and handlebar mustaches, I fell in readily with her wishes. He was very intelligent too and unlike me had acquired a superior degree of spit and polish that I hoped to emulate. But there was another reason why my nuptials could not be deferred; of late, the Master's concern for my welfare had begun to embarrass me as well as other members of the family, especially as he taken to referring to me, playfully of course, as his black rose.

After my marriage, I lived in the quarters with Robin and

only came into the house to take care of Small, who needed more attention than Madonna now, when the Master was away at work. In a few years, four years after the youngest son of the family was born and Small met with the accident, I stopped going to the house altogether, for reasons best and only known to the Mistress and myself.

It was Madam Leila who brought me out of my retirement to take care of Roma and Sheila, even though Madam Millie had rightly felt that I was too elderly for the job and had wanted a trained nanny for the girls, in keeping with the prevalent culture of the house. But Leila, always intent on fulfilling others' needs, perhaps saw the hunger of a childless mother in my eyes, and convinced her that affection was more important than efficiency, got her way and said to me:

'You are just getting fatter and lazier by the day, Lena, come and help me look after my children and help poor Robin out with a little money, instead of eating him out of hearth and home!'

That was always her way, to make a joke out of kindness, to indicate that no gratitude was expected, to treat it as pure give and take. And I genuinely tried to give the girls all the love and affection I had denied the child I had given birth to, but never called my own. Only it did not work out as I had wanted, planned or anticipated. And now I am caught in the toils of an emotion that I thought was safely buried and out of the way, and the consequent conflict, in which I cannot call on anyone, even Robin, for help.

How I wish the mistress was alive so that with a touch of her magic wand she could solve all our present problems. I still often wonder what gave her this great wisdom and fortitude and how did she not lose these qualities living with the Master all her life? The family was very unstable after she died, but we all felt that Leila would be able to take her place, and she did to a very large extent, for many years.... but now?

SMALL-SPEAK

I had asked my mother why she had called me 'Small' when Tony was younger than me, but instead of replying to my query, she had hugged me tight and said:

'As far as I am concerned, you are my smallest one.'

Although I was only four years old at the time, the reply had struck me as highly illogical, but an odd expression on my Mum's face had discouraged me from pursuing the subject. My father, the Judge, was crazy about me and took me everywhere with him; he called me his mascot and said that I brought him good luck and success. He even took me to the High Court sometimes, where I sat in his chambers and played with my new nanny, who was elderly but spoke perfect English, while he worked on one of the most complicated cases that had come his way. One day he called my mother at lunch time and said he was not sending me home, for he still needed me to be around, and I sat on his lap and shared his lunch with a napkin wrapped around my throat. Then he went back, and my nanny put me to sleep on the sofa, usually reserved for visitors. When I opened my eyes, he was back, sitting quietly in his chair, waiting for me to wake up; he looked tired, triumphant, but also, somehow, rather confused, which was very, very unlike him. I was hardly six years old at the time, but I can see his face with its odd expression so clearly, even today…

And then, a few weeks after that, everything went wrong, so terribly wrong that my entire life came to a grinding halt, even before I had taken a few faltering steps down the road…

BOBBY-SPEAK

It seems strange, even blasphemous, that today I, even though the eldest son of the Judge, am the head of this household; Bobby _____ , successful lawyer, vice-president of the bar library, well-respected in town, president of the most important club, associated with every worthwhile social initiative, calm, courteous, benign, I can never see myself stepping into my father's venerable shoes. It took me years to acquire this persona, for even after the pater was cold in his grave it seemed inconceivable that anyone should attempt to fit into his awesome shadow. I may never have dared if it had not been for Ronnie's gentle but firm insistence. Ronnie, my dearest brother and friend who is suffering so quietly today…what fun we had had as boys together.

In winter, family picnics were the order of the day; we would pile into three or four cars, family members, friends – Indian and British, servants, and leave in the early hours for a scenic spot, usually within a radius of a hundred miles, and spend the day there. We ate breakfast on the way, but lunch was prepared at the venue by the servants, supervised by my mother and aunts, and I always wondered why food at home, was never so palatable. Perhaps it had something to do with the fragrant smoke of the twigs and leaves, whose flavor permeated the meat and vegetables? After lunch, my brother Ronnie and I would disappear with our air guns to pick up partridges, herons and snipe, if there was a waterbody nearby, green pigeons if there was not, while the rest of the family went on a leisurely tour of the nearby villages. The mud-and-thatch cottages had creepers growing all over them and from them hung gourd, cucumber, bitter gourd and other creeping vegetables in unbelievable profusion. My mother would buy as much as the cars could carry, for market vegetables never tasted like these. My father, uncles and particularly white friends made it a point to speak to the local menfolk, share a smoke and village news with them, for, as Father said:

'These are troubled times, and it is good to put your ear to the ground, occasionally.'

So we too, Ronnie and I, talked to the boys and later to the younger men, and over the years the quality of this interchange had been gradually and subtly transformed, till of late, on the eve of Independence, we had come to realize that the social gap between us was fast narrowing, and that their attitude was not that of awed subservience anymore, but one of grudging acceptance. But for the accident of birth, they seemed to indicate, they were as good as anyone else. Also, our obvious and proud westernization was no longer a hallmark of quality, but rather something to be faintly ashamed of as a mark of erstwhile slavery. The women still kept sedulously away and only very occasionally did we catch a glimpse of a curious face, a bright black eye, through a window. It was clear that they did not trust us city-folk around their women, either then or now.

On this particular afternoon however, a curious pall of

mourning lay over the village of ------, and no one seemed
in the mood for conversation. The men hung about in
sullen groups, taciturn and uncommunicative, not wanting
to divulge any sort of information. Ronnie and I felt so
uncomfortable that we decided to return to the family, our
guns still loaded with shot, which was rather ironic, come
to think of it. It finally transpired that a young woman,
recently widowed, had immolated herself on her husband's
funeral pyre a month ago to protest against the unfair
judgment that had sent him to the gallows, and it was clear
that the village perceived her as a suttee and her husband
as a hero. There was a very fine dividing line between the
terrorist and the nationalist then as now, and it was evident
that the majority perceived her husband as a martyr to the
cause and not traitor to the Raj. As Father remarked in his
usual crisp, sardonic way when we tried to probe:

'Merely a matter of perspective, boys.'

But while my father and his lawyer friends scoffed at
the incident, the Police Commissioner Mr. Wilson, looked
distinctly worried, and kept saying:

'A matter of poor judgment; firearms should never have
been used in the encounter. This will cast long shadows...'

It was clear that the villagers did not consider the flip side
of the coin. They thought that the dead man was a warrior
and were planning to make use of his wife's self-sacrificing
gesture to mount a public protest. Equally clear was their
resentment of us as part of the anglophile ruling elite, and
the unspoken message:

'Unless we could help, we were not wanted and should
not hang around' came through loud and clear. One or
two village elders, who knew that our father was a judge,
attempted to consult him, but turned away abruptly when

one of the younger men whispered in their ears with a look of such searing malevolence on his face, that we were taken aback. In the end, we decided to return early to the security of the city, convinced in our hearts that this was no laughing matter.

And we may have got away with it if luck had been on our side, but one of the cars lost a fan belt and none of the drivers were carrying spares. We tried to manage with a leather belt, but it wore out within a few miles. Then my mother had a brilliant idea; she loosened her hair and offered us the braid she used to hold her plait in place. Since it was made of three separate pieces, each with three hundred strands of strong, silk thread, she reckoned it would hold till we got home, and it did, but it slowed us down terribly. We were about fifteen miles from our destination when we found our way blocked by three bullock-carts, strung in a line across the road.

The drivers tried to maneuver the cars around the blockade, but found the way impassable due to a ditch on one side and huge mounds of earth on the other; someone had taken the trouble to plan carefully. Peering through the windows we could see men carrying staves, scarves drawn across the lower part of their faces; some of them held flaring torches whose leaping flames cast bizarre shadows but little illumination, ensuring that recognition or identification at a later date would prove quite impossible even by family members. One of the drivers stepped out, but was immediately pushed back with a filthy oath and the ugly word, collaborator, hung in the air like an evil meteor caught in mid-flight. Then our father stepped out, stretched to his full height of six feet three inches, and challenged them:

'Come on you bastards, let me see what kind of mother's

milk runs as blood in your veins…I will take on the lot of you with one hand tied behind my back. Let the women and the children go, you filthy cowards! Your quarrel is with me because of that miserable rat that you plan to set up as a hero; well, let the rest of the rats feel a taste of my wickedness now!'

The flickering light made him seem even bigger than he was, his bravado was obviously disconcerting because it had the ring of complete sincerity, and when a gun appeared almost magically in his right hand, we thought the battle was over… But not quite… One of the men wrenched open the door next to which our mother was sitting with Small cowering in her lap, snatched her up and made off with her at top speed. Before any of us could react, Ronnie had jumped out and set off after the abductor into the darkness…

RONNIE-SPEAK

The second brother in a large household always has a hard time, as his role is never clearly defined and he is accused of either being too little or too much. In my case this was complicated by the fact that my redoubtable father clearly preferred me, Ronnie, his second son, over every child, except perhaps Small, though Madonna always thought she was the favorite! About Bobby, he clearly had mixed feelings, perhaps because of his staunch virtue and righteousness? Perhaps he saw in Bobby, all he himself could never be? Or did he resent the fact that Bobby would inevitably step into his redoubtable shoes, professionally and as head of the family, one day? How Bobby felt about this obvious partiality I do not know, for we have never discussed it, but what I do know is that he has never allowed it to stand in the way of his constant affection for me. Dear, God-fearing, steady, loyal old Bobby!

I, for one, had always hero worshipped my father for his satanic good looks, huge physical and mental strength, towering personality, indomitable will, and enduring worldly success. Therefore, it was all the harder to reconcile myself to his darker side, which became apparent to Bobby and me as we grew older, particularly as it was pitted against my mother's unvarying and unfaltering, yet unobtrusive goodness. Strangely, it was she against whom his major crimes were committed, which we came to realize much later, who told us that a progenitor was not to be judged, for it was he who had given us the gift of life, and that filial duty demanded that we render unquestioning obedience and loyalty. She quoted the scriptures to endorse her point:

> 'The progenitor is your heaven,
> Your father is your religion,
> He is worthy of worship at all times…'

In a way, this made things easier, since it lifted the onus of responsibility from our shoulders, and we could carry on with our own lives, secure in the knowledge that Ma did not mind and did not want us to interfere in matters beyond our purview. Certainly, she did not expect us to fight her battles, if there were any, and as our father was mostly affectionate to mother in the run of daily life and very good to us, we had little cause for complaint on any score, and the domestic scene was less stormy than one would expect.

For instance, he never stood in the way of her philanthropic activities even though sometimes, and in an oblique way, they critiqued his venerable British masters. Famines were almost an annual occurrence in the 1930s and 40s and the images of starving, skeletal, hopeless men and women, desperately dragging one foot behind the other, stumbling along in the vain hope that they would reach a big city where food was supposedly available and people generous, have been too vividly chronicled by Satyajit Ray and Mrinal Sen not to be forgotten even fifty years later; but we were some of the unfortunates who lived through this period and are compelled to remember the horrors, even though we would rather forget.

The lines of zombies, eyes glazed, clothes that were more holes than whole, rickety children with protruding bellies and lifeless, vacant eyes, passed our main gate endlessly and their only plea was for rice water that is drained and thrown away when the rice is cooked….they did not dare to ask for more… The look of incredulous delight when leaf-bowls full of khichri was put into their hands is one sight I will never forget as long as I live. My mother personally stood at the gate with gigantic cauldrons of this nectar as the indigent called it, on the floor beside her, and helped the servants dole it out bowl by bowl and place them in the stick-like hands; she also insisted that Bobby, Madonna and I do our bit, so that we would have some idea of how our fellow countrymen lived.

Sometimes Father would stand far away behind us and watch us in action, and the expression on his face was one of exasperated admiration, as though he did not know what to do with this determinedly right-thinking wife of his! He also could not get us to budge, even Madonna! And once when the District Magistrate commented a trifle sarcastically on the contrast between our mother's good works and the opulence of the table at which he was sitting, she told him very clearly that the family was cutting back on luxury items on a regular basis, even the children, to provide money for the khichri, and today's plenty was only for the benefit of the company… 'After all, someone had to do something…' It was clear that she thought that administrative failure was responsible for the debacle, and though my father quickly covered up the uncomfortable moment by commenting:

'Well you see, someone has to pay for my sins and my good wife does that...we strike a balance this way...'

The august company had the grace to look distinctly uncomfortable.

When I look back today, I realize that he was a man of gargantuan appetites and feudal mindset, who found it difficult to contain his passions within the belt of rule. Born at a different time, in a more colorful civilization, he would have been a spectacularly resplendent figure; wielding a saber, riding a magnificent stallion, he would have slaked his thirst for life with impunity and no one would have questioned his morals. But born in India at the turn of the century, into the westernized upper class with its borrowed Victorian morality and strait-jacket of hypocritical social correctness, life had dealt him an underhand deal, and although he had done his best to conform outwardly, his feudal genes had proved too strong for him at times. In a way, he was a giant among pygmies, and that is why his lapses, even the smallest, drew so much attention and covert criticism; but this neither affected him nor caused him to change in the slightest! I don't think I have ever known anybody who was less concerned with what people thought of him.

And perhaps, this is the reason why the coming of independence to India posed a real challenge for him. Fiercely pro-British, proud of his privileged social position, he did not think India was politically prepared for total independence:

'Nehru is an idiot and Gandhi, a wolf in saint's clothing,' were his favorite phrases, and he had fought for Dominion Status tooth and nail as long as it had seemed a feasible alternative, right up to the 1930s. In 1931 he had been most critical of the famous patriot, Bhagat Singh and his compatriots, terming them 'bloody terrorists', siding solidly with his British masters. But the Second World War and the Quit India movement had put paid to his hopes, and he had been caught in a cleft stick; for, the only way to maintain power and prestige for the local elite at that point was to become a British Hater, don the Gandhi cap, climb on to the Nationalist and Congress band wagon and court arrest as a satyagrahi, a searcher of truth. This prospect of a volte face went terribly against the grain for in his own way he was a man of principle, and he was hard put to make a choice, not least because the British Government, still in power in the 1940s, demanded his loyal services in situations and occasions that were certainly not in the national interest as was understood at the time by the opposition. And he hated the hypocrisy of it all. He was compelled to vacillate, and the consequent reduction of his own social and moral status left him frenzied, and caused him to slip more than once. Postcolonial angst is of many kinds, and this is one of the less discussed breeds. Although the transitional psyche has not been analyzed sufficiently, on superficial examination, confusion due to divided loyalties and desire for self-preservation at any cost, seem to stand out as the salient factors.

But to return to the family, he brought up Tony so differently from Bobby and me, did not send him away to boarding school or even the best local school, but to an old-fashioned Jesuit missionary institution. Said his horse sense set him apart from us, as we were nothing more than academics pretending to be professionals. He got Tony apprenticed to a business friend when he was eighteen and set him up in his own business by the time he was twenty-one. He left clear instructions that he be married to a very pretty girl from a lower middle class home and we had to look high and low before our wives found Rose for him. In his will he left the house and property jointly to Bobby and me, and a very large sum of money for him in case he, Tony, ever wanted to set himself up in a separate establishment. Of course we never divulged this clause to him, merely gave him the money for his business; and he too, trusting us completely, never questioned us further, and we continued to live as a joint family. All this did not pass without comment, particularly from the extended family, neighbors, friends, and attempts were made to vitiate the relationship between us. But thanks to our genuine affection for each other, our mother's unfailing wisdom and later Leila's wise, immaculate handling of this thorny situation, for our Rose certainly has 'thorns', we had managed comfortably enough till now, till this terrible trouble fell on us like the shadow of an evil raven with menacing, outstretched wings.

My first meeting with Leila was entirely fortuitous: I was traveling on business and on an early Sunday morning being driven down a quiet road to the golf course of a city I hardly knew, when my attention was drawn to a huddle at the edge of the road, where a policeman was obviously getting the worst of an argument, because his imperious antagonist though obviously at fault, refused to accept the fact. She insisted that the tree she had hit and the pedestrian she had narrowly missed, were both on the wrong side of the road! She was very apologetic to the man, though, and gave him a generous sum of money to visit the hospital just to check if he was hurt, and the altercation ended with the victim exhorting the policeman to let go of 'the case' since the young lady was absolutely right and he had been on the wrong side as had been the tree! The policeman looked even more bemused when the lady's driver obviously whispered her identity in his already humming ear, and the incident ended with the lady driving away happily with a wave of her beautiful hand and the official staring after her completely dazed!

Although I was a stranger in the city and only there on a business matter for a couple of days, I was determined to find out who she was. It was easier than I thought, for the men I met at the course knew her right away:

'It has to be Leila to say something absurd like that and get away with it!' laughed one of them.

'If her father finds out, she will be gated and her car taken away... For although he loves her too much for her own good, he is a real stickler when it comes to the law...' commented another. 'After all, he is one of the most brilliant and sought after lawyers in the country.'

'She drives well though, as a rule: wonder what happened to her?'

'Must have been singing as usual... you know how she is with a new song...'

I had to meet this intriguing character...I did... and we never looked back...

The same Leila is actually leaving in two weeks' time, forever. How can she? Can a snail live outside its shell? Can a fish survive without water? Can a bird banish itself permanently from the air? Every little detail of this household has been of urgent and paramount importance to her always; how can she cut herself adrift as though she does not care at all? Somewhere along the line I have failed her terribly, but how? If only she would speak, would share, would blame... I cannot bear her looking like a stranger, almost from another world...Leila who was so positive about life! My mother believed implicitly in God, so does Leila. If He exists, why is he hiding his face now?

They say old sins cast long shadows. Whose sins are we paying for?

TIMMY-SPEAK

The feeling that I, Timmy, oldest in this generation of the family, born to Bobby and Millie nineteen years ago, need to take a firm hand at this juncture in our family affairs is fast turning to conviction. It is evident that my Father, Uncle Ronnie and even Uncle Tony, caught in a time warp, are floundering; Aunt Madonna, tight-lipped and sardonic, will not give me the time of day, and Sammy and Sheila clever as they are, lack maturity and do not realize that this disaster has long roots snaking away into the past. This is merely the tip of the iceberg hinting at unfathomable depths, but these depths must be fathomed if the tip is to be uncovered.

I myself would never have seen clearly had it not been for Willy, a graduate student from Cambridge working on a thesis entitled: 'A Comparative Study of Socio-Political Conditions in England and India in the Final Days of the Raj'. He has been in the city for a year working in the archives and he joined our political club in the university as an honorary member when he discovered that our aims are somewhat similar, except that our foci were pre and post-independence India. Then he became fascinated by our family, saying that we were a piece of living history.

He came to the house often, charmed everyone and was charmed in turn, and by no one more than Aunt Leila and my artistic mother.

He, Willy, found the old Judge to be an intriguing character and was especially fascinated by his case. He had long discussions about my grandfather's famous judgments with my father saying that he must be very much a chip of the old block, a truly worthy son, which pleased Dad no end!

Then the blow fell, and when he found out how miserable we were, he insisted he wanted to help, and he has been pushing me relentlessly towards the past and particularly the enigmatic personality of my grandfather, the Great Judge and his cases. Willy believes that his personality holds the clues to our present trouble. This attack on Aunt Leila, he is convinced, is a case of vengeance, pure and simple, and we have to go back in time to find the roots of this poison tree. I tend to agree with him and I think I will talk to Robin to provide some facts. He knew the Old Man and the family members at that point, perhaps better in some ways than they did themselves, but whether he will open his mouth at all is any man's guess. His loyalty to the family borders on the fanatical, and he takes his cue from my own ancestor-worshipping elders, who raise their hackles the minute one hints that the past might have been less than perfect.

In any case, I must first find out whether the vengeance is personal, political, a mixture of both, or none of these, and it is certainly not easy to separate the strands when you have to go back and view half a century of murky tapestry. Also, the time frame is odd… I mean, why wait so long to wreak vengeance? Would it not have been more satisfactory to have struck out at the old man while he was vulnerable to suffering?

Willy said something very interesting the other day:

'Have you ever thought, Timmy that we create the road down which we travel every moment of our lives? Every action, every word, and every resolve builds constantly, brick by brick, to lay out the path we have to move on, yet certain choices are made almost without volition, against our better judgment and we are stuck with the consequences whether we like it or not? How formative a part does conscious will actually play in our lives?'

DAVE-SPEAK

I, Dave, do not belong to the family directly, being a second cousin, son of the Judge's brother, the engineer. Honestly, what an illustrious generation. Taking advantage of the educational opportunities opened up by the British, the brothers trained assiduously and rose to the top of their professions including, law, engineering, surgery, medicine and linguistics. And the second generation, our generation, we have not done so badly either. Bobby and Ronnie have been extremely successful in their own fields, I a doctor of some repute, my younger brother in Government service, and all our girl cousins married to illustrious men. It was only ------, my oldest brother, all of twenty-one at the time, who became a Nationalist and joined a well-known political organization that was working towards Indian independence, much to the consternation of his elders, who were all in government service and therefore decidedly pro-British. They did their best to dissuade him but he was adamant. He was particularly critical of his uncle the Judge, for he felt that some of his judgments were not only unpatriotic but also flagrantly unjust. He was involved in the Alipore Bomb Case, when an attempt was made on Magistrate Kingsford's life. Although the bomb missed its intended mark, the group of young nationalists succeeded in killing Barrister Pringle Kennedy's wife and daughter in a bizarre foreshadowing of the incident at Sarajevo in 1914. My brother was among the thirty-three people rounded up as suspects, branded a terrorist by our white masters and incarcerated. The evidence against him was thin but his fearless demeanor and his seditious words at the trial, though lauded by like-minded Indians, obviously did not meet the approval of the presiding Judge, who caused him to be arrested and incarcerated for years in the unhealthy and infamous prison at Buxa in North Bengal. He died there supposedly of malaria, as my parents were informed much later. His death caused a rift between the two branches of the extended family, for my father had passed away still grieving, and the rest of us, including our mother, felt that the Judge could have helped had he so desired, for he had extensive connections within the British bureaucracy. But he was adamantly opposed to any intervention on my brother's behalf and even after the tragedy that befell Ronnie and Small, he had no pity for nationalist heroes, even his own kin. But I also had an insistent question in my mind that would not be banished: did he have an ulterior motive in taking such a strong stand against the nationalists?

I also wondered then and do now whether my brother was not worth more than all the members of the righteous family put together. The only other person I knew who was of his caliber was Mukul, the poor relation, who also gave his life for the sake of Indian independence. While we who were rational and pragmatic, never got our feet wet and quietly feathered our own nests, they died choking on their own blood. Well, here we are today, safe and dry, and look what happened to them! Or did it seem so only on the surface, for payment was due, would not be denied and the victims were the most innocent ones: Ronnie, Leila and Small, while the perpetrator, the Judge seemed to escape scot free? But did he?

Our father always quoted a line from the Bible: 'The mills of God grind slow but grind exceedingly small.' Who did he have in mind?

So when the Judge summoned me to his sick-bed, for reasons of his own, I was too surprised, and after that I re-established connections with the family and was welcomed warmly by my dear cousins, Bobby and Ronnie, and even by Tony, who had hardly known me. For many years I was a regular visitor joining in all family engagements with enthusiasm and spending most of my leisure hours in the beautiful house. Leila and Millie too treated me as one of the family and of course I was their family physician and saw all the children, including that impossible Sammy, through their measles, chicken pox, sniffles and fevers. I remember once being ordered off the premises by Bobby because little Sheila had gone under the bed and was refusing to emerge as Doctor Uncle might give her an injection!

Then I got married and things changed; a different perspective came into play and I concentrated more and more on my profession, rising steadily to the summit. No children though, perhaps I had forfeited the right to father a child?

Is this how the 'mill ground' for me?

WALL-HANGING IN THE JUDGE'S ROOM

Sin and Virtue, sun and shadow,
Dappled on the grass,
Take heed unwary traveler
Lest you fall, so gently pass.
Pick your way with great care,
Step only on bright patches,
Fold your mantle close round you
In case the bramble snatches.

We are folks who play with words
And we weave the magic strands,
To show you castles in the air
And roads in shifting sands;
Make you believe others are wrong,
So suffering should be their share,
And safe in your tower of goodness,
You really don't have to care…

ONLY,

When you reach the crossroads dear
Beware 'Time', the patient saint,

His stories are better with a pinch of salt,
For it weakens the mortal taint!
He rolls his eyes and speaks you sooth
But in sooth, he lies like the truth.

2. Conversations

MADONNA AND LENA

Madonna: This doggerel, typed and framed, still hangs in my Father's room, and will hang there forever if my brothers have their way; it's one of the best rooms in the house, why do we have to treat it like a mausoleum?

Lena: Only God and your family know the reason for this ancestor worship; in our village we would say: one mouth less means more for the rest of us, and put that room to good use!

Madonna: How many years since you left your village?

Lena: Let me see…certainly not less than thirty-five years, doesn't seem so long somehow.

Madonna: So, you see how difficult it is to shake off the past? Your life in the village is still more meaningful to you than your present, even after all these years; how can you blame my brothers?

Lena: Oh I don't blame them; in any case, it would require more courage than they have to dismantle the Judge's room, especially with that ferocious portrait of his hanging there!

Madonna: Painted by a famous artist whom my father bullied unmercifully; I think all the artist's resentment went into that portrait, and he made his subject look even more fearsome than he actually was!

Lena: That would be really difficult; even for the most brilliant, how do you say it… cartoonist!

Madonna: You mean a satirist, but you really make me laugh, Lena, that is why I have always enjoyed chatting with you. Never afraid to call a spade a shovel, are you, particularly these days?

Lena: Well, someone around here definitely needs to, with all of you pussy footing around, walking on eggs, and being so careful! I, for one, find it difficult to breathe sometimes.

Madonna: But now that Leila is gone, don't you feel that you can breathe more easily?

Lena: No, it's much worse for the simple reason that there is not a dishonest bone in her body. She is tough, but she lives her beliefs and you know where you stand with her. Wish I could say that about the rest of the household!

Madonna: How much does she pay you for singing her praises?

Lena: I wouldn't say these things, if I were in your shoes, however jealous you may be. You wouldn't like her or I to speak out, especially to Ronny or even Tony, would you now? Anyway, I have a lot of work piled up and cannot waste time in idle gossip like some.

Madonna (*staring at her retreating back*): Horrible old hag! Wish she would go back to the quarters and not hang around Sheila all the time, as though she is protecting her. That child is strong and needs very little protection. I'm afraid what she is actually doing is filling her up with lies and turning her against her own folk. Must have a chat with Millie about this, but Rose must be kept out of it for she is canny and will not hesitate to make matters worse for the family to achieve her own ends. What she does not realize is that with Leila out of the way she is entirely at my mercy and will only fly as far as the 'silken shackles' allow her... But what of Tony? What if Lena goes to him? He has changed a great deal over the years, acquired a formidable personality and is actually setting himself up as an advisor to his brothers, and rightfully so, perhaps, for they will never have his worldly sense. Particularly ever since Leila fell sick, he has almost become dictatorial in his pronouncements and it's amazing to see both his older brothers defer to him. He will certainly brook no opposition when it comes to what he considers good for Leila.

It is I who need to watch my step...

TIMMY AND ROBIN

Timmy: Tell me something about granddad's cases, Robin; after all, your father was more his buddy than his servant and probably knew more secrets than my Dad or Uncle did or do, right?

Robin: The old master was most kind to my father and me, and my old man was useful to him in some ways, but...

Timmy: We know what these ways are, and I'm not interested. I don't want gossip; I want only the facts, facts about his cases!

Robin: Then why come to me? Go to the High Court and look up the records, or even better, go to his solicitor, Mr. Sen. He is still alive, going strong and should be able to give you all the facts you want.

Timmy: But he will only give me the official version that everyone knows. I want the truth.

Robin: And why do you imagine that the official version is not true?

Timmy: Don't be silly Robin, lawyers don't earn a living by speaking the truth; they are paid to dress the lie up to look like the truth; that is their trade and the more skillfully they can do it, the more they earn. You know that better than most, surely!

Robin: I do, but your grandfather was a judge; his job was to establish the truth without fear or favor, and I think he did just that, at least on most occasions.

Timmy: And on the occasions when he did not?

Robin: There was always a good reason for it, an honest reason, trust me. In certain matters he would never compromise.

Timmy: I have only your word for it, and I know you are biased. There are others, however, who see matters differently.

Robin: So, these 'others' have suddenly put these ideas into your head, why? The master has been gone these ten years and more, what good will the reconsideration of his cases do? Don't dig up dead bodies, Master Timmy, they tell strange tales sometimes, tales you do not want to hear.

Timmy: But I do want to hear, so I can answer my friends who keep hinting at things.

Robin: Your friends! You mean that shaggy-headed, pretentious bunch of loudmouths who go around interfering where they are not wanted, in the name of social reform? What do you have to prove to that lot, may I ask? If I had my way, I wouldn't let them through the gate!

Timmy: I know you don't like them, because according to you, 'they don't have class and are not fit company for me'! What an old snob you are, Robin, almost worse than your sainted master, and when he died, he sure left an able lieutenant behind! But you take my word for it, they are good and very committed people; they really want to leave this world a better place than they find it at the moment.

Robin: No doubt, better for them?

Timmy: And others…anything wrong with that?

Robin: Yes, everything! And what have they said to you now to make you want to dig into the past? How will the world benefit from this resurrection?

Timmy: Not everything has been done right in the past, you must admit; don't you think that our present trouble has its roots in the past? Do you think my Aunt Leila, who according to my uncle is as strong as a horse, fell sick just like that? Something has shocked her to such an extent that she finds herself totally alienated… So much so, that she actually wants to leave this house for good! Don't you think that something must be done now to repair the damage, before it is too late? Willy certainly thinks so.

Robin: Ah, Willy…so that's where it's all coming from… But tell me, how are you planning to put things right? How will you know what is right, and what divides right from wrong?

Timmy: Please don't talk in riddles, Robin; I hate it when you do that. It's so confusing! I am old enough to know right from wrong, and you cannot tell me different, I won't accept it.

Robin: And suppose for a moment, that you are wiser than all the wise men before you – and that you do know – how do you propose to put matters right?

Timmy: I will decide when I have the facts clear in my mind, but I am sure that some good will come of it. The honest pursuit of truth can never do any real harm, can it?

Robin: Did Willy say that too?

Timmy: Yes, initially; but now the initiative is entirely mine.

Robin: So he wants you to think; that one with his green eyes and dark hair is a clever one alright, no doubt about it.

Timmy: But he is right, isn't he? What harm can the truth do? Is it not always beautiful?

Robin: You will realize that it can do irreparable harm and that it can be quite ugly, but much later; at that point I may not be around to crow over you in my carnal body, but my spirit will keep an eye on you, never fear!

Timmy: And what exactly do you mean by that idiotic remark?

Robin: Merely that when I die, I will return as a ghost and live in that banyan tree by the gate, very close to my present post. How can I leave you to the tender mercies of your friends? My master would never forgive me, and I don't want to tangle with him, even in the spirit world!

SAMMY AND SHEILA

Sammy: You know Sheila, I have gone over the spot where I found your Mum with a fine toothcomb, but the place has not yielded a single clue.

Sheila: What exactly were you looking for, footprints, cigarette butts, or a highly distinctive handkerchief?

Sammy: Shut up Sheila! You know what your trouble is? You think you are the only clever one... Just because you are ahead of me in school in some subjects!

Sheila: Only the subjects that are supposed to require imagination, Sammy; in the others, like math, you are way ahead of me. And, if I am so clever, why did my mother abandon me? Tell me that!

Sammy: Oh, come on Sheila, she did not abandon you or any one of us. She just fell sick.

Sheila: So sick, that she cannot tell us what made her sick?

Sammy: If she could, the problem would not exist. Either she does not know, or she cannot, or will not tell.

Sheila: That is why I keep saying that something

happened that day after I left her. I tell you, she had not a thing on her mind as long as she was with me. Whatever upset her, she carried away with her, and tried to destroy before she destroyed herself behind that willow that she loved so much. There has to be something.

Sammy: Well, whatever! But tell me, what should I have been looking for?

Sheila: I wish I knew. For instance, you did not notice any fragments of burnt paper, did you?

Sammy: When I found her, I looked at nothing else. I will not forget that terrible pallor as long as I live; for a moment I thought we'd lost her!

Sheila: I know. I wish you could have seen your own face when you came running in to inform the family, white as a sheet, I thought you would faint or something. Thank goodness Uncle Tony pushed that swig of brandy down your throat!

Sammy: Rather good at that, isn't he? I mean swilling the stuff himself and helping others swill as well? Hey, that's almost as good as a pun!

Sheila: Very clever, considering your limitations! But to get back to burnt paper.

Sammy: Remember it was raining that evening? If there were any such pieces, they would get washed away.

Sheila: Not washed away...where would they go? No, the stuff would get into the soil or flow into the serpentine...so...

Sammy: The pieces could still be there!

Sheila: Exactly!

Sammy: Then, what are we waiting for?

SMALL AND FRIEND

Small: I always loved you; even as a little girl I would come and sit by you, hug you, rub myself against you, do you remember? Especially after Nan died and was buried in the garden? I would put flowers on her grave and then come and sit by you? Perhaps you don't, after all you are a busy man, but I who have so little happiness to look back on, remember every detail. And that is why I keep coming back, to relive and rejuvenate memories that I can share with no one else. But today I need you, for the fear that had not been so terrible the last few years has come back to haunt me again.

Only till a few weeks ago things were as usual, and I came to you only because I loved you, but after Madonna explained things to me and told me what she wanted me to do, although I'm not quite clear why, I said I would help her without consulting you. She said it would make me feel good if the people who had harmed me were punished, and I believed her, for Daddy always said that bad people should be punished, and Daddy was never wrong, was he? It's amazing how clear everything is till that terrible picnic and how hazy everything afterward, so it's hard to know what to do. But Madonna is my only sister and she says she loves me to distraction, whatever that may mean, so I must believe her, mustn't I? The trouble is I got so lonely sometimes, particularly that last month, when Leila was away with Ronnie on a business trip and I had no one but the kids to talk to, and they were busy with exams. During that month, Madonna took great care of me and told me many things I did not know, some of them very strange, but when I tried to speak to her, words came out all different somehow and she couldn't understand me, or at least pretended not to. This seems to happen with everyone except Leila; with her I don't have to speak. She looks into my eyes and just knows what I want, and now she is so sick, she doesn't love me anymore, she never looks into my eyes. Madonna says Leila loves no one but herself, that is why she is paying for her sins and must be punished, but Madonna, for all her talk, does not pay attention to me like Leila did. Then why is Leila bad? And she fell sick immediately after I carried out Madonna's instructions. Is that what Madonna wanted, that Leila should be sick? But if I ask Madonna, she just rolls her eyes, tells me not to be stupid or repeat my silly thoughts to anyone, for the results might be unfortunate. And when she speaks like that, staring me down with her big eyes, I am frightened.

That is why I have come to you, for love, for an explanation, for help, for comfort. When I hold you close and your rough skin presses against my breasts, a wonderful shiver runs through my body and I press harder, even though it hurts, then I try to wrap my legs around you and finally your odd finger finds its way inside. Then I push harder and your finger goes deeper, until the water breaks… After that I rest a while near you for I am torn and bleeding. Then I return to the house and go straight to sleep. And in this sleep there is pain but no terrible faces, no burning torches, no screams, no bodies, no Madonna, following me around like a shadow.

But today I need help of a different kind and you must advise me, tell me what to do; today you must speak, please, please, please... What did you say?

'Invite him by all means and all will be well?'

Oh, thank you so much! I have no one else I can trust so implicitly, so I will obey you and speak to Tony right away; I am so very troubled about what I have done.

The sky wept,

The wind sighed,

The tree stared impassively...

MADONNA AND MILLIE

Madonna: Millie, do you think that Leila should go away with her mother?

Millie: Well, it's really not our decision, is it?

Madonna: What I mean is, shouldn't we persuade Ronnie to put his foot down?

Millie: I don't see how we can; he's tried hard enough on his own, but made precious little headway.

Madonna: What about Sheila? Her mother used to be silly about her. Do you think she ought to try harder?

Millie: I think she is trying very hard to find out what has actually happened to her mother, and I have a feeling that between her and Sammy they will discover the truth.

Madonna: Oh they do fancy themselves don't they? 'Super Sleuths' is what they call themselves…funny!

Millie: Not so funny, children see clearer than adults sometimes.

Madonna: Is that why Sheila hangs about with Lena so much?

Millie: Lena? What does she have to do with this?

Madonna: Well, she has an axe to grind, surely you realize that?

Millie: Lena is a nanny; however long-standing, faithful and almost family, she is not, emphatically not, family. How does she come into the picture?

Madonna: You have been married and living in this family for twenty odd years and you can say something idiotic like that? Are all artists as blind as you are?

Millie: Please don't be mysterious, Madonna, it is very, very irritating. Why don't you speak out and tell me what I have been so blind about? Speak the whole truth for once?

Madonna: The whole truth? Is there such a thing? Never mind. Tell me, has Bobby spoken to Leila? In the old days she never went against him. He should be able to persuade her to stay on.

Millie: Do you think he has not tried? You know how fond he is of her and how heartbroken he is about the whole affair. He has begged of her to reconsider, practically on his bended knees, but she just stares at him and the tears continue to fall till... till he rushes out of the room.

Madonna: And you Millie? How hard have you tried?

Millie: Harder than I have ever tried for anything else in my life, I think. I did not plead so desperately with Timmy, my own son, when I wanted him to get out of that political club of his.

Madonna: Oh really? I thought it would suit you to have Leila out of the way for a bit so that you could come into the limelight. After all, she pretty much steals your thunder, doesn't she?

Millie: I don't know what you are talking about, Madonna. Leila brought me to public notice by arranging that exhibition of my paintings and ensuring that I have time to devote to my work by taking care of the household; no one else bothered, not even Bobby, and certainly not you!

Madonna: You poor simpleton! Have you considered the fact that this was a ruse to get you away from the home fires, from the real center of power? While you paint shadows of life tucked away in your studio, who controls the life of this family? Who is the one person we consider quite indispensable? Who do the menfolk, the children, Small, even the servants turn to in their hour of need? Not to you, that is for sure!

Millie: But that is because she is so unselfish, always so willing to tackle their problems, to go out on a limb to find solutions, because she loves everyone so much.

Madonna: And you don't?

Millie: Of course I do, but let us say, I don't have her capacity for translating love into action.

Madonna: And you do not regret this fringe life? This, this, what is the word?

Millie: Marginalization? But I have chosen that way of life. Don't you see? You cannot give yourself to your art wholly, if you grapple too closely with life. Without detachment, the vision is impaired.

Madonna: Oh, come off your high horse, Millie! All this clever talk is just talk, an excuse for failing to grapple with life, as you put it. Art, religion, poetry are creations by the weak, for the weak, the ultimate refuge of the emasculated!

Millie: That is really too much, Madonna; what is your stake in this, that you are so fierce about it?

Madonna: Nothing, really. I'm sorry I flew off the handle like that. I'll talk to you later.

Millie: No, you tell me right now!

Madonna: Well, I just want you to have your rightful place in this house that is all.

Millie: And out of this purely altruistic motive, to ensure my rights, you were trying to poison my mind against Leila? You expect me to believe this nonsense?

Madonna: Don't, it's your funeral, anyway.

Millie: Wonder what she meant by that parting shot? Not content with ruining her own life, she is determined to cause further havoc here. I will have to speak to Bobby. Maybe she should have her own establishment instead of living with us, and then she can grapple with life all she wants!

BOBBY, RONNIE, AND TONY

Bobby: Come on Ronnie, pull yourself together, this incessant grieving will not get us anywhere.

Ronny: Nothing is getting us anywhere, anyway. I just cannot face life without Leila. What will happen to the girls?

Tony: Why are you looking at the worst scenario? We have to find a way of bringing Leila back to life and keeping her in her own home, that is all.

Bobby: That is all! As usual, Tony, you go to the heart of the matter with admirable accuracy, but the modus operandi? How is this to be achieved? Do you have any concrete ideas?

Tony: You don't have to be sarcastic; this is not your courtroom but a family conclave about a very serious matter. This has to be tackled right now, or we will lose Leila forever. I do not think that we should waste any more time.

Ronnie: But we have tried everything.

Tony: No, you have not, because you have allowed yourself and your self-pity to get in the way. You are more concerned about your own future than about Leila, even at this moment!

Ronny: How can you be so unfair?

Tony: Look what you said just now... 'I cannot face life without Leila,' not, 'How will Leila live the rest of her life?' Your main focus has been your own misery ever since this happened, rather than your wife's acute unhappiness, and there lies the problem. I also think that this has been building for some time. Exploded rather dramatically, that is all!

Ronnie: So you think I have taken Leila too much for granted, and for some time? On the contrary, I have been extremely appreciative of all she has done. Leila says so herself!

Tony: Of course she does, to make you feel good about yourself. She has polished your halo so consistently that most people have come to believe in your saintliness and no one more so than you, yourself!

Ronnie: Look Tony, this is too much. You know very well what a wonderful relationship we have had all these years, and now, just because she has fallen sick, you say it is my fault, entirely? How come you never uttered these words of wisdom before?

Bobby: Yes Tony, you know that Ronnie and Leila have shared a relationship that is almost idyllic in its perfection; how can you question that now, because things have gone wrong for some purely extraneous reason?

Tony: Because reasons are never extraneous, because I do not believe in idylls, because I do not trust perfection, because Camelot never has, does not now and never will exist on earth! You claim that there was complete trust between you, then why has she turned away from you in the hour of her greatest need? Tell me why this lack of confidence in the great King Arthur on the part of his loving Guinevere?

Ronnie: Well…if you are trying to provoke me…

Tony: I am trying to puncture your bubble of self-esteem and trying to make you look inward for a change!

Bobby: But Ronnie carries self-awareness to the point of obsession and analyses all his actions more minutely than I ever do! Then why are you picking on him?

Tony: Your wife has outlets that Leila never had and has not suffered a breakdown in consequence; besides she does not have to cope with an armchair philosopher who is the most vulnerable creature on earth and quite impossible to live with. Have any of you ever realized how he has compelled Leila to be pleasant at all times, to contain all her frustrations, to never lose her temper? Is this natural? Why, he has never given her the satisfaction of a single, full-blown, no-holds-barred quarrel, ever!

Ronnie: Well, your domestic spats are famous in the neighborhood. I do not choose to emulate you in this respect, if you don't mind.

Tony: Naturally, you are too civilized for that. But it is your wife, not mine, who has had a nervous breakdown! You know what your problem is? Life has been too easy for you: a fine brain, tremendous good looks, talents galore, parents who loved you to distraction, a wife who spoiled you rotten… No wonder you cannot cope with the first crisis in your life! But believe me, this is due to a failure on your part; somewhere along the line, you have let her down terribly, so terribly, that she has withdrawn into herself completely and turned her back on all of us.

Bobby: Tony, you are very fond of Leila, aren't you? So are we all, but is it fair to blame it all on poor Ronnie? After all, it is not his fault that he has been fortunate, is it?

Tony: Oh, I know that you think that I speak out of envy, because Ronnie is everything that I am not, and how often have I heard people say that! But believe me, I have never envied either of you. Why should I? Deprivation is a precious gift I have always cherished, for it has given me perspective. 'Only those whom the Gods damn, they make unvaryingly fortunate and virtuous.' Proverb; do think about it.

Bobby: What proverb is that? You just made it up!

Tony: What if I did? Does it not have the ring of truth? Remember our father's famous phrase?

Bobby: Who can forget? But explain the bit about virtue, please. What on earth…?

Tony: Virtue is man's second nature, never his first, do you agree? That means behavior that is acquired rather than reflexive, right? Have you ever thought of the tremendous pressure the virtuous man labors under, living up to his second nature, fighting to sublimate his natural predilections, constantly playing a part? He has no safety valves, simply because he has discarded them as weaknesses! On top of that, if he is unvaryingly fortunate he has lost the last excuse for lapsing into his natural mode, and no man or woman can take such a strain indefinitely... Something has to give!

Ronnie: And that is your explanation of Leila's illness?

Tony: It may not be the whole truth, but a pretty fair chunk of it, I'm sure. You see, you never gave her an opportunity to be selfish, rude or just plain wicked, by setting yourself such impossibly high standards and expecting her to follow suit, and for so many years!

Bobby: Well Ronnie, what do you think? Perhaps you have been rather exacting, both on yourself and Leila? I do know for a fact that the whole family has demanded a great deal in emotional and spiritual terms from both of you, and you have given without reserve, but perhaps the strain has been too much for her, and you too, though you have never let us feel it?

Ronnie: What did Tony say, that suffering confers perspective, something that I lack due to my good fortune? What about my experiences as a child during the Case? I think I paid a large enough premium then for future insurance, and though Tony was too young to remember, surely you have not forgotten, Bobby? In any case, if there were arrears, I believe I have made up for those in the last few weeks. And from my new-found vantage point I am now wondering whether Tony's moral indignation on Leila's behalf comes only from his affection for her, or whether there is a deeper cause? Don't worry Bobby, I will get to the bottom of this, if it's the last thing I do, but some people may wish that they had kept their own counsel better, when I get going.

Bobby:　　Oh God! What have you started now, Tony?

Tony:　　I'm neither afraid nor sorry. If this helps to bring them together again, I don't care how much he hates me now. This shake-up was needed; we have been living in Never Never Land forever. High time we took off our wings and walked on our feet!

ROSE AND SMALL

Rose: Why don't you spend more time with me, now that Leila is sick? I am sure that you must feel very lonely at times.

Small: I do, even though Ronnie, Sammy and Sheila do their best, and Bobby, Tony and Millie try hard too.

Rose: I care for you too, please believe me.

Small: Sure you do and mainly because of Tony, I know that; only…

Rose: No one is like Leila, right?

Small: Quite right! She is one in a million you have to admit!

Rose: Wish I had her magic touch, and then you would say such things about me too.

Small: Yes she has magic; she can really make you feel good about yourself; help you forget that… forget that you are terribly different from everyone else…

Rose: But we are all different from each other, aren't we? So what is special about that?

Small: Just look at that mirror on the wall, Rose, and tell me what you see.

Rose: The two of us sitting on the bed and chatting.
            What else do you expect me to see?

Small: You see one very beautiful woman who is very
            aware of her own attraction, and you see a
            misshapen, stunted, wild-haired creature, who
            is also supposed to be a woman. Why do you
            pretend that there is no difference?

Rose: But, but…

Small: But what? That is taken for granted, right? Do
            you remember how you reacted when you came
            into this house and saw me for the first time,
            even though Leila had warned you? You clung
            to Tony, closed your eyes and said 'who is that?'
            as though you were in the grip of a nightmare.

Rose: I admit that I was young and stupid, but later…

Small: You had to put up with me didn't you, because
            the family, particularly Leila and Ronnie, would
            not have things different? But you never touch
            me if you can help it, even today. Will you ever
            be able to hold me to your heart as Leila always
            did? Would you trust me with your baby, as
            Leila did with both her girls when they were
            little? You can't ever understand her magic, leave
            alone duplicate it, for it is love, pure and simple
            love, of which you have a very little, and that
            too only for yourself and for those you consider
            your own!

Rose: That is not fair!

Small: Yes, it is! Have either you, or Millie, or even
            Madonna noticed how long and unkempt my
            hair is looking, leave alone do anything about it?

Rose: We have all been so busy…sorry! I will take you

for a haircut this minute; come, we will go now!

Small: You have lived in this house for so many years, and you don't know that I am terrified of knives and scissors? Do you know that my hair used to hang to my knees in knots till Leila came, because I could trust no one after my mother passed away? But somehow, I could trust her around me with a pair of scissors after about six months persuasion, and she gave me the smartest haircut ever. After that she regularly trimmed my hair, till, till she fell sick.

Rose: Shall I try?

Small: Give me one good reason why I should trust you over others, over my own blood?

Rose: Well, if you put it like that, I really don't have an answer, but you could give me a chance now that Leila can no longer be of use to you, may never be of use to you anymore.

Small: So that is your little game, is it? That Leila will be permanently out of circulation and that you will take her place? Well, you are wrong on both counts. One: It is not what you do, but who you are that matters, and you can never be Leila! Two: She will get well again, and that is a promise I have made to myself; it will take pain, it will take atonement, it will take resolve, it might even take blood, mine and others', but Leila will be her wholesome self again…

Rose: You are giving me the creeps, Small, whatever do you mean by 'blood, yours and others'?

Small: Wouldn't you just love to know?

WALL-HANGING IN THE LIBRARY

The Pursuit is relentless,
The pursuer insistent,
The feet pound endlessly behind,
The victim flees helplessly,
The maze twists ruthlessly,
The mirror deceives perpetually,
The path circles inexorably,
The mind reels tiredly,
The body struggles weakly,

TILL

Evasion is impossible,
All escape routes are blocked,
Shelter is withdrawn,
Space closes in, claustrophobic,
Breathless, coffin-like,
No space to turn away,
Face to face at last with the pursuer,
Known and not-known...I...?

This is a face familiar, and unfamiliar,

The features seen and not seen,
The contours glimpsed, merely hinted at,
Tantalizing, teasing, tortured, troubled,
Defying recognition, hinting at reversal,
Beautiful, but half eaten by leprosy,
The eyes semi-open with vision impaired,
The sharp, scarred edge of truth, at last!

Anonymous

3. Rumination

MADONNA LOOKING BACK

I loved him with a passion that is impossible to recall now, for the body of the impetuous sixteen-year-old is no longer mine, but even today the effort of coping with sudden, unbidden remembrance while carrying on a correct, purely casual conversation, is difficult as it causes a stirring in my heart and loins that is so intense, so uncomfortable, that I have to push these feelings away determinedly and ensure that my spotless, white outfit remains white, spotless, chaste, colorless, for there are many sharp eyes that would love to spot a discrepancy between who I was, who I am, or who they think I am.

But on a listless Sunday afternoon when the light is sad and touches my skin so the wrinkles become apparent under the outwardly smooth surface like dark shapes beneath calm water, when the carefully nurtured lustrous hair shows patches of dry gray, when my arms are empty and my soul desolate, then it is impossible to keep memories at bay... They rush out of their dark caves, attack me from every possible angle, and I am helpless against their fierce onslaught.

I was so proud of my control of self, my renunciation, my self-abnegation, my ability to hide my bleeding heart, of being able to live up to my father's created image of a twentieth century Madonna, one who could sublimate her passions, her forbidden love and wait patiently for the holy flame to be ignited within the bonds of an immaculate marriage. Only a child of sixteen is capable of such absurd faith, naively believing that her supreme self-sacrifice will be rewarded, recognized, that pity will penetrate the armor of an angry god and he will relent somehow, someday, somewhere, in a heaven for fools. What would have happened if I had spoken out and rebelled? Run away? I think at one stage I might have taken an extreme step if I'd had even a speck of encouragement, but it never came. For one day I spun him a tale about two people in a similar situation, and the look of horror in his eyes, the sheer contempt of such immorality was warning enough. For him it was marriage or nothing, and I went back to warring with myself endlessly, convinced that I was pleasing him, and that tenuous conviction was sufficient to make me persist in my folly. Later, much later he begged me to do what I had wanted in the first place, but by then it was too late and the angry God had got his way.

Sufficient to make me accept passively what was considered a wonderful match: the eldest son of an elite family, politically very well connected, with a huge estate about two hundred miles away from our home. The father practiced in the Supreme Court, was an important member of the Congress government and spent most of his time in the capital city of Delhi. The elder son, a successful barrister, had his own house in town and lived there for extended periods, for he practiced at the High Court. I would live there and would be required to visit the ancestral home only during state occasions. When I think back today, I am convinced that my father had a very fair inkling of my state of mind, and therefore tried to make it up to me by fixing the most spectacular match he could find. Only, even he did not possess a crystal ball.

When Sunny came visiting with his parents, I was impressed despite my misgivings. Dark, aquiline face alive with intelligence, courteous in every gesture and word, swift, agile, manly, he had the family eating out of his hands in no time. Ronnie and Bobby liked him immensely and even Tony, all of five at the time, pronounced his approval:

'Sis can marry him if she wants!'

What particularly inclined our family in his favor was his sensitive handling of Small, and the way his family included her in every event without a hint of intrusion.

As I got to know Sunny better he reminded me more and more of 'him' in the oddest way… Looks or background wise there was no similarity at all, but something at the core of both human beings was alike. I was too rebellious and confused to analyze further at the time, but looking back I now realize that it was the main factor that tipped the balance ultimately. I am sure, too, that my father also shared this knowledge and used it consciously to get his way.

When two eminent families are allied in matrimony in India, a certain element of rivalry, though subtle and understated, seems to be inevitable. The one-upmanship is particularly evident in the extravagance of the presents that the families exchange, the jewelry that is given to the bride and the groom, the scale of the banquets and festivities, the variety of entertainment provided. And I have to admit that my Father came off second best despite his best efforts, especially in the area of ornaments and guest lists, for even he could not hope to match the ancestral glory or the political history of Sunny's family. At the reception in their city residence, a small affair compared to the show on their estate, I was covered in gold and jewels from head to foot, and needed assistance from a cousin to get to my feet from a reclining position! My mother-in-law said to me later, rather apologetically, that it was the family custom to put at least five thousand grams of gold on a new bride! The coronet, studded with diamonds, alone took care of two hundred grams and my slender neck held it up more by will power than natural strength! Anybody who was anybody, Indian or British, was present, and _____, the governor of the Reserve Bank, pronounced us one of the handsomest couples in India.

An auspicious beginning, I wondered?

The journey to the ancestral home would take two days by train, boat and car. We would break journey at _____, where the family had yet another house, spend the night there and leave in the morning, cross the river and arrive at the estate by the afternoon. I would spend these nights with my sisters-in-law and nuptials would only be solemnized the night we reached home on the bed used for the purpose by generations of Sunny's forbears. This gave me the breathing space I needed, and an opportunity to get to know Sunny better and gauge perhaps the level of his physical need, for that was my main fear; would I be able to go through the motions without betraying myself? Sunny was eight years my senior, a lawyer with very sharp eyes, no doubt more experienced in man-woman matters, would he be taken in by my feeble efforts? In any case, how did he expect me to behave? Normally, a girl of my age would have gone with her instincts, allowed her body to guide her, but how would I react to his advances when every nerve in my body apprehended his touch?

The journey by train was uneventful, but the increasing lushness, the dun and brown giving way to myriad shades of green, fascinated me, as did the water-birds on the fast-increasing number of ponds and lakes. I wanted to know their names but the girls did not know; finally Sunny not only supplied names, but little rhymes to go with them; for instance:

> The snipe looks for worms in the mud,
> The kingfisher dives swiftly for fish,
> The mallard floats majestically by,
> The stork, on one leg, is quite still.
> The heron picks his way in the lake,
> The 'dark one' with its divided tail,
> The blue jay with its flashing blues,
> The occasional oriole and the quail….
>
> (My translation)

This unexpected aspect of his persona made me look at him with renewed interest, and I also noticed what a charming smile he had, the way the corner of his mouth puckered and his eyes lit up when he looked at me.

We were running behind schedule, and late at night the train stopped with a jolt and woke me up. I looked out of the window and realized that the halt was unplanned, for we were in a deep, dark wilderness, everybody was asleep, the night lights were burning low... A wild thought crossed my mind: if I got down quietly and walked away now, no one would know. The future did not enter the picture...all I could think of at that point was that I would not have to face Sunny on the night. What was I afraid of? That I would not be able to bear his touch or that in my growing attraction for Sunny, I might prove disloyal to 'him'?

Oh, the follies of youth!

I got up quietly, put on my slippers; no one was awake or stirring. Very, very carefully I picked my way to the door; the door handle turned easily, and I was down the steps in a flash and standing on firm ground staring into the darkness. What next? If I managed to get away would I be able to find my way to him, for I had a vague idea that he operated somewhere in this area... I had barely taken a few, faltering steps when a quiet hand fell on my shoulder and I turned to see Sunny looking down at me, not in anger but with genuine concern.

'Running away? Running from me or from you? Have you a plan of action in place? Where will you go?'

So many pertinent questions, and I did not have an answer to a single one! So I shook my head dumbly and my tears splashed on to his hand in a steady trickle.

He took me firmly by the shoulder and said:

'Get back in the compartment before other people wake up, find out and create a scene. You have nothing to fear, believe me. We will sort things out once we get home, I promise.'

Even before he had finished speaking, my older sister-in-law poked her head out of the window, wanting to know what was going on. Sunny caught me to him in a bear-hug and said with a sheepish smile:

'Nothing sister, just explaining things to Madonna, she has never traveled in this region before.'

'Oh, I see, a lesson in geography, nothing more, and that

too in the middle of the night? How very thoughtful you are, Sunny!'

Amidst more banter in this vein and much laughter, I regained my compartment, lay down and tried to sleep, but sleep would not come. The beating of Sunny's heart against mine was too loud in my ears.

The river was a revelation in terms of expanse and turbulence; the waves that rose and fell with unerring regularity were more reminiscent of the sea and I wondered what sort of craft would take us across these vast waters and what kind of terrain awaited us beyond. My fears were partly allayed when a houseboat with the family name flying on the pennant hove into view, and I was conducted with much ceremony by the steward to the Victoria Suite done up in blue and gold brocade. An English breakfast complete with fried eggs, liver and kidneys, honey and blackberry jam with hot buttered toast, made me realize how hungry I was, and I tucked in with a will that was perhaps unseemly in a bride, but Sunny did not seem to mind and kept me company throughout, as did his sisters and only brother, Josh, who was training in the medical profession. His sense of humor appeared quite irrepressible, and soon the room was alive with witty conversation and laughter. An hour later I suddenly realized that I was no longer sad, and also, more strangely, that I did not hate the idea of being alone with Sunny.

Very suddenly, as is usual in the foothills of the Himalayas, the sun hid its face in the clouds and the wind changed from a gentle friend to an angry demon, blowing hard as though it wished to capsize the boat. We women were hard put to hang on to our seats but the two brothers walked out onto the deck and I noticed with growing confidence the easy authority with which they took charge, how dexterously they managed the helm by turn and saw the boat through the rough patch; also, how implicitly the crew trusted them and deferred to their judgment without demur. The relationship that existed between masters and men was one of a different equality than I had been used to in my own house, and I suddenly realized that these men were gearing up for a new, democratic India that was emerging from years of colonial rule, trying to reduce the social gap that had existed during the days of feudal and then British rule between man and master. Used to tirades against the great unwashed and longing for the civilized days of the Raj in my own family, this took me by surprise, and I decided then and there, to conform to this new code in my new home. After all, my mother was very different, Lena had been my good friend at my mother's insistence, till she was sent away, and what of Robin, without whom we could not manage for a day? Besides, had this insistence on equality not been at the heart of 'his' being, his very soul that had so set me on fire? When the brothers returned we went back to the ready badinage as though there had been no interruption, and I think this aplomb and lack of fuss impressed even me more than their obvious courage.

The estate was a vast sprawling affair, well over two thousand acres, with orchards, fields of grain and vegetables, a poultry farm, a huge lake for fishing and a haven for migratory birds, rows of neat cottages for the farmers who lived and worked there, a primary school for their children and a hospital for the entire neighborhood. All this came into view while we drove in the family Rolls from the landing stage of the river to and then through the estate. The family mansion, built in the early colonial style, boasted a hundred doors, a hundred and fifty windows, and fifty tall columns that supported the massive edifice. My entry and welcome was not merely magnificent with the blowing of a hundred conch shells, but replete with affection and genuine feeling, and when the elders pronounced me 'just right for Sunny', I felt a surge of pride in my heart that was not perhaps entirely unexpected, but surprisingly welcome.

The night found me resplendent in red and gold on the ancestral, flower-bedecked bed in a room that had seen every nuptial of the men-folk of the family for more than a century. After seating me on the bed, my mother-in-law had blessed me and simply said:

'May you be as happy as I have been in this house and may you have a son as wonderful as Sunny.'

When I touched her feet and then looked up into her face, I found to my complete astonishment that the one prayer in my heart was the echo of her own blessings.

Somehow, her words, her complete faith in me and the future, had gone straight to my soul and brought quick tears to my eyes, and I had thought to myself:

'I cannot let these people down; they do not deserve to be hurt; an old loyalty must make way for a new one and I must do my best to make the lie true.'

In my glorious romanticization of self, I turned a blind eye to the fact that I had almost fallen in love with Sunny and that to be a wife to him in the real sense of the term would be no great hardship! What adepts the young are at self-deception, particularly when it shows them up in an impossibly virtuous light. How would I have reacted if I could have brought my present cynicism and self-knowledge to bear on the situation? Thank God, I will never know.

As soon as all the clocks in the house had struck the

midnight hour in perfect unison, my mother-in-law shooed all the young people from the room like a bunch of chicken and insisted that they leave us alone. She also reminded us that a visit to the family temple had been scheduled for the morrow and that we would leave the house by 7:30 a.m., as it was an hour's drive from the house. Benediction writ large on every line on her face, she closed the door gently on us, and I am sure it was only my hyperactive imagination that detected an element of acute anxiety that underlay the good will?

Sunny sat down next to me and put his arm around me; how he interpreted the tremor that shot through my body I never got to know, for he smiled at me and said:

'I have not forgotten that you were trying to run away the other night, and though I want to know why, I will not question you till you want to tell me of your own accord. The day you do, I will perhaps have a story of my own to tell you, but that is in the future. For the present, why don't you change into something more comfortable and then we can both get some sleep?'

He quietly withdrew his arm, and if he had an inkling of my fierce disappointment, he certainly did not show it. In twenty minutes we had both changed, the light was out and I was pretending to sleep although it had never been farther from my eyes. Sunny's even breathing soon indicated his deep slumber and my humiliation was complete. The prima donna had been neatly upstaged and no one the wiser! What had I expected? Grand scenes of passion and attempted seduction, quiet, dignified surrender on my part in the line of duty, which he would appreciate and cherish as a sign of my saintliness? But, the Madonna undone and no applause, this had never been part of the scenario! Hot tears of shame flowed into my pillow till the gods of fatigue and sleep took pity.

For the next three months the pattern of our relationship remained unvaried: easy camaraderie, sharing of common interests of which we had many, growing closeness with each other's families, my increasing interest in nature under his tutelage, learning about his cases and the ramifications of the law. We traveled frequently between the estate and our town residence, and with my mother's help I began to acquire the housekeeping and hostess skills that were expected of me as the elder daughter-in- law of an elite family and the wife of a barrister with a fast-growing reputation. But through all this we remained polite strangers, who never disagreed, never lost tempers, never let guards down, never got to the marrow of things, and who knew nothing at all of each other's innermost, personal thoughts. Sunny did not seem to mind, though his smile slipped a little occasionally, but the strain for me was getting unbearable.

To add to my misery, it had begun to dawn on me that I just could not face the thought of life without Sunny, that I craved his closeness with passion, but also that this closeness which was once mine for the asking, would now only come at a price due to my own folly on that silly night, and the terrible fear that I might lose him altogether if I made a clean breast of things, that I might have to return to my father's house in shame, pushed me practically to paranoia. Close to breaking point, yet in the throes of this terrible indecision, I remained precariously poised but quite passive and yet another month passed.

Through all this I was learning about certain unsuspected or un-thought-of characteristics of this family. My father-in-law, though educated abroad and a very successful lawyer, much courted by the Raj for his influence in the area, was first and last a nationalist, a supporter of Purna Swaraj even in the revolutionary sense, and there were clear indications that his sympathies lay with the revolutionaries who were making a violent bid for freedom. He was very strongly against the Dominion Status that my own father advocated so fiercely, and felt that blood and iron were needed to loosen the foundation of British rule in India. He deeply admired Aurobindo Ghosh, and rumor had it that he worked with him and his party. Both the sons took their cues from him, and though thoroughly anglicized, had a great love of their own language, literature, history and philosophy. This reminded me poignantly of my own mother, her divided loyalties and of course, of 'him'. I really had to watch my step and my tongue in many ways.

One evening I was dressing for a party and I managed to get the clasp of my necklace entangled in my hair. Normally, I would have called the maid to assist me, but this was her evening off, and try as I might, I just could not get it free, for the clasp was old-fashioned and complicated. I was contemplating a pair of scissors when there was a knock on the door, and Sunny enquired whether he could enter. Though I was clad only in a blouse and petticoat, I threw caution to the winds and asked him to come in. He took one look at me and was about to turn away when I walked up to him and asked him to undo the clasp. With infinite patience that was characteristic, he untangled each strand and then asked, very business-like, whether he should place it round my neck and press the clasp. He had been so absorbed in his task that he had failed to notice that I had been observing the entire tableau in the mirror in front of us, and seen the look of intense longing he had cast on me once or twice; so instead of saying anything, I turned around, hugged him close and begged him to forgive me.

My pathetic little confession came out in a flood of tears causing a definite aloofness on his part initially, but then, strangely, a curious sense of relief and easing of tension became apparent in his body language as I continued to hold him close. But when I assured him that the whole thing was over and done with and that he was the only man I would ever love, a look of infinite sadness overcast his features that took me by surprise. Did he not believe me after all?

But he returned my hug and said:

'Let's get the party done with and then, later, we can talk.'

And later, deep into the night, when the moon was full and flooding the earth with its radiance, he held me close, buried his face in my hair and told me his story:

As children, both brothers had all played with the sons of the farmers on their estate, and while Josh and he had initiated them into the mysteries of football and cricket, they in turn had taught them to hunt, to lay traps for animals, to handle boats, to find easy paths up the steep mountains, to look at birds' nests and eggs without disturbing the owners. During school holidays in winter, a regular shikar or hunting trip would be arranged and they would spend anything up to a week in the mountains chasing bear, boar, tiger, cheetah and leopard. At night they would camp in tents, light a fire, and sit around it late into the night, singing and exchanging stories. Then they took turns to ensure that the fire, which was their lifeline, did not go out while the rest slept the dreamless sleep of the brave and the fatigued. The easy relationship between the owner and the tenants and their sons that had impressed me on the very first day, had been forged in these years. Sunny said rather wistfully that those were the happiest days of his life and for some reason, the use of the past tense struck an indefinable chill in my heart.

The year Sunny had turned fifteen, the Governor of Bengal had come on a visit, and Sunny's father had arranged a magnificent affair complete with lavish tents that had carpets on the floor, adjacent bathrooms and petromax lighting! About a hundred people had gone on the trip apart from family members and guests; beaters, cooks, guides, runners, carriers, cleaners and gun bearers. The women of the house, including Sunny's mother, had accompanied them, and so, professional hunters had been called in to take care of the unforeseen. So does man propose.

On the third night stakes with sharp tips had been driven firmly into the ground and several goats had been tied to them to lure a leopard who had been seen in the area, and whom the beaters with their assortment of instruments, including drums and tin cans, were driving steadily towards the machan or eight-foot high platform, on which the shikaris or main hunters were seated with their hunting rifles and binoculars. Sunny and Josh, who were not permitted to be on the machan, had hung around hoping for a glimpse of the magnificent animal before it was shot down. With agonizing slowness the thud-thud of the drums, the plunk plunk of the tin cans and the whining of the banshee had moved closer, yet closer. The two boys had strained every nerve to penetrate the darkness before others, to catch the first glimpse. Then, unaccountably, the cacophony had moved away, dwindled and finally died down. The hunters exchanged anxious glances and runners were dispatched to make enquiries.

Unable to bear the suspense, Sunny had stealthily climbed the tree under which the platform had been built to get a better look; Josh had wanted to follow suit, but severely repressed by his brother, had stood sullenly at the bottom, awaiting an opportune moment when his back would be turned. Sunny climbed about thirty feet, ensconced himself firmly in a convenient fork, and peered around. The darkness appeared solid, impenetrable to begin with, but as he continued to stare it was pierced by innumerable points of light and it began to resolve itself into branches, leaves and other shapes he did not recognize; for like the end of a kaleidoscope, the fireflies formed a million patterns as they flew around continuously and Sunny was so mesmerized by their display that he failed to notice a pair of bigger lights moving towards him. The leopard would have got him if it had not been for Josh who had begun the climb, gone up about fifteen feet when he had noticed the animal and shouted out a desperate warning. Sunny had seen the fierce face ten feet from him and in a blind rush to get away had slipped and fallen headlong.

The fall saved his life but marred it permanently, for he fell not on the ground but on one of the stakes that pierced his trousers, sliced neatly through his genitals and went into his left groin. He had hung impaled there like a grotesque, broken doll for ten minutes, his life's blood draining away, before the shocked family had got its act together.

It had taken five hours on an improvised stretcher in a jeep to get him out of the jungle and another five to the hospital. By the time the doctors got to him they had given up hope, for vital nerves had died and they had no way of bringing these back to life. However, they had reckoned without the boy's fierce determination, rock-like will power, excellent health and his mother's prayers. The pair had fought back steadily and within a year Sunny was back on the football field as good as new, only not quite. Although he might manage an erection occasionally, he would never father a child in this life.

He had agreed to the marriage after much soul-searching only because he had perceived my innate reluctance and imagined that I would welcome a physically understated liaison. However, if now I felt betrayed because my feelings had changed, he would set me free without delay, although it would really break his heart to do so. When he pulled away and compelled me to look at him I was totally taken aback, for I had never imagined that such poignant anxiety could be reflected in a pair of human eyes, and I only hoped that the irony of the situation would not strike him too forcibly, and that he would never realize to what extent the situation had reversed.

I can still recall with immediate poignancy how the moonlit garden had turned a smoky gray and the singing petals in my heart had withered and fallen on hearing these words; how tears had choked me completely and I had insisted on burying my face in his chest as tightly as I could so that he would not see my disappointment. But my mind was racing too. Suddenly the time for silly, romantic pretenses was over; this was real, the greatest challenge life had thrown at me, demanded true courage of me, and I was not about to fail this time. At the least I would give it my very best shot. So I put my hand on his thigh and said:

'I have never made love in my life…will you show me how?'

And he did.

Contrary to expectations, our relationship for the next

ten years was quite idyllic: Companionship matured into friendship, there was little recrimination and the give and take of sex continued to be exciting, passionate, of waxing desire, even though it did not lead to procreation. Perhaps I was not the most maternal of women, for I did not miss having a child of my own, particularly after Josh's wife, who produced two boys in quick succession and insisted that I relieve her of the burden of excessive motherhood and take care of one! The boy, Joy, became the center of the universe for Sunny and the little fellow called him Dada from day one, and that was that. I was quite content to be surrogate mother as long as Sunny continued to love me and accept me as Joy's Mum. Life continued to flow, tranquil on the whole as I learned quickly how to gain the unconditional love of the child, a fact that delighted Sunny no end. In any case, these were busy years, for coping with the changes that the country's altered political situation brought, kept the menfolk busy and traveling a great deal. At Sunny's insistence, I involved myself in various social projects that kept me busy, imparted a sense of fulfillment, but also compelled me to rub shoulders with the great unwashed.

For instance, I was member of a Ladies' Club with many British members who donated time and service to eye-camps that were held all over the country from the fifties onwards, to help poor villagers to get the cataracts removed from their eyes. Primitive in the extreme, these camps were nothing but makeshift tents, sheets of torn canvas draped over bamboo frames. Inside were trestle tables covered with old sheets or blankets, often blood-stained, and a series of patients lay on them one after the other, pretty much like fish for sale on stone slabs in markets, patiently awaiting the doctor's arrival. These eye surgeons were busy people, some donating time out of conscience, others most unwillingly in the thrall of the idealistic wave that was still riding high in the country. They usually came in late and then went through the tents like whirlwinds, never spending more than five minutes on a patient. We, ladies, shone a torch in the patient's eye while the assistant perfunctorily swept a wad of cotton-wool faintly smelling of disinfectant and obviously not pristine, over it. Then one of us held the eye open while the doctor made a quick snip in the cornea with a pair of scissors and pushed out the cataract like a thick brown button. A stitch if considered necessary, another swipe of the cotton-wool, a piece of gauze taped over the eye and the operation was complete, the doctor striding down the aisle to the next patient. Five minutes later, a relative came in, bundled the person into an adjacent tent for three days of post-operative care. This consisted of providing an eye-patch, a prescription for spectacles and khichri twice a day for three days. After which, they were transferred on to bullock carts for the long haul back to their villages, absurdly grateful to the Sarkar, us ladies and the kind doctors for the free medical services provided. Strangely, I still cannot get the stench of their long unwashed clothes and bodies out of my nostrils and their blessings: bathe in milk and produce sons, so terribly ironic, out of my mind. Yet, in a strange way, those were some of the best years of my life.

But in the long run it was not enough to dress in borrowed feathers. After the thirtieth birthday, which the family celebrated with great fanfare, I woke up late. On the way to my bath I caught a look at myself in the same mirror that had proved a turning point for me twelve years ago, and stopped dead in my tracks. It was as though the mirror image was someone I did not know, a totally alien being looking back and mocking me, my so called adjustments, my courage, my resilience, all the flattering attributes I had given myself, pointing out that I had merely found palliatives for hypocrisy, and lack of self. The face was older, contemptuous, not the person I knew or thought I knew to be myself, at all. I hurried away to shower vigorously, but when I looked in the mirror again, water dripping from my hair on to the carpet, it was the same face, and the sound of the dripping water grew louder and louder and beat like a hammer in my brain till I lost consciousness.

Fortunately, I came to in a few minutes, picked myself up and tried to carry on as usual, but though the image did not appear in the mirror again, it haunted me the minute the lights went out, constantly, contemptuously, and mercilessly. I began to suffer from frequent bouts of depression and occasional blackouts that I was at my wit's end to account for, and just could not fight off the despair that enveloped me. The feeling that I had made a compromise that was not worth it, began to grow on me. It is not that I loved Sunny less, but the quality of that love was changing inevitably as he focused more and more on the child, and the innate sterility of the relationship became only too obvious. What did the future hold, except more compromise, more pretense that all was well, and a false sense of fulfillment in having a son who was not mine, after all? Sunny had the same blood running in his veins and could perhaps believe Joy was his son in spirit as well as flesh, but I could only pretend a love I did not feel and hold my breath that I would not be found out. For the next thirty years? Why? This was not heroism, but cowardice and a negation of life. Was it for this that I had turned my back on every hope of true passion, sense of oneness, the flowering of fertility? And the more I thought about what I had lost, the more I hated this trap of false motherhood.

I think the first to react was Joy; children operate on instinct and for no apparent or good reason, Joy began to go to Sunny for his homework and to his own mother when his Dada was busy. When I tried to hug him, he could not control the tremor of revulsion that ran through his little frame, though he too, did his best to pretend otherwise. The conflicting messages that his instincts and consciousness were sending him were confusing him and causing him considerable pain. But one day when he broke down and told his Dada that he wanted to sleep in a separate room with him and not share him with Mama, Sunny turned to me with a look I did not like, and I realized that a choice would ultimately have to be made.

According to a Spanish proverb, every man should plant a tree, build a house and beget a son. It says nothing about wives. Joy was Sunny's ticket to immortality, but he was not mine. And I did not think that the situation would change with time, for Sunny was against sending Joy to boarding school and wanted to bring up his son himself. I certainly did not want to give up Sunny, partly because I still loved him a great deal and mainly because no alternative was available that could compare with my present lifestyle. Habits of social eminence and luxury seduce unobtrusively but surely, and my father's home, once the epitome of all that was gracious, now seemed shabby by comparison, and was today very much the domain of my brothers and their various wives, particularly Leila, who held the whole family in affectionate thrall and who was so good to me when I visited. But this welcome was so warm perhaps because I visited rarely, and in style? How would she react if I went back as an inmate, a refugee? Besides, I had been thoroughly spoiled by Sunny's patience and forbearance. Convinced that I had made the supreme sacrifice of my life in standing by him, he had put up with my recent moods and tantrums with a loving equanimity, which was nothing short of Olympian. I certainly did not see my redoubtable Dad being as patient with me, particularly if I decided to give up my wonderful life and went back on a permanent basis. What choices did I have? Carry on pretending for the rest of my life till the pretense merged with the reality, or till I failed to perceive the difference? And I might have done just that, had it not been for Joy.

I really did my best for a couple of months to get back on the original footing with the child, to woo him back to the games and activities we had shared, to get him to listen to his favorite stories, to lure him with the tarts and pastries which only I could once make just right for him, but to no avail. It was as though an invisible wire had snapped, casting him adrift on a sea of alienation that I could not navigate. It was not so much what he said or did that spelled out estrangement, but the way he looked at me. His limpid, hazel eyes darkening with an emotion akin to terror, and then the withdrawal into himself, without movement, as though he had remained still and a shell had formed around him. I was not used to people spurning me, and the child's recalcitrance, which Sunny observed quietly, upset me and made me angrier than I cared to admit, even to myself.

Winter arrived with a bang in a flurry of wind, rain and hail, the windows rattled, the curtains billowed; closing so many doors was not easy and we ran around like mad with the servants battling the elements, which seemed to be in their true element that night. When I arrived in my bedroom near midnight tired, footsore and seeking comfort, Joy was tightly curled up on his side of the bed, the quilt drawn firmly over his head to keep out the thunder. He was like a cat and the hair on his head bristled with electricity just as a cat's fur does, and it terrified him. Recognizing his frame of mind, I felt for his hand under the quilt but he said very quietly:

'Mama, I'm so glad you are here, now I can go to sleep.'

And he lay perfectly still under the quilt.

So I went to my side, put up my feet and leaned back against the pillows. There was a momentary lull in the storm and both of us must have dozed off, when suddenly a shrill clap of thunder sliced through the silence and brought me to my feet. At that moment Sunny came into the room and before I could say a word Joy flew past me straight into Sunny's arms, weeping in sheer terror, his short-cropped hair crackling with static.

It took half an hour to calm him down and another hour to get him to sleep; Sunny spent all night cradling Joy in his arms and only when the fingers of dawn were creeping across the sky did he put him down on the bed, turn to me and ask, despite his own fatigue: 'Were you scared too?'

Suddenly it was all too much and clinging to him I wept my heart out and Sunny comforted me just as he had Joy, but his face was troubled.

Out of the blue, my father fell seriously sick, and Sunny, Joy and I rushed back to town, to his bedside. The stroke had robbed him of his towering personality and left him uncharacteristically vulnerable, with a pleading look in his eyes that none of us could account for, as he steadily refused to admit what, if anything, was troubling him. While I spent most of my time with him, Joy became a part of the family and hardly came to me or even his Dada. He followed Sammy and Sheila all day, slept with Sammy at night and of course, clung to Leila as he had never clung to me. It was quite embarrassing as Sunny noticed it all, and I had to send urgent signals to my own family members to indicate that all was well, but I don't think they were convinced.

Finally, on the night the doctors told my brothers that the end might be near, although patients in his situation could also spend the next ten years in bed, practically a vegetable, Father sent for me and indicated that the other family members should leave us alone. His eyes were closed, and as I sat quietly by him, the nature of our relationship, our many silent conflicts which had always ended with capitulation on my side, his unrelenting ways, yet unexpected kindnesses, his desire to compensate me for some indefinable lack, yet the iron discipline he imposed on me, passed through my mind in silhouette, like shadows on a revolving glass.

His joy when my marriage was solemnized and when I came back to the house with Sunny to pay an extended visit. He had spared no pains to make that visit memorable, show his complete approval of Sunny, and made sure that the entire family bent backwards to do their bit. As I mulled over those happy days, I suddenly realized his eyes were open and that he was looking at me with a strange, indefinable expression. What was it, a terrible pleading or pity? And in a moment I remembered that I had seen the same expression once, and once only before in his eyes, on that memorable visit. With the joy there had been a touch of poignant anxiety in his eyes, which had given way gradually to increasing relief as the days passed. Why? Like a clap of thunder followed by sheet lightning that irradiates the entire landscape for a second, realization flooded my mind and I saw clearly for the first time:

My father had known about Sunny's disability all along, and despite that had gone through the motions.

I held his right hand in both mine, and the agonized question fell from my lips like blood-red embers, burning as they fell:

'Why, Father, why?'

And he put his other hand over both mine, summoned his last ounce of strength, and told me why, but added, Prophet like:

'I know that you have lost a great deal, but very few people have even as much as you do. Make sure you keep what you have by following in your mother's footsteps, not mine. Give Joy all the love she gave Tony and all will yet be well. Otherwise, I can only see an inferno ahead of you.'

He closed his eyes and did not speak to me again till I left, even though I begged and pleaded every day. Why Tony? What did he have to do with anything in my life in this context, particularly, Joy? But supremely arrogant and playing God till the last, he chose not to explain.

The last time he spoke to me was just before he passed away ten years later, but by that time too much water had flowed under the bridge.

DAVE REMEMBERS

I had been summoned to the Judge's sickbed at his own express command. I thought he wanted to make peace, although he had told his sons to summon me for my medical skills! As I stood looking down on his emaciated frame, my brother's face, still etched in hot iron at the back of my mind, came to the fore and I was tempted to speak my mind for once. But just then his eyes opened and the pleading in them was so desperate that the angry words died on my lips. He just put out his one workable claw-like hand, clutched mine in a fierce grip and held on for dear life, while desperately trying to point with his other hand at Madonna.

As the doctor, I had been just outside the room, overheard some of the conversation between father and daughter, and I did my best to talk some sense later into Madonna, to persuade her to let sleeping dogs lie, but she turned on me in fury and slapped my hands away vehemently! I will never forget her flashing eyes and heaving bosom as she spat out her resentment and told me exactly why she had agreed to marry Sunny in the first place or why she had agreed to be mother to Joy. Not that I did not have an inkling, but the vehemence of her emotions only became clear to me on that day, and I also recognized the futility of reasoning with her. Or maybe I did not wish to try too hard and was content to let matters take their own course, content with the reversal of fortune, happy to leave the old sinner hoist on his miserable petard. A life for a life?

I realized later, too late in fact, that the Judge had been pleading not merely for Madonna, who desperately needed a safety valve, but mainly for himself, because the situation in which she found herself was entirely of his making, and now he was in no condition to influence the aftermath, the future course of events, or her decisions. He recognized, I think, the same quality of ruthlessness in his daughter that had once allowed him to leave my brother to languish in Buxa Jail till his death. The Judge, therefore, had an inkling of the intended victim and the lengths to which Madonna might go to achieve her purpose. The irony was breathtaking, the master strategist outfoxed by his own child and unable to lift a finger to save her or the intended victim, whom he truly loved. He had used everybody, including his own children, all his life, but had not expected the tables to be turned so devastatingly by one of them, especially when he so desperately wanted to forestall the writing on the wall, but had no recourse to his usual resources. He did not want his daughter to repeat the mistakes he had made, because he was on the rack himself, every fiber of his being inflamed by pain, but it was too, too late. I think this was one of the high points of the corrosive process of guilt that had begun with the death of his wife and was to continue for many years to come.

4. More Conversations

SAMMY AND SHEILA

Sheila: See, Sammy the great, I was right, after all!

Sammy: Well, we have found some burnt paper trampled into the mud and floating in the water, but since they were indecipherable, I don't see that it takes much further. However, it proves my point that someone gave your Mamma a letter or something that upset her so much that she burnt it, and that caused her to go into shock. But tenable as the hypothesis is, do you think the elders will take us seriously?

Sheila: I know two people who will; your father and mine. They will pay attention to us, all right!

Sammy: How can you be so sure?

Sheila: Because they care the most and because I have proof!

Sammy: Proof? What sort? You never told me!

Sheila: I found this under the bench as we were walking away, and I did not tell you because I wanted to think about it first. I am sorry!

Sammy: Well, never mind, tell me now, quickly!

Sheila: Look at this piece…can you see the letters on it?

Sammy: Only 'ONN', what does that prove?

Sheila: Who is the only person in this house in whose name these letters occur?

Sammy: BONN, DONN, HONN, SONN ... Oh my God! You mean RONN or Uncle Ronnie! But how can that be?

Sheila: Why ever not? You know how Mamma felt about Daddy; it was a family joke, for heaven's sake! Now if she were told something really terrible about Daddy, I think she would react like this, violently!

Sammy: But why would she believe in this nonsense? Wouldn't she check? She is too sensible to fall for something idiotic like a poison pen letter, surely!

Sheila: Wouldn't that depend on what was said and who said it? And more importantly, by whom it was conveyed and how? I don't think the person who did this was an idiot, not a chance. On the contrary, he or she must be almost diabolically clever.

Sammy: You mean that neither the communication nor its mode of conveyance could be doubted? But then, it would have to be a family member or a very close friend, someone she trusted implicitly. But since everyone in the family is crazy about Aunt Leila and no one would want to hurt her so cruelly, I'm certain it was an outsider.

Sheila: That is what I would like to believe, with all my heart, but Robin is very sure that no one had passed the gates between five thirty and seven that evening, except the milkman and one of Timmy's friends, and he went straight up to

Timmy's room and stayed with him the whole time. As a matter of fact, Rocky joined in the search and did not leave till you found Mama.

Sammy: What if old Robin had dozed off for a bit, and someone sneaked in?

Sheila: Through a closed gate and wired fence? You know that there is only one switch and Robin alone operates it! Even Uncle and Daddy have to have his permission. You are just clutching at straws, Sammy, and you know it!

Sammy: But this is terrible, Sheila, how can we suspect our own people, all the folks we love and grew up with? I won't be able to trust myself any more, after this.

Sheila: This is the hard part, Sammy, the hardest part. When you took on the search in the spirit of adventure, I was scared that you, who did not appreciate the implications fully, would soon find yourself at this terrible and painful juncture and want to give up. But I was so alone, I did not have the courage to go on without you, and so, did not warn you. But now that you know the deal, you can choose, Sammy, I will understand.

Sammy: You are so brave, Sheila, you break my heart, but if you think you can shake me off just when the mystery is deepening, you can think again! Just as long as we two and our parents are okay, who cares? In any case, joint families are steadily going out of fashion and most of my friends consider us anachronistic. How can an entire tribe live amicably together year in and year out? The old tartar and his lady held us captive by sheer will force, but now that they are gone, what is going to happen to this family?

Sheila: That's just it, Sammy; somehow, I feel that the roots of this trouble stretch back to the old man and his terrible will. Did he foresee the aftermath of his own decisions or actions, I wonder, and did he even care how it would affect his progeny?

TIMMY, BOBBY AND RONNIE

Timmy: Dad, Uncle, may I speak to you both for a moment?

Ronnie: You know you are always welcome, why do you ask?

Timmy: I ask because things are not what they were when Aunty Leila was here to answer questions and to show us the way. One is so lost without her, somehow.

Bobby: We realize that better than anyone else, but if there is any way in which we can help, we would be glad to.

Timmy: Dad, do you ever look at the underbelly of the world, you know, pay attention to the unwashed and unpleasant?

Bobby: Well, as a lawyer and judge, I think I have a fair knowledge of and contact with the seamy side of life. Why this sudden interest in my affairs?

Ronnie: Don't get on your high horse Bobby; the boy has asked you an honest question, give him a straight answer.

Timmy: Exactly! I mean, don't you think we still live too much in the shadow of the Raj, instead of India of the 1980s?

Ronnie: We have done our best, I think, to give all of you a well-rounded view of your own culture and that of the West?

Timmy: Oh, you have certainly done that, but it is of your India, the India of the Tagore and the Gita, but not the real India around us. I mean, why do all of us have English names? Why not Ramprasad, Shambhu and Priya, for instance instead of Timmy, Sammy and Sheila, in the name of God?

Ronnie: We did not realize the names bothered you. Why didn't you tell us before?

Timmy: And if we had? What would you have done? Changed our names?

But could you have changed the people who have grown into these names? We are fastidious, sensitive, and unable to compromise on matters of principle? Do you realize people make fun of us? Say we are washermen's donkeys, who neither belong to the house nor to the waterside? And Willy feels the same way, says we have failed to formulate an identity!

Bobby: Willy said that? But surely that is very extreme coming from him? Why, he says he is fascinated by our culture and is studying it for that reason. Besides, all our friends are westernized people, and their kids seem to be doing all right, so, what's with you? I think it's only your shaggy haired political friends who are trying to influence you!

Timmy: And what will these kids do? Make a beeline
            for universities abroad, get an education, get
            a job and make their life there. And the void
            that they will create with their exodus will be
            filled by my shaggy haired friends: the inheritors
            of independent, modern India. What if we do
            not want to run away? What if we want a niche
            for ourselves here? You have equipped us in no
            way to compete with them! We cannot go for
            the throat like these people do, nor stifle our
            precious consciences!

Ronnie: Look Timmy, come clean; something specific is
            bothering you, that is clear. Why don't you tell
            us the truth instead of beating about the bush?

Timmy: Are you sure you have not heard ANYTHING
            untoward?

Bobby: This is really getting tiresome... untoward...
            about whom, for Christ's sake?

Timmy: About Grandpa, for one?

Ronnie: Look, Timmy, your granddad has been dead
            these many years. Nothing that anyone can say
            can hurt him or us now. He was an extraordinary
            man and you know that!

Timmy: Yes, of extraordinary talents too, if my friends
            are to be believed.

Bobby: And what is this extraordinary allegation they are
            making? And, do they have a basis for making
            it?

Timmy: That he was a secret agent of the British Raj.
            That he manufactured evidence and wrote
            judgments against his own people and he sent
            many innocent people to the gallows.

Ronnie: Look, Timmy, the transition was difficult for all of us, particularly those who had been born and raised in the system, an identity crisis of sorts if you like, and divided loyalties; but none of us would do anything to hurt our own countrymen, surely you believe that and not the idle talk floating around?

Timmy: Not even if the odds were overwhelming?

Bobby: What the hell do you mean, Timmy?

Timmy: Well, they are planning to appeal that the archives be opened and the facts be made available to the public; that the Great Judge is to be judged by posterity, by the great unwashed; ironic, eh? Let me see how you people tackle this one!

5. More Rumination

RUMINATION, MADONNA STYLE

With Leila out of circulation, old enmities are surfacing, guilty memories raising their ugly heads, and tensions are becoming palpable. Things have certainly not worked out the way I had expected, quite the contrary, in fact, I wish I had not been so hasty and vicious again, but with the die cast, now I have nowhere to turn.

Truth to tell, I never expected Leila, educated and sensible, to fall for the story hook, line and sinker in this manner. I thought she would be troubled, go to Ronnie to vent her suspicions and for once they would misunderstand each other, quarrel, be unhappy, and their Eden would be soiled as mine had been with black intent. But I had reckoned without Leila's brand of innocence and her complete trust in Ronnie, which caused her to crumble at the first onslaught and made her explore the ramifications of the accusation till she drove herself mad. This madness and innocence also prevented her from investigating the source, which was good for me, but the respite did not last as the whole household turned into a band of sleuths, including those very smart kids. And they are not innocent; on the contrary, they have a healthy appreciation of evil and are beginning to look my way.

I will have to write to Josh, telling him I wish to return, and I know he will be very happy to have me go back, for he has never been pleased about my decision of living in my father's house, now that Father is no more. I wonder whether he would let me live in my town residence, the one I had shared with Sunny many years ago? It would be no worse than the present, with dustsheets and a caretaker, and I would live as quietly as a ghost in this ghostly world with my memories. But one thing I cannot do is go back to the estate, not after that afternoon.

We had returned to the estate a month after my father had recovered somewhat, and I tried to go back to the old days, particularly in view of the revelations of that fateful evening and his burning anxiety. I wanted to believe that Father at least had not been disappointed in his hopes, although my future and happiness had hung in the balance for it, and now my brothers would continue to accept the façade for the truth.

Let some permanent good come out of this tragedy, had been my quixotic stance, and it might have just worked if it had not been again for Joy. This time I gave Joy no cause to distrust me, for I genuinely wanted to win back his affection and through him, Sunny's trust, and the child began to respond to the change. We played long hours with the new toys I had brought for him, plucked and ate forbidden, unripe fruit from the orchards, went for walks along the lake on which we sailed paper boats, things his own mother never did with him. Within two weeks we were back on the old footing and at the end of the month he told his Dada that he would like to sleep with both of us.

The look of incredulous joy on Sunny's face on that fateful day is one of my guiltiest memories. But at the end of six months of pretense and self-deception, it became clear to me that I had lost my primacy with Sunny, and that he lived now for Joy, his son. All his plans were for the boy and his future: education, friends, career, and this had given him a stake in his own future and perhaps a promise of continuity? He now worked twice as hard as before, for he had to catch up with his grandiose plans for the boy, and as Josh and his wife never interfered, this sense of oneness remained unimpaired. Even I, critical as I was, could see how genuinely delighted they were that Sunny had someone to call his own, someone to live for. Their affection for Sunny had allowed them to make a sacrifice joyfully, that I could not match, but could only envy and resent endlessly to the point of obsession.

At the end of a year the choices were very clear: either I would play second fiddle all my life; or, Joy would have to go, never to return. I would not lose out, again temporary aberration or onset of madness? Who knows?

DAVE'S CONFESSION

Sunny, Joy and Madonna left for the estate last evening and it was only after their departure that I realized that I was terrified, not for her, but for people around her. Ever since she was a little girl she had this passion to win, to be first with everyone, to be loved better than all others; she wanted what she could not have to desperation, and this passion for forbidden fruit has driven her like a goad all her life. It made her a person of impossible loves and hates, capable of the most impossible loyalties and betrayals, quite beyond the normal ken, yet strangely enough, few people have stumbled to the fact. Is this because she was adept at dissimulation or because this was a family that took virtue for granted? Or was this due to the fact that we always look for drama outside the immediate vicinity and never within the family circle?

Two people recognized this trait in her though, her father and I – for obvious reasons as an onlooker, rather than participant. Perhaps Mukul had also guessed, tried, been betrayed and so moved away? Her Father did his best to contain these desires and give her the primacy she wanted, for he recognized himself in her and knew her for a potential time bomb; but in the end he too ended up using her and adding to her cup of bitterness.

Should I have warned Sunny, for I had great admiration for him and was fond of Joy, a lovable little fellow? Today I know that this omission was my greatest sin and I will carry the mark till I die, but at the time I never gave myself a choice because I was too intent on my own nemesis. I wanted to leave a more indelible mark on this family than anything Madonna could dream of: a life was to be given for a life taken. In the end I was no better than Madonna and my attempts just as futile; neither of us got away with anything.

6. Points of View

BOBBY, RONNIE, AND TONY

Tony: I have spoken to Lena, and decided to call in this soothsayer for the want of a better word, a man of God, for you anglicized brothers of mine will not accept the local term, Jyotishi or sadhu, will you?

Bobby: Why are you on the warpath all the time these days, Tony? Why don't you explain and give us a chance to communicate, instead of condemning us out of hand?

Tony: Simply because your western education has made you skeptical of anything that is not perfectly rational, and faith is not rational, is it?

Ronnie: Listen to yourself Tony! Are you not as biased in favor of western education as any of us? Why are your children reading in missionary schools, then? And this is a fairly recent, post-nuptial phenomenon, right? You were educated in a missionary institution yourself and used to visit the chapel regularly with your white, Christian friends, remember? And even today, you prefer a good beef steak to the best example of Indian cuisine, so, why this sudden pretense at Indianness, including a reversal to an imaginary, bucolic, non-western, past? But, most important, do you seriously believe that this soothsayer has occult powers that can solve our problems?

Tony: Lena says that he has brought peace to many troubled households.

Bobby: Oh, Lena, and what does Robin have to say?

Tony: And you say I am biased! Well, for your information, Robin swears by this man, says his observations and predictions are quite uncanny as are his powers of healing.

Bobby: Then let us have him in by all means. If the devil himself can restore Leila to normalcy and peace, I will welcome him with open arms.

Tony: Just a minute, brother; remember, I said he is a soothsayer? Well, the truth, particularly his truth is not always palatable. Secondly, he will want to meet all the family members; do you think they will agree?

Ronnie: You mean he will hold a kind of séance with all of us sitting in a circle, holding hands? That should be interesting!

Tony: If you are going to turn this into a joke, I will call off the whole thing right away; in the end it's your funeral more than anyone else's, and you talk like this? I sometimes feel you don't want Leila to get well.

Bobby: This is really too much, Tony! Just because Ronnie does not whine, don't underestimate his sufferings. You apologize to him this minute and take back that offensive remark you made.

Ronnie: Let it be, Bob. I am who I am. I cannot go about all day, braying about my misfortunes; I have to make a joke out of the most serious calamity. Had I not been able to do that, I would have gone out of my mind many years ago, and no one knows that better than you. And now that Leila, my other self is involved, I cannot change, and if my failing makes me appear the culprit to some people, too bad! But like you, Bobby, I would do anything, however irrational, to bring Leila and myself out of this terrible shadow of suspicion. So, please request Tony to call in any one he damn well pleases, and I will ensure that everyone in this house attends. No one in the family will deny me this chance, of that I am absolutely certain.

Tony: Very pretty speech Ronnie, very well made, as usual. Once I have got you angry enough to go on the warpath, I will not allow anyone else to stand in the way of the revelation, of that you may be sure. I owe you Ronnie, and I owe Leila and I don't forget that our mother trusted me to take care of you. Now we shall see what we shall see and hear what we shall hear.

SHEILA AND SAMMY

Sheila: The entire household is buzzing madly with the coming of this soothsayer; what if he turns out to be a soot-seer and paints everything, everyone black?

Sammy: Wish I had thought of that! But you get in first every time!

Sheila: Never mind Sam, it's a stupid pun anyway, and I'm only good at it because once upon a time Daddy, you and I used to play this game all the time.

Sammy: Yes, what fun it was, and talking in rhymes and riddles, particularly at dinner table! Remember how livid Aunt Rose would get because she could not follow?

Sheila: But Mamma helped her out every time, before anyone noticed.

Sammy: Amazing isn't it, how her eyes were everywhere?

Sheila: Yes, everyone but herself! If she had not fallen so completely for the rubbish that was written on that foul bit of paper and talked to Daddy, she would never have lost her mind like this.

Sammy: That's just it! What could be devastating enough

for Mamma to have a complete breakdown? And now that she is better, why won't she talk about her experiences? Do you think she will see this man uncle Tony is bringing in?

Sheila: She has agreed to be present because Uncle Tony has begged on his bended knees, but I don't think she will participate in any way.

Sammy: Well, it will be interesting to watch how other family members react. Some of them are very tense I can tell you, especially Small; wonder why she is so concerned.

Sheila: Remember, she was the last person to see and talk to Mamma before this terrible thing happened? Perhaps she has something to hide? Or, much more likely, has seen the significance of some word or deed she did not before? You know hindsight?

Sammy: That is very possible and I think that is the reason for her new-found confidence as well. I was quite happy to hear her telling off Aunt Madonna in no uncertain terms about her future course of action, and Aunt taking it all quietly.

Sheila: Yes, it's not like Aunt Madonna to allow any statement to go unchallenged, then why this sudden deference to Small's pronouncements? Do you think we should tell her to watch her step?

Sammy: Yes, we should definitely warn her and if possible, get her to share her thoughts with us. You know, there is safety in numbers.

7. Secret Thoughts

ROSE

I don't know why Tony is getting together with Lena to bring in this man. That Lena has an axe to grind is obvious, but Tony is only thinking of Leila, as usual. That I, Rose, his wife, for God's sake, do not want him to do this, does not penetrate his thick skull, and for obvious reasons I cannot spell it out. Is this man a mind reader, by any chance? Will he gauge my true feelings for Leila and tell the others? I will not look into his eyes, whatever happens. Maybe I can pretend to be sick? But, how can I be sicker than Leila, and she has agreed to come to the session. Oh, God!

MILLIE

That fatal year before Leila came into our lives, how I wish I could turn back the clock. And yet, my Sammy, handsome, intelligent, loving, outspoken, silly, old Sammy, no life is possible without him, either for Bobby or me. Such a contrast to Timmy and yet so alike in some ways, but completely indispensable! Why is Tony doing this? Did he get his idea from that silly bit of verse that hangs in the old man's library? What if that is proved true and this man lies like the truth? I, Millie, have nothing against Leila. I love her dearly. I want her to get well and return to her former position with all my heart. I have done nothing wrong and have nothing to hide in this matter. But what if this man strays into uncharted territory? Oh, Lord, how and to whom does one pray?

LENA

I, Lena, have carried this burden too long and been taken advantage of at every twist and turn of life. I put up with it quietly as long as there was no opportunity to make capital out of my secret, but now, at the tail end, when opportunity has come without my asking, putting Leila with her fierce sense of family out of the way, why should I hold back and not do my duty to myself? Yes, duty, for the few years of life I have left. The trouble is that I cannot discuss this with Robin for I never told him, and now if I do, who knows how he will react? But I will take the plunge and do what I can for the only human being for whom I am responsible, which is why, this soothsayer business came to mind, and thank God, Tony fell for it, though for entirely the wrong reasons.

But what about the flip side of the coin? How will everyone react if the truth does comes out, and where will I stand after my last and only bolt has been shot? It could go either way. After all, what is one guilty secret among many? Who notices a slingshot in a hailstorm? Robin has very sharp eyes and has been watching me very closely; he is one person who will not thank me for messing with the family and might reject me altogether. Perhaps I should have stopped at only hints and judicious blackmail, after all.

SMALL

My friend, I have come to visit you today, but I have no time or wish to love you. My heart is too heavy and my mind very disturbed. Madonna explained to me about the soothsayer and told me what to say if he asked me questions, but I am afraid that I will not be able to lie convincingly, especially about Leila, for I love her too much. Darling Leila, she was so good to me. Why did I have to listen to Madonna? She said it would help Leila and Ronnie to understand each other better, but just the opposite happened. I, Small, will listen to Madonna no longer. If the soothsayer asks me the right questions I shall speak the truth as I know it and not pretend. You, my friend, are my witness and judge since my Father passed away, and I will come back and report to you day after tomorrow, and I promise again that I will speak nothing but the truth.

TIMMY

I, Timmy, seem to have got carried away and opened up a regular can of worms, thanks to my stupid democratic ideals and so-called love of truth. What started out as political naiveté has boomeranged as a huge blunder that is going to cost not only me dearly, but my entire family as well. The adulation suited me fine, and to be told that I was different, a realist, not an effete aristocrat by Willy was flattering to say the least, but Robin, in his usual blunt way, had warned me:

'No one praises anyone unless they hope to get something out of that person, and I don't trust your revolutionary friends one bit, not even Willy. You be careful, Timmy!'

But of course I was too lofty to pay heed. Sammy and Sheila too did not like them and made fun of my green political ambitions, but I ignored them as pesky kids, which they are of course, but now it seems they have their heads screwed on the right way after all; and strangely enough, they were not as impressed by Willy and his clever talk as I was. What will the archives reveal? After all, in politics, today's hero is always tomorrow's villain. Will we all end up paying for his sins, or mine? Rocky is asking for a huge sum of money to call off the hunt, but how will I get it? How

I wish Aunt Leila was not sick; she always had a solution for my problems in the past, and I know exactly what she would have said:

'Don't be afraid of the truth, Timmy. Nothing can be hidden forever, and Truth will out, some day some time. Instead, be happy that you are the agent and once it is out, we will face the consequences together, as a family.'

That was always her way; but now without her support, do I have the courage? And on top of all this, the wretched soothsayer business is upon us. Should I confide in Aunt Madonna? She's as rich as Croesus and could help out if she liked. But will she like? Not if I know her! Should I go to Uncle Ronnie? He will understand and help, but with Aunt Leila in this condition, should I disturb him? But the million-dollar question really is, should I stoop to bribery in the first place? And would I be able to?

I don't believe in God and I can't pray, but I will go mad if something does not come up soon. Damn Willy and his insinuating ways; he put me on my mettle and I did not want to turn down the challenge and now where is he? Still insisting we go through with it, but it's not his skin, it is mine.

8. Ordeal by Water

MADONNA REMEMBERS

Almost like an answer to a prayer, Josh called today of all days to say how pleased they would all be if I went 'home'. Said he understood my reluctance to return to the estate, and would be happy to help me settle into the town residence, where they would visit frequently, for with their son in a boarding school, he and his wife have more time for travel. But he also had an alternative proposal: He is winding up the estate and decided to turn the mansion into a school-cum-orphanage in Sunny and Joy's name. Josh would be delighted if I would run the place. He felt my intelligence and energy needed an outlet and this would also, in a way, be a compensation for my love of Joy, my only son, of whom I had been robbed. Besides, by turning the mansion into an orphanage, the family would still own it. Said it would be a real favor and he was just waiting for me to give him a date.

Dear Josh, as stable, trusting and honest as his brother, will he ever realize the terrible irony inherent in his suggestion? I could go tomorrow and get out of this ordeal I have called upon myself; but how would I face him and his wife day in, day out, and survive? Particularly, could I look into the eyes of his wife, Joy's mother, without giving myself away?

Today it seems inconceivable that I could have got into a frame of mind so frenzied and violent, but at the time nothing would suffice but Joy should no longer be part of my life, nor usurp my place with Sunny.

Noticing the child's interest in sailing, Sunny had made for him a miniature sculling boat that required considerable skill to balance, leave alone navigate, and Joy went through a lot of ducking and heartache before he could even stand upright in it. But pluck, skill and determination won out in the end, and he was soon managing the boat easily, with a specially designed scull. The boat was firmly tied to a nearby tree with a fifty-foot steel chain and Joy could only move in a restricted circle of a few hundred square feet of shallow water. The chain that held the boat had a lock, of which Sunny had one key and I the other. Joy also had firm instructions to use the boat only when Mama was present, which meant that I spent half my day at the lakeside. Not that I minded; it was pleasant to sit in the fragrant shade of the giant tamarind tree with the filtered sunlight splashing on my body, warming my heart that was permanently cold, thinking, reading, dreaming. One day I dreamed that Joy had disappeared, that Sunny wanted only me, his only succor, his only comfort. He took me back to town, and life was again idyllic, where I came first.

The lake had a patch of reeds where herons nested, and which therefore, was never disturbed. Sunny had warned me that neither Joy nor I were to go anywhere near this patch, for the substratum was quicksand and so, very, very dangerous. While chatting with Joy one day, I gave him the idea that he might be able to peer into the nests and see the eggs and baby birds if he could get close enough in his boat, for naturally, nothing could be seen from the banks. His eyes glistened, and I could see the plans whirring in his head. So, I told him off sharply and said I would report to Dada if he did anything foolish. This ensured that Sunny would have no inkling of the background or my involvement if something did happen. After all, Sunny was no stranger to accidents, one accident in his boyhood had decided the course of my life; now another would rectify it. The simple give and take of life!

Sunny was out for the day, so Joy and I decided to carry a picnic lunch to the lakeside. We invited his mother, but for some reason best known to the boy, he did not want her to come. In any case, she said she had other fish to fry and did not want to sit by the lake all day and get splashed! So she packed us a delicious lunch of roast mutton sandwiches, fruit, chocolate and lots of lemonade; funeral meats and wine? The idea tickled my sense of humor: Ironic, but strangely apt.

Hamper in hand we arrived at our favorite spot, and while the boy rushed to his boat I spread the table-cloth on the picnic table, took out the goodies as Joy called them, one by one, and laid them out covered with linen napkins. I laid the table very carefully, even artistically, creating a centerpiece with wild flowers and placemats with leaves from the near-by Travelers Tree. Who had laid out the Last Supper, I wondered, Judas?

When I look back today, I can only remember the cold calm determination, so beloved of novelists, that had me in its grip. I don't think I hesitated for a second, not even once.

Finally Joy was hungry enough to join me, and he noticed the decorations right away, and cried out:

'You are the cleverest and sweetest Mama in the world,' and hugged me till I nearly choked. Then we both tucked in with a will till everything was gone, except the lemonade. Again, Joy said:

'Mama let's save some of the lemonade for afterwards for we will get thirsty on the way home. Then we can put everything back in the basket and take it with us. You always say we must not waste or litter, don't you?'

He was trying so hard to please me and I agreed gravely with what he said, particularly about litter.

Normally the key to the chain never left my pocket, but today it fell out with my handkerchief and lay twinkling on the grass. Joy was all eyes, but I pretended not to notice his keen attention. Then as he went back to his boat, I fell asleep, and did not wake up when he crept away with the key, turned the lock, and drifted away in the boat. My last but one memory of him is standing up in the boat, straight and sturdy, sculling away in the direction of the herons.

I woke up and pretended to miss him about half an hour later, and I immediately set out calling his name, but in the wrong direction. By the time I retraced my steps, Joy was halfway down in the mud, and calling for me desperately. His face lit up as he saw me and I cried out that I was coming and gingerly stepped into the water, trying to look purposeful. It was at this point that a flying shape rushed past me and plunged into the lake, swimming with incredible, superhuman speed towards the boy. Sunny had returned early, heard about our picnic and come down to escort us home.

He never made it, nor did Joy, and as I stood rooted to the spot in terror, words of caution frozen on my lips, they went down, father and son, arm in arm, clinging to each other, Joy no longer afraid and Sunny turned around once to look at me at the last minute, and I knew then that he knew it all.

They found me unconscious among the reeds and took me home, but I could tell them nothing of what had happened. The doctors said the trauma had been too great, and in any case, what was the point of a postmortem? The damage was irretrievable. Fifteen days later, still unable to speak, I indicated my desire to return to my parents' home, and my dear brothers, who were entirely broken by the double tragedy, took me away.

My gall still rises when I think of the terrible irony. Why, with me, always? The balance must be restored and that is why someone who has not been deceived by fate as I was over and over again has to pay.

CONJECTURES: RONNIE

It never rains but pours, and at the risk of sounding clichéd I have to say that Bobby could have deferred the urgent meeting he has called this evening for just the two of us, to a more opportune moment. I wonder what the reason is for this urgency and why he is so insistent. Does he want to prepare for the wretched soothsayer business? But he and I have nothing to hide, and will welcome the truth, as always, so why this urgent need for a preparatory session? He gave me no clue about its significance and just said:

'A packet containing papers of great importance has arrived in my office in our joint names, and therefore it is only right that we should open it together.'

Dear Bobby, always so serious and correct, but then once a lawyer, always a lawyer, and I would not have him change for anything!

The rendezvous is at six this evening, in the library, without the body, I hope? How impossibly melodramatic it all sounds; and yet, I have to admit, I am a trifle uncomfortable, particularly with no Leila to hug me and tell me that all will be well.

MILLIE AND BOBBY

Millie: Bobby, what is this meeting with Ronnie about this evening?

Bobby: It's about this case that is to be re-opened.

Millie: And...?

Bobby: Nothing else, really, we just need to strategize.

Millie: Then why do you have to be so secretive about it?

Bobby: Hardly secretive, Millie, everyone in the house knows, don't you dare make it sound so cloak and dagger!

Millie: Well, if rumor is to be believed, there were plenty of robed men and a dagger in that famous case. Only one is not sure which role was played by whom?

Bobby: Oh, rumors! You know how people talk, Millie, their lurid imaginations running riot.

Millie: Stop treating me like an unstable witness, Bobby, this is not the courtroom. If you think that I will believe that a mere case has had you looking green in the gills for the last two weeks, you are mistaken. I know you too well and also the signs of battle, when you scent a problem and go in

for the kill with your pennant flying; you enjoy
that more than anything else in the world. But
this time you are scared, why, because it is too
personal and goes against the grain, rather?

Bobby: Who is acting the prosecuting counsel now,
Millie? You sound quite fierce you know. Why
are you so concerned, all of a sudden?

Millie: Because strange things are going on in this
house and it is all connected to this damn case.
After what happened to Leila I am terrified for
you, Ronnie and the kids. The menace has been
building steadily and is now coming to a head. I
can't sleep at night for whenever I close my eyes
all I can see is Leila's white and lost face. She was
so strong, if she could go under like this, what is
to prevent the rest of you falling prey?

Bobby: You are not scared for yourself?

Millie: No, I'm not; you see, I am not important or
particularly strong, and as you are aware, the
blight always goes for the lustiest. I lead a shadow
life that does not invite hatred or envy. I'm safe.
But the children are not, particularly Sammy
and Sheila. All this creepy sleuthing stuff they
do, and they are so smart and perceptive, they
could easily stumble on the truth, and then.

Bobby: And then?

Millie: Why don't you tell me, instead of trying to
sound me out like an unwilling accomplice? You
are not as lofty and unconcerned as you pretend
to be, Bobby, you are as afraid as I am!

Bobby: I am and I wish I could, Millie, believe me, but
this time I am truly and completely in the dark.

You know, I deal only in facts and they are not always the best guides. Someone has said that the best key to the understanding of life is through fiction, for it uses the third eye of imagination. Well, you are a painter, can't you look beyond the veil that Ronnie and I find impenetrable, and discover the truth for all of us?

Millie: That is the biggest compliment you have ever paid me, and to justify your faith in me and for our own safety I will certainly do my best. You know what the main problem is? There are too many strands in this skein, too many colors on this palette.

Bobby: And...?

Millie: It will take time to disentangle, to decipher...

Bobby: And time is one thing we do not have, right?

Millie: No, we do not; I feel like Eliza in the folk-tale with an axe hanging over my head on a tenuous thread; disaster around the bend in the road...

Bobby: I have never heard you speak in this melodramatic style before, and I only hope it's the artist in you speaking and not the 'prophet'. Anyway, I'll tell the kids that you have joined their investigative firm!

Millie: Well, I am solidly behind them in all their sleuthing as they call it, for they have taken action while we have only talked! My Timmy too, however politically green he may be, he has not bowed to pressure. Tell them I will be honored it they accept me as a member!

ROSE AND TONY

Rose: Tony, why are you not attending the meeting in the library this evening?

Tony: What meeting are you talking about? I know nothing of a meeting!

Rose: My point exactly! Why don't you ever know anything about anything? Your brothers are meeting at six this evening in the library, to discuss some important documents that have arrived a few hours ago.

Tony: Look Rose, must be business that does not concern me. Pretty academic I'm sure, not exactly my cup of tea. If they see the need, I am sure they will inform me. In any case, how did you find out and what is your interest?

Rose: Well, as a member of this precious family, do I not deserve to get a glimpse of some of the skeletons?

Tony: What makes you talk silly like this? Have you come across any secrets before? In this family, we don't operate in hole and corner ways.

Rose: Oh, I know all of you are too high and mighty, elite and moral, beyond suspicion, but after the

| | Leila business, I'm not so sure anymore! If only you were less blind, Tony! Even those pesky kids know and are talking about it, but you… |

Tony: Shut up Rose! It's none of your business, and you know it very well. And don't you dare call those motherless kids pesky! My brothers have never let me down, and they won't, now. More importantly, I have no intentions of letting them down by distrusting them, particularly at this point. In any case the soothsayer is coming, isn't he? Can't you wait one more day for your precious skeletons? God, women!

Rose: You are impossible with your trust in your brothers…have you never read the Mahabharata? If you had, instead of imbibing all the junk that your missionary school fed you about trust and honesty, you would pay more attention to me today!

Tony: And what a tragedy that would be!

SHEILA AND SAMMY

Sheila: Will it be very wicked if we hide in the library and listen?

Sammy: Have you lost your mind entirely, Sheila? How can you think of such a dishonest thing? Not like you, at all!

Sheila: You think I don't feel ashamed to even plan such a thing? Would I have thought of such a plan six months ago? But I can't bear it any longer, Sammy, my wonderful, beautiful Mamma…

Sammy: Come, come Sheila, here, wipe your eyes, it's clean, I promise!

Sheila: Don't be an idiot Sammy, that makes two of us! There, I feel better, now…really…

Sammy: Just think of what Aunt Leila would say, and let that be your guide.

Sheila: We all did that, always, didn't we? But then, how come Mamma got let down so badly herself?

Sammy: In that case, why don't you listen to what Robin 'the wise' always says? That there is solid evil in this world, and it won't go away by pretending it does not exist, but we cannot fight evil by becoming evil ourselves. Strange how we turn to him for advice sometimes, rather than some family members!

Sheila: If he says so, why are you lecturing me? What I said was evil, but the only way to cope with evil is to face it head on! Isn't that what he says? As for family members, the less said about some of them, the better.

Sammy: I agree on both counts; we must destroy evil by facing it, challenging it, but not by becoming weak ourselves! In any case, why do you think that this has anything to do with the family? It could be pure business.

Sheila: Because I know something that you do not!

Sammy: I knew there was a catch to it! Tell me quickly!

Sheila: The packet came to the house first and our Aunt Madonna was dying to get her hands on it, saying it had come from her family. But Robin seeing Uncle's name on it, redirected the courier to his office.

Sammy: Courier? Not the postman?

Sheila: No, a man from their estate; you know how distinctive their uniform is, olive green and red with the sleek turban? One can't miss it!

Sammy: In that case...

Sheila: Exactly!

MADONNA-SPEAK

What has Josh sent to Bobby? It was quite a bulky packet...
The man recognized me, saluted, was coming straight to
me when Robin clanged the gate shut and held him up!
Then he turned to me coolly and said:

'Sorry, Madam, the packet is for Mr. Bobby.'

I was sure that the papers had to do with the school
project Josh has been talking about, but before I could get a
word in, he had sent off one of the gardeners to accompany
and escort the man to Bobby's chambers. And the man
never came back to the house. Bobby put him up in the
office quarters and sent him home with a massive tip, or so
I've heard.

Why this urgency to avoid contact with me? Why this
secrecy, this reluctance if the matter does not concern me?
Has Josh found out about Joy after all this time? But it
cannot be, I spoke to him only yesterday ...Or... is it
something to do with Father's deal that has come to light?
In that case what should my stand be? Both players are
dead, and only one of the pawns is left, who was never part
of the game anyway... 'Injured innocence' I think is the
right stance...but will it work?

What if a connection is traced between the past and the

present, between the political and personal, what if the soothsayer's revelations light up the murky past and point to the cause of our present trouble? What if Small spills the beans? Oh God!

9. In the Library

RONNIE-SPEAK

We met in the library at six p.m. shut the door, chased out Timmy who was browsing and brooding, and settled down in our comfortable, leather-backed chairs. Bobby, clearly nervous, poured us a couple of drinks, and we sat back for half an hour and tried to relax. Bobby's pale face really disturbed me, and I wondered whether he had an inkling of what the packet might contain. After all, he was six years my senior, and knew of matters that had transpired before my time. In the end, his hands were shaking so badly, that I slit the sealed manila envelope with the sharp, Moroccan paper-knife that our father had once used, and which had lain on the huge, polished work-table for many years along with other accessories.

What fluttered out first was a letter from Josh, but inside the first envelope was another sealed one which was addressed to our Father, and failing that, to Bobby and me in Sunny's father's clear, bold hand-writing. This was sealed with old fashioned, red sealing wax and stamped with his signet, the 'lion rampant', which we both recognized, for it was not the British lion, but the Indian one, an emblem of the strong rising India of his dreams. He himself had been a king among men, and we both, and even perhaps Father had often felt dwarfed by his presence. All of a sudden both of us shivered and looked over our shoulders…the fleeting sense that he was actually in the room with us was strangely, very strong…

Josh's letter was a simple one and it went like this:

Dear Bobby and Ronnie,

As you may be aware, I have decided to divide up the estate among the men who have tilled the soil for generations and to give them full ownership of the same in keeping with my father's dictum:

'The land belongs to the man who tills it.'

I am not sure that my only son will ever live here, for he is a town-bird first and last, and as you know, of the family, Sunny and his son Joy were the ones fiercely attached to the estate. So, after the terrible tragedy, all three of us have found it difficult to reconcile ourselves to single ownership. We will keep one of the cottages with its garden for old time's sake, but the land will go to the men who have nurtured it all these years. We are, however, turning the big house into an orphanage and school for local children with special provisions for the disabled, and it will be in Sunny and his son's name. Sunny had many good ideas about developing this area and we are hoping that this is a step in the right direction: Let other children benefit from the nurture Sunny would have given his son, if they had both lived. In this context, I have also spoken to Madonna to request her to come here and run the school... Perhaps it will assuage the pain a little to give to less fortunate children the love she still hides in her heart for Joy? I also feel that since she has not re-married, this occupation might help to take her mind off her own tragedy?

Therefore we are clearing up, and to deal with the remains of a century is not easy, as you can imagine. In the process, we came across this envelope, of whose existence I was unaware. Perhaps Sunny knew, but he never got an opportunity to talk to me about anything...

I am sending this envelope to you by courier for I have no doubt that it is of great importance. If there is anything in it that concerns our family and I can be of help, please don't hesitate to tell me. In the meanwhile, if more papers addressed to you come to light, I will dispatch them to you immediately.

It is strange, but I still feel you are family even though Sunny and Joy have left us; this is perhaps because Sunny never drew a dividing line between in-laws and family, and his love for Madonna and Joy was like sunshine that warmed us all equally.

Let us hope this never changes
Best regards,
Josh

Bobby and I read the letter through twice and for a moment both of us were overwhelmed anew by the terrible loss. Dear Sunny and dear Joy, the finest father-son duo that ever lived, so wholly good and so very affectionate. Sunny had been a fourth brother to us all along, and had stood by us like a rock after Father passed away. As for Joy, he was the nephew we had never had, and the whole family loved him like a son of the house, particularly Leila, of whom Joy was inordinately fond. We had even suspected twinges of jealousy in Madonna sometimes, and Sheila had laughingly warned her mother:

'Hands off Joy, Mum; Aunty does not like any of us to get too close to her son!'

And then, this terrible tragedy took place within months of their return to their estate. We were not very clear as to what had happened though we rushed there immediately, except that it was an accident in a treacherous patch of quicksand. How and why Sunny and Joy had ventured there no one knew, for the lakeside had been quite deserted in the siesta hour, and Madonna, the only witness, was too traumatized to remember, let alone being capable of rendering a coherent account. Even today her eyes glaze and go vacant if either of them is inadvertently mentioned… As for Josh, the loss is obviously as acute as it ever was, which is why he has taken this momentous decision. That grand estate and majestic mansion parceled and divided among strangers? Somehow it seems impossible and neither of us can imagine or visualize that wonderful place without the once vibrant ＿＿＿＿＿＿ family. But perhaps Madonna will take up his offer and help to keep memories alive?

Bobby's voice had strange undertones as he asked rather cryptically:

'Is this the march of democracy or the march of doom?'

And I just stared at him wordlessly.

Finally, Bobby picked up the knife, pried open the seals of the second packet and pulled out some documents that were obviously legal in nature. On closer examination, this proved to be a copy of a judgment signed by our own father as one of the judges in a case some years ago. Accompanying the document was a single, typewritten sheet signed by the grand old man, as we had always called Sunny's father. So we decided to read that first:

I, ＿＿＿＿＿＿＿ ＿＿＿＿＿＿＿, in complete possession of my faculties; do hereby admit to my complicity in the miscarriage of justice that the accompanying document represents. This was done, against my own better judgment, to save the reputation of the close friend who wrote the judgment in order to eliminate a serious threat to himself and his family. Two of his children were in serious jeopardy, their entire future threatened by complete ruin. In addition, he had a claim on my gratitude, for he had given me the gift of life for one of my own children. I am not sure whether this was a deliberate ploy to gain my support, but even if it was, I still owed him.

He could have got away with it in any case with the help of his British masters, but because the case took a political turn and the entire area was up in nationalist arms, he needed the support of a man above reproach, a true patriot. The irony of it almost broke my resolve, but in the end I yielded to the silent appeal in my son's eyes, the son who had never asked me for anything, and endorsed this verdict. I did wonder later, though, whether my son would have appealed, if he had known the entire story.

What followed however was something I was entirely unprepared for, something I could not have anticipated as I had never guessed at the unplumbed depths of ferocity within the man, and the lengths to which he would go to achieve his desires, and protect his progeny. I had never thought that the entire village would pay for the sins of a few. It was a holocaust, mass execution almost, and the excuse was the suffering he and his children had undergone. But he seemed to overlook the salient fact that he himself had set the ball in motion by ordering to the gallows the young man who had supposedly thrown the bomb at the magistrate's car. After all, no one had died, even been injured, and the terrorist was only twenty-two! A life sentence should have surely sufficed? Then, after his hanging, the lad's eighteen year old wife had set herself on fire by climbing the funeral pyre and been hailed as a suttee, almost a deity, and the local people had bayed for the blood of the judge and his family.

I am not very clear about what happened that particular night, but I saw the living proof of the atrocity on his second son and youngest daughter, and I admit, my blood turned to ice. How would I have reacted in a similar situation?

The entire business has weighed on my conscience, and I must leave a record of what actually did happen and why it happened, that is, to the best of my knowledge, for I know the matter has not ended. Like the phoenix it will rise in the future to plague his inheritors, and at that point, it might help to have a witness from the past.

I will leave this in the custody of my eldest son, the wisest of us all, and he in his wisdom, will choose the time and mode of presentation.

_____ _____

The 9th day of August, 1942

SHEILA AND SAMMY TRAPPED!

Sheila: We have to get out of here fast, for if they catch us, it will really be the end!

Sammy: But how? There is only one door that serves as exit and entry to the library; the others are locked on both sides.

Sheila: Yes, but aren't there windows?

Sammy: Wait a minute…there is one window that opens out on the lawn …I can jump out quite easily.

Sheila: While I stay here and suffocate?

Sammy: Well it was your idea to get into this old moth eaten cupboard!

Sheila: And a bad idea…we really know nothing except that Uncle Josh sent some legal documents that pertain to the family…so? Big deal!

Sammy: But have you noticed how white both of them are? I have a feeling that not only is it serious but it also has to do with our present trouble. Small too has been on tenterhooks ever since the man from Uncle Josh arrived. I think she has an idea of the contents but is too scared to ask her brothers.

Sheila: But why? They are always ready to listen to her.

Sammy: Because she is involved in some way and is afraid of the consequences; but never mind, first we have to get out of here and I have an idea that might just work; listen,

I will jump out and create a diversion with Robin's help and when our Dads step out to investigate, you can streak out!

Sheila: And do you know who will be waiting to catch me, our dear Madonna! She knows very well that we are up to something. No, if we have to jump, we'll both jump! Come on, give me a hand and make sure I don't break a leg.

Sammy: Well, it's your leg!

BOBBY-SPEAK

Ronnie and I decided to mull things over and meet again in the library in two hours' time. The responsibility is too great as it affects the entire family, even the children. This is what Timmy's friends have been plaguing him about, and perhaps Madonna has been so agitated because she has some inkling of the matter? Robin has been warning us for some time now that some trouble is afoot, but we have not taken him seriously enough, as usual. Well, what is the worst that can happen? That our father's image will be tarnished a little more and we will be ostracized in certain quarters as anglophiles, who condoned the death of our countrymen at the behest of the white rulers, for no one will believe today that we did not know. We cannot be held legally responsible in any way for we were all minors at the time; however, our reputation for honesty will certainly take a beating from which we will find it hard to recover. I can imagine quite well the barbed comments and snide looks that will come my way in the bar library from those colleagues who profess to be my friends, but are, unfortunately, less successful than I am! But that I can ride out...what is more serious, will my clients trust me as implicitly as before? Can I look a man likely to be condemned for murder in the eye, and assure him that I will do my best to save his neck? Or will he think:

'This man might sell me down the river? Why ever not? Didn't his father do the same thing? And I bet some money changed hands there!'

That is something I just cannot face, for I have been considered an exception to the rule in the legal profession heretofore. No one will think of the differences in situation, time and character; all they will see is the taint of blood, damn them!

Yet, to prevent this from happening, the whole truth must be told; but that will cause unbearable pain to many people I love very much and who in no way deserve the torture that will ensue. Completely sinned against and not sinning, they are victims all the way...yet, will anybody believe the truth? What is that terrible doggerel that still hangs in the old man's, now our library? Something about:

'Time the patient saint who rolls his eyes and speaks the truth'...but actually he 'lies like the truth'?

So very apt! Did the old sinner hang that thing up in preparation for this day? I certainly wouldn't put it beyond him!

But what on earth do I say to Ronnie when I see him in half an hour?

10. Fresh Perspectives

RONNIE-SPEAK

I never thought this story would have to be told after so many years, but I now realize that time certainly does not bring oblivion, merely, distortion. Had the truth been laid bare then, it would have been painful, but we would perhaps have managed to live it down in time...then why was it suppressed? To spare us pain, we were told, but now I wonder, was it to save father a lynching? Sunny's father calls it miscarriage of justice but to me it seems more like revenge, pure and simple, and the subsequent suppression of evidence! But was the revenge purely on our behalf? Again, that is what was said, but now we have living proof and cannot get away from the fact that the whole process was initiated by our sainted father, for more personal reasons!

Our mother, wise but patient to a fault, disagreed with her husband on practically every serious issue, but chose to turn a blind eye to his more obvious misdemeanors, particularly those that concerned her. I think she had stopped caring a long time ago. But when it came to her children or her principles she could be a tigress, something many people did not know or appreciate. And now it falls into place, why that night, she fought him tooth and nail to make him speak the truth… Went so far as to blackmail him if he would not agree… He was completely taken aback and did not know how to deal with this pure woman, who yielded to no bribe, was afraid of nothing and was implacable in her demands:

'Have they not suffered enough, my children, because they have you for a father? And will you store up further suffering for them now to save your own miserable skin? Over my dead body! If you do not rescind that order you have passed, I will go out tomorrow to the public and tell them the truth!'

It was at this point that he struck her, and truth be told it was the first and last time to the best of my knowledge, but she got up, blood spurting from the cut on her forehead, and calmly said:

'You will have to do that many times before I die…'

Madonna, Bobby and I, staring through the window, were petrified, and though I wanted to run in and protect my mother, the other two held me back, Madonna clutching me in a vice-like grip and whispering fiercely in my ear:

'Don't be stupid, Ronnie, he will kill you too!'

And exactly at that moment we heard our mother say:

'How many people will you kill to save one worthless carcass?'

He was almost beaten, and he knew it, and he bowed his head as though in acquiescence, and we imagined the battle was over…but not quite …

He suddenly pointed to Small sleeping through all this, because she still needed to be sedated almost a year after her terrible ordeal to prevent screaming nightmares, and said something none of us could catch because he was whispering… Then we heard our mother cry out:

'No, no, no, even you cannot stoop so low!'

And he laughed sardonically and asked:

'Would you like to find out? And now do you see, that it is not one carcass but several that are at stake?'

After that all the fight went out of our brave mother and she lay down quietly clutching Small to her heart, her face averted, and so she did not see what we saw:

That sardonic, handsome, cruel face cleared of all emotion except a terrible pity...

What actually happened that fateful night of the picnic, I really do not know, but when I peer through the mists certain things stand out:

The uneven ground was so difficult to run on despite my tennis shoes; that I kept falling, picking myself up and running again till my knees were completely skinned and bleeding. The thorny bushes clutched at me and tore at my clothes. The darkness was a curse and a blessing, for though I could not see the ground at my feet, I could clearly see the burning torch carried by one of the hooligans who had carried off Small in the distance. The comfortable feel of my Swiss army knife in my pocket, given to me by Father on my tenth birthday, quite a weapon if one knew how to use it, was the only source of comfort. The thought that grew insistent with every step I took was that I was moving away from the protection of my family and into unknown territory, but also that Small must be saved at any cost.

I never got an opportunity to use my knife, for one of the men must have seen me running, but for reasons best known to him, he allowed me to get close to the place where the men were sitting with their hostage. The torch was planted in the ground; the men were sitting in a circle allowing the little girl to run and then catching her just when she thought she had escaped. All of six years, she was as innocent as the jasmine flower she resembled, had been named after, and this was her first encounter with fear... The look on her face made me call out to her against my better judgment, and I will never forget her eyes widening with hope as she cried out in complete faith:

'Ronnie, Ronnie, come to me and help me, save me!'

Then one of the men jeered at her, held her up high and said:

'Just watch your brother help you...'

The blow to the back of my head laid me out, but not before I heard the thud of Small's tiny body hitting the rocky ground as the man who was holding her up just let go of her like a sack of garbage...

I woke up in hospital, and found out later that we had both been found lying unconscious on the ground in the small hours of the morning, far away from the spot where we had lost consciousness, by the search party my Father and some villagers had organized. The police had arrived soon after and managed to trace some of the men involved in the game. In the magistrate's court the personal angle was understated and the enormity of the 'rebellion against the Raj' emphasized. The press said that the children had suffered because they were the progeny of the 'loyal servant of the British Government', and we became heroes overnight in official quarters.

What no one talked about or questioned was the fact that our mother had gone away with Small to our country home, and our aunt had left her own home to come and take care of the household with Lena's help. Also why every mirror in the house was turned to the wall, covered or discarded before our mother returned with Small some eight months later.

But something I questioned endlessly and never found an answer to, and something I don't know to date is:

'What did my father say to my mother that night to subdue her so completely?'

11. Old Sins and New

MADONNA-SPEAK

I almost gave myself away when Small retuned from the country with our mother, Tony and Nan, for she looked like a distorted shadow of herself due to the terrible scars on her face and body. Scars that had blinded one eye pulled up her lip exposing broken teeth and shortened one leg, causing her to walk with a limp. Her tongue protruded through the gap in her teeth making her look like an idiot, in the real sense of the term, and she constantly twisted her still delicate hands together. But in other ways she was the old Small, bright, affectionate and chirpy, who sometimes wondered why 'her Madonna' seemed different. It was apparent, said doctors, that her conscious memory had rejected the incident and attempted to erase it from her mind as far as possible to protect her sanity, but at night, the story was different; screaming nightmares had her in thrall and only mother could soothe her out of them. Cosmetic surgery was unknown at that time and false teeth were declared impossible for one so young, so all we could hope for was that time and nature would heal her to some extent. It was going to be a long haul, but the doctors said that if we could keep Small from seeing herself as she now was till her old image had faded from her memory, there may not be serious or permanent psychological damage.

It was about a year later that I came running in response to a scream of pure terror to find Small lying in a faint on the floor, in front of a large panel of glass built into a door. When she came to, she insisted that a monster lay hidden in the glass, and that we should all be careful for it might pounce on us at any time. Delighted that she had not connected herself to the reflection, the doctors advised us to preserve the myth, even turn it into a game, and we did our best to comply:

'Shall we play monster-in-the glass, Small? You know we cannot play without you for he will cooperate with no one else!'

Ronnie or I would say, and she would come running because she was the only one the monster obeyed and imitated...

I think this game conferred a sense of uniqueness and power that enabled her to deal with the truth about a year later, or perhaps the truth had lain dormant all along and merely surfaced with the passage of time, but she took the blow with great equanimity when it fell.

It happened quite innocently and naturally: Tony, who had few early memories of his sister, was playing the monster game with us, giving the monster all kind of instructions, and when it failed to comply, he turned to Small and demanded impatiently:

'Small Sis, why don't you obey me and do what I tell you to do?'

I froze in my tracks and remonstrated:

'Tony, you mean, why doesn't she make the monster do what you want?'

'No, I do not mean that! Sis is the actual monster, isn't she? And she is not listening to me at all!'

While we stood petrified, Small calmly turned to me and enquired:

'Madonna, this is true isn't it? I had thought so from day one, but I played along with you people because I trusted you… Well now I know.

And that was that. We could not get her to discuss herself with any of us ever again. She lived her own life on her own terms, conforming outwardly, but never allowing anyone entry into her own special world. She never attained puberty because her inside had been injured beyond repair by multiple rapes at a tender age, and she stopped growing after this incident. So, the name 'Small' continued to apply in a bizarre fashion and we almost forgot that she had once had another, 'Jasmine', perhaps because it was too ironic? Then I was married, our mother had a stroke, and though our brothers did their best, Small seemed condemned to solitary confinement within her own misshapen body for the rest of her life…till Leila came into our lives.

From the day Leila stepped into our home, Small became the object of her special care and love. She did not allow Small's initial rejection of her advances to stand in the way, but persisted for a whole year till the ice began to melt… She trimmed her hair, changed her lifestyle, insisting that she continue with her education and go back to the books she had once loved so much. Her smart, specially tailored clothes and made-to-order shoes gave her a chic look, that was oddly arresting and Small began to regain some of her early confidence. Most importantly, she began to speak again, to communicate, mainly with Leila, but also her brothers and Millie. But Leila's master stroke was yet to come: when Roma was born Leila handed her over to Small, telling her that she must care for the baby and keep an eye on her because she, Leila, was too busy, and she could trust no one else. She would leave the baby in the crib and Small would sit by her and watch over her like a hawk by the hour. It was the same with Sheila, and to date the girls feel that Small is their second mother. The day Leila placed Sheila in Small's arms, Small made a comment about her own past for the first and perhaps the last time in her life:

'I know why you want me to look after the girls, so that what happened to me, should not happen to them…and I will make sure it does not… You can trust me Leila.'

She has never spoken since of this, but ever since Leila fell sick, she has been very unsettled. Spends all her time in the garden hanging about that knobby old tree she calls her friend. It seems to me now, that I made the biggest mistake of my life by asking her to run that fateful errand, but at that point I could not bear to see Ronnie's wife, Leila, so happy and the happiness all of her own making, when I had pushed myself beyond the point of no return and had nothing to look forward to. Millie with the sword of Damocles hanging over her all her life, I could still forgive, but not Leila. Truth to tell, I had not imagined that the consequences would be so severe; I had merely wanted her to be miserable, as miserable as I was, to besmirch her ivory tower with black suspicion and let her take the consequences, suffer as I have suffered all these years, that is all… If the truth ever comes out what will Small's reaction be? How much does she actually remember of that terrible night almost thirty years ago?

I have to find out before the soothsayer comes tomorrow, but how can I get Small to talk without giving myself away?

12. Consultations

DAVE AND MADONNA

Dave: Why the urgent summons? Are you sick? Ronnie and Bobby did not seem to think so and Millie was quite taken aback at the suggestion!

Madonna: Stop playing the fool, Dave, this is deadly serious.

Dave: It usually is, whenever you are involved; whose head is it going to be this time? Who has dared to be good or happy?

Madonna: Why are you always so cynical when it comes to me, Dave?

Dave: I cynical, with you around? Don't make me laugh! You invented the word, remember? But tell me, what is worrying you now? I thought your master card was played and you have the family just where you wanted them, worried and miserable?

Madonna: What master card? And why should I want my own family to be miserable? They have been so good to me…

Dave: Which is why…doesn't it work that way with you, always?

Madonna: Dave, I have explained to you many times that I

cannot stand conscious virtue, because it is just another name for hypocrisy. But in this case...

Dave: You made a mistake in going for Leila, for she is the rare exception who believes in not only doing right, but thinking right. However, she misjudged you completely like others before her, and so fell into your trap; by the way, how did you spring it, exactly?

Madonna: So, you too are besotted like the rest of the family?

Dave: No, only clear-sighted, because knowing you as I do, I have no problem in believing the worst of you. But I think you will find that this time the others too will be more reluctant to fall in to the trap. Did you expect Tony of all people to take a hand and call in a soothsayer, for instance? I think I will turn up on the day just to watch the fun.

Madonna: I hope you have fun Dave, but for all your cleverness, there is a vital point you have missed.

Dave: And that is?

Madonna: I am not the only culprit, there is someone else who is intent on wreaking revenge and he is in deadly earnest.

Dave: He? Oh you mean Timmy's political friends? But they were mainly interested in hush money and now that Timmy has managed to stand up to them and decided to face the worst I think they are losing interest; petty blackmailers are not dangerous once their bluff has been called.

Madonna: No, this is someone with a deep personal grievance, quite ruthless, will not desist till all the pus has flowed out of this terrible sore…I cannot put a face to the presence yet, but I am absolutely certain.

Dave: Do you really believe this or are you merely hoping that the guilt will be divided?

Madonna: No, just think clearly for once; if my objective had been Leila's misery alone, why would I push for the case to be re-opened? If the truth comes out it will probably take away the cause of her misery and defeat my purpose altogether.

Dave: So your house of cards is built on the shifting sands of falsehood after all? One would think you would have had your fill of quicksand by now…step back, Madonna, there is still time.

Madonna: No, time has run out for all of us Dave, even for you.

SHEILA AND SAMMY

Sheila: Well, I did not break a leg, and no thanks to you!

Sammy: Crass ingratitude! If I had not held on to you, you would have fallen on your face, and you know your nose could not have stood that challenge!

Sheila: Just because you have a more aquiline face, you don't have to show off!

Sammy: Stop throwing those big words at me! Is aquiline like leonine or is it something worse?

Sheila: You stop being an idiot, Sammy, and think. We have just a few hours before all hell breaks loose.

Sammy: I think we are pretty much in hell now, Sheila, only we don't know how bad it is.

Sheila: Well, one thing I do know, Sammy, and that is we need to keep an eye on Small.

Sammy: On Small? But how is she involved?

Sheila: Haven't you noticed how unsettled she has been of late, wandering about in the garden and muttering to her tree-friend all day? She hardly speaks, even to me, and you know that we have always been good pals.

Sammy: But she has been upset ever since Aunt Leila fell sick, the last six months…so, what's new?

Sheila: You notice so little, Sammy, you have no micro-vision. Through the last month, ever since we found the remains of that letter and realized that Mamma had tried to take her life, she has been getting more anxious by the day, but the soothsayer business has turned her wholly paranoid. She is obviously terrified of something, or someone, and my concern is that she might come to harm due to her anxiety.

Sammy: But who on earth would want to hurt Small in this house?

Sheila: The same person who succeeded in hurting my mother so badly that today she is beyond the pale of recovery. Someone who cannot afford to have Small come out in the open and speak the truth?

Sammy: If you are thinking what I am thinking, let us go and talk to Small immediately!

13. Introspection

It's amazing how hard it is to keep the ideal in life apart from the personal, and how quickly political and patriotic zeal disappears when faced with a personal crisis. How the noble pursuit of truth becomes a millstone round one's neck that one would shake off at any price! Robin had done his best, had warned me that I was about to open the box of sorrows that once opened, could not be closed. When I asked him where he had heard the story of Pandora, he had replied:

'Oh, the master of course, who else would bother with me, Timmy? Any little wisdom I may have today is his gift. He told me this story when Baby (Small) was sick, and I a mere boy of sixteen. It was late at night and when I was about to repair to my quarters, he said something that I have never been able to forget. He said, watching my face very carefully to check whether I had got the meaning: Every household has such a box and it should never be disturbed, for no good can ever come of it. You remember that Robin, for your horse-sense seems to be one of the few guarantees of sanity in the future for this crazy family that I have raised, and I want you to be around when the box is opened in this house for it will be very difficult to stem the flow.'

And I should have paid heed and stopped right there, for the old man knew and taught Robin more of life than this entire family put together, except perhaps Aunt Madonna, who could have pulled me up in my tracks if she had wanted to; however, she did not warn me at that point unlike Robin, but sneered at me much later, telling me that every sorrow that has befallen the family is my fault. Why? What is her stake in this business, I wonder?

Whatever, realization has come at a terrible price and too late. I have always taken Uncle Ronnie, courageous, honest, straight as an arrow as my role model, and was so proudly determined to face the consequences of my search, to convince my political friends and Willy that our illustrious family had nothing to hide... And now, the case will be re-opened, Aunt Leila is at death's door, Uncle Ronnie on the very brink and little Sheila going quietly mad. As Aunt Rose says rather cattily:

'People who live in crystal houses should not throw diamonds of wisdom at other people.'

Oh God, What have I done?

LENA

What a fool I have been, crowing over everyone and hugging my secret to myself, thinking I have the power to make people tow my line and make the killing of a lifetime. Never thought about the fallout deeply enough to realize that the only person I care about and can call my own will suffer horribly through this exposure and certainly not thank me, Lena, for jerking out the world from under his feet. And Robin; he may not hate me for what happened, he is too wise, but he will never forgive me for the hurt my revelation will cause the family if I bring out the truth after all these years. Is a large sum, even a huge sum of hush-money and a few years of luxury worth breaking a heart?

The soothsayer, what if he really has the power of divination? What if he comes out with the truth before the family members? I would rather die than face that shame. But now, even if I wanted to, I cannot stop him from coming because I arranged the visit in the first place.

What is it that the old master always said?

'Look before you leap, Lena, not after you have leapt into nowhere…!'

The cunning bastard leapt all his life and left us all holding the can!

14. Questions

SMALL, SHEILA AND SAMMY

Small: Sheila, don't ask questions to which I do not have answers. I said nothing to your mother that evening to make her sick and that is final.

Sammy: We know you did not say anything, why would you? You love Aunt Leila best, and everyone knows that. But did you carry a message for someone?

Small: No, of course not! You know very well that I never leave the house since Leila fell sick, so whom would I carry a message from?

Sheila: How about someone in the house? Someone who wanted to use you as an intermediary?

Small: Your imagination is working overtime again Sheila! Why would anyone do that when they could talk to Leila directly, any time they wanted?

Sheila: So you would carry the responsibility and the blame, naturally!

Small: But I would cheerfully give my soul to save Leila pain, she is one person I would never hurt, surely you know that?

Sammy: We do indeed, but so does everyone else,

unfortunately. Hence, you are the ideal courier; don't you see? You are one person who is beyond suspicion.

Small: Oh, my God, I never thought of that! But she promised…

Sheila: So, there was someone…Who is she and what did she promise? Tell us before it is too late, please!

Small: But I can't…I also promised I would tell no one! How can I break my word, tell me?

Sheila: Just this once, Small, for our sakes? For Mamma's sake, please? You have always thought of me as your child…will you not grant me this one request that matters more to me than anything else in the world? How can you bear to see Mamma suffer like this?

Small: But it is only an assumption on your part. How can you be sure that the message is the cause of this terrible trouble?

Sammy: Now you are talking like my Dad, arguing like a lawyer. We don't have time for arguments Small, we need to take action before it is too late!

Small: If this is true, how come neither Ronny nor Bobby has said anything to me? Why should I believe you two, half the size of nothing?

Sammy: Because you know very well that we kids see a lot more than our Dads do through their moral screens, always wanting to do what is right and ignoring the need to take action! We are closer to the ground because we are half-size, and that helps.

Sheila: I beg of you Small, please!

Small: Okay, let me talk to her and I will get back to you.

Sheila: I wouldn't do that if I were you. It could be dangerous.

Small: Dangerous, for whom?

Sammy: For you, naturally.

Small: But why me? I have done no one any harm.

Sammy: Are you suggesting that Aunty ever harmed anybody in her life? Yet she is at death's door today. Cause and effect are not always clearly linked Small, or why did you suffer so much, a little girl of six?

Small: So, you know?

Sheila: We don't know the details, but we know it was something terrible, mainly because of the way you have guarded Roma and I all our lives.

Small: Yes, I have, and it seems my guarding days are not over even though you are clever enough to advise me now, you especially Sheila, for you are Leila's child. Well, give me a little time to talk to my friend, and I will be with you very shortly.

Sammy: Which means you are going into the garden. Well, you watch your step and make sure you speak to no one else. Should I come with you?

Small: Don't worry Sammy, I can take care of myself; in any case, I have nothing to fear from anyone for I have nothing more to lose.

Sheila: Don't say that! You have me, Sammy and Roma.

Small: Yes, my child, I know that and I have no intention of losing any of you like we once lost Joy. I see much more clearly now, and I think I know what I have to do to give you back your

	life and bring your mother back to all of us.
Sheila:	Oh Small, if you only could!
Small:	If I don't, it certainly will not be due to want of effort, for I feel my friend will agree wholeheartedly and help me in every way.
Sheila:	Then go talk to him quickly and tell him I sent my love.
Sammy:	Just hold on a minute Small, why Joy? Why do you suddenly speak of Joy now, after all these years? What does he have to do with our present problem?
Small:	Never mind, Master long-nosed Sammy!

LENA TO SMALL

Lena: Small, I just heard you say to Sheila that you
          would bring her mother back! How will you
          make this possible, and so easily, when all these
          months of untiring effort by family members,
          doctors, even her own mother has got us
          nowhere? I don't think you should give that
          child false hope only to let her down in the end.
          Her heartache is complete; she cannot take one
          more disappointment.

Small: I know you brought us up Lena, and took
          care of Tony and me like a mother, but you
          don't seem to have noticed that it was a long
          time ago, and that we have grown up since and
          become responsible people! Do you seriously
          think I would let Sheila suffer any more? I will
          now make sure that her heart is whole again by
          putting an end to this nightmare. I should have
          done it a long time ago, only I did not realize
          earlier what I had to do…but now I do.

Lena: But now? What have you realized that you did
          not before? Does this mean that you know who
          is responsible? And how can you be so sure?

Small: Because, in a stupid, indirect way the whole
          thing revolves around me! Mind you, I'm as

much a victim as Leila, but even then I cannot shrug off my share of the responsibility. I have to make amends, and I will.

Lena: Please be careful Small. With the mistress gone and Madame Leila in this condition, there is no one to take care of you, and I am so helpless without her! Why don't you leave this alone? It's not your business. Haven't you suffered enough that you want to buy more pain?

Small: Exactly, Lena; I am no stranger to suffering, so what is one more capsule?

But in the process, if those children smile again, it will be a small price to pay. Don't you agree?

Lena: No, I don't! I could not bear to see my first baby in trouble! Don't you realize that what Sheila and Roma mean to you, Tony and you mean to me?

Small: Oh, I know about Tony of course, but I too? Never thought of that!

Lena: What do you mean by that remark, Small? Why should I love Tony more than you? I took care of both of you to the best of my ability and the mistress trusted me implicitly, you know that!

Small: I do indeed, but you were wet-nursing Tony, weren't you, because Mamma refused to nurse him? I wondered about that even at the age of five!

Lena: She did not refuse, she was unwell.

Small: No doubt I got it wrong then, and you would know best, wouldn't you?

Lena: Is something seriously wrong Small? It is not like you to speak in riddles. Please tell me how I can help.

Small: No one can help anyone but oneself; it took Leila's predicament to make me realize this simple truth! And it is only now that I am beginning to find answers to many thorny riddles that have pricked me all my life. Well, see you around Lena!

Lena: I have never known her to speak like this. Can it be that she has actually guessed after all these years? If so, how will I deal with the inevitable confrontation? Oh God, help me in this hour of need for that _____ is not around to answer questions, as usual. How can I stop her from speaking to Madonna, Tony or even Millie about this?

But she has not done so in all these years, so perhaps she will continue to hold her tongue? One thing about these siblings, they will do anything, bear any hardship to spare each other pain, and in this respect they certainly did not take after their father. All except Madonna, that is.

So I had better not take the initiative and get myself into a bigger mess. What is it the Master always said?

'Never forget your station in life Lena; it does not pay to get too big for your boots.'

15. In the Library, Again

BOBBY AND RONNIE

Bobby: The library seems so odd and gloomy today, Ronnie, maybe we should have asked for a fire to be lit. Somehow I did not feel so cold outside.

Ronnie: The cold is in your heart, Bobby; the thermometer hanging there will tell you that the temperature is perfectly normal, bearable, and does not call for a fire. Besides, it is too early in the year. Remember, we never light a fire in this house till Halloween, All Soul's Day? Rather appropriate in the present context, with so many ghosts flitting around, don't you think?

Bobby: About time we changed some of the things we have always done in this house! I've just about had enough of the venerable past vitiating our lives, Ronnie!

Ronnie: What you mean is, we have had enough of 'pussy-footing around the truth' as Sammy would say! You know, Bobby, kids have such an uncomplicated view of things that they make the intellectual leap in a way we never can. So, before they find out anyway, maybe we should do the needful? That way, the initiative will still be with us, at least partially.

Bobby: But what do you want from me, Ronnie?

Ronnie: The truth, raw, simple, unvarnished. What
            was the famous political angle? Why was this
            damned case hushed up in the first place? What
            role did Sunny's father play in this affair and
            why? Who else but you is aware of the truth?
            And most importantly, why this sudden urge
            to re-open this case after thirty years? Who is it
            that will not let sleeping dogs lie, in both senses
            of the word? For that there was a lie perpetrated
            seems beyond doubt, but by whom and why?

Bobby: You are the one who should have read law,
            Ronnie, you with your uncanny ability to
            cut through the peripherals and lay bare the
            essentials. Those questions go to the heart of the
            matter, and I can see that you have framed them
            as plainly as possible, but have you forgotten
            that the truth is never simple, and not to be
            found unvarnished? As a lawyer, I know that to
            my bitter cost, and in any case, I don't have the
            answers to all your questions. Besides, we need
            to prioritize; not all the questions are of equal
            importance.

Ronnie: Bobby, are you trying to escape, again? No
            purpose will be served by further prevarication.
            Give me the answers you do have, then.

Bobby: For me the most important question is:
            Why this sudden urge to re-open this case after
            thirty years, and although the obvious answer
            is Timmy's silly political club and Timmy's own
            quixotic attitude, it is not the whole answer. Their

efforts have been very carefully orchestrated and brought to a head, and I have no idea by whom.

Ronnie: Well, we are a very successful, and worse, a very united family, and because we brothers, our wives and even the kids get on so well, it is difficult to find a chink in our armor. Besides, we do not have too many skeletons in the cupboard, either, so it is difficult to get at us. I could think of a dozen people who would be delighted to see us taken down a peg or two and squirm socially. Perhaps it is some political or professional rival, Father's, yours or mine, or even a business rival of Tony's?

Bobby: No, Ronnie, that kind of jealousy or mal-intent is easy to deal with and would not worry me in the least; but there is a personal angle to this that is very disquieting. Why else would they have begun with an attempt to destroy Leila?

Ronnie: Leila? You think she is a part of this strategy, but why and how? I don't see the connection.

Bobby: You know Ronnie, Tony was half right when he called you an armchair philosopher and the most vulnerable creature on earth. I shut him up that day, but I too have come to realize that this determination of yours to see only the 'good' in everybody, family and friends, and completely ignore the 'evil' that is in all of us, makes you an easy target. You never see the pitfalls because you refuse to acknowledge them.

Ronnie: Bobby, these attempts at diversion are getting us nowhere, so please tell me in simple, unequivocal language exactly what you mean. I have always believed that to deliberately seek out what I perceive as evil and criticize it from the vantage point of conscious virtue, is tantamount to the annihilation of self, and I am not about to think differently because things have gone wrong. But how are my beliefs and their failings relevant here?

Bobby: Well, you have always given people the impression that it is I, as the head of the family, who has held this joint family together, but only insiders know that it is Leila's doing more than anyone else's. Therefore, a family person alone would realize the far-reaching damage that would be caused by getting her out of the way and proceed to find the best way to do so.

Ronnie: And the best way would be?

Bobby: To damage her faith in you, to make you fall so irrevocably in her eyes that nothing anyone could say would restore that faith, something so unspeakable that she would not be able to talk about it, but just pine away in misery. With Leila out of the way and you not far behind, the field would be clear for others strategies, like the re-opening of this case.

Ronnie: Which brings us to my first two questions: What was the political or nationalist angle if there was one at all; and, most crucial, why was the case hushed up? If I know our father at all well, I would say that cowardice was not one of his failings and that he was never the one to avoid confrontation or refuse to face the consequences of his actions; then why in this particular case? I'm sure you remember how desperate our mother was that the truth be told?

Bobby: Then you will also remember what desperate means he took to ensure her silence? It was not easy for either of them, and Father would never have gone so far if he alone had been under fire.

Ronnie: So, who else was involved, Bobby, and what were the stakes that made him behave in this uncharacteristic manner? You have to tell me, and that too, right now!

Bobby: I have gone back into the archives as far as possible, but the main papers are still protected by the Privacy Act, and I so have only allied information and my own memories to fall back on. And that is the crux of the matter; these people know that time is running out and soon the information will be public property, and then...

Ronnie: And then?

Bobby: Whatever the information be, it is bound to be highly inflammable, and we will have had no time to prepare due to lack of prior information. That is their trump card, and you can now understand why it is making me paranoid.

Ronnie: No, I still don't understand. However damaging the information be, it cannot hurt our father except by besmirching his reputation, and that is not making you paranoid because he was always and still is a controversial character, and in any case, no one can touch him now as he is dead. No, what is worrying you is much closer

Bobby: to the knuckle because it affects the living. Now, tell me who?

Bobby: Do you remember the atmosphere in the village on that day where we went for our last picnic?

Ronnie: Not too well, because what happened afterwards has dwarfed previous memories; but of course, that was the aftermath, I realized that even at the time...

Bobby: Exactly; the village and its anger constituted the root cause of all the subsequent misery. At that time we thought the boy who had been executed was a terrorist in the British parlance of the times, and that our father, staunchly being on the side of his masters, had failed to take into account the evidence in the victim's favor and helped to pass an unfair judgment. He had been hanged almost too quickly, the boy's wife had immolated herself and the Nationalist Press had really gone to town on the case, setting up the boy as a great patriot killed by the anglophile Judge!

Ronnie: Yes, and if I remember correctly, they were planning a rally that day, which would come into town to protest against the judgment, and because their mood was ugly we left early. But what I did not understand then, and don't now is, if the cause was purely political, why the personal attack, and that too on a child and a girl child at that? In those days such things were rare in rural India, and even under extreme provocation, children were usually spared.

Bobby: You are absolutely right, but what if there was more than one cause, and a strongly personal one at that? Might it not then be a case of an eye for an eye, and a tooth for a tooth?

Ronnie: You mean one of Father's by-blows? Oh my God!

Bobby: Exactly! But by a strange quirk of fate, he was not guilty this time, or he would never have gone to this village in the first place nor touched that case. Let us say, he did not know that he was guilty.

Ronnie: Come on Bobby, between him and Robin's father they had a pretty good thing going and that garden house was seldom unoccupied till this incident occurred. His genes were too strong for him!

Bobby: I agree about the appetites, but this time the circumstances were not of his own making. Shall we say that fate decided to take a hand and show him that he was not the master after all?

Ronnie: So, whose sins are we paying for, if not his? And who was the protagonist and who the victim? Do I know them?

Bobby: You will never believe this, but the circumstances were created by our mother, and the supposed victim was Lena!

Ronnie: If that is meant to be a joke, let me tell you it is very ill-timed and in very poor taste.

Bobby: A joke? I only wish it were, Ronnie, but in this case the truth is stranger than fiction, however trite that may sound!

Ronnie: But I always thought that Lena ran away from the village to avoid her father, who was planning to sell her off, and that our mother took her in out of the goodness of her heart and because the old singer, who had brought her to the house in the first place, begged of her to do so. Later she decided to let her take care of Small, and remained with us.

Bobby: You are quite right and that is how it actually happened; but no one knew that _____ was the village she had belonged to, and that her old man, on finding out where she was, had been laying a trap to blackmail her employer. When this unfortunate incident occurred, he saw his chance and inflamed the whole village against him, and Father's reputation made that unfortunately easy.

Ronnie: And they took it out on Small when they found he was unafraid because he was not guilty, and ready to take them on single-handed? The bastards! But then, where was the need to hush things up? Everyone would have sympathized with us, in any case.

Bobby: They would have if matters had not been distorted, twisted out of recognition in a filthy manner that left a man as fearless as our father cowering, and with no choice but to do their bidding. It was a plan as diabolical as it was simple, calculated to choke the great Judge in his own bile.

Ronnie: Why Bobby, you sound quite Old Testament… it must be very ugly indeed, to provoke such courtroom language! Come on, share as we have always done since we were children; it will make you feel better and lighten the burden.

Bobby:	That is the one thing expressly I do not wish to do!
Ronnie:	Why on earth? Oh I see; it concerns me then, exclusively?
Bobby:	That would be easy to fight wouldn't it, and the Judge would never have hesitated; but they thought of that and made Small part of this terrible plan.
Ronnie:	What plan? We know Small was terribly violated and all my efforts to save her had come to nothing, but there was nothing that either of us could be blamed for, surely?
Bobby:	Not unless the whole thing was misrepresented.
Ronnie:	Bobby, please come clean, I cannot bear this anymore.
Bobby:	Nor could I, and it took all my resolve to appear normal when I did find out about a week ago.
Ronnie:	And how did this revelation come your way?
Bobby:	Entirely by chance. I had gone to see Mr. Sen, our family solicitor, on business, and we obviously got talking about this case, and then quite suddenly, he said: 'Bobby, your Father had given this sealed letter into my keeping many years ago, hoping that it would never have to be opened; but since the letter is addressed to you, I think the time has come for you to make your own decision about its contents. Perhaps there is something in it that could help you?'
Ronnie:	And the letter said?
Bobby:	Here are Father's very words. I'll read the letter out to you:

To Whom it May Concern

My wife did not forgive me till her dying day for what happened, and I would have done the same had I been in her position, for when it came to the children, we had always seen eye to eye up to this point. And this has been on my conscience ever since, because she forgave me so much.

Not only that, I have a feeling that though I may have managed to stifle this outburst for the moment, managed to cut down the poison tree, it will put out leaves again and bear ominous fruit someday. For in the process of destruction I have inevitably given a hostage to fortune, and against the day of discovery, I pen down the complete truth as it was, so that the suffering may be somewhat redeemed, even though in the process my image, particularly in the eyes of those I brought into this world, will be further besmirched, and they will see me for who I am; an arrogant sinner trying to play God. Ronnie, I think, has always known my weaknesses, for he is as sharp as I am and has the courage of his convictions like his mother as I do not, and of course Madonna for reasons of her own, knows me only too well. Bobby and Tony, who determinedly avoided the reality out of their blind love and admiration for me, will suffer terribly. But it is my baby, my Small, who had paid the terrible price for my folly once, and whom I used most unmercifully a second time to save my own worthless carcass, who weighs heaviest on my conscience. She must and should know her Father for her greatest enemy and betrayer. Maybe when she spits on my memory and cries out imprecations to heaven, the scars will begin to bleed afresh on my soul, for they never can heal, and nor do I ever want the pain to subside. Expiation is not possible, but perhaps my redemption lies in eternal pain.

When the children were ultimately found lying in close proximity among some bushes, they were both unconscious, had terrible signs of atrocity on their bodies, particularly Small, hardly any clothes to cover their shame and it was clear they had been left there to die. We would have missed them altogether, if it had not been for Nan, our trusty old Alsatian, who had indefatigably followed her nose, leading the police dogs in ever narrowing circles, till she found them. Then she sat beside them and whined and barked the place down till everyone came running. Even the hard-bitten Mr. Wilson, the Police Commissioner, had paled at the sight and sworn vengeance on the spot, and I knew then that if the children lived, they would have justice.

The medical examination revealed that they had been given doses of Datura, the Indian original of the Jimsonweed, which fuzzes the brain and produces terrible hallucinations. Very clever insurance against future evidence in case they survived, for anything they said would carry very little credibility. Not that they remembered much; Ronnie was very clear about events before the blow on the head, but had no recollection of the aftermath and Small stopped talking altogether, only expressing her terror in screaming nightmares.

Mr. Wilson, good as his word, had the ring leaders of the attack in irons within a week, and it was clear that they were in for rigorous sentences; no judge or jury who had seen the children would forgive the perpetrators of the atrocity. In the process the public, focusing on the children, were turning away from my sins and the hue and cry against me was beginning to die down. Was I glad of this? Surely not, but in honest truth, I am not sure. A mother may put her children before herself, Solomon and many others, strong patriarchs all of them tell us so, but there are no instances of such sacrifice on the part of progenitors to the best of my knowledge. As a matter of fact, in mythology and all great literature, stories of children, sons and daughters, sacrificing themselves for their father's and brother's succor, are legion; Antigone, case in point. The men obviously wrote these pieces to endorse the society they were creating for their own benefit. For instance, the Vedic Prayer about a Father's semi-divine qualities, worthy of prayer and total worship, to be obeyed at all times, not to be questioned or refuted!

Words that my wife dinned into her children assiduously, absolved men of the greatest crimes that they had committed in the cause of being begetters. Lear and Gloucester turned so easily against their progeny, but the wronged ones came back to save them against their enemies that their blind elders had considered as friends. Was I wrong in not being an exception, allowing blind sentiment to stand in the way of self-interest? My wife was horrified when I told her this, but all her tears and reproaches did not manage to convince me otherwise when it came to the crunch.

For, just as I had begun to assume that I was out of the woods, the hydra reared its ugly head again; the public prosecutor, a Gandhian, and a long-standing adversary, pounced on the very point I was at pains to keep in abeyance and began to work on the Lena angle, an angle that I could in no way allow to be explored, even though Lena had come to the house of her own volition and been willing party to all events thereafter. If the case came to trial and these facts came to the public, my children would get justice all right, but my credibility would be in tatters, irredeemably. My masters might just withdraw their support, for they had strange notions of justice and would insist that to avenge the children was the main purpose, and that the Law should take its course in all matters to achieve this end. They themselves were under threat in India and other colonies and would not wish the image of British Justice to be tainted, especially if it was not at cost to them. They might even make an example of me to polish their own haloes, since matters had played so conveniently into their hands. I just could not take a chance.

So, counter measures; a rumor to be countered by another rumor that would be so heinous, it would shock the public into changing sides again, and the only pawns who could achieve this for me would be the same children who had saved me once before, for I was sure I had no other cards left. The only question was:

Could a father use his children in the same way his enemies had done?

The answer, after some superficial soul-searching and a battle to end all battles with my wife, the children's mother:

Yes. This father could and would do so.

But most unexpectedly, Robin's father, who had served me so faithfully through the years, been my procurer and boon companion in drink and debauchery, had bailed me out of endless scrapes at cost to himself, and on whom I had based my strategy, baulked at my plan this time and remonstrated strongly:

'You can't do this, sir; people might believe the rumor-mongers and then, two lives, lives of your own children will be irrevocably ruined. Even if that does not happen, a shadow will always remain. No, I cannot agree to this; I love Ronnie and Small too much to allow this horrible idea to get about. We must think of something else.'

'But you don't seem to realize that no one will know that the idea is coming from us. They will put it down to the evil intentions of the opposition and the sympathy they are arousing at the moment, will be nipped in the bud. That is all we want, isn't it'?

'That is what you want and hope sir, but the idea, whatever the source and however unlikely, will get to the public, and do you know what they will say? An extension of what they have always said:

'No smoke without fire. Like father like son; spares no one, not even his own kin.'

'Ronnie does not deserve this for he is not in the least like you, and I will not allow this to happen as long as I am alive.'

And that was that. Nothing I could say would budge him and the children concerned were not even his own! In the end however, I got him to arrange an attack on Mr. Wilson's wife, who always went for a walk with her dog in the afternoon, and being self-reliant with complete trust in the natives, refused to take a bodyguard with her. What he did not know was that his attack would coincide with the very rumor campaign he had been at such pain to avoid, and that this person would make no mistakes, for her own self-interest was at stake.

I had also been in constant touch with Sunny's father, and it looked as though things were going to work out between Sunny and Madonna. Another child would be sacrificed for the well-being of her father, and he would get out of all charges that may be leveled by capitalizing on her quixotism and persuading her that the move was a benison in disguise, and poor monkey, she would accept it. I needed the great man's support and no price was too great to pay, as long as I did not have to do the paying.

So, Mrs. Wilson's dog was shot, and she herself, torn, lacerated, was left by the roadside to die in a grim and grotesque replay of the earlier incident; this had been deliberately done to link the two events in Mr. Wilson's mind, to shock him into frenzied activity, and it achieved its purpose admirably; finally, when the rumor that Ronnie, depraved as his father had committed the outrage on his sister rather than the alleged miscreants, began to make the rounds, he was convinced that he was dealing with a group so diabolical, that nothing but a holocaust would suffice.

At least thirty people died in the battle that ensued, and many, some of them women who had started the whispers, were maimed for life. All those even remotely connected with the case were permanently silenced and no one knew that most of the killing was done by hired men rather than the police, for they knew their targets. When the case came to trial two months later, Mr. Wilson came in with his wife's photographs to point out the similarities between the two happenings, for she was in a state of permanent shock like Small and could not speak. The last cobwebs of doubt were swept away by the grand old man's thundering rhetoric, and the standard-bearers of the nationalist outrage, their banner in tatters, their arguments appearing more and more like a sick ploy of personal enemies of the poor Judge were shamed into silence, and finally withdrew the case.

The final judgment was passed by an English judge, and I managed to stay out of the picture pretty much except as a victim.

What I never could get out of my mind is the expression of complete disbelief in Mrs. Wilson's eyes when we found her... and a year later when she could speak, she never stopped re-iterating her conviction that the entire incident had been planned to use her for personal reasons, for the common people of this land, which was hers by adoption, would never break faith with her in this ugly manner. But by that time it was too late for the case to be re-opened and her husband, terrified for her safety, would not permit it, but she remained a constant threat and a thorn in my side, till she and her husband died in a road accident a few months later. On their way back in a police jeep from a meeting in a nearby village, an over-laden lorry mowed them down in the twilight just outside the city, and disappeared without a trace. He had been a good friend, but his wife was too outspoken for comfort.

And that is the truth, the whole truth, and nothing but the truth, so help me God.

Signed: _____

15th June, 1943

The shadows which had been lengthening on the lawn for some time were now beginning to run together, coalesce and turn into continuous darkness and the pattern was repeated within our minds, leaving us numb. Madonna had lit the great lamp with its thirty-five wicks in the Puja room, a practice from our grandmother's time, which our mother and then Leila had performed till taken sick, and the sound of the conch shell calling the faithful to prayer reverberated ironically through the house. On cue, one by one the lights came on in the big house, a ritual observed for the last hundred years, since the days of oil lamps and then gas and electricity, casting faint illumination on the lawn, but Bobby and I sat on in the darkness, afraid of what we might see in each other's face when the light came on, for we too were fathers.

Then we heard Sheila and Sammy at the door, clamoring to be let in and I jumped up, switched on the lights and opened the door.

Sheila: What are you two up to? Holding a séance? Uncle, you look as though you have seen a ghost, and Daddy, you look pretty weird too!

Bobby: Well, we have seen ghosts, and not one but two. Please do look in the mirror, both of you!

Sammy: Well, you can't blame us in view of what is going on downstairs!

Ronnie: Now what, for God's sake! Why is there not a moment of peace in the house?

Sammy: Because the peacemaker is sick, that is why. All hell has broken loose regarding the visit of the soothsayer tomorrow!

Ronnie: Why? I thought all arrangements had been made in the hall downstairs?

Sheila: We all thought Aunt Millie was in charge, and she has arranged the room beautifully, in her own artistic way with just the right atmosphere.

Ronnie: Then, what is the problem?

Sammy: The other ladies are the problem! Aunt Madonna wants the visit cancelled immediately as does Aunty Rose. Lena is saying she doesn't mind if that is what the others want, pussy-footing around the matter as usual. Small definitely wants the man to come, and Uncle Tony is threatening to throttle anyone who does not agree, for he cannot bear to see his dear sister-in-law like this any longer and is determined to get to the bottom of this hell-hole! Mamma is worried, but wants the man to come if he can help Aunt Leila. Daddy, you will have to do something as the head of the family, and now!

Ronnie: Bobby, we have been living in the shadow of the past too long. But now, the man cannot tell us anything we do not know, or worse than we do know, so to hell with it! If the man is what he claims to be and does speak the truth, we are in for some muckraking, but if it will help cure Leila by clearing her mind of cobwebs, I am prepared to have a mud bath! Please go and tell the good ladies that our plans stand, and that nothing will stop us from seeing the man tomorrow.

Bobby: That's my boy! I will go and inform them with the greatest pleasure!

Sheila: Spoken like a man, uncle! Now we will see some action! Daddy, do you think Mamma will get well now and we will be able to go back to the old times?

Ronnie: One thing I can promise you kids, if it does not happen, it certainly will not be for the want of trying on our part.

16. The Night Before the Morning

INTERCHANGES

Small: What are you doing in my room so late Madonna? You should get some sleep, given that the man of truth will be on our doorstep bright and early. Robin promised to get him here by eight o'clock, sharp, don't you remember?

Madonna: Yes, yes, I remember all right! As a matter of fact, I can remember little else. I really wish we had not got into this tomfoolery!

Small: If that is all it is and you have no guilty secrets to hide, why are you bothered? Just enjoy the fun! I mean to do that and so should you!

Madonna: I wish I could Small, but I can't stop worrying about Leila.

Small: Too many people worrying about her including me, so you can relax. We will all sort it out together. It is not your fee grief as Shakespeare might say...or is it?

Madonna: How come, you are suddenly so chirpy and spouting Shakespeare all around, particularly at me?

Small: Well, it was Leila who brought me back to my books, you know that, and ever since she has been missing in action I have done more reading, understanding and thinking too, and I am quite amazed at the parallels I have found between his stories and our own. See how well his phrase fits you, or actually, does not fit you?

Madonna: Look Small, exactly what are you getting at?

Small: What makes you think I am getting at something? Merely a manner of speaking, I assure you.

Madonna: Hoity-toity, as we said when we were children... why this sudden elevation in tone, this calm assurance, this assumption of superior knowledge? To put it simply, what is it that you know that I do not?

Small: Not a question of knowledge, dear sister, but of conscience...Now if you have 'a bosom franchised and allegiance clear'...Shakespeare, again!

Madonna: Stop it this minute, and come clean at once, Small! What is all this talk about conscience, yours or mine? How do we come into the picture?

Small: If we do not, what are you doing prowling about in the middle of the night, looking for the entire world like 'withered murder' or Lady Macbeth? If someone sees you, he might actually wonder what you are up to. For Heavens' sake, Madonna, go back to bed and switch off my light as you go. We'll play Shakespeare quizzes in the morning with the soothsayer, if you like!

Madonna: I'm warning you, Small, don't take a joke too far...there is a time and a place for everything.

Small: Exactly, now you are quoting the Bible; the

devil himself will turn to the scriptures in time of need, isn't that what they say? But for some people, time runs out before its time, like it did for Joy and his Dad, right, Madonna? Well, this time I will not let that happen, whatever happens, for I have nothing to lose, anyway! Now please go and leave me in peace, though not eternal peace, please! You do understand, don't you, Madonna, that there are more ways of buying life insurance than policies? There is a letter for Bobby and Ronnie; if anything should happen to me, that letter will certainly reach them.

MILLIE AND ROBIN

Millie: Please put the daybed closer to the dais, Robin,
            so the man can hear what Madam Leila says…
            her voice is so faint now…

Robin: Yes, Ma'am, and I will put a couple of extra
            cushions too to help her sit up.

Millie: The flowers are beautiful, Robin, particularly
            the lilies that Leila loves so much.

Robin: The gardeners insist that they have fewer blooms
            all-round the year ever since Madam Leila fell
            sick. Today they have practically denuded the
            garden to fill this room as you wanted.

Millie: I thought it might help, if she were surrounded
            by flowers and children, all the things she loved.

Robin: And your wonderful paintings, Ma'am.

Millie: Ah yes, she loved those too.

Robin: That painting of the woman and the snake in
            the garden, it is recent, isn't it?

Millie: Yes, done just a month ago. Fancy your noticing
            the painting!

Robin: I always pay a lot of attention to your work
            Ma'am, for in a way, they are a record of our
            daily lives in this house, and now I can see that

you have used Madam Leila as a model for the woman. May I ask you a question, Ma'am?

Millie: Certainly, Robin. Please go ahead.

Robin: If you wanted a model for the snake, whose face would you choose?

Millie: Why, a snake face as I have done. Why would I choose a human face? But I think you should leave now, Robin, it is past ten o'clock and you need to get some sleep. It is a long way and it will easily take you an hour and a half to drive there.

Robin: Yes, Ma'am, right away!

Millie: What will the next twelve hours bring? I cannot live to see horror in Sammy's eyes, neither Timmy nor Sheila's for that matter. And Bobby, dear old, steady-as-a-rock, reasonable and moral to a fault, Bobby, can I face him? Ronnie is the only one who knows and he has held his tongue because of his brother and his own compassion, but now when it's a toss-up between Leila and I, who will weigh heavier? Must Leila's restoration be at the cost of my eclipse? How absurdly melodramatic that sounds! But we do not often remember how dramatic life is, how violence lurks just beneath the surface, how terrible a price passion exacts by compelling us to give hostages to fortune.

Should the truth be told even if the outcome is suffering, particularly for those who are neither involved, nor remotely culpable?

Dear God, come to my aid now or there may not be a second chance.

TIMMY AND RONNIE

Timmy: Uncle Ronnie, please tell me honestly what your premonitions are about tomorrow? Your clear thinking might help clear the cobwebs cluttering my brain. I am so terribly confused.

Ronnie: As a reader of history Timmy, I should have known better, should have realized that man was never meant to lead an ordered existence; should have known that the boom and bust cycle of business is true of personal life as well, and prepared accordingly. Where we go wrong is when we believe that sowing and reaping are connected…well, why do we have so many famines then? Why does the most industrious farmer suffer the most from every possible natural and man-made calamity? It seems Nature cannot bear order, for it leads to decadence which stifles her fierce passions, her turbulent creative energies, and her mania for change, the more violent the better. The idea of disaster management makes me laugh! Disasters should not be managed: they should be welcomed as the threshold for the new and the unexpected.

Surely our mistakes through the century provide ample evidence of our total rout in the face of nature? And I think, in our domestic arenas too, we too get tired of goodness, of conformity, of the ordered life, of doing what we ought, and then the urge to throw a spanner in the works becomes inexorable. Nature takes over and all goes dark.

Something like this happened to us and I am just beginning to get the glimmerings now, but look at the rest of the family, they think we need a soothsayer to show us the truth when all of us have the power to get at it ourselves. However, knowing the truth and acknowledging it are very different, so maybe this man is the badly needed catalyst? The need for miracles and magic is basic to all of us, and we would rather trust in the oracle than find the truth ourselves. So be it then, I am prepared for all eventualities and will fight like blazes tomorrow, even against my own, to bring Leila out of the woods, for I owe her.

Timmy: I believe our Grandfather was a great proponent of the nature versus nurture debate, and strongly upheld the importance of the latter over the former. I have heard that he used his arguments in favor of upbringing and the lack of it as irrefutable causal factors in court and won many a case due to his masterly arguments and Machiavellian interpretation of facts. It appears that this is when he became the master of manipulation, and playing God with his clients led him to believe that he could actually play around with the lives of his friends and even family members. This happened mainly in his lawing days. Later, when he became the Great Judge, I think the power went completely to his head, and he felt he was the dispenser of, but above the Law himself. Worse, I feel sure he used his children as guinea pigs to prove his point. Absurd as it may seem, nothing else explains his diverse handling of his progeny or the terrible legacy he left them and us.

Ronnie: So, you think that this case has to do with the family?

Timmy: Pretty obvious, isn't it? But I also believe that there are two separate issues here, both personal and both born out of vengeance; however, they are interconnected.

Ronnie: How come you are suddenly able to see so clearly?

Timmy: It took Willy to show me that I am partly responsible for this debacle, questioning the tip without an inkling of the iceberg beneath. I will be glad when the ordeal is over; when the pitiless light of truth lays bare the slimy shingle that has lain dormant, festering under the still waters of falsehood, hypocrisy and social convention; ugly and deceitful. One can face that, for one has to fight when there is no way out, but the constant innuendo, the vicious whispers, the endless waiting and the imminence of the crash I cannot take any more, and nor can most other family members by the look of it. The kids have had enough and Dad and Uncle Tony are fed to the teeth. It's only the women who keep on blabbering about family prestige and tradition. But what kind of prestige is this that condemns an innocent woman to living death, that needs a blanket of lies to keep it warm, alive and breeding venom? If this family believes in rectitude and morality, it should be prepared to test these values in the fire of fire.

Ronnie: Willy has certainly done a great job, Timmy and I am proud of you! I only hope you can hold on to your convictions throughout the coming ordeal without breaking your heart.

SMALL, LENA AND ROBIN

Lena: Who is that at the door? For the love of heaven, it is four in the morning…stop knocking, we've heard you, so don't wake up the neighborhood! There it goes again…what uneasy soul is this breaking down the door? Wait, wait, I am coming…give me a moment… Robin, will you please take a look?

Robin: Must be the family in the third room; remember, the wife is expecting a baby very soon?

Lena: But not so soon; perhaps she has had a miscarriage? By the way, if I go with her to the hospital, I can escape the soothsayer, can't I?

Robin: You know you don't mix with the other servants as you think you are a cut above them…then why this sudden desire to be of help? And why are you so scared of the man of truth?

Lena: Not for myself, Robin, only to spare the family embarrassment.

Robin: Of course, the family always comes first with you, I know that.

Lena: There goes the knocking again… Robin please open the door!

Robin: All right, all right! Why, Small, what are you
            doing here so early? And why didn't you send
            someone or ring the bell instead of coming
            yourself at this dark hour?

Small: Because I thought Lena might know what to do,
            Madonna is very sick.

Robin: Then we must get the doctor. Lena you go with
            Small; I'm coming in a minute and we'll have
            Master Bobby call the doctor.

Small: I could have done that myself, Robin, why would
            I bother you? No, Madonna needs someone she
            can talk to, and remember, Lena took care of her
            when she was little? With Mamma not around, I
            think she will be most comfortable with Lena.

Robin: Strange! Why a servant and not her own kin?
            She has her brothers, or Madam Millie, or even
            you?

Small: For a very intelligent man, you are really stupid
            sometimes, Robin! Tell me, why does Timmy
            talk to you and not his dad or uncles about
            things that bother him?

Robin: But he did talk to Madam Leila when she was
            around.

Small: Exactly! Everyone spoke to Leila; she was the
            safety valve-in-chief; but not having recourse to
            her we must all make do with second best, surely
            you see that?

Robin: You know Small, it's very strange, but your father
            used to say the same thing, that sometimes
            when we are sick, we need someone to talk to,
            someone who understands, rather than a doctor.
            He found that out in his law practice days,

and always allowed his clients to talk without interruption even if they were rambling.

Small: And no doubt he discovered more about them through these ramblings than proper conversation. I remember sitting quiet as a mouse in his office when he spoke less than listened to people, making notes on his jotting pad all the while. Did you know that Shakespeare spoke these words of wisdom three hundred years ago?

Robin: There you go with your Shakespeare again; is there anything the man did not say or know? And how do you know so much about what he said?

Small: Father again and then Ronnie and Leila. Oh Lena, there you are; let's go.

Robin: Yes, you two carry on, and I will follow in ten minutes. In any case the chauffer and I have to get the car checked out for we have to leave at six to pick up the soothsayer. His ashram is a fair distance.

Small: I too am looking forward to his coming; do you really believe that he can do what he claims, Lena?

Robin: Why would Lena recommend him so strongly if she didn't?

Lena: Come on Small; Robin will stand there and talk forever, if you give him half a chance!

TONY-SPEAK

I, Tony, have known all along that I am different from the rest of my siblings and I began to feel it even as a kid when I found that my mother's eyes, for all her affection, lit up differently on seeing me than they did, say, for Ronnie. She loved me, did more for me when I needed her than she did for the others, but I always felt that it was out of duty rather than affection, and could not understand why. But when I think back now I realize that this was mainly due to Small's accident, for she never did get over the terrible experience, and gave all her time and love afterwards to her unfortunate child as long as she lived. Strangely however, she seemed to care more for me after this happened than before, and concentrated on the two of us to the exclusion of the older ones. It was my happiest time in our country house for eight months, where she went after the accident with Small and I. In that house with its large garden, clear pond, grazing cows, and Nan our Alsatian who came with us, we had a lovely time; Small slowly began to heal and her nightmares began to fade. While we played together in the sun and our mother just sat there trying not to cry, it was really Nan who took care of us and prevented us from straying. It was as though she felt that the enemy was not too far away, even then, and she never left our side. After all, the search party might never have found Ronnie and Small if it had not been for Nan, and it seemed as though she was making sure that there would be no repetition of the outrage. Small just clung to her and very often would go to sleep on the grass resting her head on Nan's side, and Nan would not twitch a muscle till she woke up. Dear, dear Nan; we have had other dogs since but not a single one with her regality, intelligence or affection.

But our mother died the day she brought the three of us home from our country house. Something happened that night, which shocked her to such an extent that the indomitable spirit that had enabled her to withstand Ronnie and Small's terrible tragedy and made her work indefatigably for their recovery, crumbled, and she lost all hope. After that she just withered away and lived on like a shadow till Leila came to the house; then, as though absolved of all responsibility, she passed away and her funeral pyre was lit. I still remember standing between Bobby and Ronnie holding the burning wood and refusing to touch it to my mother's face till Bobby just gave my hand a push and the terrible ritual was done. Then my paternal uncle came and took me away, but when I looked back I had a clear vision of my mother standing behind the pyre and looking at me sorrowfully.

It was Ronnie who took me up to the terrace that night and holding on to my hand firmly, though his own voice was not quite steady, he pointed to the stars and told me that stars were really the souls of people who had passed on, and that the brightest star to the east was actually our mother. He said:

'She can hear you but she can't reply, so if you want

anything you just ask her and leave it at that. You can also talk to her as much as you want.'

And he was so right… Everything I asked my mother for appeared miraculously by my bedside in the morning for many years after that. It took me many more years to figure out why either Ronnie or Bobby always kept the key to the terrace in their possession.

And perhaps for the same reason, Father always made a special effort to compensate and gave me every opportunity to be independent and to think for myself. When he found out academics was not my cup of tea, he put me into business, and he always conversed with me and made me hold my own in arguments. But for all his bravado, he was a different man after our mother died, and by the time he passed away ten years later, he was a specter of his former vibrant self. I am very aware that if it had not been for my brothers I would have never survived or become the man I am today, because I lack their superior intellect. I keep up this façade of mock rivalry that does not fool them one single bit; as a matter of fact, it keeps the relationship strong and dynamic. Rose does not understand of course and I choose not to explain!

The one person who understood and became my best friend from the time she stepped into this house was Leila. Our greatest pleasure was to sing together, while Ronnie tried to join in, alas, hopelessly inept! I had always enjoyed music but had never taken it seriously till Leila arrived. She of course had a beautifully trained voice but insisted that I would do just as well with practice. It also seemed to please Ronnie that there was something I could do better than he and he was always arranging parties and family get-togethers where he and Bobby insisted that Leila and I sing, singly and in duets. We were all very happy together even after Rose arrived, because Leila saw to it that she was seldom embarrassed, and we continued pretty much as usual.

And then this blow… That evening we found Leila she looked just like my mother had after that night, white and destroyed, soulless, somehow, and I was and still am terrified, for my mother had never recovered. But I'm damned if I will allow the same to happen to Leila and Ronnie and of course those kids. In any case, it makes good practical sense to solve the problem, for in their recovery lies our salvation as a family, and let no one tell me different.

I am standing on the terrace tonight after a long time looking at the stars, as bright as they had shone on the night Ronnie had taken me up, and have realized anew that I owe him and Leila. I have taken their love for granted, time I did something in return. My dear mother, if you are up there as I desperately want to believe you are, please help us now.

17. Early on the Fateful Morning

Timmy: That dratted telephone! Who can it be, calling at five in the morning? Hullo, yes, who is it? Please speak up…can't hear you…Who? Oh Willy…in the name of… why so early for Christ's sake! Is there an emergency? … We have an emergency? …What emergency? …Oh, the soothsayer? …That's hardly an emergency; we are ready for the guy and will take him on collectively, don't worry. … It is more complicated than I imagine? Perhaps, but my Dad and Uncles are very determined to get to the bottom of things, and I have no doubt will handle it perfectly; my biggest mistake was not to confide in them earlier … You want to come? …Why? …To help? …How can you help? This is a family business and you have no role to play…You feel like you are family? …Very kind of you but I doubt other family members would agree…If I could talk on your behalf? …But why would I? This is a very serious matter involving my Aunt, and my Uncle is a very private person…I could try? Why? He would never agree and I wouldn't make such a silly request even for you…No, Willy, sorry! It just won't work this time and you will have to be patient and wait till I report to you. Bye for now!

Willy is really too much, barging in where he is not wanted…surely the soothsayer is not part of his research? Or is he? I will have to look into this a little more carefully and find out why Willy was so insistent on coming …

SMALL, SAMMY AND SHEILA

Sheila: Small, feel how cold my hands are, just like Mamma's; I don't think they will ever be warm again unless Mamma recovers.

Small: Hush child! Both you and your Mamma will be as warm as you were before, and that is my promise to you.

Sheila: Did your friend tell you that? But if you had had things your own way, this would never have happened, yet it did. So how can you be so sure?

Sammy: Small always has her reasons, don't you Small, because you see things that others do not? But I am not scared of what the soothsayer might say, and somehow feel that this visit is not meant only for Aunt Leila but for the whole family. He is the magician who will put matters in perspective.

Small: And what do you mean by that intelligent-sounding but cryptic remark?

Sheila: I know what he means. It's just like Aunt Millie's paintings! Why are they so arresting? After all, she paints everyday things which we see all the time. It is the way she looks at them and presents them that makes them different. That is what 'Art' is all about, isn't it?

Small: Don't forget, 'Art' carries two words in tow – artifice and artificial.

Sammy: Exactly! So each person has this gap between seeing and presenting and though we are not all 'artists with colors', all of us are with words. And who knows how much artifice each one of us uses and how artificial our presentation is?

Small: You have left out something; you should have said 'how much artifice one uses consciously', for there is a whole subconscious world we are not even looking at...

Sammy: On the dot as usual, Small, and it is supposed to be the most important area if Freud is worth anything, but even so, who knows the difference?

Sheila: The soothsayer, supposedly?

Sammy: Right! And that is why I am hoping for some action today!

LENA-SPEAK

I, Lena the 'nanny', came running from my quarters, but Madonna refused to see me. Kept me waiting at the door for an hour and then said she was feeling better after all... Which means she has some new strategy up her sleeve. She's a survivor if ever there was one and knows how to find her way out of any trap, even the ones she lays herself. She must have panicked seriously to have asked for me in the first place, but ultimately, she is too proud to take help from a servant, for that is how she thinks of me even after all these years, and she is one who will break but not bend. I have not forgotten how imperious she was even as a child, how quick to remind me that she was the boss, just like her sainted father!

As I stood at the door I remembered how in a family competition of making up riddles, the kids asked their father to be the judge, to guess the answers and to give away the prize, which was a bottle of boiled sweets. This was a tradition created by their mother to keep the siblings and their cousins entertained and close to each other and they were always writing and putting up plays, or singing and dancing, or arranging competitions, especially in the summer holiday when the boys were home and their cousins visited. This time there were six cousins, two sets of parents, and a big family party.

It was all happening on the lawn outside, boys versus girls affair, and Madonna was torn between openly letting Ronnie win and so appear magnanimous rather than inept, or trying desperately to win by fair means or foul. Winning was always very important to her and she never counted the cost. In the end she bribed Small to get the answers out of Ronnie for he could never say no to the little girl, and so managed to win! No one was deceived though, least of all the Judge but no one gave the game away; such was the loyalty among the children. Only little Tony, too young to understand and always one to call a spade a shovel, said very innocently:

'How did Sis get to be so clever suddenly?'

And his Father said:

'Because of Small; I think the prize should go to her...'

But Small piped up:

'I don't want any more sweets, I have had too many already!'

'And who gave you the sweets?'

'Madonna did, from that bottle in your hand!'

The Judge looked down at the bottle in his hand and found that the purloined sweets had been cleverly replaced by rose petals so no one would notice the difference... But before he could say anything, Bobby and Ronnie jumped into the fray, said the sweets should be distributed equally among them as they had all played and tried very hard, and winning or losing was not important anyway... And that was that; but I have not forgotten the look on the faces of either father or daughter...

Madonna had used Small then as she has now because she finds herself again in a very tight corner, but will her brothers bail her out this time, at cost to Leila?

SMALL-SPEAK

This could be my last visit to you, my friend, and if we do not meet again I will pray that we will be united in our next birth. There has to be another birth, right, or how will the terrible inequalities of life be balanced? Jasmine became Small and lived as Small, but should not Jasmine have another chance? Unlike Madonna, Lena and Millie – who all made conscious choices, Leila and I did nothing to ruin our chances, and yet, here I am and there is Leila, suffering wordlessly. That is why I am so afraid that she will not get better, things will not return to normal though we are fighting so hard, and the kids will continue to pine through no fault of their own…for it never did get better with me…

Our father was a Judge who seemed so easily to sit on judgment on others, passing sentences righteously and with impunity, yet in his own actions are the root from which this poison tree has sprung; each one of us has paid for decisions and actions taken by him and yet it is true that he loved us all… Is it this love that is the root cause of all unhappiness? Animals do not love, except for Nan, and they are never unhappy, but we – caught in the snare of self-love and love-of-others – are never at peace. That is why it is so peaceful to be with you, for there is no expectation on either side...

And yet, to know what lies beyond the next bend down the road, to hope endlessly against hope, to believe that there is a right way, is this what life is all about? In the Mahabharata, Yudhishtir, his brothers and Draupadi got to know the truth only at the end of their climb; is this enlightenment granted to all, or is the road itself the only truth?

DAVE-SPEAK

I, Dave, turned up to watch the fun as I had promised Madonna, to some consternation on the part of the ladies of the family, but I think Bobby, Ronnie and Tony were quite happy to have an independent witness to the proceedings and welcomed me before the women could get a word in edgeways! If looks could kill, I would be dead meat now, and initially I quite enjoyed their discomfiture! But when I looked at Sheila's tear-stained face, her hands clinging on to Sammy's as though to a life-line, Small sitting as though turned to stone, Millie's face, a battleground of compassion and despair, and finally Leila coming down the stairs on her mother's arm, a shadow of her former radiant self, to take her place with dignity on the day-bed, carefully avoiding eye-contact with her heart-broken husband, Bobby and Tony turning away to hide their tears, Timmy, the picture of anxiety and guilt, I felt a terrible anger rise within me; none of them deserved to be in this state for none of the misery was of their own making…And isn't that what we had been always told to believe:

'As you sow, so shall you reap', 'the biter bit', 'hoist on your own petard', 'sow the wind and you shall reap the whirlwind'…?

Words of wisdom were legion, all assuming the equation between sin and punishment, virtue and reward; all assuming we could control our own destiny and that of others. But when I looked at Madonna, haggard and grey, Lena ready to collapse, even the cunning but obtuse Rose, an uncharacteristic fear etched on her face, the perspective changed. Some of us are naturally austere and conventional, virtue comes easily to us, but what of those in whom passion is a rampant stallion, desire a searing flame, and the love of self all consuming? Tossed on a dark sea of cross currents, without guidelines like a rudderless boat, the human soul tries to find the shore, as much a victim of circumstance as of its own unruly passions. So where is the famous principle of justice we are so proud of? I suddenly remember Madonna, an innocent sixteen-year-old, trying so hard to contend with her wants, desiring to please, almost succeeding, then failing when she least expected to. Lena surviving the only way she knew how; Millie, bored, unable to find an outlet for her creative energies, turning for excitement where angels fear to tread. And Rose, suffering from a crashing sense of inadequacy, envying and planning revenge endlessly. And almost all of this was the outcome of the Judge's machinations, himself the epitome of justice! Honestly, the ironies of life are just too much for me sometimes!

St. Augustine certainly knew what he was talking about when he said:

'Only a sinner can be a saint.'

For the virtuous have never known temptation or the endless suffering that comes with it, and sainthood is not attainable without the cleansing. What are we in for today, a blood bath or gentle de-mystification? After all, this man is a man of God and surely he should have the answers and be merciful?

Hullo, what is Willy doing here? He is coming, almost forcing his way in, and I can see that Timmy is very uneasy about it…Surely he has no place in a family affair, or does he? I wonder, wonder very much. Another sinister shadow from the shadowy past!

18. The Soothsayer

I, the rational Ronnie, had agreed to this plan of Tony's almost out of desperation, a last stand before the deluge swamped us, for I firmly believed that the floodgates would open with Leila's departure. She, my dearest wife, had held the family together after our mother's death in a way neither Rose nor even Millie would have been able to, which is why our mother had spoken her last words to Leila when she was moistening her parched lips and throat with water from the Ganges:

'Peace and goodwill among brothers…'

The age-old but futile prayer of every mother since man came on to this planet, beginning with Eve! But Leila had taken the admonition with great seriousness and managed to maintain peace due to her constant vigilance and her own endless fund of goodwill; even now she has agreed to meet this man today because, despite her own misery, she still cannot say no to me or Tony. The person who had struck her down had a wider target than was apparent at first, the entire family at one fell swoop and nothing less. If this person is unmasked today my purpose will be served, and pray God it be so.

I can hear the car rolling to a stop in the porch and

Bobby going forward to welcome him. He steps into the hall, tall, spare and serene, looking around with obvious approval at the flower-filled, incense-scented, and gracious ambience. Bobby leads him to the chair at the head of the room but he asks for an aasan or prayer-mat on the floor, which Lena silently provides from the Puja room. The most striking feature is his white skin, more Anglo-Saxon than Indian and piercing blue eyes to match. Dressed in the traditional saffron, he is indeed an arresting figure. We have been told by Robin that he has his ashram or hermitage in the hills of _____ where he and his team serve the entire community within a radius of twenty miles. They come down very occasionally to the plains, either to attend spiritual congresses or when they feel that the need of a particular human being in pain demands their attention.

Although he speaks Hindi, his intonation reveals his British and particularly Oxford origins very clearly, and after a while he says:

'It is obvious that my native tongue is also yours and that we would all be more comfortable in the language. Shall we switch?'

One can almost feel the power emanate from him and the impression that he has a window on every soul in the room is very strong. Does he know the whole truth, and if so, how much will he reveal and in what manner?

By this time we have all taken our seats on the carpets and trying to look as comfortable in our new-found postures as he does in his lotus pose on the aasan, spine erect, shoulders thrown back, hands folded on his lap, immense energy barely contained in the powerful physique. Eyes level, he is looking at all and yet each one of us feels that he is only looking at the individual. Finally he calls out to Sammy and Sheila and tells them to come in and sit next to him. He holds each child's hand in his own briefly, then lets go and tells them to sit like him, which they do effortlessly, their eyes never leaving his face. He turns back to all of us, and says:

'Let me tell you a story:

'A hero on the playing fields of Rugby, a scholarship student at Oxford, and then a young lecturer in the same august institution at twenty-three, spouting Patriotism and Empire. Free, White and Ruling, as one would say, and you have a clear picture of a naive and vainglorious young Englishman who had it all and needed no one to tell him what to do with life. Then the First World War came along and he went in with his pennant flying to earn a Victoria Cross, and his faith in himself was further endorsed by the fact that he had spent three hard years in the trenches in Belgium coming to terms with reality, as he told himself with pride. Now he knew all about suffering, as he had come through unscathed and was more certain than ever that all it needed was a little will power to come to grips with life. The only dissonant voice was that of a close friend, fellow student at Oxford, a conscientious objector who had refused to fight on moral grounds, and who had done his best to persuade his friend to desist. But the tag Yellow was too daunting, and our young man did not have the courage to wear it despite occasional misgivings; it was easier to face the Germans in the trenches. When he returned to an exhausted England, he found the Empire Flag showing distinct signs of wear, mainly due to the onslaughts of Gandhi, the Naked Fakir from India, and his objector friend ready to set sail for that very country. His objecting days were over and he had paid the price of his cowardice by losing his position at the _____ School. Our hero of course had his position waiting for him at Oxford so he could mold more students in his own impeccable image.

'All was well at first, but he soon began to find out that the Halls of Oxford were not spacious enough after the trenches, that his students had begun to speak a different tongue and were not particularly impressed by him or the great wartime leaders. They actually felt that the War had been one of the most futile in history, where the petty squabbles of the European nations had grown out of proportion and set the whole world ablaze. The real defeat at Versailles had been for the allies who had been revealed in their true, selfish colors throughout the Empire, present and erstwhile, and were now being held to account. Somehow, all of a sudden, he did not have all the answers. So when his friend wrote to him from India inviting him and the University at _____ offered him a lecturer's position, he took a year's leave and set sail without much ado. India was a revelation for him as it was for most foreigners, who did not know very much about the country except for the rope trick and rajahs. But he was fortunate and a most significant gift was granted to him that transformed his life.

'Life, after all, is largely a matter of perception and how we see life actually makes all the difference between happiness and sorrow, for things remain as they always were and will continue to be. The well-to-do Indian was invariably materialistic, but a trifle uncomfortable with the dichotomy between Bhog and Tyag, or unbridled enjoyment and austerity, as the latter was held in higher esteem by educated Indian society. But the West, freed from the shackles of traditional Christianity which had been equally puritanical, and now with its conscionable and relentless pursuit of material success in the guise of modernity, endorsed the preferred view that enabled the educated Indian to loosen the constraints of the traditional plain living high thinking philosophy and espouse a way of life where the individual is only happy with what he wants, and never with what he already has. And of course, the list of wants is endless, so he is never happy. For instance, failure makes us unhappy, but only till we see it as a challenge and a second chance to make good, creating more objects of desire in the process. We put our faith in things and people, never appreciating that both are time-bound, entirely ephemeral, and it is only when we hitch our wagon to the eternal that we begin to realize what happiness even means.

'I can do nothing to help anyone directly, but I can tell you things that will enable you to see from a different perspective and tap the spiritual resources that lie dormant within you. Also, please bear in mind that your greatest strength so far has been your family unity, a legacy which you have treasured in India and which the West is fast destroying at great cost to the social fabric, so that is one page you do not need out of their Book of Knowledge. After that it is up to you.

'Now I shall pray for help so I can do what is required of me today, and I want all of you to pray in your own way along with me, so you can work out your own solution to your problems after this session. Remember, every solution lies within you and the God within you, not in an extraneous factor. As the great philosopher Tagore says:

'"I have hitched my soul to yours with the bonds of song," and "I will sail the tumultuous sea through the storm fearlessly, in the boat you have made for me…"'

He sits, spine erect, folds his hands, palms upward on

his lap and begins the chant in his deep sonorous voice: 'Om Namah Shivaya', invoking the great Shiva's mercy and power, so He might help the seer to achieve his purpose. As the voice rises in pitch and volume, it seems to fill the air, resonate off the walls, escape outside and permeate every atom of consciousness. There is nothing else but the chant, all else is lost in oblivion and the image of the terrifying Shiva with his tangled hair, poison-blue throat, tiger-skin draped over his body, hand resting lightly on Nandi the Bull, his mount, a benign smile touching his lips but fading out in the eyes, rises before all of us. The irony of an Occidental Christian achieving this miracle for us does not strike any one, only the fading smile rivets our attention: Why does the smile fade? What have we done?

After an eternity the voice begins to lose intensity, the blood in our veins begins to flow again and we open our eyes to find Shiva gone and only the seer looking at us with the faintest smile on his lips.

He then begins to speak and addresses us one by one:

He first speaks to Bobby:

'You have had a difficult role to play and discharged your part with conscience and courage. You have nothing to fear. However, if personal pain comes your way like Ronnie, don't lose faith. Stand by life and life will stand by you.'

To Ronnie:

'You have suffered a great deal through no fault of your own, except perhaps reluctance to see weaknesses in your loved ones. Your suffering will be alleviated but only at the cost of further pain. Don't lose faith; stand by your principles as you have always done.'

He turns to Tony:

'You have shown great wisdom and steadfastness in

calling me in today. I know you have done this in the face of much opposition and only out of love. Even so, a price must be paid for love, however unfair it may seem. Don't lose courage; what you will appear to lose is only illusion, the reality is deeper and will remain unchanged.'

He says rather grimly to Dave:

'The sins of the father are to be visited on the children, eh? You must do as you think best, but do consider, is revenge worth the price?'

To Millie:

'You have managed to conquer fear with love and your feat today is nothing short of heroic; continue to trust in love, it will not let you down.'

With a smile to Rose:

'Cast envy out of your heart; you have enough and you shall have more if you are unselfish and generous. Try to see the good in others, rather than yourself.'

To Small with infinite respect and compassion:

'On such sacrifices as yours, my dear Jasmine, the Gods themselves throw incense. I bow my head before you in acknowledgement of your superior spiritual stature. You have made one inadvertent mistake, which is nothing in comparison to the suffering you have undergone on its account. Do not fear; all will yet be well with the children whom you have protected so fiercely.'

With a smile to Sammy and Sheila:

'You have done a superb job, fighting and not giving in, and your efforts will be amply rewarded; you will forget these hard times like a bad dream, so stop crying both of you and continue to be brave and chase the truth.'

To Timmy:

'Keep up your search for the Truth always my boy without

fear of consequence, something that deters the bravest among us…the outcome, though painful, is necessarily beautiful, right? You have a long way to go, my boy.'

To Robin:

'Such loyalty and wisdom is rare indeed, and your old Master must have been quite a character to inspire it. Continue to stand by your brothers, for in the next few months they will need all your strength and support.'

To Lena:

'You have a great husband, be content. Do not desire what was never yours to begin with, or untold suffering will ensue. Do not open the floodgates.'

To Willy:

'What did you expect Willy, particularly when you found that I was your countryman? Did you think I would help you to gain your end? You don't need me for that, as you can do it yourself. And you should reveal the truth, for you have suffered much; only see to it that the innocent do not pay the price for another's crime, for that would be to impair the very justice you are fighting for.'

To the cowering Madonna sternly but sadly too:

'Why did you attempt to make others pay for your and your father's sins? An eye for an eye and a tooth for a tooth only leads to terrible blindness; you know that better than most, and even so, when you had your chances you chose not to take them. All your victims have escaped you but you will still try to find a scapegoat, won't you? Don't. You owe restitution for your own salvation and no one else's.'

And finally to Leila, taking her delicate hands in his own, tears trickling down his eyes, he says:

'Such suffering no one deserves and certainly not a human being of your ilk. But you too have paid a price for a crime of omission. You also failed to realize that there was a larger target, the aim was to wreck the family by putting you out of the way, and the family you have loved and managed to hold together against many odds. You lost faith in life itself and life cut you adrift. You are a fighter, why did you accept defeat so easily, particularly as there was no precedent? You must know that the persons you thought responsible have suffered as much as you if not more, and you owe it to them to put the record straight. Come my child, begin now!'

And as we watched in stupefaction, he wept with an abandonment that seemed entirely out of character, holding Leila close to his heart. And as he wept, Leila's misery seemed to flow out of her to be replaced by a new-found courage, a sort of energy osmosis, and gradually she raised her head in the same proud stance as before and said:

'I am sorry; I understand. It will not happen again.'

He hauled Leila to her feet, walked her to my side, put her hand in mine, and Leila turned to me and smiled the shadow of her once dazzling smile.

Then he walked to the door without another word and Robin ran out after him. In a few moments we heard the car wheels crunching on the gravel drive and then saw the cloud of red dust that marked his departure.

We all knew instinctively at that point that we would never see him again. We also knew we would, none of us, ever be the people we had been before this encounter. We had been face to face with our own truth, if only for a moment and that 'sharp scarred edge' had cut through much illusion and made us strangely averse to returning to self-deception. A Soothsayer who did not make dramatic revelations but influenced perceptions permanently by revealing our own truth to us... Sooth indeed!

THE AFTERMATH, TIMMY'S VIEW

The 'Case' of 'The State' Versus _____(deceased) opened ten days later, and it seemed odd to find my Father, not addressing witnesses or conducting proceedings, but waiting quietly in the audience with his brothers, to be summoned along with them as witnesses. They had decided to speak the whole truth as they knew it, and Mr. Narang, Father's colleague and good friend, strongly recommended by Mr. Sen the solicitor to defend the case on the family's behalf, had approved wholeheartedly. He agreed that rumors did more harm than the real thing and only perpetuated the misery. The catharsis would be painful for the proud family but it would be an end of sorts, and it would help dispel the shadows that had loomed over us for so long.

What had transpired between Uncle Ronnie and Aunt Leila behind closed doors after the Seer's departure no one quite knew, but it was enough for all of us that she was not going away, was coming down for her meals with us and very gradually, beginning to take an interest in her household duties. As my mother said:

'I can't wait for you to take back your responsibilities, Leila, so I can get back to my studio! How do you manage all this work so quietly and efficiently?'

At which Aunts Madonna and Rose merely rolled their eyes in exasperation but did not pass comment!

However, there is a clear if clearly unexpressed conviction among some of the womenfolk that now that the immediate problem has been solved, the Pandora's Box should be closed and we should be left alone to get on with our lives; that this is not possible is chiefly my fault and their ire at my unwarranted interference is barely veiled. It takes Aunt Leila's strength of conviction, as before, to stem this flood of innuendo:

'Timmy has opened up an old festering sore and how can we now stop the pus from running? We did this before and look where it landed us. For God's sake let us not try to cover up ugliness and make it look pretty; let us all have a chance with a clean slate, even though my husband will suffer the most for no fault of his own, again, and my dearest Small who has paid the most heavily for other peoples' sins and will continue to pay, but perhaps she will have peace of mind at last. I mean, look at me, now that we have paid, Ronnie and I, we will hopefully have a clear run till the end of our days? What do you think?'

Stunned silence greets her words but the poisoned arrows stop coming my way for some time.

Sheila and Sammy have decided to go into the sleuthing business seriously when they are older and are busy designing the terms for their partnership. Only, every hour or so, they run to Aunt Leila as though to ascertain that she is still around.

Uncle Ronnie is back to his strong self and the three brothers are prepared for any eventuality. They would like to keep the women-folk out of court as far as possible, but if they must appear, even Small, who is no longer afraid, then so be it.

Robin has stood by me like a rock, not perturbed any more by my immaturity or shaggy-haired friends; he has actually said that all that happens is for the best and he is glad that I decided to pursue the truth, despite his own repeated efforts to dissuade me.

Somehow, the Seer has left us all stronger people than he found us.

The Reckoning

AS TOLD BY TIMMY

The Public Prosecutor, Mr. Purohit, very senior and experienced, an old family friend, is definitely not enjoying his present commission. Completely devoted to duty he will be perfectly honest in his mission, but iconoclasm is repugnant to him in any form, particularly when a three-generation association is at stake. His father was a judge too, a close friend of our Old Man and he and my father have crossed swords often, but never where personal issues were involved. He has been assured time and again by our family of our complete trust in his devotion to justice, but this has only made things harder for him. They have all found that the old-boy network, though it has its merits, is not always an unmixed blessing and sometimes, as now, a serious moral disadvantage.

It is also very apparent to him that this case is intricately layered and that the personal and public are intermingled almost inextricably. How to separate the strands and keep family secrets that do not touch the main issue intact is Mr. Purohit's major concern. The entire picture or story is like an ancient piece of tapestry, colors muted, details blurred, and threads running into each other, quite indistinguishable. Particularly the underside of the piece, where the beginnings and ends are, is only a medley of knots and the skeins are so dusty that who knows where one ends and another begins? One false step and the true innocent could become the cynosure of a thousand accusing eyes. Not an easy task.

There are still many people who remember the Judge's anglophile values only too well, so any attempt to counter that would smack of falsehood and Mr. Narang, Defense Counsel, is too canny to fall into that trap. As a matter of fact, he agrees with all that Mr. Purohit has to say and adds to the image with his own memories of the Judge's eminent British friends, his lavish parties, shikar trips, even the garden house which was the setting for crazy frolics, inevitably bacchanalian in character. It is said that there was a special fountain in that house that ran with wine on special occasions, and many dancing girls and singers who are famous music and dance icons today, had made their debut there. There were also exhibitions of martial arts, and while there was a shooting range for his British friends, his own entourage of men who walked on stilts, were swordsmen and stave wielders found a platform for the display of their skills. Mr. Narang says that some of these men twirled their staves so fast that it seemed there were a hundred of these stout sticks blurring together in a wheel in one pair of hands.

He recites facts and figures that support the old man's image of near-fanatical loyalty to his white masters but also as a scrupulously dutiful judge, who dispensed justice without prejudice or favor on most occasions. The case of Uncle Dave's brother comes up inevitably and he is called as a witness, whereupon he calmly takes the stand and confidently utters the oath to speak the whole truth.

Dave says: 'We were in Chittagong then, a district in

British Bengal that is a part of Bangladesh today. As my father was the district engineer, we lived on this magnificent tree-clad hill in a spacious bungalow that commanded a view of both sea and forest. My mother called the place the land of eternal spring as it was never too hot or cold, flowers bloomed wild all year round and the forest was evergreen. The people too were green at heart and despite terrible poverty, the sound of drums, melodious voices and dancing feet resounded through the year, fueled by the energy of the intoxicating punch distilled from the Mahua fruit. The bears too loved the sweet fruit and were to be seen on moonlit nights reeling drunkenly around after a feast. The forest teemed with bird and animal life and we never got tired of tramping around in this flawed Eden.'

Mr. Purohit asks: 'Do you have any personal reasons for that particular turn of phrase?'

Dave replies: 'Well, it was the kind of place where intense nationalism seemed to take root and flourish, much to the chagrin of our masters, whose police found it difficult to track offenders down, for neither the forest nor inhabitants would betray the youngsters who belonged to the Surya Sen and Pritilata Wadedar clan. Surya Sen had been a teacher in the local school and commanded a huge fan following among students, who cheerfully risked their lives to do his bidding and my brother was no exception. My father, a government employee, was at his wit's end with the lad and was planning to send him off to boarding school, when Surya Sen, Priti and Kalpana Dutta were betrayed; they had been hiding out in Savitri Devi, an elderly widow's house and an informer betrayed them. They escaped in the nick of time because three boys raced ahead of the police and warned them, but the boys were not so fortunate. All three were captured, my brother among them. He was all of seventeen.'

Uncle Dave stops abruptly and we can see he is trying very hard to exit from the time warp in which he finds himself and regain his composure. Mr. Purohit is busy settling his papers on his desk and when he looks up, Dave is back to his slightly cynical, smiling self.

Mr. Purohit prompts: 'And then?'

Dave answers: 'Since nothing was conclusively proved, the boys were kept in custody in the infamous prison at Buxa in North Bengal, but the case was never re-opened and the damp cells and malaria soon made short work of the three boys. Our Uncle, with his connections, could have brought the case to court, particularly as my brother was a minor, but he paid scant attention to our prayers. When I look back I feel that perhaps at that time he had too many problems of his own to bother with us, even his brother whom he loved very much. Perhaps he had favors of his own to beg of his white masters and our need would have tilted the balance against him? But today it seems retribution is catching up with his progeny for crimes they did not commit but inherited…old sins certainly cast long shadows.'

Mr. Purohit says: 'Crimes is a very strong word, Mr. _____, would you mind explaining more fully?'

Dave replies: 'Well, that nationalist incident is too well known to sweep under the carpet, and most people have felt all along that the political angle was mostly eye-wash on both sides as very serious personal issues lay at the heart of the conflict. However, I would not like to comment further, as I am as much in the dark as you are about the truth of the matter and anything I might say in my ignorance is bound to cause pain to people for whom I care a great deal.'

Robin takes pretty much the same stand, and says he had been too callow and inexperienced to understand all the implications. However, anyone who could harm children the way they had, deserved hanging and worse. In any case, an English Judge had finally passed the judgment after the English Commissioner of Police Mr. Wilson had insisted on strong action in view of the terrible outrage. This point about the English Judge had not been mentioned so emphatically before and it strengthens Mr. Narang's hand considerably.

Mr. Purohit agrees. The Judge himself could not take independent action, as his kin was involved. However, the opposition had alleged that the Old Man had unduly influenced the decision due to his friendship with the Sitting Judge.

My Dad comes to the witness box and tells us with the exactitude of a practicing lawyer precisely what had happened on the day of the fateful picnic: the young woman who had immolated herself to protest against her husband's death penalty, the hostile men-folk and angry women, the car losing its fan-belt, the road-block, Small's abduction and Uncle Ronnie's pursuit of her.

Uncle Ronnie takes the stand and continues the story of that terrible night with calm resignation, but in eloquent and graphic detail up to the point he lost consciousness. His words conjure up the scene perfectly, and everyone in the room can see in his mind's eye the dark night, uneven, difficult terrain, the flickering torches, the pitiless men with their faces covered; and the sturdy little boy running fearlessly into the jaws of hell to save his flower-like sister.

And after this, when the compelling voice stops, the audience does not find it difficult to imagine in gruesome detail the terrible sequel.

When Small comes to stand next to him, there is not an eye that is not moist in the courtroom.

Aunt Madonna cuts an impressive figure in court as she testifies in ringing, sincere tones as to how Small had almost lost her sanity after the unthinkable experience and how she had fought back mainly because she did not want to let her father down. His terrible burden of guilt had been unbearable to her, young as she was. However, she skirts the political aspect adroitly, saying she was too young and inexperienced to understand the ramifications.

The first two days pass in this manner and just as we are beginning to breathe easy the axe falls: Mr. Purohit has a new witness, whose testimony he believes will clinch the case against the Judge conclusively.

A dark overcast morning finds our cars speeding toward the courthouse; I have opted to drive because steering through dense traffic helps take my mind off the questions that have been hammering in my brain all night:

Who is the witness? Where has he been all this time? Why has he not come forward before this? How was he involved in the case? How reliable will his testimony prove? How will his revelations affect us, the living? They say, let the dead past bury its dead, but does the past ever die?

However, the first witness of the prosecution today is Mr. Desai, a well-known political activist and a historian of Indian nationalism. He has been my teacher in college and I am familiar with his sharp brain, formidable analytical skills, and passion for truth. His latest book, a series of micro-studies of eminent people caught in the cross-fire – like our old man – has proved revealing and amply supported his central thesis that at an individual level, the National inevitably takes second place to the personal, at least in India. National movements had to be mass movements to make a difference, for the common man alone had a stake in changing the status quo, given that the elite can play both sides with skillful agility. Several eminent heads have rolled due to his revelations and I realize with a sinking heart that we must have been on the anvil for quite some time.

Mr. Desai catches my eye, smiles reassuringly at me and I try to smile back, but not very successfully. I know he believes that I share his passion, is banking on me as an ally, but the irony of the situation seems to elude him completely! He takes the stand with the confidence of a man with a mission and it is clear that he has spared no pains in putting his evidence together and means to use it as damningly as possible. Here is the perfect example of a man I have always aspired to be like, pursuing the truth without fear or favor, completely uncolored by personal bias, and I find myself wishing I had never met him! My first exercise in idealism outside the pages of a book, and I am gasping for breath, looking desperately for a way out of the trap I have sprung!

Mr. Desai puts together a jigsaw puzzle with deft strokes of his verbal brush, building up context, situation and character not only with great accuracy, but managing to imbue them with life and emotion, till we have a living montage moving before our eyes. His imagination fills in gaps so convincingly that we begin to feel that things could have happened in no other way.

'The man should write novels, not history,' whispers my mother to Aunt Leila, who concurs, saying:

'Absolutely, his imagination is wasted on mere facts!'

But Aunt Madonna, my Dad and Uncle Ronnie are beginning to look more and more anxious as Mr. Desai moves towards the denouement, the part of the case that is shrouded in mystery, the part that the Judge actually played in bringing the miscreants to justice; for according to Mr. Desai, the Judge had brought the whole thing on himself and his family and his children had paid for their father's misdeeds.

Mr. Narang does his best to flog the near-dead Nationalist Horse, saying that they had punished the Judge for sending a man who had attempted to assassinate the Deputy Collector of the district by throwing a bomb at his car, to the gallows, but Mr. Purohit counters this strongly by saying that the man had got nowhere near the car and that nothing had been conclusively proved against him. The Judge had indeed made a revealing pronouncement on the occasion:

'This sentence should be exemplary and dissuade others from dastardly action.'

Mr. Desai concurs and says the man had been hung with indecent haste as he had some knowledge that was so damning, that even the Judge's British masters would have found it hard to overlook the matter. He says:

'It may be a terrible thing to say, but the attack on the children actually proved a boon for their father; it deflected attention from him to the children and in the consequent hullabaloo, the original miscarriage of justice was forgotten, as people felt that folks who could perpetrate this terrible outrage on innocent children, must be capable of the sickest ploy and deserved to be punished anyway. Some even say he was egotistical enough to welcome the reprieve, although I would not go so far.'

Mr. Purohit, however, does not agree fully:

'You may not be aware Mr. Desai, but another attempt was made to reopen the case because more evidence had come to light, which would conclusively prove that the judgment had been motivated by purely personal factors, and the Judge was in a really tight corner because it seemed that in the 1940s the beleaguered British would not tolerate their image being tarnished, even by a favored flunkey.'

'And it is at this point that the trail disappears, for the nationalists began a whisper campaign of such a vicious nature against the same children, that all sympathy was diverted away from them. What is not clear is why they would do something so unsavory when they seemed to have the case all sewed up?' wonders Mr. Desai!

Mr. Purohit smiles knowingly:

'Exactly my point and this is where my new and most unexpected witness will be able to enlighten us. Mr. Wilson, please take the stand!'

And as we watch in stupefied silence, Willy strides forward to replace Mr. Desai on the witness stand.

I am half out of my seat, about to protest, when Uncle Ronnie holds me back by gripping my arm in a tight, almost painful grip and whispers fiercely in my ear:

'Let it go, Timmy; let all the ugliness come out once and for all and let there be an end to this nightmare. We've just about had enough, all of us!'

It seems to me that this is a Willy we do not know. Gone is the gentle and admiring friend, the amiable academic in search of historic truth; he is no longer one of us. In his place stands an implacable young man, determined to have justice. We had all prayed for justice at different times; now it seemed we would get more than we had bargained for.

He places his hand firmly on the Bible and takes the oath to speak 'the whole truth' in a voice that does not falter in the slightest. I look at him steadily but feel that he is avoiding me, for he refuses to meet my eye. He carefully arranges some papers on the lectern and places markers as when preparing for a lecture. It somehow comes as a surprise that his last name is Wilson, for I had always assumed that his nickname was an abbreviation for William. In today's ambience of easy camaraderie one gets on first name terms immediately, no one bothers with details, and with us it had been Willy and Timmy from day one. His full name, now it appears, is Richard Leonard Wilson and the nickname is an inheritance from the Public School he went to. I find my Dad and Uncle Ronnie exchanging meaningful glances when the full name is announced and my uneasiness mounts. What can he possibly know about the case? He was born long after the whole thing was finished and done with. Why, he is only a few years my senior and has never been to India before. In God's name, what is this fresh can of worms and what further miseries have I let my family in for?

He creates a favorable impression on the entire court, including the Judge, with his amazing clarity and exactitude, gift with words and complete sincerity. The Judge, Justice Mehta, a friend of my Dad's, is a regular visitor in our house; his son reads with me in college and knows Willy well. It is clear that he is as surprised to see Willy on the stand as we are. However, he also realizes that only something of paramount importance would bring Willy to the stand and is waiting patiently for the denouement.

It is at this juncture that Willy turns to me, looks me straight in the eye, and smiles warmly. Then he holds up both his open hands in the age-old gesture of peace, known in Sanskrit as the boon of freedom from fear, showing that he is holding no arms, and suddenly, I am no longer afraid.

Mr. Purohit guides him skillfully through his narrative with judicious questions, and as he proceeds, the etchings of growing disbelief stand out clearly on every face including ours; but the most pathetic is Small, her misshapen face twisted in incomprehensible agony, for this is her beloved Father that they are discussing. In sheer sorrow her face attains a beauty that is almost ethereal. Her eyes have retained some of their early limpidity and remind one of a glimpse of clear pools hidden in the tangled weeds, and now the tears drip steadily welling from the pools, down her cheeks onto her shrunken chest. Finally Aunt Leila moves to her side, takes her hand in her own and they sit together, still as statues, the beauty and the monstrous beauty, perfectly attuned. Very gradually, the tears stop flowing but the eyes are now glazed.

It appears that a couple of letters found among Willy's grandfather's papers after his death had put Willy on the trail of our family. The letters, written more than thirty years ago, had been penned by the old man's brother, who had been in Colonial Service, a Commissioner of Police, at the time of his untimely death in India. Aware that Willy was planning to visit India, his cousin Geoffrey had sent the letters to Willy along with some Indian artifacts. The first letter had mentioned a particular Nationalist Case, which had caught Willy's interest, and he had decided to delve into the matter on his arrival in India. But it was the postscript in the second letter, which he had almost ignored, for it had been scrawled at the back of the last page, practically as an after-thought by Mr. Wilson's wife, which had actually struck an ominous note and helped him to make up his mind.

In Willy's words:

'The matter cried out for investigation and yet nothing was done; I had to know why?'

The first letter is produced, marked as an exhibit and read out in court:

Dear David,

I do hope this finds you and yours in good health and spirit. I have not written in a while as things here are really boiling like a witch's cauldron and one has to be on one's toes all the time. At all hours of the day one is on duty and there is no routine or respite to speak of. But one copes; the stiff upper-lip culture still holds and one is trained not to complain. It seems ironic that our glorious Empire Builders chose us, the smaller men, to pick up the pieces after their heroic exploits had blazed a path that is still blazing.

Terrorism is rife and the local populace lauds every ruffian who throws a bomb at us as a nationalist hero. As always, the bombs are thrown nine times out of ten to achieve private ends, but only we know that. The few educated Indians who work with us also come in for a lot of flak and a few are defecting... Not so, Justice _____, who has stood by us like a rock through the Nationalist Case, where the hero's wife immolated herself on her husband's funeral pyre in protest, causing a huge furor, even though personal tragedy has marred his life irrevocably in the process: Two of his children kidnapped and tortured, and though the boy has weathered the storm with great fortitude, the little girl will never be normal again, nor will her mother by all accounts. The man has paid a terrible price for his loyalty and although he is a notorious debauch, one somehow cannot help respecting him. There is real steel in that man.

However, there is yet another India that still loves us and

thinks we are great; does wonders for our morale, I can tell you! The men who serve us, the soldiers, the constables, the batmen, personal attendants, the butcher, the baker, the candlestick maker, still trust us and would be loath to see us go...perhaps they think their own Indian masters would be worse? Well, in a country where a man is whipped because his low caste shadow has darkened the path of an upper caste aristocrat, what can you expect? My wife, my brave Winnie, who has been by my side through thick and thin and loves this strange, beautiful country, swears by these people and still goes for a walk alone every afternoon, only accompanied by her dog, completely unafraid. May her trust never be broken!

Doomsday is around the corner, the writing is on the wall and the days of the British Raj are numbered; I can only pray that we go out with a show of colors and not a whimper.

Why not pay a visit while I can still arrange a shikar for you?

Yours truly,
Richard

The words linger in the air and for each one of us they conjure up different images: for our elders, familiar with the ambience, a rush of memories but for Sammy, Sheila, Roma and myself, a view from the other side of the fence. How did it feel in an alien land boiling with discontent, to try and maintain an order one did not believe in? These patriots who had done an unpleasant job they abhorred, only out of loyalty to their own country, had actually carried the white man's burden. Hated and reviled for a process they had no hand in but merely inherited, they had tried to uphold the tottering edifice and desperately believed that the hatred was not universal. It seemed clear that at a personal level they believed they did have friends, but how trustworthy had they proved in the long run?

Not very, if one read the second letter, written almost a
year later:

Dear David,
Forgive me for not replying to three of your letters, but I have
been just too depressed to respond positively or rationally
even to the people I hold most dear...

Why Winnie? The bravest of the brave, the truest of the true,
with complete faith in the people of her adopted country?
The Memsahib who went into the servant's quarters to deliver
the ayah's baby? Who regularly visited the homes of the poor
people living in the tenements close by to check on their
needs, educate the mothers and their children and impart
simple rules of hygiene? Her greatest battle was for fresh air,
persuading these people to open their few windows to let out
the fetid air and admit the life-giving oxygen. Who worked
alongside her domestic staff so they would not feel menial?
So, why was Winnie attacked? Her beloved dog shot and she
herself, abused and torn, left to die by the roadside?

It was this modus operandi that dispelled my last doubt about
the identity of the miscreants, for it was a replay of the earlier
incident with the children. In any case, the rumor circulating
about the kids, that it was the brother who had abused the
sister under the influence of datura and that the nationalists
were not to blame, was vicious enough to warrant a reprisal,
and this time I made no mistakes. A combing operation was
carried out and any one even remotely connected with the
case was not spared. It also emerged that the woman the
villagers had thought to be a victim of the Judge's lust, was
actually a servant of ten years standing in the household, and
had left the village voluntarily because her father was bent on
selling her to an old man for opium money. The Judge's good
lady had given her sanctuary.

Winnie could not speak for six months, but the pleading in
her eyes was unmistakable and in the end many of the original
sentences were muted, because I could not ignore her pleas.

She is convinced till date that the villagers had played no part in this ugly incident; the people who had hurt her were thugs who had been hired by the conspirators to make it look like a 'nationalist' outrage. She argued that the attackers were not angry, emotional people, merely ruthless, who did their job with mindless efficiency. There was no idealism involved. But who were the conspirators and against whom was the plot directed? I still do not have an answer.

I never thought I would volunteer to leave India, but now I have applied for repatriation because I am afraid, and am impatiently awaiting transfer orders on compassionate grounds. Hope we can leave without further incident.

Looking forward to meeting you soon,

Yours truly,
Richard

At the back of this missive is Mrs. Wilson's cryptic note:

David,

I don't care what Richard says; I am convinced that I was not the target. The whole job was too well rehearsed and efficient. There was no sense of vendetta or retribution, just a neat job to achieve a desired end. In any case, why me, and why my dog, before the attack on me, when he had done nothing to annoy them? A dangerous witness eliminated? To the best of my knowledge, there was no ill feeling towards Richard, who if anything, errs on the mild side due to his feelings for the common man of his adopted country. No, this was a diversion orchestrated to get Richard mad enough to rush in to precipitate action. And that is exactly what happened. I am convinced that the Judge is somehow involved, and let no man tell me different! You have only to look into his eyes.

I devoutly hope we can get out of his evil clutches soon, although leaving India and all my friends will not be easy.

Win

This opens up a completely new line of enquiry, and I can see that both the Defense and Prosecution are doing their best to re-orient themselves. Willie however, does not allow the hiatus to lengthen and takes up the narrative smoothly:

'Imagine my horror when I found out that husband and wife had been killed by a speeding lorry that had mowed down their police jeep and escaped without trace, within days of mailing this letter. They had been traveling in convoy, but not a single other vehicle was touched; just this jeep was singled out, mangled out of shape and the Police Commissioner, his wife, the driver and the orderly were annihilated; no doubt another neat Nationalist endeavor?

'It was at this point that I made up my mind to investigate this murky chapter of Indian Nationalism, which like every country caught in a struggle for freedom, has its share of martyrs and self-seekers. Not everyone is a Gandhi, just as not everyone is a Winston Churchill.

'What almost defeated me was my friendship with the Judge's family. They were so kind to me, and having no idea of my intentions, perfectly open with me. As a matter of fact, the cultural parity almost took my breath away, I felt completely at home and I certainly did not relish the role of a traitor in these conditions. Then gradually I found out that Timmy too was very concerned about this shadow of the past, particularly after his aunt fell sick and he became convinced that the cause lay not in the present. Also, the entire family, particularly his uncles, seemed unafraid of the truth, or they would never have allowed the soothsayer to visit. It was at this juncture that I decided I would do the family a service by bringing the truth to light and so release them from the shadowy prison of doubt and rumor mongering in which they had been trapped for so long. I do hope they will understand that my intentions were entirely honorable.'

The pleading in his voice is unmistakable and I am not surprised to see my father take the stand soon after and admit that Willy's version is very close to the truth. He also says that there is an extant document protected by the Privacy Act that corroborates Willy's reconstruction closely, but it cannot be made public yet. He has no objection however, to the lawyers and the honorable Judge viewing it before passing judgment.

Post Script

BOBBY

That was more than a year ago. Our father's letter was not read out in court, but the presiding Judge's words left no one in doubt of the Old Man's guilt. He had sent a man to the gallows on the thinnest of pretexts to scotch a rumor about his own debauchery; he had used his own children shamefully to protect himself. He had definitely engineered the death of the Wilson couple because Mrs. Wilson had begun to voice her doubts about the attack on herself, aloud. He had been true to no one, friend or family, least of all to himself.

Our family name took a terrible beating and what hurt the most was the ghoulish relish with which his memory was desecrated. He had made too many people feel like pygmies and they were hardly likely to pass up such an opportunity, even after so many years. Our children took it very hard and we sent off Sheila and Sammy to boarding school for two years to live these memories down. Timmy however, refused to budge, weathered the storm with aplomb and courage till he had won his friends back, and through this difficult time Willy stayed by him constantly. They left six months ago for England, Timmy to study for the bar as he was determined to be as eminent a judge as his grandfather someday, minus the stigma. Strangely, his imagination continues to be fired by his enigmatic ancestor despite all the beating that Old Man's image has taken in the last few years. Is this what charisma is all about? The original word is karishma and the meaning is magic or supernatural power; does the devil confer his graces on people he considers his own?

Many people have commented on the fact that Ronnie and I, and to large extent Tony as well, are very different from our father, especially the fact that we are painfully moral people, and they put it down to an immaculate inheritance from our mother. I cannot explain to them that our Father was a very moral person too in his own way, and made us toe the line relentlessly. The rules only changed when it was a question of success versus failure. He could not accept failure at any cost and at that point, no ruse was too heinous, no action too ruthless if it would achieve the desired end. Does this paradox have a rational explanation? The doggerel still framed and hanging in the library, might it provide a clue? After all, these people standing at the crossroads of history had little to guide them as far as ethos building went; old mores had been discredited and replaced with uneasy Westernization, only to be discarded in turn for an even more uneasy nationalism or Indian-ness. To which star would they hitch their wagon? What would be their guiding principle? Had the sharp, scarred edge of truth necessarily and inevitably eluded their search under the circumstances?

It is a measure of the complexity of the case that it took a whole year to be resolved. However, we were certainly not at the end of the road, any of us; we had just struck out on the long path to discovery and introspection. The case was a mere catalyst and the worst was yet to come, the sharp, scarred edge had yet to cut through layers and layers of self-deception that enveloped the members of our family.

There was in particular one chapter that none of us had any idea of, and which explained so much; it would completely change the way we had looked at each other through the years and enable us to see through the mist of incomprehension. Particularly, it would tell us why the Judge went through a process of conscious and constant self-flagellation in the years between our mother's death and his own demise.

It would not be easy, but travel the road we must.

20. Long Shadows

LEILA-SPEAK

A week after the case was closed with the verdict of guilty, I could not find Small anywhere in the house. She had stopped communicating and kept to her room ever since we had returned from court and though Madonna and I, her much loved Leila tried to talk to her, she shied away from both of us. In the end it was Sammy and Sheila who had been her sleuthing buddies in recent days and whom she seemed to trust, who took her meals up to her room and tried to coax her back to life. Perhaps I had wasted too much energy grieving to have a reserve left over to share, and Small realized that her Leila had lost much of her old magic and strength? Was this draining of energy a result of mindless self-absorption? Why had I fallen so neatly into the trap laid for me, I who am fairly rational and pride myself on my knowledge of human nature and motivation?

Anyway, this morning it seems as though we are back where we had started a little over a year ago, only the missing person is Small, not I; again it is the kids who know where to find her and run to the garden like homing pigeons, saying she must be with her friend, and even the madness that follows, though perhaps purer, bears a bizarre and macabre resemblance to my past.

Their ashen faces when they come pelting back, breathless and terrified, augurs disaster and I keep calling out to all family members as I run after the kids back to the garden. Fortunately it is too early for the men to have left for work and very soon the pounding feet behind me reassure me somewhat, till I reach the tree that Small has always called her friend.

Small is hanging impaled on one branch of the tree, which appears to be her only anchorage. Her entire body is leaning out at an angle of almost thirty-five degrees but on closer inspection we find that the arms have caught on smaller branches and are spread-eagled. Her head is lolling like that of a broken doll; the beautiful pool-like eyes are open, reflecting her last agony. The whole tableau is that of a crucifixion, which either chance or happenstance or deliberation has created. The stunned silence is broken by Bobby who says as though on cue:

'Small has always been the Christ figure in this family; paying endlessly for others' transgressions; whose sins has she paid for now?'

However, it is Tony, always practical, who notices and says:

'Hey folks, she is breathing...we have to get her to a doctor!'

After that people swing into action: very carefully they extricate her from the branches, lay her down on the rear seat of our biggest car and rush her to hospital, with Millie and I crouching on the car floor supporting her. Strangely, Madonna does not want to come with us. With Tony driving and Ronnie beside him urging him on and waving traffic out of the way, both horns blaring, they break every traffic rule to save ten minutes, which the doctor said later had proved vital. She is already in the ICU when Bobby and Timmy and Lena screech to a halt in the portico. Yet a third car arrives with Robin at the wheel with the two kids tumbling out even before the wheels have come to rest. Robin says helplessly:

'I know I should not have left the house, but we just had to come...'

Small has some serious internal injuries, has lost a lot of blood, but pulls through miraculously, mainly, say the doctors, due to her indomitable will to live. In her delirium she keeps muttering about her friend, the kids and her duty to keep them safe, not let any harm come to them, and we all realize that it is this sense of mission that is causing her to fight for her life so determinedly. Small has never learned how to lie, her word once given, is written in stone, and the fact that she herself is handicapped and has limited capability never enters her mind. 'I gave my word to Millie and Leila,' is her constant refrain. Against all odds she begins to heal and doctors decide they will keep her in hospital for a month; after which they hope she will be able to go home and resume normal life.

In the meanwhile, we find that Madonna is planning to leave even before Small returns. She is taking up Josh's offer to run the school in the old house and Josh and his wife are delighted with her change of heart. They have never been happy about her decision to live with us and feel that she is now returning to her rightful position. Surprisingly, her brothers too are not terribly unhappy to see her go and although they assure her repeatedly of her welcome, they do not protest vehemently. Madonna notices this and says in her sarcastic way:

'Enough is enough, never outstay your welcome, that is what I believe.'

To which Rose retorts, sotto voce: 'Well, you certainly took your time about it!'

Her farewell visit to Small is hurried, even furtive. She refuses to meet her sister's eye but tears pour from her eyes as she strokes her hair, her own face firmly averted. Small makes no attempt to speak, just looks up at her quietly, steadily. When Madonna rises to leave, Small just asks one question:

'You know why, right, Madonna?'

But Madonna does not reply and glides away from the room.

Two days later Sunny's Rolls Royce arrives with the driver at the wheel and an attendant to see to her needs, both in the distinctive uniform of their estate. They are deferential and their response to her orders make it clear that she is going back to a warm welcome, and after days Madonna looks happy and relaxed. Her goodbyes are characteristically unemotional, and she rolls her large eyes and says:

'Never thought I'd live to be a ruddy teacher, but then that is life; square pegs in round holes!' Cursory pecks on our cheeks and hugs for the kids, she only clings to her brothers for a moment. Then the smile is back in place, she is in the car, the large vehicle purrs to life, is sweeping down the drive, and with a wave of her hand she is gone. All of us know in the heart of our hearts that we will not see her again in a hurry.

ABOUT LENA: ROBIN-SPEAK

I think my father knew all along about the great family secret, or at least had a very fair inkling, which is why he went the whole way to help his sainted master out of a very tight place and at great cost to himself. Not that this was anything out of the way, his mission in life was to extricate his master from the endless scrapes he was always getting into, but the scenario here was different, because in this case I was involved and the mistress had the final say.

When she asked me to marry Lena, I did not object because she was attractive and lively, already a part of the household, knew the ways of town life and would not pine for her village and family like my cousin's wife, who hardly ever came to the city, making it very hard for her husband to maintain his moral purity. She did not care that he visited brothels and was quite happy bringing up her three children in the village with the money he sent, for as head gardener he made a good salary. I did not want to follow in his footsteps or for that matter of all our kin who earned in cities and stayed away from their women-folk eleven months in the year. I wanted my wife to be a companion as I had heard Master Bobby say when he married Madam Millie against the Mistress's wishes. He had said he wanted a well-educated mind to communicate with and did not care if she came from a different community. The mistress had given way but the wedding had been a quiet one, nothing like the lavish show that was put up for Master Ronnie or Miss Madonna. This is also perhaps why Madam Millie has always maintained a low profile, even though she is the eldest brother's wife and should have taken the Mistress's position after her death. But I think she preferred her shadowy art-world to the fray of everyday life and was happy to leave the manifold problems of a joint family in Madam Leila's capable hands.

But to get back to Lena, she was a lot of fun with her sense of humor and caustic tongue, very attractive and pure magic in bed, but she was entirely loyal and never looked at another man after she married me. Our life together would have been quite perfect if only we had had a child, but years melted into each other and her womb remained barren. Doctors were at a loss to explain this infertility for we were both healthy people. As time went on, Lena looked more and more to the household children to assuage the pain and so did I, but while my favorites are the second generation, Timmy, Sammy and Sheila; for Lena there has never been any competition for Master Tony and Small, whom she had looked after since they had been born, especially Tony who still looks on her as a kind of foster mother. The reason for this is that after Tony was born, the mistress was unwell for a long time and Lena raised him almost single-handed. In a very fair-complexioned household, Tony was the dark but very handsome one and Lena always said he was Krishna for her, the dark avatar of the mighty God Vishnu, and she his foster mother, or Yashoda. I did not realize the significance of this statement till last year when Lena was diagnosed with pelvic cancer and the doctors said that she just had three months to live.

MARRYING FOR LOVE: MILLIE-SPEAK

We married out of love and Bobby crossed all barriers, brooked all opposition to bring me into the household. Perhaps at that point neither of us realized that it was the great challenge, the adventure and the novelty of defying authority that had driven us rather than our innate attraction for each other. All said and done, and for all their vaunted anglophile ways, Bobby had been raised in a traditional household where his father's peccadilloes had been frowned upon severely. The boys had always supported their mother who, strong and independent minded, had never asked for their help but this dichotomy had the effect of turning them into puritans who questioned every bit of fun they had, particularly Bobby. He had told his parents that it was right that he should marry me, not that his joy lay in the association, and after an initial objection caused by difference in caste, the Judge had agreed, mainly due, I think, to my westernization, an asset in his social circle, and his wife had followed suit, albeit less willingly.

The daughter of a well-reputed scientist working in the Research Wing of the Armaments Department, I had spent my childhood in Germany, but in my early teenage years our family had been interned in England due to the Second

World War. Those years had been formative in many ways: we had learned to make do on very little, survive on potato soup and bread day in and day out, live under a constant cloud due to our German antecedents. I will never forget the blond, bearded, sharp-eyed inspector of police who always asked me the same question every week:

'Well Miss, heard from your German friends lately?'

To which I always replied in the negative, but I don't think he quite believed me. My parents were almost housebound, lived on a pittance granted by the British Government and chafed under constant surveillance. As my father said bitterly:

'We are doubly suspect: first due to our Indian origin and second, our German association, none of it of our own choosing, but the situation really couldn't be worse!'

I was not allowed to attend school and would never have survived the loneliness if my father had not turned our one room into a school for me. Here he gave me a regular school day with special emphasis on mathematics and science, while my mother taught me how to draw, paint and embroider. Pencils were not available so we used pieces of charcoal, paper was scarce so we drew on the floor, and silk skeins could not be had so we used wool unwound from old sweaters for our tapestries. My father's infallible memory took the place of books and the floor was covered with diagrams and formulae and ultimately it became the most exciting time of my life! But best of all, this school won me a friend, Isaac, who being an European Jew was also suspect, incarcerated, and as lonely as I. He would creep over and join us when the police had done their daily rounds and together we would explore the worlds of Newton, Euclid and the Brothers Grimm.

He taught me how to weave a basket and I crotched a multi-colored headband for him.

Ultimately, we were allowed to return to India after the Armistice was announced, and the only one I clung to in desperation before leaving England was Isaac, as I knew I would never see him again.

Back in India our lives were not easy either, and though we had a home with our uncle and I was allowed to join college, my father could not find a job and prospects were bleak. Ultimately, he and my uncle set up a company for manufacturing and marketing scientific instruments, one of the first native enterprises that proved very successful, but it took many years and my uncle and I benefited more from it than my parents. I met Bobby at a social gathering and his attention was arrested because I was different, speaking English and German with equal aplomb, and all my wartime stories... I soon realized that a better catch would never come my way and spared no pains to turn his fascination into infatuation. When he proposed marriage and his parents objected, the project took on the dimensions of a holy crusade and Bobby was prepared to fight every windmill to marry me. In the end, it was Ronnie who finally persuaded his parents to relent, and I from my natural obscurity was catapulted to the eminent position of the Great Judge's first daughter-in-law!

In the beginning it was exciting to be a part of this wealthy and powerful household, to be given precedence in all spheres, particularly in contrast to my early anonymity, even ignominy. But by the time Timmy was two years old, Bobby was rising steadily in his profession and keeping very long hours in his office. Madonna was married and leading the most exciting life with her charming Sunny. Ronnie was doing very well and was soon to be married to a girl very different from me in every way, one of whom the family approved thoroughly. My perspective began to change. My mother-in-law's health was failing and more and more responsibility devolved on me, including caring for Small and Tony. The glamour was definitely waning; there was no time or opportunity to paint or read, let alone have fun, and it seemed this terrible sameness would eternally blight my life.

At this difficult juncture, the serpent entered my garden… unobtrusively, but holding out promise of a very different lifestyle.

21. Ordeal of Paternity

STRATEGIZING: SHEILA AND SAMMY

Sammy: It seems we are back where we were five years ago, with everyone whispering behind my back, the family's back; why won't they come forward and speak, bring matters to a head?

Sheila: Did they do so before? No; Sammy, people enjoy the discomfiture of others too much to be so kind.

Sammy: Then what shall we do? We can't carry on like this forever…

Sheila: We will find a way as we did before, don't you worry. You see, you were the clown of the family, always getting into scrapes and no one took you seriously. But now that you are not as ugly as you were before and on your way to being an engineer, people don't like it, do they?

Sammy: Well. None of us is doing badly, come to think of it, including you, so why pick on me?

Sheila: They probably think I'm only a girl and I've had my share with all the wicked innuendo about my own Daddy and Small, and Mamma almost dying of grief because of it. Roma and Timmy are too far away to reach, besides…

Sammy:　Besides?

Sheila:　Promise you won't hate me if I speak the truth?

Sammy:　I shall try very hard.

Sheila:　Well, it is true that you resemble Uncle Dave more than you do your own Daddy, not feature by feature, but the same turn of head, the same easy gait, a large share of his male magic?

Sammy:　If that is all, family resemblances are strange things. You look more like Aunt Madonna than your own mother, don't you?

Sheila:　That is genetic, girls always look like their aunts on the Dad's side and boys like their maternal uncles. Uncle Dave does not fit the bill, does he?

Sammy:　No, he does not, but what about freak cases? Look at our cousin Toto; he looks European with his blond hair and gray eyes, but his parents are like anyone else in the family, so?

Sheila:　Well, you know what Toto himself has to say, that he is a throwback and the genes of Portuguese mistresses his ancestors acquired on a regular basis have surfaced in him! The other day I was out with my friends and we stumbled on Toto. You should have seen the faces of my friends when he gave me a hug, but Toto himself could not care less! That is the way to deal with jealous gossips!

Sammy:　So Toto gets away because of his anonymous ancestors and I get stuck because of a freak family resemblance? Not fair!

Sheila:　Look, Sammy, I think we all made an unspoken pact to stick to the truth five years ago during the… the fire-trial, as they say in local parlance, when the case was re-opened. Why should we deviate now? If I were you, I would confront your parents and find out once and for all. They will not let you down, believe me.

Sammy: I know they won't nor am I afraid of their letting me down, but doesn't it show a lack of trust on my part to ask such a question?

Sheila: What is the alternative? Don't you remember how Grandaunt Miranda spoke at dinner the other evening?

'Bobby dear, what a charming child Sammy is, much more handsome than you ever were my dear or even Ronnie for that matter. He is almost the spitting image of Dave, isn't he? Wonder how that happened?'

Sammy: Poor Daddy was getting so flustered; you know how he cannot be rude to older people, even under extreme provocation, but...

Sheila: Small turned the tables so neatly on her; I could have died when she said, so sweetly:

'Aunt Miranda, you are so right! Talking of coincidences, we all wonder why your only grandson bears such a marked resemblance to your old gatekeeper, Ravi, who has been with you for years like our Robin, my brothers tell me. Now, he is not even family, so did your daughter have a crush on him or something? Or is it pure happenstance? I only ask, since you brought the matter up.'

Sammy: And though Aunt Leila did her best, Miranda would not stay for dessert! Besides, she could not say anything, because of Small's privileged position in the family! Besides, ever since Aunt Madonna left Small has become a different person, have you noticed?

Sheila: But the old cat will not stop talking and spewing poison behind our backs, so I think we should lay the ghost, once and for all.

Sammy: Okay. It is going to be awkward and embarrassing, though. Will you come with me?

Sheila: Of course…don't forget I am an old hand at this game of family whispers.

BOBBY TAKES THE PLUNGE

Sooner or later Sammy will bring the matter up. He has been unsettled ever since Aunt Miranda's visit and all her wicked talk. Yet Aunt says she loves her brother's family like her own; well, she did till I outstripped her son-in-law career wise, and she has just that one daughter whom she cannot bear to see unhappy. I feel sorry for her as I know what envy can do to a person's psyche, particularly after what it did to Madonna, but what do I tell Sammy, my dearest son, who dotes on his father and wants to be like him in every way? Best if Millie and I confront him together; then he will see that we have nothing to hide and that we are not afraid of the truth. I must discuss this with Millie tonight.

Millie and I sit in two deck chairs in the balcony on the first floor adjoining our room, which looks out on the garden. This is our favorite spot, not only because we can see the clear water of the serpentine that stems from a natural spring shining through the tracery of willow leaves, but also the waterfall that it feeds. Old ferns growing along the watercourse on the rock-face dip into the water, creating miniscule rivulets that birds and squirrels drink from, and the tiny wild plants that cling

precariously to the bare rock flower in profusion. Millie
has planted orchids, jasmine and ornamental caladium
in pots on the balcony, and the plants trailing over the
balustrade add to the magic of the garden. This used to be
our mother's room and after her death Ronnie and Leila
had insisted that we move in as heads of the family and
Tony and Small had concurred happily.

We are unbelievably fortunate that we are together, that
we survived the crisis five years ago, trust in each other
unbroken, and I only pray that nothing in the future will
ever dent this amity.

But tonight Millie and I face our personal crisis that
concerns no other member of the family but our two
children and us; they have questions to which we must
provide convincing answers, but to do that we have to
resolve our own confusions, something we have allowed to
hang fire for the last twenty odd years. Why, simply because
we lacked courage and resolve, or was it because we had
accepted the fait accompli as an inevitable part of creation
and woven it into the fabric of our day-to-day living?

When I had found out about Dave, my resentment had
been megalithic; I had wanted to tear down the family
fabric, have a showdown, send Millie back to the obscurity
from which I had rescued her, but Ronnie's wisdom and
indomitable will power had held me back:

'You must wait for the birth of the child,' he had said.

Then Sammy had been born, all bloody and slimy and
funny, his hair sticking up, mouth bawling lustily, and the
nurse had handed him to me saying:

'Another son sir. Congratulations! You can hold him
now.'

And at that moment I had forgotten everything but that

I had been granted a healthy child, my very own, today to us a son is born. And I had clung to him wordlessly. Within three months it was clear that Sammy loved me best and responded to me in a way Timmy never had; Millie, often at her wits end with the recalcitrant child, would hand him to me saying:

'Here, Bobby, see what you can do with him, I really can't manage this terrible brat of yours!'

If he was sick, I had to miss work to be by his side; if we went trekking he would only hold my hand; I had to gore his first air gun for him. Once he was to go on a trip with Ronnie, Leila and the girls; he was just ten years old and till the last Sammy could not make up his mind; finally Ronnie said:

'Why don't you think that for the next ten days you will be my and Aunty Leila's son, that will solve the problem, won't it?'

'Okay,' he replied, 'but you have to promise to return me to Daddy as soon as we come back! I will only go on this condition!'

Neither Millie or I realized when the awkwardness melted away, all discussion became redundant, nor when Sammy became our son, but tonight this untold tale will have to be told; meaning have to be assigned, and answers have to be provided. The scarred edge of truth at last. Poor monkey, I hope he won't take it too hard.

On a moonlit night the view from our balcony is spectacular, but tonight there is no moon light and we have to find our way in the dark all by ourselves. The foliage in the garden is gray and colorless in the dark, waiting for the sunlight to kiss it and bring it back to life. In the fairy tales our grandmother told us when we were young, there were fairies with golden and silver rods, a touch of which restored people to life and sanity; how would we find our salvation? Who would play fairy godmother to us?

Finally, the silence is broken:

Millie: Tell me Bobby, when did you guess?

Bobby: Guess what? That you were having an affair with Dave, or that he was Sammy's father?

Millie: Stop trying to be brusque, Bobby; it's not your style.

Bobby: Well, the question is valid enough, isn't it, though it may be stylistically inaccurate?

Millie: Bobby, are you going to be sarcastic, stuffy, and horribly logical, carry on in your tiresome courtroom manner? In that case...

Bobby: Well, you married a tiresome lawyer entirely of your own free will and...

Millie: And one of the most successful and that is where the problem lay!

Bobby: My professional success is a problem for you, would you prefer it if I were struggling and impecunious?

Millie: Of course not, I enjoy the perks too much! But you have to admit that when you were rising to the top, life was hard and lonely for me...

Bobby: So you fell promptly into another man's arms to allay your boredom?

Millie: I did not! Just a moment's pique, a moment's flattery, a moment's weakness and the deed was done! I never went back to him; you know that, don't you? Or don't you believe me?

Bobby: Strangely enough, I do, because Dave told Ronnie the same thing as well. That he too lost interest because he had achieved his purpose.

Millie: Purpose? Ronnie! Dave discussed this, discussed ME with Ronnie?

Bobby: Oh yes! Dave was so proud of his planning and strategy and it would all have been pointless if we had not known or suffered on account of it.

Millie: I, I don't understand.

Bobby: Naturally not. But you are an artist, and at times subliminal feelings emanating from your subconscious find expression in your paintings. Tell me, what did you have in mind when you painted that painting you called Serpent in Eden, which you refused to sell even though you were offered a fantastic price?

Millie: At the time I painted it I had no idea what drove me, but later I thought maybe Madonna's machinations had inspired it.

Bobby: I don't think so; I think you had Dave in mind, for you have known all along that he used you, but you refused to acknowledge it.

Millie: Used me, how?

Bobby: Sounds Biblical and absurd, but it was a case of a 'life for a life'.

Millie: That is not only absurd but horribly melodramatic as well, and it makes no sense at all!

Bobby: It does, though bizarre; tell me, why was Dave so mad with our Father?

Millie: I thought it was because of his brother whom your father made no attempt to save.

Bobby: Exactly! A life had been taken, and he would retaliate not by taking another, but by planting what he imagined would be an unwanted one.

Once he achieved his purpose you were no longer attractive to him. Sorry to be so brutal, but this is why I never brought it up before, because I did not want to hurt you.

Millie: And you Bobby? How could you take it all so calmly? How could you carry on as usual, as though nothing had happened? Were you not hurt by my infidelity?

Bobby: I was, terribly; ready to tear the world apart...it was Ronnie who held me back and said I must wait for the baby to be born.

Millie: And?

Bobby: The rest you know. The moment I set eyes on Sammy I knew he was mine, and the matter of his paternity, a biological accident, did not matter in the least! Also, I knew that Dave's worst punishment, in time, would be to know he had a son on whom he had no claim and to whom he did not matter. After all, I am not a lawyer for nothing! And look, he married in the end, but he never was able to father another child, although his wife is much younger and perfectly fertile. Life has a way of sorting things out, Millie; it is we who lack patience and cannot wait for life to complete the cycle.

Millie: So, you forgave me because of Sammy?

Bobby: Partly, but also because I love you, Millie, and know that you have never, truly, broken faith. If I felt that you cared for Dave with your whole heart, I would have stepped back and let you go.

Millie: Well, thank goodness for that, I always realized that you were a very kind human being, but never knew you were such an old romantic, Bobs! And Ronnie, how do I ever thank him for saving my life?

Bobby: Don't even try; he has just got back his own life and is still reeling from the impact!

Millie: So now, Operation Sammy?

Bobby: Operation Sheila and Sammy, they are both waiting!

SMALL-SPEAK

'Trust God, see all, nor yet be afraid.'

I hope I got that right? Ronnie's favorite line from Browning's poem, Rabbi Ben Ezra, that I had learned and internalized even as a child, but as I grew up it became harder and harder to know who was endorsed by God and so could be trusted, for they all said they loved me. And they did of course, or thought they did, especially after the accident, when they began to confuse love and pity and became extra protective. As long as Mamma was around, there was no confusion; she loved me best and I know, died out of sorrow for me. But after that, it was very turbid… Father, who had been like a rock for as long as I could remember, began to crumble somehow, and avoided me; it was as though he could not meet my eyes or bear my company, something I found very hard to take. Lena loved me, but loved Tony better, perhaps because he was younger and a boy? Bobby and Ronnie were always there for me, whatever the circumstance, and they told their wives clearly that Small came first with them and their ladies must follow suit. Millie did her best, but she found it difficult to communicate; however, I knew she would rise to the occasion whenever required. Madonna was married soon after the accident and came home rarely. When she did she claimed that she mainly came because of me, made a huge fuss about taking care of me, buying presents without consulting me and wanting to take me to places I hated because there were inquisitive strangers there; but when Sunny suggested that they take us, me and Tony, to the estate for a holiday as his parents were very keen and both of us really wanted to go for we loved and trusted Sunny completely, it was Madonna who demurred, saying she did not wish to impose, whatever that meant. Sunny was very hurt and kept insisting but it never worked out. I realized much later that Madonna did not want the estate people to know that she had a deformed sister.

So, it took Leila, with her heart full of love, to make a human being out of me again, and after the girls arrived and became my special charge, I never looked back till Madonna returned to her father's house, this time without Sunny or Joy.

At that point neither of us had an inkling that Madonna would be compelled to return to the estate one day, for Sunny's home would be her last and only refuge or that I would pay the long over-due visit; both events took place but under circumstances very different from what either of us had imagined.

LENA AND ROBIN'S ENCOUNTER
WITH TRUTH

Lena had always had a bad back but lately it had been threatening to cripple and confine her to bed, so Master Bobby fixed up an appointment with the best orthopedist in town and we, Tony and I, drove her down to the hospital one morning. What had promised to be a routine check turned into a full-fledged investigation with a barrage of diagnostic tests and in the end the ailment was diagnosed as the terminal stage of pelvic bone cancer. The family insisted that she be transferred to the best nursing home available so that she would have the right medical care and be reasonably free of pain in the short time that was left to her. They all took turns to visit her but Madam Leila, Small, Tony, Sheila and I went every day, and I sometimes twice a day. On such a day when I was alone with her, a lovely spring evening with the cuckoo singing its heart out in the mango trees that filled the compound, she held my hand in her own warm, too warm ones, and told me her story:

'As you know Robin, I ran away from my village to escape my father and ended up here thanks to the old singer and our kind Mistress. It was the happiest time of my life, playing with Madonna and helping to take care of Small, the most beautiful baby in the world, and of course, being teased by you and hoping you would take real notice of me someday. You did not know, but I lost my heart to you the day I set my eyes on you, but the Mistress who noticed everything, had her own plans for both of us all along.

'I think I must have been born under an uneasy star and was never meant to have an easy life; the Master had always been kind to me but now his kindness was taking a turn that made me uncomfortable. Said I was a black rose in his garden of white ones, the prettiest, the hottest, said my fragrance was driving him mad. The Mistress did her best to protect me but to no avail and one night he waylaid me just outside Madonna's room and said he would wake her up if I did not yield. This molestation went on for three months and at the end of it I was pregnant. By then he had had enough of me and was planning to send me back to the village after an abortion, when the Mistress found out, and not unexpectedly, dug her heel in very firmly:

'"Lena was under my protection for I took her in and she will not suffer and I will not allow her child to die because I have an immoral husband. The child will be born, but the world will know me as the mother, and Lena as the wet nurse. We will go to our country-house for a few months to facilitate matters."

'Only she could think of such a solution or have the courage to pull it through and I only stared at her beautiful face in dumb hero-worship till she put her hand on my head in benediction and said:

'"Sorry Lena, that you will only be Mother Yashoda to this Krishna, but also think of the advantage of compelling the Master to be his legitimate father! He will get a taste of his own justice and I will love the child as well as my own children, you believe that, don't you?"

'The Master threatened and scolded, literally begged at her feet, for he was sure that this act would come back to haunt him in some way, but the Mistress was adamant and threatened to tell the older children if he did not agree. In the end he gave in, though with very bad grace. There was great jubilation all around, for the mistress had said that Small would be her last child. The children were thrilled and the boys vied with Madonna saying the baby would be a boy and so their team would get stronger. Early in the seventh month the ritual of 'saptamrit' (the seven elixirs) was held and after that your father drove us down to the village for the last lap.

'Those few months in the country-house were some of the happiest in those sad times; the Mistress took care of me like a daughter, no ominous shadow hovered and the whole village celebrated. The Mistress's generosity to the poor was legendary and there was a whirl of activity with Pujas, festivals and 'Daan', giving food, blankets and clothes to the villagers. I stayed indoors in swaddling clothes, taking care of Small, while the mistress, stomach firmly padded, held center stage. I think it was at this time that it struck me that the first step to sainthood was taking responsibility, even when the debacle was not of one's own making; when you made amends for someone who had wronged you terribly, but you thought the other had been wronged even more. As long as I live, I shall never meet a saint like the Mistress and it was due to her that I was able to endure the ordeal with equanimity.

'Three months blurred by and when it was time for the laying in, a hatchet faced doctor and an equally dour nurse arrived from the city. When my labor pains began, they closed all doors and windows of the chamber firmly and only allowed me to attend on the Mistress. It was an easy birth and Tony the handsomest baby. I was reminded of the many stories Madonna had told me of kings and queens in India and Europe, who due to infertility had often fallen back on village wenches to supply the need, and then these girls then stayed on in the family as nurses for the baby. Apparently, I was the rule rather than the exception.

'The rest you know; you were kind enough to marry me and life was very fulfilling till I realized I would not be able to give you a child. I think the doctor who attended me, no doubt on the Master's initiative, ensured somehow that I would never have another child. So here I was with a son who would never be mine and unable to give my husband, who loved children, a legitimate child. It was at this point with the Mistress dead and no one to guide me on the tortuous path of right and wrong that the greed for power got to me. For once, I the mean, the lowly, the used, would turn the tables on my tormentor. In the last few years I think I became quite paranoid, even obsessive, and managed to torture the Master unmercifully; and he, physically paralyzed but mentally alert as ever, with enough on his own conscience to worry about, was terrified of further exposure. I put him through pure hell and the more he groveled, the more creative I became. It was sweet music to my ears to hear people, mainly visitors, praise me for my devotion and service to the Master.

'Like a daughter is the cliché they inevitably used, and to know that he was squirming with terror all the while was supremely fulfilling. Very often I sat alone with him on lazy afternoons when the nurses were dozing and turned the knife in the wound till I had no more energy for cruelty and left him with glazed eyes that were like a dead man's.

'In the end though, I gave up because I realized that I was hurting myself more than my victim with the corrosion of hate and more importantly, that I was putting myself in considerable danger, for Small walked in one afternoon to check on her Father and though she had not heard my words she was too canny not to diagnose the look of terrified supplication on his face. She held both his emaciated hands in her own for a long time and when he fell into deep slumber, she left the room without a word to me. The next day a nursing supervisor, Ms. McDermott, Scottish, dour and terrifyingly efficient, appeared on the scene, took complete charge and no one napped or dozed around her except her patient! Small merely told me very sweetly: "You are getting old too and you don't need to take care of Father any more Lena, I will sit with him every afternoon, and Ms. McDermott will be in charge round the clock."

'And that was that! Very few people realized at that point that a dramatic restoration was in progress and that Small, after years of shelf-life, was finally coming into her own. I think her mother's illness and death made her realize that she needed to take responsibility for her own and the family's emotional well-being. Even her siblings did not cotton on to the fact that an exceptionally sharp brain was back at work behind the pathetic façade or that nothing about her was small any more except her physical stature. Perhaps her early experiences had given her a ground view and the ability to size up people for who they were? The Old Man always said she would be an exceptional Man of Law and took her everywhere as his mascot, till that fateful night. After her mother's death she went into a shell, but even so, took close note of all that went on in the house and her brothers trusted her implicitly and over everyone else. However, she allowed no other family member to get close or through to her.

'But when Madam Leila came into the house and insisted that they communicate, Small began to trust herself and her own judgment again, particularly when Leila encouraged her to do so by leaving her own children in Small's charge. Her growing sense of responsibility and the feeling that she was needed, did wonders, and Small was soon on her way to becoming a personality to reckon with. No, I would certainly not like to cross swords with Small.

'Then when Madam Leila fell sick and the household was suddenly unstable as never before, I thought I would try a spot of blackmail to get more out of the family for my son and an elevated position for myself. But Tony was so upset about Ronnie and Leila that the last person he had on his mind was his old nanny; in the end I was compelled to acknowledge that he would not thank me for adding to the burdens of the family. He had always been very kind to me as his old servitor, but would never, never accept me as a mother and might even come to hate me for demeaning him. The only person who caught on to my intentions again was Small and she warned me in her characteristic cryptic style:

'"Don't try to dig up the dead, Lena; you will never be able to breathe life into them. Not only will you suffer but many others along with you. Look at my life, my mother's real, youngest and dearest daughter, and be content with what you have. At least what you have is whole."

'I think she had guessed all along, because she had been with us in the country at the time of Tony's birth.

As a matter of fact she had once asked me whether I had not been Tony's wet-nurse. But I was too far-gone in my madness. Robin, you did not understand, but I called in the soothsayer hoping he would bring matters to a head and was delighted when Tony backed me up; but he was doing this for Leila, Ronnie and the girls, not with any other motive or intention. He was certainly not thinking of me, but I refused to accept that! Thank God, the soothsayer was so wise and warned me in the nick of time not to follow my wicked and foolish inclinations. He blessed me with the last few years of happiness, as your wife and nanny to all the children in the household including Tony, the roles I had been assigned by Providence and played best all along.

'And then last month the doctor came and I found that the day of reckoning had come and I must pay for my sins. With my days on earth numbered I understood how futile the attempt to right a wrong in the same manner as the wrong was originally perpetrated, could prove, and that the only access to right was within my own soul. I thanked God and the Wise Man with all my heart for pulling me back from the edge of the black chasm of evil intention and enabling me to leave the earth without the great blot on my conscience.

'Now only you know, Robin who has loved me best, and if you forgive me I shall die content, having made a clean-breast to you before facing my maker.'

I found on looking down later that our hands were wet with tears, and then realized that the tears were not all Lena's.

22. Operation Sammy

BOBBY, MILLIE, SAMMY AND SHEILA

Bobby: Come in you two, and please try to look human and not like two scared owls!

Sheila: You are laughing at us again, Uncle...but this is a serious matter. Sammy is...

Millie *(very concerned)*: Really Bobby, you must take these kids more seriously...why, Sheila is almost seventeen!

Sammy: You don't know how hard it is to have these horrible cats whispering in vicious huddles at these stupid family gatherings, and then have them move apart when you walk in, to look innocently at you as though they love you best and have only your welfare at heart.

Sheila: Yes. Why this pretense? Why don't they ask us outright?

Bobby: Don't you see, as long as the mystery persists, they have the power to intimidate you, but truth liberates you and then you have nothing to fear. Surely the case has taught you that much?

Sammy: It has taught us not to fear the truth, and that is why we are here today, to settle the question, once and for all.

Millie: Okay, no more beating about the bush. Let us
            begin with Sheila. Sheila, if you find out that
            Uncle Dave is Sammy's natural father and not
            your Uncle, how will it affect your feelings for
            Sammy?

Sheila: But…

Millie: No 'buts'. Just close your eyes and think.

Sheila: Well, it feels kind of strange, but I don't think
            it will change my feelings for old Sammy in any
            way.

Millie: So far, so good. Now, will it affect your feelings
            for your Uncle?

Sheila: Most definitely not! Uncle is my second Dad,
            how can anything in the world change what I
            feel for him?

Millie: And me? How will this affect our relationship?

Sheila: 'Let me think. You know Aunt Millie, while you
            have been a second Mum to me, you have also
            been my friend; you have taught me to look at
            the world differently through your paintings, a
            curious upside down way, if you know what I
            mean?

Millie: And?

Sheila: And all your childhood stories about making
            the best of things when life was so difficult and
            dark for you, have made me realize how lucky
            we are to have such a wonderful family and
            childhood…besides…

Millie: Besides?

Sheila: You are stupid old Sammy's and learned old
            Timmy's Mum, how can anything in the world

change that equation? I can never love them less…they are all the brothers I have and you are their mother, so…

Millie: Thank you Sheila from the bottom of my heart, whatever that might mean, does the heart have a bottom? But that is light-headed and does not suit the occasion. I must be solemn; now Bobby, it's your turn.

Bobby: Tell me Sammy, does it hurt a lot?

Sammy: It does, rather, mainly because I have never liked Uncle Dave much; all of you must have noticed that?

Sheila: I have, and have always wondered why?

Sammy: Primarily because he is sly and never looks you in the eye…and I don't like the way he sucks up to me. I told him never to bring a gift for me unless he brought gifts for all of us, yet he actually had the gall to offer me a bike for my sixteenth birthday. I told him, 'Thank you very much, but Aunt Leila and Uncle Ronnie are taking care of that!'

Bobby: Ouch! That must have hurt!

Sammy: It did! You should have seen his face, but I was glad of it!

Bobby: But what if you found out that he was your actual father? Wouldn't your feelings and attitude change?

Sammy: What are you trying to tell me Dad? Is this an academic discussion or are you saying that these old cats are right, after all? Don't play around with me Dad, please; it is a matter of life and death for me!

Bobby: I can understand, but just supposing they are right?

Sammy: Then I suppose I will just go and kill myself, or something I, I, can't face this shame!

Bobby: Steady, boy! Tell me, is it only the social angle that is bothering you? What people will say?

Sammy: Naturally…plus, plus…

Bobby: Plus what?

Sammy: I cannot face the fact that you are not my Dad!

Bobby: Now, who has said anything about my not being your Dad? Tell me, what does the word Dad mean to you? What do you understand by or expect of the person you call by that name? Never thought about it? Well, come on Sheila, you tell us.

Sheila: Come to think of it, we all have certain preconceived notions about roles that are assigned to us in life, and we play them basing our thoughts, actions and attitudes on these assumptions to a large extent; I mean social constructs rather than individual, independent responses. That is what you mean, don't you uncle?

Millie: Yes, Sheila, you just said Uncle is a second Dad to you, what did you mean by that statement?

Sheila: Well, I guess it means someone who knows your weaknesses and strengths yet accepts you unconditionally, someone who is always there for you, someone you can turn to in any kind of trouble, who just loves you totally, I guess!

Bobby: Well that's a tall order, but I too guess that I do my best; what say, Sammy?

Sammy:	Of course you do, which is why…
Bobby:	Which is why an accident of birth is going to change nothing, at least for me; it did not before and it will not ever; as far as I am concerned, you are my dearest son and will always be sine qua non, legally and morally.
Millie:	Bobby, no courtroom language, please!
Sammy:	But Mamma? How could she?
Bobby:	You are too young to understand now, but believe me, pure boredom or a spell of depression can cause an accident like this; your mother has never stopped regretting it and I have never forgiven myself, for it's my fault too.
Sammy:	How can it be your fault? They deceived you! Doesn't it make you angry?
Bobby:	When you are older Sammy, you will realize that the predominant color of life is gray…here, let me tell you both a story.
Sammy:	I am in no mood for a story!
Sheila:	Shut up Sammy and listen! These are the kind of stories Uncle tells in court, and since you are turning this into an inquisition.
Sammy:	You don't know how terrible I feel. I wish I were dead!
Sheila:	Time enough for that! Now pay attention to what your Dad has to say.
Bobby:	I made all of you read the Mahabharata some time ago, tell me why?
Sheila:	At the time Timmy was facing his dilemma with truth and you told us to read the book because it has answers to all life's problems. It certainly seemed to help Timmy, for he said he realized

that life was not meant to be easy for anyone and he was no exception. It gave him his favorite phrase: 'survival is a matter of technique'.

Millie: And he did survive and helped us survive too, it brought Leila back to us.

Sheila: Well, I never really understood what had made Mamma so sick, except that it had something to do with Daddy. Was it something like this?

Millie: No, a thousand times 'No'! There was no truth on that occasion; a bunch of cruel malicious lies told by a very wicked person was responsible for all our misery.

Bobby: But to return to Sammy's story tell me, why did Devavratha the prince, come to be called Bhishma?

Sheila: Because he made and kept two terrible promises to please his father.

Bobby: And what were these promises?

Sammy: That he would never claim the kingdom even though he was the heir and that he would never marry so that his sons would not be able to make a claim.

Bobby: And why did he do this?

Sheila: So his father could marry Satyavati, who wanted her sons to sit on the throne. Why was his father so stupid? He must have been old when he married Satyavati who was only sixteen! He could have married the girl to Devavratha!

Bobby: No, that was never the idea, but everyone knows the story so far, tell me what happened afterwards?

Sammy: Who knows and who cares? In any case, where is this rigmarole getting us?

Sheila: Have patience, Sammy! Uncle is making a point.

Bobby: Do you know what the great irony was? After all this rigmarole as you rightly call it, Satyavati's son Vichitravirya sat on the throne with great fanfare, but, could not father a son to take the dynasty forward because he was impotent!

Sammy: Oh my God, and then?

Bobby: Satyavati had to call in Bhishma and beg him to beget sons on her two daughters-in-law, the same princesses whom he had won in battle for his stepbrother!

Sheila: And did he agree?

Bobby: Of course not! He was promise-bound never to take a woman, remember?

Sammy: So?

Millie: He advised Satyavati to call in her other son, the Sage Vyas, to get her the grandsons she needed!

Sheila: And did he oblige?

Bobby: After much persuasion, and only to keep the dynasty going. He never bothered with the boys Dhritarashtra and Pandu, for a day, and it was Bhishma who undertook their nurture, because the family was of primary importance to him; he took care not only of these boys but their children, the great Pandav and Kaurav warriors as well, and to the end of his days he remained the true patriarch of the great family.

Sammy: So, what does this story have to do with me?

Sheila: Everything, you idiot! Don't you see, the father

	who begets is not really important, but the father who nurtures is all-important? Right, Uncle?
Millie:	Right as usual, o wise one!
Sammy:	But what about genes and heredity, don't they matter?
Millie:	They knew about that too, which is why the begetter was always chosen from the same family. In any case, boys take more after their mothers, please to look in the mirror!
Sammy:	Please Mamma, don't try to be facetious I am not amused. I don't give a damn about whom I resemble as long as I can be a human being like my Dad…and what makes you think I want to look like you, anyway?
Sheila:	Come on, Sammy…
Sammy:	You shut up, Sheila; do you know how it feels to know that my mother sold my Dad down the river and took away from me the chance to be his true, begotten son? How would you? Your parents are still crazy about each other!
Bobby:	Sammy, would it surprise you very much to know that your mother and I are still very fond of each other?
Sammy:	Yes, it would! You are not claiming sainthood now, are you?
Bobby:	God forbid! Saints are quite insufferable…but to fall back on a cliché, just as 'one swallow does not make a summer', one affair does not kill a marriage.
Sammy:	Not even if it produces a bastard son?
Bobby:	How dare you call my son a bastard, Sammy, my beloved son whom I have nurtured with my

life's blood and loved with all my being? The son whose smile is my sunshine, whose tears are my darkest nights and whose future my greatest rainbow? The son who is dearer to me than my first born, Timmy, from the moment I held him all bloody and slimy in my arms at the hospital? Oh Sammy, now you are breaking my heart in a way your mother never did!

Sammy: ...And what makes her so wonderful?

Bobby: Her endless repentance and endless suffering to which only I have been witness...her sleepless nights by the window, thoughts chasing each other like squirrels chasing their own tails through her poor brain till it throbbed mercilessly, the eternal terror of discovery, the eroding, constant self-recrimination, the never-lifting burden of 'if only'. She has paid many times over for what was after all a mere slip in a weak moment, never repeated. She has never forgiven herself, Sammy, which is why you must.

Sammy: I must nothing! She should have thought of all this before she had her fling! Why aren't you angry, Dad, why don't you knock that vase down? I feel like breaking something, slashing my wrists or someone else's!

Bobby: Hold on, Sam! Violence is not the answer! It is terrible to be angry with others but much worse to be angry with oneself, believe me!

Sheila: I have to agree with Uncle. I have watched poor Daddy trapped in a similar situation, blaming himself for Mamma's suffering, when he was in no way responsible. I thought it would kill him! And Aunt Millie has been torturing herself for nineteen years! There is no sin in the world that this kind of penance cannot expiate, and Sammy, you are a benighted idiot if you can't see it all on her face. Don't you understand that her greatest fear is that she will lose you?

Sammy: Okay, okay, Madam Oracle, enough of your famous wisdom! I can be wise too, you know; when occasion demands. Who held your hand through the entire case episode, may I ask? But it hurts, Sheila, it hurts like the devil to think that by law I am not my father's son.

Bobby: But you are, Sammy; the name of your father on your birth certificate is mine; it's my name on all your school documents, in all property matters, in all legal transactions. Legally, there is no shadow of a suspicion. Don't forget, I am a lawyer and I made damn sure that should the question ever come up, nobody would be able to point a finger. We don't have to admit to a damn thing and we can tell all the cats in the world to go to the devil with impunity!

Sammy: But how could Mamma let a man like you down, Dad? I can never forgive her this transgression, never in a hundred years!

Bobby: Oh yes, you will Sammy…some day you will stand in her shoes and realize how helpless man is; how hard he has to fight and that too with the poorest tools. You speak of transgression, but who lays down the parameters? What parameters were there for a little girl trapped in a concentration camp? You know that saying,

Sammy: 'The mills of God grind slow, but they grind exceedingly small'? Well as a lawyer, I know better than most people the truth of that saying. None of us shall escape calumny, none of us, so how can we presume to sit on judgment?

Millie: If you only knew Sammy, how hard I have tried to forgive myself and failed; that is the hardest part, as you will perhaps find out some day.

Bobby: Don't overlook the fact Sammy that someday perhaps you too will need to forgive yourself and earn the forgiveness of those you love, and on that day maybe these memories will come to your aid?

Sammy: Dad, you are not such a successful lawyer for nothing; not only are your arguments masterly but the wisdom that informs them irrefutable, and since a man must trust his lawyer, doctor and priest, another of your sayings, I will roll all three together in you, put my complete trust in you and try to make peace with my mother. I will give it my best shot, but if it does not work out then both of you will have to forgive me. Come Sheila, let's go. I shall suffocate if I spend one more minute in this bloodless room!

Millie: Oh Bobby, you tried so hard, but the young are so passionately righteous! I don't think either of them will ever forgive me in the core of their hearts.

Bobby: They will my poor Millie, but it will take
            time; unlike us, they have not learned to make
            compromises with their feelings, yet.

TONY: MY TRUTH

I, Tony, knew all along that I was different from the others. I was dark like my Father but handsome in a raw, tribal sort of way distinct from his regular good looks; quite different from my brothers, particularly Ronnie who was extraordinarily handsome too, but an aristocrat with his ruddy skin and aquiline features, very similar to our mother. While they excelled at academics I pulled along, never failing but not doing too well either; truth to tell, I found books removed from life and boring and right from the beginning I was determined not to let others dominate my life. Life herself is a much better, a more trustworthy teacher, and I put my trust in her from day one.

But what set me apart most from the others was our mother's attitude: Small was called Small because she was supposed to be the youngest and everyone treated her with special affection, particularly Father who took her everywhere with him and called her his mascot. I was an accident and often teased as such by Father, but especially by Madonna, who said I was a changeling and had been smuggled into the house in a warming pan like many famous monarchs! To Bobby and Ronnie however, I was their baby brother for whom nothing was too good, and for whom their steady affection has not varied for a day, bless them! But our mother, not only did she love me best, but it was almost an obsession with her to ensure that I lacked for nothing. She brought the house down when Dad decided not to send me to boarding school like the others, and it took me a whole week to convince her that I did not wish to go, mainly because I did not wish to be parted from her. When I told her this she hugged me and broke in a storm of tears, which was very, very unlike her. I felt sometimes that because she had allowed the accident to happen she felt she owed me. When she knew her end was near she looked at Leila and said: 'peace among bothers', then she called me and said:

'Tony, I leave this family in your charge because you are the strongest; great trouble will come but if you keep your head all will be well. Take care of your brothers, take care of Small and take care of yourself.'

I could not speak, just nodded, but I wondered even then why she had not spoken of Madonna…

I could not at that point fully understand the import of her words and thought perhaps her mind had been wandering a little? In any case I was inconsolable after she passed away. The sense of loss was overwhelming and I would not have weathered the storm without my brothers, especially Ronnie's vigilant care despite his own grief. Lena tried to speak to me once or twice, some rubbish about how she had been a second mother to me, but I lost patience after a while…second mother, indeed! If anyone was a second mother it was Leila and when she fell sick I realized what my mother had meant and decided that I would fight till the last to redeem my word to her.

This is why I am convinced that she put the idea of calling

in the soothsayer into my head by somehow making Lena suggest it. What I also found out at that point from Robin was that my mother had visited the Sadhu's ashram secretly after Ronnie's and Small's terrible ordeal and returned somewhat healed and stronger. Our father had no inkling of this because Robin had taken her secretly from our country home. Now in this critical time it seemed that she wanted us to take the same route and I was determined that nothing would stop me from making her wish come true.

That night I went up to the terrace after a long gap because I remembered Ronnie's words to me the night my mother passed away about stars actually being souls and the brightest being our Mother. That night I needed confirmation of this; I needed to communicate with her.

The night was starlit as there was only a crescent moon and they hung so low in the sky that I was almost able to reach out and touch them. Then the clouds floated away and they suddenly became even brighter and reminded of the song Leila and I always sang together, because it had been a great favorite of our mother's, and then Ronnie's:

'In the deep darkness of my silence,
My inability to communicate
Or express my thoughts,
Your feelings are like guiding stars that
Teach me what I want to say…'

And there it was, my mother was telling me to follow my instincts at all cost and not deviate from the path of truth out of fear.

Today when I look back, I am convinced that my mother had the gift of second sight, knew how I was different and had dealt with me accordingly. That she singled me out for this singular honor and that I was able to do my bit is proof of her trust and my greatest reward.

Strangely enough, I find that even my clever brothers, since the sage's visit, don't make a move without consulting me; perhaps they have come to the conclusion that the rough-hewn road is easier to navigate than the one complicated by too many moral twists and stiles? Well, they could certainly do worse…as the saying goes: better late than never!

MISTAKES: SMALL-SPEAK

I, Small, despite my vaunted wisdom, fell for Madonna's ploy and gave that letter to Leila, but I was completely dumbfounded by the outcome! Never in my wildest dreams could I have imagined that an innocent trick for a bit of fun as Madonna had described it, would almost kill Leila! What did that letter say? I should have read the letter of course, but childhood habits die hard, and my mother's admonitions about prying are still fresh in my mind. Obviously Madonna had not forgotten either, or she would not have trusted me to be errand boy. Ironic, how good only leads to bad! Ronnie said later that Leila was a bloody fool to trust Madonna, and I should have checked with him in the first place, but I know that Leila did not tell him the whole story, she could not bring herself to utter the abominations that letter contained, mainly because it had something to do with me? Why me?

When Leila suddenly fell sick and wanted to go back with her mother, I like everyone else, lost the ability to think and never made the vital connection with the letter, but I did notice that Madonna, when she thought she was alone, looked just like a cat with all four paws in a bowl of cream, and I began to wonder. It dawned on me that with Leila out of the way, she would have all of us exactly where she wanted, lord it over her brothers, their children, the entire household as a matter of fact. Millie and Rose would never be able to stand up to her and I did not count, naturally! But all my hindsight would have been useless if those kids had not found those burnt scraps of paper. Madonna was petrified initially, but since no one could take it further as the case was on everyone's mind and Leila refused to open her mouth, she recovered her aplomb pretty quickly. Tony proved the real hero of this story and ever since he decided to call in the soothsayer, Madonna lost her sleep completely. She also noticed that I noticed, tried to intimidate me, failed, and was at her wit's end. She reminded me at that stage of a hooded cobra, ever watchful, ready to strike down any one who came in her way.

The soothsayer came and went, Leila began to recover and Madonna knew her days in this household were numbered, but she still could not resist a final act of retribution.

That night I had gone out to confer with my friend. It was a dark, moonless night with a hint of storm in the air, clouds hanging menacing and low, unmoving, no hope of rain; the kind of night when cats hide for the electricity crackles in their coat. A night when shadows walk the earth and seek to establish primacy, a night of stifling closeness that does not allow one to breathe, a night when banished, lost souls come to life with an eerie sense of mastery.

I explained all this to my friend who understood perfectly as usual, whispered a severe caution saying I was in grave danger and should not expose myself, and I was just about to turn away and go inside when a great surge of desire overcame me and I felt that I just had to feel his presence within me; if only for a moment. I just could not explain it either to him or to myself, perhaps the witching night had something to do with it but against his wishes I climbed up and sought the finger. It hurt, as usual but it was delicious pain and I was poised on the pinnacle of release when a blow to my back impaled me on the tree, the finger cutting through my innards, the pain excruciating. As I faded into unconsciousness the image of Christ on the cross, carved in wood by Millie and hanging in her studio, stood out on my minds screen in bold relief.

I should not have lived, but the doctors said that the offending twig had bent back on itself against all laws of nature and saved my life. Instead of going through my kidney and spinal cord it had lodged itself in soft tissue. They called it a miracle and I agreed, but they did not know that it was a miracle wrought by my friend to give me back the gift of life. When I heard this, I decided to fight back and I survived, a second time.

Even if I had not seen the edge of Madonna's black shawl out of the corner of my eye that night, I would have known purely by elimination, for it could have been no one else; besides, the pallor of her face and the terror in her eyes confirmed the story. I also think that Leila knew and Millie had her suspicions as did Sheila, but my brothers were convinced it was an accident and in turn they convinced the police. In any case the manner of my impalement was embarrassing and would be difficult to explain rationally, so the family heaved a sigh of relief when the matter was dropped. I had recovered, was going home, and that is all they cared about. The extra heavy padlocks on the doors did not escape my notice on my return, neither did Robin's grim smile. There was to be no repetition.

Madonna had never thought that I would survive and

now that I was to return home, could stand it no more, all those eyes looking askance and quickly averted out of fear of detection. The police being called off was a great relief, but she always knew that no one had been taken in. She also knew the siege would never end for trust was irrevocably broken. Even her brothers, despite their best efforts at normalcy, were uncomfortable and no one objected when she offered to leave. She was brave to the last but the family was heart-broken, no one more than I, particularly when I remembered her endless care and affection after my first accident. She who had nursed me back to life had tried to take the same life? Why? Where had we all gone wrong?

23. Back to the Riddle

RONNIE-SPEAK

After the events of the last few years, I, Ronnie, have increasingly been teased by the riddle that was my father. Instead of falling back on genetic and social clichés as I tended to do earlier, I have tried to find a rational explanation for my father's life. That he was a very rational man and seldom acted on impulse alone had been clear throughout, but his choices and the reasons for those choices had blurred endings that refused to dovetail. Where did these contradictions have their roots?

For instance, his great independence of spirit and his anglophile ways, his respect and affection for my mother and continuous debauchery, his legendary generosity to his loyal servitors and harshness to the point of cruelty to those who dared to question his decrees, his complete devotion to his progeny but intolerance of their individuality were difficult to reconcile. How, and even more why, did he harbor these polarities within himself, and did he even recognize them? His ego compounded by his appetites was an enormous force he had to contend with, but set against that was his initial training in morality by a village schoolmaster father, who by all accounts was a saintly man well versed in the scriptures. After the village school and at his own insistence

Father had read five years in a government school beginning at the age of ten to pick up English and learn something of the world around him. Soon afterwards he had won a scholarship to read Political Science in a city college and then train in Law. His abilities had found him a place in the Judicial Service and he had risen steadily through the ranks to become one of the first Indian High Court Judges in India. His British Superiors, well aware of the value of his support, had wanted him on their side in the upcoming nationalist struggle and had put their stamp of approval on his career by knighting him. He had accepted gratefully, though his mother and our mother, inspired by Tagore and Sir Surendranath Banerjee, had staunchly stood up against it. I realize how difficult it must have been for Brown Sahibs like him to cope with the constant challenge of colonialism, its material pressures and blandishments, and the moral pressures of nationhood, for people looked to him for leadership in the political area too. I know, as it was pretty hard for all of us as well. It was not merely an intellectual or spiritual challenge but a problem of day-to-day living. Did he, for the want of a better option, train himself to believe like Bismarck, the Iron Chancellor of Germany, that 'wrong undertaken for the benefit of the State could only be right'? But he mostly read self instead of state for 'his State' was not actually his. And was this then a conscious shift of paradigm or a gradual slip? For me it was an investigation with interesting possibilities: how had western thought and philosophy impinged on a traditional Indian mind to create and resolve moral dichotomy? What authorities had he fallen back on in his dilemma? Where had selfhood, that convenient buzzword, begun and ended for him?

For many years we did not disturb his room but kept it

as it was, almost like a museum or memorial. Somehow it seemed sacrilegious to sleep in his bed, recline in his armchair or write at his escritoire. The garland on his massive portrait was changed every day and incense lit before it twice a day This routine was first disrupted when Leila fell sick for Madonna did not always remember, and then after the case it seemed rather pointless to resume. Finally, Tony said his girls were growing up and needed a room for their personal use and we suggested that he and Rose move in to Father's room and let the girls have their present one. Only Rose had the requisite insensitivity to atmosphere and consequent courage in the family to dare for she had never met him, and was quite delighted to have the best room in the house! Tony, who understood the strategy perfectly, grinned wryly and said:

'Sometimes a thick skin is not a bad thing, eh? My Rose has certainly taught me a thing or two about getting on in life. In any case, I never hero-worshipped the old blighter the way you and Bobby did, Ronnie; you see, I always saw through his poses, which is why he left me alone and never invited a showdown; it would have been too mortifying for him to know exactly what I thought of him. And now, I wonder how he will like my sleeping on his bed, that ugly canopied four-poster so intricately carved? I know he would prefer you to do the lying Ronnie, and I would throw it out now if I did not know that it is a priceless heirloom and won't go through the door! Look, you people had better move that portrait, that silly poem and all other memorabilia before I move in. I will only take on this terrible legacy if I can begin with a reasonably clean slate!'

Portrait and poem went to the library; clothes and linen were given to the poor, papers burnt after Bobby had glanced through them, and only a pile of books on his bedside table remained: The *Bhagvad Gita*, a King James Edition Bible, Freud's *Civilization and its Discontents*, the *Ramcharit Manas*, Tagore's *Gitanjali*, Gandhi's *My Experiments with Truth*, Kautilya's *Arthashastra* and Machiavelli's *The Prince*, all well-thumbed and obviously often revisited. Realizing that this collection had formed part of the core of his guiding principles, I took the books to my room. They would bear more detailed study.

LEILA RETHINKS

Madonna has broken silence after a year and invited Sheila and Sammy to visit her school and spend a few days on the estate. She said that Josh's son, Rob would also be home from college and the kids could have fun together, boating, fishing, and trekking in the hill. Although her words are characteristically laconic, the longing for her own family is quite clear and the children want to go tomorrow. We, the parents, have no problem but Small is making a huge fuss, saying they can only go if she goes with them. So I phoned Madonna and Josh's wife Bunny, who took the call, invited Small most warmly on the spot, saying they would love to have her. She then transferred the line to Madonna and greeted her with the fait accompli; Madonna had no alternative but to agree, but did so with very bad grace, I knew her too well not to catch the sourness in her voice as she said, though apparently in jest:

'So, no one trusts me anymore, not even you, Leila?'

But with Bunny around she could not say too much and had to give in.

Truth to tell, I had felt bad about Madonna's exile even though she had brought it on herself, and this seemed like an ideal opportunity to reestablish contact. Other family members were, however, less enthusiastic and Tony said in his usual round fashion:

'Really Leila, you are a fool to beat all fools. You really want a rapprochement after all the misery she put you through? What are you made of, woman?'

I could not explain my growing conviction that there was deep down in Madonna's heart a well of sorrow, of deep disappointment, of self-recrimination that made her strike out at people, even those she loved, as though their misery would in some measure compensate for her own. I also believed that though the death of Sunny and Joy constituted a large part of this unhappiness, they were not the whole story. She needed to talk, she needed to confess and be granted absolution. But she would not open up to anyone. Perhaps the sight of the children in the territory where she had sustained her greatest loss would help to loosen her heartstrings?

So I told Tony that he was becoming a real tyrant and that he should not rob the children of a wonderful holiday just because of his own fears, and fortunately Bobby and Small backed me up. In the end it was decided that the threesome would go by car and Robin would drive them there and bring them back; Tony insisted on that, saying these children needed a strong hand as they were too gullible like their foolish parents; besides, Robin needed a break after Lena's passing.

Increasingly, Tony is setting himself up as the head of the family and strangely enough, none of us likes to cross him.

SHEILA TELLS A STORY

We have to admit that Aunt Madonna has done an impressive job with the school and even though the students are officially on holiday, they are constantly in the premises, working on various projects. The latest for the older boys is a hatchery for which a small pond has been earmarked. The students will drain, dredge, deepen the pool, plant rushes and other eco-friendly plants that will invite and feed edible worms and maggots, various microorganisms that form fish-food, and finally re-fill the pool. Then the enclosures for the young fish, made of bamboo paling and polythene netting, will be constructed and installed by the students. After this they will stock the pool with baby fish or fry and when these begin to mature they will be transferred to bigger ponds and lakes. Uncle Josh is delighted to see us and says:

'For a "city girl", your Aunt Madonna is amazingly at home in the country, Sheila; she has the gift of not only teaching the kids but enthusing them by putting some money in their pockets. We should have thought of this a long time ago.'

We spend most of the day on the lake boating and fishing, and during the evenings we eat crisply fried fish. Rob is a city kid like us and is enjoying this break as a welcome change. We go for long walks and trek in the hills, but always accompanied by members of the estate personnel; no one talks about it but no one forgets for a moment, how tragically Joy and his father had died in the treacherous quicksand. At Small's desire to pay her respects we visit the place only to find that the access to the patch has been sealed off with a heavy cordon of posts and chains, which makes it all the more ominous. Small sits down on the grass and closes her eyes, while we look around trying to reconstruct the scene. Both of us remember Uncle Sunny as a wise, kind and fun person who loved children. We always had a great time when they visited, even though Aunt Madonna had been very possessive about Uncle Sunny and Joy. He was very athletic and so was Joy, excellent swimmers both of them, and even at the time it had seemed strange that they should drown so helplessly; and now that the place is before our eyes, it appears more unlikely than ever. They knew about the quicksand, so how did it happen? It seems that the shadow never lifts completely and Uncle Josh and Rob are still caught in its meshes. If only Aunt Madonna, the sole witness, could remember something.

Finally Small opens her eyes with a strange expression on her face, and says very quietly to Uncle Josh: 'Thank you for giving me this opportunity to commune with Sunny; he was always very kind to me and, and I loved Joy just like the others. I am glad father and son went together, for neither could have lived without the other.'

She says no more and we all walk back silently, but Small keeps glancing back and continues to look as though she has seen a ghost.

While it is obvious that Aunt Madonna is delighted to

have us here and does everything in her power to indulge and spoil us, it is obvious that she is not completely at ease with us, particularly Small. Uncle Josh and Aunt Bunny are much more like family, taking care of us and making sure we have a good time, but putting Rob and the two of us firmly in our place if we transgress, particularly in matters of safety. They sit and chat for hours with Small about the old times, Uncle Sunny and Joy, obviously delighted that someone remembers them with the same affection and fidelity as they do. Aunt Madonna is never part of this circle, saying she cannot bear to think about the tragedy, much less talk about the people concerned, but she keeps us under constant surveillance trying to eavesdrop whenever possible. She reminds me of a nervy cat, ever watchful, swishing its tail, on the lookout for a storm or an ambush. What is she afraid of?

Rob is very keen on a moonlight picnic on the lake and begs Uncle Josh to allow the three of us, just for one night. The moonlight here is nothing like it is in the city, blurred by smoke and dust; here the moon shines like a halo of pure light in the velvet sky and gains radiance with its light reflecting on myriad bodies of water. The effect on the main lake is pure magic with the tracery of the newly planted trees creating delicate images in the water: Merlin's castles, caves, creatures, and solid blocks of darkness like gothic mansions housing demons, made by the boles of ancient trees. We have been enchanted by this view from the banks and feel that a night out in this magic world would be an unforgettable experience. Rob has never been allowed, but now that we are here, surely we can all go.

Aunt Madonna is on our side, lends us unstinting support, and in the end Uncle Josh gives in, but insists that we take the big boat and that two of the boatmen come along, they will handle the boat but stay out of our way. At the last minute however, Robin comes to know of our plans and puts his foot down: either we take him along or we don't go at all. We know Robin too well to argue and Aunty Bunny is delighted at his insistence! However, we know that Robin is good fun on the whole if we obey him and since he is coming along we are allowed to make a day and night trip! So it is in high spirits that we sally forth on our great adventure early in the morning of the night when the moon is to be full.

The boat is really large, actually a houseboat, and Aunt Madonna has told us that she had made her first journey as a bride to the estate in this boat for there had not been motorable roads at that time. The decks are spacious enough for table tennis and quoits and the suites are opulent, even luxurious. There appears to be an inexhaustible supply of good food freshly cooked on the boat and the day flies by in a whirl of activity and eating! We are not allowed to swim in the lake but the pool on the boat is sparkling blue, good enough for us and we are in and out of it all day. Before we know the day is gone, evening is upon us, the sun is setting and a chilly breeze has come up. Robin says:

'You came for the moon, right? Now get ready to greet it on arrival.'

Wrapped in shawls, sprawling in deck chairs, deliciously tired after the long day, I am almost asleep when Rob whispers: 'Look' and I open my eyes to a magically transformed world where 'nothing is but what is not'. And Sammy, the unromantic, practical, irrepressible Sammy, misquotes almost involuntarily:

'The moon on the hill forgot to die,
The lily revived and the dragonfly
Came back to dream on the river.'

He takes the cover off his guitar and begins to strum and Rob and I hum and sing louder and louder, while Robin keeps time on an upturned pail; gradually the boatmen below join in with metal on metal surfaces.

A rare moment of togetherness encapsulated in time.

They had cut the engine some time ago and allowed the boat to drift using an occasional oar to keep her on course, but in the last hour the slap of the oar against the water had been missing and the boat had floated downstream at its own will almost to the middle of the lake. The water here was molten silver, shadows like charcoal paintings and the sleepy choir of bird calls the only matching music. We wound down involuntarily for it seemed to all of us that we should just look, listen and absorb quietly, as such enchantment would not come our way again in a hurry. Only the calls of sleepy nightjars broke the silence and the gentle lapping of the water against the sides of the boat; I felt as though a stage had been set and a spell had been cast and we, without volition, were playing a part assigned to us. No one wanted to break this spell, now or ever.

It takes a bump that goes shuddering through the boat to jerk us out of our stupor and Robin is on his feet shouting to the boatmen, saying we have run aground and that they should start the engines and pull the boat out. I think we all realize simultaneously that we have hit the patch of quicksand for the chains and posts are clearly visible on the bank, and the sheer panic that overtakes us is clearly reflected on every face, even Robin's. All the stories and movies about boat and ship skeletons being discovered years after they had sunk in treacherous sands race through our minds, clear graphics reducing us to jelly. Robin is the first to recover and even as he is turning to go down to the engine room, we all freeze in our tracks. A figure is rising out of the water, a hooded, mantled figure waving its arms, not breaking the surface but sort of floating, it appears to be warning us to go no further, very vehemently, then its gestures change and it seems it is trying to tell us how to extricate ourselves. Although many of his gestures are meaningless to us, Robin and specially the boatmen seem to understand perfectly and soon we hear both the engines start with a roar and begin to accelerate while gears reverse furiously. For a while nothing happens, no movement, only the powerful engines screaming their lungs out manically, and just as the hope that had surged in our breasts is subsiding in sickening disappointment, the big boat pulls itself free with a great sucking sound and we are afloat once more. The figure is still there telling us to go back in a more easterly direction, but as the boat rights itself and begins to move away on the designated path, the figure disappears as suddenly as it had come. For many moments we are too shaky to speak, then Robin remarks, trying to restore common sense:

'You kids know what that was? Can you see that big tree, its branches swaying in the wind? At the angle we were stuck in, the moonlight made the shadows of those two branches appear like a figure with waving arms, but now that we have moved away, it is no longer visible. It definitely was a great coincidence that probably saved our lives, but a coincidence after all, so stop looking as though you have seen a spirit!'

Rob objects: 'But the figure came out of the water, not from above.'

Sammy joins him: 'Yes Robin, we all saw him rising out of the water, didn't you?

Robin says: 'A trick of the light, boys. Don't you know that moonlight plays strange tricks on the imagination?'

I break in:

'Tell me Robin, if it was merely a shadow, why did its movements change to suit our requirements? That figure told you guys what to do, right? And all of you did his bidding without demur or hesitating even once, tell me why?'

Robin is saved the embarrassment of trying to find a plausible explanation by one of the boatmen, who has come up. Refuting Robin, he says with calm certainty:

'No, Robin Sir that was our Sunny Sahib who came to our rescue. He has been seen here before by people in danger and tonight he came to save his own.'

He has articulated our confused thoughts and Rob is now weeping openly, it is clear that he believes every word, and somehow this explanation seems more credible to us too, even Robin who has been fighting the idea steadily so far looks convinced. Why?

As many have said:

There is no absolute truth or falsehood but thinking makes it so and a miracle is an act that creates faith.

In the end we decide to cut our trip short and go home.

At home, comforted by the blazing fire, Rob and Robin tell the story. The family has no doubts at all and is abjectly grateful for the timely appearance, which they seem to take almost for granted. Aunt Bunny speaks quite simply:

'Sunny just had to come, not one but six lives were at stake and three of them his own children; he could not stay away under any circumstance.'

Uncle Josh agrees:

'Whether Sunny is physically with us or not makes no difference, his vigilance and concern remain unchanged. I would have been surprised if this incident had not taken place.'

He looks at us closely, perhaps finds some of our expressions slightly skeptic, and says with greater assurance

'We have had many proofs of this; if you don't believe me, ask Madonna.'

Aunt Madonna does not speak, so Rob enlightens us:

'Aunt Madonna almost stepped on a scorpion in the bathroom, whose bite could have proved lethal, but she felt someone push her away with such great force that she fell five feet away and the scorpion escaped. Of course later she denied this and said that she herself had moved away, but the first version is what she told Mama when she found Aunt cowering and weeping hysterically in a corner of the bathroom.'

Aunt Madonna still does not react but when Small says:

'I am not surprised either; I felt a very strong sense of Sunny's presence under the tree by the lake the other day.'

Aunt Madonna can no longer contain her anger and lashes out at her furiously:

'Don't talk like an idiot, Small! What do you know about it? This family is obsessed with Sunny and sees his shadow everywhere; he may be dead, but we are never free of his or Joy's presence, not for a moment. I have tried to fight this phobia tooth and nail, but failed. Now you, an outsider, are adding fuel to the fire, why? You know jolly well that what you say is impossible, the dead are dead, and they do not, cannot come back and creep around as shadows.'

She breaks off, bosom heaving with passion…

I cannot help coming to Small's rescue for she is more embarrassed on Aunt Madonna's behalf for her unwarranted outbreak before the family, than for herself:

'I am sorry Aunt Madonna, but what happened tonight cannot be ignored. In a few hours you people would have been organizing search parties who would never have found us, just as they never found Uncle Sunny and Joy, have you realized that? You have lost more than anyone else to those terrible sands, aren't you happy and grateful that there has been no repetition? As for Small, you know very well she is psychic, and that she does not know how to lie, so if she says she felt his presence, it has to be true.'

But she is too incensed to listen to reason, and forgetting her customary caution continues to rail:

'You know why I was so keen on letting you kids go on this trip? Because I thought that you would come back and tell these benighted people that there is nothing mysterious or occult about the place, that the lake is only a lake, the trees only trees, the shadows natural phenomena. But no! You had to come back with this bizarre story that only strengthens these crazy ideas. Are you sure you are not making the whole thing up just to make my life difficult? After all, I have to live here.'

For the first time Uncle Josh interjects:

'Why should these stories as you call them disturb you so much Madonna? Aren't you happy to believe that Sunny and Joy have not left us, but are around to help us, even protect us? It's merely a leap of faith that you have to make, and I would think you more than anyone else would want to make it for your own sanity. Instead you want to disprove it, push your loved ones away. Why would you who loved them most, want to do that?

Here Sammy breaks in:

'Why don't you ask Robin if you think we are making up stories? He is practical, not obsessed like the rest of us and he will tell you the unvarnished truth.'

The acid in his voice does not escape our Aunt but she turns to Robin with faint hope; however, Robin seems to have made up his mind and speaks out clearly:

'I too tried to believe that it was a mere coincidence, mulled over the sequence of events in my mind several times, but found in the end that there were too many discrepancies, too much that could not be explained rationally. I don't know who or what saved us, but the incident that took place tonight was nothing short of a miracle.'

I will never forget Aunt Madonna's ashen face as she stared at him and then at all of us by turns. The hunted look in her eyes was particularly disturbing. Somehow we, her own family, had let her down, and she would never forgive us this infidelity.

But who or what was she running from? Having failed to free herself from the toils of memory by her own efforts, had she looked to her own family to demystify the situation by scoffing at the mystic experience? Had she hoped that our failure to believe would make a dent in the family's faith and thus help her to escape the shadows of the past? But what were these memories that she so desperately wanted to devalue or escape from? Was it guilt of some sort that was driving her? Or was she too strong to take refuge in what was essentially irrational, an emotional crutch, and truly wanted to brush away the cobwebs of the occult?

Out of nowhere a line of poetry written by a very sad man flashed through my mind:

'Each man kills the thing he loves…. the coward with a kiss, and the brave man with a sword…'

We leave three days later but not before Small has made Uncle Josh and Aunt Bunny promise to visit us along with Rob. Aunt Madonna is distant, even cold and says little by way of farewell or future plans, but when I give her a bear hug before leaving, she clings to me wordlessly. As for Rob, he has become a life-long friend, as people who have held hands and stared death in the face together cannot be anything else.

24. Riddle Unraveled?

RONNIE-SPEAK

I went through all the books on my father's table and found that the *Arthashastra* by Kautilya had been visited most often and the pages that dealt with the neutralization of enemies or opponents had been assiduously perused; hardly surprising in view of his real-politicking ways and practices in manipulation, but what was interesting was how he had used and adapted the four basic principles of Saam, Daan, Danda and Bhed to his own needs, to extricate himself from difficult situations that had been mainly created by him in the first place. It would be no exaggeration to say that his philosophy of life had been culled mainly from these principles.

Saam, the lure of equality and wealth; Daan, generosity and largesse; Danda, punishment; and Bhed, creating a rift among enemies and sometimes friends, were all measures meant to ensure the survival of oneself.

At first reading the utility of these measures appeared to be fairly obvious and that even people with devious common sense who have not had occasion to commune with Kautilya's great mind, have successfully used these principles in both matters of family and statecraft. His European counterpart, Machiavelli, had advised the Heads of State many centuries later to use similar strategies in order to attain complete power. I now wondered very much whether the colonial British had not taken several pages out of this book to aid their understanding of the Indian character and then used these very principles to divide and rule the Jewel in the Crown successfully for a century. And when they finally withdrew, they left a permanent thorn in the heart of the sub-continent with the Partition, the apotheosis of Bhed.

However, on matching our father's actions with the finer points of these axioms I became aware that he had studied the implications thoroughly and fine-tuned the system till it had come to comprise the core of his power. Then I took it a step farther and an ugly possibility became sickeningly clear: The efficacy of these measures and the success they brought him in his professional life had gone to his head and he had begun to use the same methods with his family members not only on the occasion mentioned by him in his confessional but on a regular basis, and long before his own great trial began.

That he had been outstandingly successful in material terms could not be denied by even his worst enemy. Although his forebears had been substantial landowners or Zamindars, the family fortunes had steadily declined due to too great a penchant for wine, women and song. His grandfather had found himself with a few acres of land, a big unwieldy house and very few skills of survival. His wife, however, was very thrifty and had the gift of making a little go a long way. She also came from a family of humble Babus or clerks who had been working for British 'Factors' for the last three generations. They had been forced into this service because they had no assets to speak of except for very sharp brains, which had enabled them to learn the foreigner's tongue with remarkable speed. Rising from humble, almost menial origins they had, in the second generation, become indispensable to their masters, who were busy emulating the Zamindars with whom they consorted. By the third generation they had amassed a private fortune almost equal to their masters but they continued to maintain a low profile and work hard.

None of this had escaped the astute lady and when she found her husband deep in debt that would only be redeemed by selling the ancestral home she made a bargain with him. She would ask her father to lend them the requisite sum of money provided he would agree to send her sons to her father's house to be educated. It went against the grain terribly to be indebted to his socially inferior in-laws and send away his sons to them, but he did not have an alternative. And that is how the family remained solvent and the two sons wound up as a schoolmaster and a pleader in the lower courts, respectively.

However, all this was a far cry from the phenomenal success that had been my father, his name almost a household word in colonial India, and undoubtedly most of it had been of his own making; if others had taken a hand, he had conveniently ignored the contribution. He knew all about and was an adept at image building, his own and others.

As though on cue, a sequence of events passes before my eyes like a montage:

There is a banquet in the house, the list of guests reads like the who's who of the country, the long drive up to the house has been freshly graveled in red, and the trees cast graceful shadows on the lawn, that gleams like a jewel in the light of the declining sun. On tables with gleaming white napery and cut glass is laid out an array of drinks, cocktails and wines that would do credit to a royal cellar. The cars and carriages drive up one by one and stop by the lawn where our father, tall and handsome, stands dressed impeccably in western clothes with our beautiful mother by his side in a simple but elegant sari, welcoming the distinguished guests. These guests are mainly British and they are quite delighted by the western correctness of the occasion. They are particularly impressed by the lawn and Lord L _____ tells the Judge that his piece of green matches 'the best lawns of the British Isles', whereupon our mother reminds Lord L _____ in her gentle way that 'Bengal Dube' (grass) is after all the best lawn cover in the world and is used now widely in England, and he, realizing the truth of her statement, agrees sheepishly!

After the wine and cocktails, the Sahibs are perhaps expecting a sumptuous western meal, but what greets their startled eyes quite takes their breath away. Long, polished mahogany tables have been laid out with silver utensils and black stoneware in the traditional Indian style: One salver, six bowls, one glass for water and one for sherbet, a finger bowl and a set of napkins for each guest, set out alternately, the color contrast is unique and invites much appreciation. There is an array of cutlery available, but the message is clear: In India, eat like an Indian. The food too, when it arrives, is Indian cuisine at its best, and the Sahibs, mellowed by the cocktails, fall to with a will. They prove pretty deft with their fingers, the cutlery lies untouched and the food disappears fast.

Lord L _____ particularly thanks his charming Hostess for an 'unforgettable experience', before he leaves and quoting Kipling he says:

'In your care "the twain" met so effortlessly, why can't we all master the art? You should start a school Lady------.'

But it is our father who responds, saying he is 'overwhelmed by Lord L------'s graciousness in appreciating their ideas...'

Our mother's smile never slipped for this was customary: our father, turning his wife's unique brand of nationalism and immaculate taste quietly to his own best possible advantage, and then claiming the entire operation as his own!

One area where he had failed signally though was with Bobby and me; despite his best efforts to divide us, he had not succeeded, and his Kautilyan strategies had been of little avail. Why had he invariably pitted us against each other rather than encourage togetherness as our mother always had done? Perhaps he had not wanted us to equal him in any way? Or had he wanted to put us in molds of his own choice to prove that he could control nature and human uniqueness? Unfortunately for him, our mother's indefatigable emphasis on thinking for ourselves and principle of 'peace among brothers' her last words to Leila, and our own predilections had proved stronger, and he had finally been defeated by our gentle but iron-willed mother. Had this humiliation impelled him to go out on a limb, as he never had before?

I had not tumbled to the truth about Tony's parentage till I had caught his reflection in the mirror one day when he was standing behind me smiling. It was the smile that did it and for a moment it was Lena and not Tony smiling and staring at me. The shock was so great that I almost gave myself away, but the thought uppermost in my mind was: 'Tony must never know, it will kill him if he finds out.'

So I got up, punched him in the stomach and told him

not to creep up on me like an evil spirit and frighten the daylights out of me!

He punched me back amicably and we sparred for a bit, then he said he needed some help with a business matter, and if 'I could bear to tear myself away from my books for a moment it would help.' In his usual sarcastic way, and that was that. But I could not sleep for days afterwards and finally Bobby and I made a pact that if the matter ever came out, we would fight it tooth and nail as mere idle and malicious gossip. Fortunately it never did and we accepted the matter as one of our progenitor's more vicious peccadilloes. But I now wonder whether this had been meant as a deliberate challenge to Mother, to test her fortitude and bring her to her knees? If so, he had failed signally, for if anything, she had been fonder of Tony than us. Later with both our parents passing away and more recently, Lena dead, the possibility of discovery appeared remote and we stopped thinking about it. But I suddenly find myself wondering today whether this too had been one of his many stratagems? He was too old a hand at the game of fornication to have fathered a child inadvertently, so it must have been a deliberate act. But why; why would he give a hostage to fortune by fathering an illegitimate child and that too under his own roof? Was this an exercise in Bhed that might weaken our Mother and lead to a rift between brothers?

Hailing as our mother had done from a family of intellectuals and patriots, her father a national hero whose speech in the British Parliament had become legendary as much for its courage as caustic wit, her uncle an author whose songs and plays were a constant thorn in the side of the British, a brother-in-law who was a barrister and indefatigably fought every nationalist case, it obviously had not been easy to adjust in an environment as determinedly anglophile as the judge had created, and it had gone terribly against the grain when the judge had ruthlessly sentenced mere boys to life imprisonment or worse for acts of terrorism, that to her had been nothing more than courageous bids for national freedom. She may never have survived had it not been for her mother-in-law, who had taught her the arts of subversive moral warfare. Lessons once learned, she had never looked back and the judge had been stuck with the gentlest but most determined antagonist in his own backyard!

It must have irked him terribly at times to be married to someone who was as determinedly spiritual as he was materialistic. Her logic had been simple:

'We must distinguish between I and the eye. If we keep our eye on I it will never spin out of control. Where and how we locate that I is what makes us who we are, unique and individual. Therefore, to walk the straight and narrow is the only way to strengthen and make the I survive, to avoid sleepless nights, to live with oneself. So I do it entirely as a matter of policy, rather than adherence to rectitude or consciousness of virtue.'

She dinned this logic into us with countless stories, poems, jingles and example till it became second nature to us, and the most confirmed disciple had been Tony, for he was crazy about her and never had much time for his progenitor. He had also been more outspoken than the rest of us, and in time, the judge had often winced at his trenchant remarks, usually prefaced with:

'Father, you know what Mum would say to that. She would never agree to an untruth and neither will I.'

The son she had never borne had become her greatest admirer and champion, and I can now imagine the frustration and sheer rage our father must have felt at all his calculations going awry and the tool of Bhed turning into an instrument of retribution for him. Our Mother, by never faltering in her love for Tony, had turned the tables on him with what appeared to be her usual acumen and aplomb, but I realized now that she had not consciously strategized, but merely done what her instincts had told her to do.

Poor Madonna had not been so fortunate, and because she worshipped him it was easier to manipulate her. Very beautiful, a near perfect face and body, the mirror had been her constant companion since the age of three and, our mother noting this with alarm, had tried very hard to move her away from the looking glass and get her interested in books and sport. And Madonna had complied readily, been a star student and head girl in school, but every visitor to the house, all our relatives and we too had conspired against her by expressing frequent and unadulterated admiration. Despite this, however, and very strangely, vanity never touched her to begin with. If she had looked at the mirror, it was because she was fascinated by the perfection of the image that looked back at her as one might be by a painting. Given an opportunity with our mother, she would have come to terms with her own beauty, accepted it humbly as a gift from God and learned to handle the admiration. But this battle was one our mother lost perhaps because of Small. So complete had been her absorption in the unfortunate child that she had practically turned a blind eye to the pressures her other, more fortunate daughter was facing. And noting the dichotomy between the Eye and the I, our father had seized the opportunity and deliberately encouraged the rift till it had split her personality; and this division, I fear, persists till date. There had ultimately been and are two Madonnas, the original, and the one our father created and nurtured so carefully, entirely for what he imagined would be his own benefit.

Bhed was to be the agent and the object. So we thought then, but we were to find out much later that our Mother had actually tried very hard and this by Madonna's own admission, but it was an unequal battle that she had lost due to reasons that we had no idea of. When one is in the thick of things, one does not notice other people too much, and after my brush with the nationalists I had taken a while to lick my wounds. Bobby and Madonna had stood by me and done their best and I was grateful for their help and support, but later, looking back, I had realized that Madonna had been changing during that period, albeit very subtly, and her attentions to me were somehow different, more personal, even beseeching. It had made me uncomfortable and I had shied away from her advances, causing her considerable hurt as she told me very angrily. But I did not want to be her special friend and share her secrets. I had troubles enough of my own and lacked the resolve to fight her battles for her, especially as our Father appeared to be the chief opponent. I think she went through a similar experience with Dave, who also moved away in discomfort and fear. For my part, I had clung to Bob and that bond has never faltered till date, thank God, and Tony's advent had only strengthened it. None of us had realized that she was desperately seeking our support in her one bid for happiness by trying to cross an impassable barrier. After a couple of years matters seemed to normalize and we had gone back to an amicable relationship, but not like the old days, if anything, the rift had widened under the papered surface. Somewhere along the line, both Dave and I had failed her when she had been crying out for help and it was as though a part of her soul had died during that time and she had hardened in to a new shell. I have often wondered to myself in later years whether this was the reason for Madonna's dislike of Leila. She certainly was not happy with the way the whole family had welcomed Leila, including my parents, and Leila had not improved matters by winning every heart including Small's, the confirmed loner, whose only confidante up to this point had been her Madonna.

Yet, even if we had tumbled to the truth at that point, what could we have done to help her? The choices were impossible. In retrospect it seems that she was 'born to endless night' under an evil star, and the circumstances in which she had found herself more than once had relentlessly pushed towards further darkness.

Had our father realized that Danda or punishment meant for his opponents would boomerang so severely on his own progeny and himself? And if he had, would it have made a difference to his course of action in the long run? It seemed Saam and Daan too had failed him in the end, because even with a lifetime of camaraderie and the biggest bribe, he had not been able to persuade Robin's father to implicate us in his second fracas, nor had he agreed to orchestrate the attack on the Wilsons. How did a man like him with no apparent moral code acquire this sense of right when the great Judge had failed so signally? Was it because he had less to lose, or was in the end more rooted in his own ethos and fear of God than his Machiavellian Master? Or was it a case of affection and gratitude, pure and simple? We found out later that Mrs. Wilson had met him several times in the course of her walks and given him valuable advice on various health issues, particularly sex-related ones, and he had benefited greatly. Also that she had never divulged the facts, even to her husband. Robin found out at his father's deathbed but never told us because he did not want to hurt our feelings. How did father and son get to be such moral giants, towering over their venerable master at whose feet they had worshipped all their lives?

25. Roots of the Poison Tree

MADONNA-SPEAK

The children and Robin left a week ago, clearly convinced that Sunny had saved them that terrible night, and their attitude to me since that incident had been distinctly cool, though Sheila hugged me fiercely before she left. But they have been very warm with the rest of the family, who have reciprocated in kind. As a matter of fact, Josh, Bunny and Rob are planning a trip to my home quite soon, but have not mustered up courage to ask me whether I will accompany them. Of course I can't, and the family I once called my own seems permanently lost to me too. How did I get to this point? None of my other siblings seem to have lost out totally as I have, even though their trials and tribulations have been no less, whether it is Small, Ronny, Tony or even Bobby? What is this fatal flaw that sets me apart and is it entirely of my own making?

My story cannot be told while I live, for I cannot face the consternation, realization, efforts at understanding and reconciliation that will inevitably follow; quite frankly, I cannot bear any one pitying me, nor can I go back to the people I once called my own, for the thread is broken and cannot be reconstituted. My expiation must be among strangers and I am grateful to Josh and Bunny for giving me the opportunity. But the story, for whatever it is worth, must be told so that Small, Leila, Ronnie, the people I hurt the most, and the others too, might have some inkling of my actions.

My childhood had been quite idyllic in our beautiful old house and the garden with its whispering trees, rolling lawns, rainbow flowers and the mysterious serpentine meandering among the willows. It had been pretty much my mother's domain, for she loved plants and had an understanding of their needs that was almost intuitive. She had a passion for the rare and the exotic, but the humble hibiscus, jasmine, oleander and periwinkle were allowed to rub shoulders with English annuals, a huge variety of roses, rare cacti, succulents and rock plants. Her almost proverbial green fingers and their creations very clearly reflected her personal philosophy: 'To walk with kings yet not lose the common touch.' Kipling wrote the line but she lived the principle. Her team of six gardeners adored her and took enormous pride in the garden, for she made them feel that it was their territory first, and then the family's. We children were routinely ordered off the lawns by Gulab, the head mali, who allowed us to jump on the mounds of fragrant grass after mowing the lawns, but not on the lawns themselves; said he had not created these spaces of parrot wing greenery for pesky children to run amok; and in any case, the Flower Show was round the corner.

The British had brought their own proud gardening tradition with them, a bit of magic that all Europe had sought to emulate, including the unfortunate French Queen, Marie Antoinette. On their arrival in India they had been greeted by the breath-taking spectacle of the Mughal gardens, the Nishat Baghs and the Chashme-Shahis, and out of this encounter had grown the English Indian garden, the first of which became the hub of Lutyen's Delhi, which is at present part of the President's residence, so not readily visible to the public. Along with William Mustoe, who planted the trees, they created a blend of the Mughal and the Victorian garden aesthetic that became unique to India, as the British in India enthusiastically adopted this model. Small or large, all gardens worth the name sported a patch of water, lawns, mixed borders, rosaries, parterres, seasonal flowers, annuals, biennials, perennials, and rockeries, and into this framework the homesick Englishwoman poured her passion and ingenuity, and her genius found free play. Stories are legion of mad memsahibs falling ill with heatstroke, weeding their lawns in the scorching midday sun, but they came up with creations that were nothing short of extraordinary, and the apotheosis of these efforts as well as their testing ground was the annual Flower Show in the capital, the provincial headquarters, the smallest town where there was a British presence. Gardens were entered under different categories as was garden produce, flowers, fruits and vegetables, and as judgment day neared, expectations rose to a hysterical pitch. The highest and the most coveted rewards were the special prizes awarded for ingenuity and creativity by the Chief Justice and Magistrate and these routinely went to the British, for there was little competition, but the winners of prizes for the largest cabbages, cauliflowers and potatoes were invariably Indian, giving rise to much jubilation in one camp but also snide comments in the other:

'Typical Indian mentality...quantity before quality... large is beautiful...!'

But our Mother penetrated the British bastion very successfully; her roses and orchids won her the most coveted prizes and cost her competitors many sleepless nights. She had a prize collection of succulents, less known than now, that she collected avidly and with discernment, and flowering plants and variegated foliage that grew wild in the mountains of India began to find their way into the plains. On her travels when India's elite moved to hill stations, during family holidays and during shikar, she was always on the lookout for exotic plants – and the baskets in which she carried rich gardening soil to place them, always came back bulging with spoils of war. Some took immediately; a few died, but most survived an initial period of shock under her care and then thrived in the thatched greenhouses that she designed, for she recreated with cooling systems of her own invention, their natural environment – as far as possible. These artistic greenhouses covered with flowering creepers were the biggest draw for visitors in a garden that was pretty spectacular in any case. In the end another category was added to the Flower Show itinerary, that of Flowering Succulents and Mountain Plants, and created a rush to the mountains of the mad memsahibs on collecting sprees.

Later she went to a judicial conference with her husband to Jaipur in Rajasthan, and while he and other eminent jurists put their heads together over the amendment of the Penal Code for a Free India, she went traveling on camel back with Robin's father and found the Yucca in its many varieties growing wild in the desert. These plants, growing to a height of fifty feet and more, covered with waxy bell-shaped white and pastel-colored blossoms from base to tip, took her breath away and launched her on her most ambitious gardening project. She brought back as many specimens as she could find in baskets of sandy soil and on her return had the sunken rose garden dug up, placed the roses in another rosary and used the pit in the sunniest spot in her property for a desert garden. Filled with sand and loam, watered very judiciously by pipes laid beneath the surface of the soil, she managed to recreate the natural habitat of the Yucca, and they repaid her efforts handsomely by growing and flowering as though in their own home, interspersed with desert cacti that had blooms of the more vibrant colors of red, yellow and orange; it brought to mind the original Eden, complete with snakes, for they loved the area, compelling our mother and gardeners to walk around in gumboots in the driest season!

As usual, our father gave her free rein for it brought him vicarious distinction, but also because I think now, he thought that it gave her a harmless outlet for her creative energies that could be dangerous if channelized along different lines. I always accompanied our mother to the Flower Shows and received the prizes on her behalf, and the ripple of comment that ran through the gathering, comparing me favorably with the blooms all around, was very complimentary and gratifying. Indeed, this is how Sunny's family got to hear of me in the first place.

But alas, we could not hold on to our childhood indefinitely, I had to leave home and almost inevitably our mother's gardening mantle fell on Leila's shoulders, who made the territory her own from the day she arrived in the house. Her father was a passionate gardener and had passed on his love of plants and all living beings to her. Whereas Millie had always preferred the shadowy world of her own imagination to living things, Leila proved an apt disciple, meticulously followed our mother's advice and became a great favorite with the gardeners. It gave our mother great pleasure in her last days to know that she was leaving her treasured creation to a worthy successor.

However, I did not approve even though it kept Leila from scrutinizing household matters too closely when I returned to live here again, thus giving me freer rein, mainly because it forged another bond between Leila and Ronnie and made my task more difficult than ever. But why did I set myself this task in the first place? Leila was the only one who had loved me genuinely, respected me as an older sister, deferred to me constantly when I came back so that I should feel wanted; her children had done the same to begin with and she had compelled Rose and Small to follow in her footsteps. Millie knew me too well, was her usual, inscrutable, ironic self and I was careful not to cross her path too often, but the boys, Timmy and Sammy, never took to me, and gradually I think Sheila began to fall under Sammy's influence. My brothers were uniformly courteous, careful to make my stay pleasant by reiterating often how happy they were to have me back, but in the end, distant, for they were the centers of their own stories now, quite comfortable sharing their brotherhood, being husbands, fathers and uncles. They did not particularly want to make too much room for an alien who had returned unaccountably. Good sense dictated that I cling to Leila and so find my way back to Ronnie's heart, but the thought was too demeaning, it would leave Leila even more secure, one more scalp on her belt. No, she had to suffer, or better still go permanently, like Joy, only then would I be able to secure my rightful place in this household, replace Leila with

Madonna – that was the plan. It would have worked with Joy except that luck had been against me, but this time there would be no mistakes.

Superficially, Leila and I had many similarities with respect to our good looks, intelligence, tact, social skills, and there was no apparent reason for common jealousy or envy; as a matter of fact, we should have been good friends, then what was it that repelled me and made me feel inadequate? Was it that I still wanted primacy with Ronnie as I had in my childhood and later with Sunny? But not really; in any case there was no guarantee that he would put me first if Leila were no more. He was very close to all the kids in the house and his brothers and I did not really figure that much, then why?

One day I was standing in front of the large mirror in my room doing my hair when Leila came in, told me to hurry up for we were all required in the living room for a family photograph. This was done every three years and went up on the wall, 'another piece of dubious history permanently trapped' as Timmy would say. Leila came and put her arms around me, her face over my shoulder, and for a moment we stared at our faces, near-perfect, next to each other, and I found my face, almost without volition, changing its sour lines to a warm, real smile and I realized that I was standing on the brink of a precipice. If I did not act quickly, Leila would wean me away from my bitterness, my only reason for living, with her great capacity for love and its power of healing.

But that could not be true, there was no unselfish love in the world, my father had told me so and he was never wrong; there was only winning and losing, put out of the way or go under yourself, kill or be killed. Leila had become an adept at deception to the point that no one saw through her anymore and took the façade as the truth. But she was just biding her time, once she had us where she wanted us, she would…do what? That was the point, I did not know, but it could not be good for anyone but herself. In any case, someone had to pay for the uniformly unfair hand life had dealt me and why not someone who seemed as uniformly, almost obscenely fortunate?

Why did things come to her so easily but to me always at a price? Why was simple happiness not only available but acceptable to her, whereas I was always faced with impossible choices?

He had come to the house through my mother, a promising but impecunious distant relative whose father had begged my maternal grandmother to help educate him and ultimately find him a job. In those days, this was customary and my grandmother had assumed without qualm that my father would help him. And he had invited him to share one of the rooms downstairs with another protégé – there were several such inmates on the ground floor – and take his meals with them. His college fees would be paid, his material needs taken care of, and he would get a pocket allowance of five rupees a month. To this needy young man it was an answer to an impossible prayer and he arrived within two days of the invitation, humble and grateful.

I might never have noticed him had it not been for the fact that my Mother called him to her room sometimes to ask about her family members whom she rarely met. Both her brothers were part of the nationalist movement, had been interned, were very often on the run and so their entry to our house was strictly forbidden. My maternal grandfather was dead and my grandmother kept her household together with great difficulty, but she was too proud and principled to accept financial help from our father, although he had repeatedly offered it. I think he felt guilty about this, which explains why he acceded so readily to my grandmother's request to help Mukul.

Slim and lithe, a head full of curls, but sharp face already marked by lines of hardship, he was not remarkable in any way except for his eyes: very bright, intense, almost fanatical, they mesmerized you completely like a snake and you could not look away once his glance had locked with yours. But he never allowed this to happen with family members and always looked deferentially at the feet of those who rarely accosted him. Only once, when he was talking to my mother sitting on the floor, did I walk in and he looked up, his eyes locking with mine, but he broke away almost immediately and went out of the room. I had laughingly asked my mother whether I had frightened away her favorite protégée and she had said rather enigmatically:

'I don't think he is easily frightened, but best to stay out of his way.'

However, Bobby soon realized what good company he was, clever, well informed and different, and insisted on making a friend of him, and since Mukul was also planning to read law they shared many common interests. One of these was history, but in this field their areas of interest were at complete variance: While Bobby had neatly swallowed the civilizing version of colonialism dished out in approved text books, ably seconded by our father, and was convinced that India had gained on the whole by the presence of the British, Mukul's historical lore, mainly learned from elders and school masters in the village, was concerned with nationalist heroes like Shivaji, Tipu Sultan, Rani Lakshmibai, Nana Sahib, Mangal Pandey, and an independent India was his greatest dream. However, they sparred amicably enough and though Mukul never allowed his enthusiasm to get out of hand, I had noticed the glint in his eye when a particularly derogatory comment was made, usually echoing my father, about Indians. After one such occasion he came and told my mother that he would like to pay for his food and when asked why, he said that he was earning some money teaching night school and wished to contribute to the family funds in a small way. My Father would not hear of it, but he looked distinctly thoughtful, even more so when Mukul took to bringing gifts for us, which we could hardly refuse, for they were always books.

To my share fell Bankim Chatterjee's *Rajsingha*, *Ananda Math* and Munshi Premchand's short stories, all in translation as English was practically our mother tongue. I was fascinated by the wonderful stories and pined to read them in the original, but little help was available either at home or in school. Raised on a steady diet of Walter Scott, Jane Austen and Dickens, I had some idea of reading literature and was thoroughly intrigued by the new world these books opened up. But I was also confused:

Where was this country these authors were talking about? Was this my India? Why did none of the people I know match the characters in these books in any way?

It did not occur to me until much later that these books constituted a preamble to an attempted cultural revolution, but it did strike me that the only person who had firsthand knowledge of this India in the house was Mukul. I vaguely remembered the stories Lena used to tell me when she first came to the house, the rhymes she had taught me and how my mother had encouraged her, but Lena had never gone back to the village; on the contrary, she had picked up the culture of the house only too well to become a traditional nanny or 'ayah' as they were termed by the British. In time, while Small and Tony were growing up, she came to know and narrate the stories of Snow White and Cinderella better than her own.

'Fox that got a thorn in his nose trying to eat brinjal' or 'the tiny bird who defied the king's command'.

Thus the tenuous thread of communication was broken and another opportunity had neither been sought nor found. So, after so many years and on reading the books I kept a lookout and when I found Mukul sitting on a mat on the floor talking animatedly to my mother seated on her bed, would sneak quietly in, sit in one corner and listen avidly and, strangely enough, Tony was always with me.

Mukul's main concern, however, was not so much the English people, for he felt that they would be on their way out of India very soon; his anger was directed against the Brown Sahibs, who, if anything, were more dismissive of the needs of their fellow countrymen than their masters, and in his opinion were just waiting to inherit the colonial mantle doffed by the British to further their own interests. This elitist landowning class would make common cause with the politicians and bureaucrats to maintain the stranglehold on the peasant and the worker. Democracy was eyewash, only intended to impress the West. Unless there was a people's revolution nothing would change. One had only to look at the Soviet Union to realize the truth of this.

Today in a world thoroughly disillusioned, particularly

with the Soviet Union and communism, these arguments sound like a string of outworn clichés, but at that time it was revolutionary and very thrilling for an ignorant sixteen year-old with no exposure to national or democratic sentiments. In any case, the youth never learns and when I hear Timmy haranguing his friends and anyone who cares to listen now, his face alight with enthusiasm, I am reminded powerfully of Mukul. It is the conviction that they are right, that they have all the answers, plus the generous dose of genuine idealism they throw in, that makes heady brew out of their words, particularly to hearers as naïve as young students are, and I was, frankly, mesmerized. The plight of the poor people, their hunger, lack of hope and total vulnerability painted in powerful imagery, brought tears to my eyes and I was determined to fight alongside Mukul, shoulder to shoulder. I think my mother too got carried away and allowed this friendship to develop against her better judgment.

He also gave me an idea about how naïve, politically innocent and God-fearing the average Indian in the villages was and how he believed implicitly in trusting his superiors, whether the Indian landlord or the British Sahib. He was so imbued with the ideas of obedience and guidance that it hardly ever occurred to him to take independent action. The Hindus, dominated by their thirty-three million deities all their life, happily added Queen Victoria to their list of Avatars and her lithograph often jostled for space among the household Gods in the Puja Room! So naturally, when the nationalist movement broke out they had serious qualms about dislodging the queen from her venerable position. If something was to be done, the first need was political education for the young before they fell into the trap of white sahib and native sahib worship. But how was this to be achieved? Money was in such short supply and even volunteers had to eat.

I started saving money in all possible ways, and one day when I refused to go shopping with my aunt and requested my Father to give me the money instead, his eyes narrowed, but he asked, very gently:

'Why this sudden austerity in one so young, and more importantly, why this sudden need for money?'

Before I could come up with a suitable excuse, Tony rushed headlong into the breach:

'Father please give her the money, she wants to give it to Mukul dada for all the poor people in his village!'

In the same level voice he looked into Tony's eyes and enquired:

'Has Mukul asked for the money?'

Tony, just about eight years old, was indignant:

'Of course not, you know Dada has no love of money! Didi just wants to help the poor people through him!'

'And who are these poor people, your Mukul dada's friends and relations?'

By this time half the household is listening and I am ready to sink through the floor with mortification, for I knew that Mukul would be mercilessly interrogated, would not be able to take the humiliation and leave the house.

At this juncture Bobby speaks up:

'Father, you know Mukul better than that! He will hand over the money to his club for flood relief. I know you are a busy man, but remember, many villages are under water at the moment?'

The sarcasm in his voice seems to flick my Father on the raw and he retorts:

'Well, if they will live and till right at the waters' edge like ignorant animals, what can you expect?'

'And where else would they be allowed to go? Will the landlords allow them to live and till in the safer parts of the villages? These are mainly untouchables and no one cares if the river swallows them, ask Bobby if you don't believe me!'

Mukul's angry voice cuts across the silence like a whiplash.

'Yes Father,' Ronnie breaks in, 'we cycled down to the _____ Bridge yesterday and saw a young woman with a baby in her arms, looking at the swirling waters as though she would jump in. When we spoke to her she said that the entire chunk of land on which their shanty had stood had been washed away along with sleeping family members by the flood; she had only escaped because she had been tending their goat and nursing the baby in the pasture nearby. It was heartbreaking.'

Bobby corroborates:

'Finally the headman of the village turned up, mainly because he had been informed of our presence and he told her to go and live in the cremation grounds, and he would see to it that she get her husband's job of helping to cremate the dead. She just walked away hopelessly, her baby clutched to her chest.'

With several pairs of pleading eyes fixed on his face, it is our Father's turn to be embarrassed and he mumbles:

'I will have a word with the District Magistrate and see what can be done for flood relief in the neighborhood of our city to begin with.' His voice trails away.

'And how will that help? The DM will speak to the landlords who will spin him cock and bull stories and produce some cosmetic families who will swear that they have been taken care of, and there the matter will end.

Ever since Lord Cornwallis handed over our peasants to their landlords' tender mercies, the story has not changed and I am convinced that it will only get worse when the Brown Sahibs take over from the British, for they will make common cause with the landlords.'

Mukul has now thrown caution to the winds and is speaking without fear for he knows that reprisal will be swift, irrevocable and he has nothing more to lose.

Father's eyes narrow dangerously:

'What do you know about Cornwallis that makes you say this? Do your history books give you this impression?'

Mukul does not bat an eyelid and replies calmly:

'No they do not, for they are very carefully edited, but it is not difficult to read between the lines; the Raj could not afford paid tax collectors so Cornwallis farmed out taxing rights to landlords, thinking both the government and the peasant would benefit. Perhaps he had no measure of the rapacity and dishonesty of those he trusted. Or perhaps he did, and this was a ruse to create a permanent conflict situation on the basis of his Permanent Settlement? Very possible, after all, divide and rule was a principle that had served them pretty well in all areas.'

Voice dripping with acid, Father retorts:

'I was forgetting that you are educated, but has anyone told you that a little learning is a dangerous thing and that you are in danger of seriously misjudging your present rulers? The nationalists say that the Zamindari system will disappear as soon as India attains independence, and you will certainly live to see whether things will improve or not, even if I don't. But at present I have serious doubts.'

'Exactly my point sir, things will only get worse, for the Brown Sahib is more greedy than his white counterpart and by demanding a cut out of the peasants' earnings will actually make their lot quite intolerable; there has to be a people's movement to restore the balance, don't you agree? We appear on the same side of the fence after all Sir, so what are we arguing about?'

My father is quick to see his advantage and moves in neatly: 'And what makes you think that the people who will come to power as a result of this movement will be any better than the Brown Sahib? Remember, they are a deprived lot, money and power hungry, how do you know that they will not feather their own nests and leave their brethren in the lurch? Have you noticed idealism and impotence always go hand in hand? But afterwards, matters change dramatically; you have read enough history to know the truth of that, surely?'

The silence lengthens, Mukul is suddenly uncomfortable and shifty-eyed, but Bobby, sensing his friend's discomfiture, rushes into the breach:

'Father, why don't we come with you to the District Magistrate and offer our services for a fund-raising campaign? Ronnie and I could get our friends and I am sure we can set an example that others will follow. We still have a month before we go back to school.'

Very graciously Father relents but his eyes are thoughtful.

The boys manage to impress the District Magistrate, who is British, with their plans; he says this initiative is exactly what he would have expected in his own country and promises to help the boys in every way he can. He is particularly impressed with Mukul's powers of organization and capacity to enthuse his friends. The girl and her baby are found and given a place in the camp the boys have set up with the help of the villagers and the money they have raised. The fact that the Judge's sons and nephew have organized the initiative helps considerably to loosen purse strings. Mukul says enthusiastically that none of this would have been possible without our father's help, and he agrees gravely and deprecatingly adds one more unearned scalp to his belt.

I too am allowed to participate and this propinquity allows our acquaintance to ripen into friendship and then very quickly into what we imagine is love. Because it is forbidden, it is all the sweeter, and neither of us stops to think of the future. Days fly and its soon time for my brothers to return to school. They leave with many exhortations to us to keep the project going in their absence and promise to work on their schoolmates for more assistance. Suddenly we have found a purpose that is worthy and our lives appear transformed.

A few days after they leave Mukul comes to me in the evening, his face ashen, and begs me to meet him in the school room after the house is asleep. Before I can ask questions he disappears down the passage. I manage to survive poignant anxiety for the next few hours, lie in bed heart pounding, till the clocks in the house strike one o'clock in unison. Then, my face covered with a shawl like a criminal in a bad film, I creep down the long corridor into the large study area we still call the school room.

Mukul is waiting for me and plunges into speech without wasting a minute:

'Madonna, your father thinks I am a terrorist and he is not far wrong, for I would not hesitate to resort to violence if the cause were worthy enough, but it would have to be really worthy; he also suspects that I am corrupting you and that is adding to his anxiety in no small measure. However, I must leave immediately or I will be arrested and incarcerated like Dave's brother, perhaps in Buxa? I only wanted to know whether you will come with me, for I must go tonight.'

'Come with you, where?' My head is reeling...

'Anywhere, who cares as long as we are together?'

'But, where will we live?'

'In each other, the best destination!'

'Don't we need a home?'

'There won't be an opportunity...we will be on the run most of the time...'

'On the run, from whom?'

'The police, of course! How dense you are, Madonna!'

'But why would they chase me?'

'Not a very clever question! If you are with me, you can hardly escape the taint! Didn't you say you wanted to work with me?'

'Of course I want to, but...'

'Yes, but...' his voice is sharp with disappointment. 'It's one thing to raise money for the District traveling in your Father's car, public praise ringing in your ears, but quite another to run from pillar to post hungry, footsore and in constant danger, right? I knew you would not agree and would never have come to you if it had not been for your mother...' his voice trails away.

'My mother, she told you to put this proposal to me? I just cannot believe this!' I sound indignant even to myself.

'You can check with her if you like! Actually, she said something very strange...said that this is what she wanted to do all her life...wanted to do something real, not live in a hideous fool's paradise, but no one had given her a chance and she had been stuck in an intolerable situation. Her useless life would be "redeemed" if her dearest Madonna could fulfill her greatest ambition ...which is why...'

The cynicism and the echoes of my father's sarcastic tone in my voice are evident even to me:

'How very generous of my mother to want me to carry the burden of her noble ambitions when she has lived all her life in the lap of luxury provided by my less than idealistic father. Do you know what he says? "You cannot make love lying on a torn quilt," and I tend to agree with him. What are you offering me, Mukul, a life of uncertainty and danger, which will perhaps be a complete waste? The likes of you will not succeed in fighting the system simply because you have no bargaining power; all you can boast of is large doses of empty idealistic emotion, which will achieve nothing in the long run. Educate yourself; equip yourself, then maybe...'

Mukul breaks in:

'How easily these glib phrases roll off your lips Madonna, just like a well-trained parrot, but think rationally for a moment, isn't that exactly what I tried to do? And look what happened! No Madonna, I must escape before I am clapped in irons.'

Desperate, I clutch at straws:

'If you promise to give up violence I will talk to Father, he will listen to me!'

Mukul is incredulous:

'Listen to you? You don't realize that you are the main reason for his branding me a terrorist? How else can he get rid of me without blackening his own precious image? Talk of innocents...but you are downright dumb, Madonna!'

Perhaps the incomprehension on my face gets to him and he mutters:

'Look, we are talking at cross purposes and losing invaluable time...I have to go now...'

He hugs me to his chest for one fierce moment and then he glides from the room silent as a shadow.

Father's obvious displeasure and disappointment at the news of his disappearance next morning confirms beyond doubt the truth of Mukul's statements and suddenly when I realize that he can never return, that I will never see him again, I am overwhelmed by emotions I don't in the least understand. All I know is I have lost my greatest opportunity of happiness, that my body is crying out for him, and that in life there are very few second chances.

Father watched me like a spider, every move was carefully scrutinized, every expression read and even when I was with my mother, Lena always hovered. In any case, my mother did not have much to say to me. I covered my pillow with a piece of oilcloth at night so my tears would not betray me and returned blank stares when Bobby and Ronnie, back from school for a vacation, quizzed me about Mukul. Father told them that Mukul had 'disappeared under suspicious circumstances and his connections with a well-known terrorist group was a recorded fact.'

They were, on no account, to make an effort to contact him.

Rebellious to begin with, the boys bowed under pressure and tried to carry on with the project as best as they could, and the generous help from Father in this respect went a long way towards dissipating their enquiry and resentment. After three months the vigil was slightly relaxed and I was allowed to visit my friends or go shopping unescorted, though only with Robin, who drove me everywhere. But the trail was completely cold; I had no means of communication and no one to help me. Also, the will to fight, the energy was gone. As a class we had been seduced by material comfort, social eminence and the desire for safety at any cost.

Only one mutilated postcard found its way to me via Tony, who still pined for Mukul. It was short, obviously penned in great hurry and part of a series:

You have not replied to any of my letters and I did not expect you to, for where would you send the letter, even if you wanted to write? Perhaps they did not reach you at all? We are planning carefully and our next strike should prove effective but the police are very vigilant. Keep your father away from the _____ _____ area if possible, for I do not want him to be hurt. Write to me at Post Box No _____, the letter should reach me.

Life is wonderful and I wish you were with me.

Mukul

I did not write back for I did not wish to betray his whereabouts, but the letter, almost crumbling, was my most prized possession for many years. Ah first love, so pathetic, 'wild with all regret' but so sweet, 'piercingly sweet'!

Father missed nothing; he knew my state of mind for he read all the letters, knew how strongly I was affected and having failed to influence me by separation, he tried another tactic:

When Ronnie and Small were attacked by the so-called nationalists Father claimed that Mukul was a part of the group and that he, Mukul, had tried to wreak revenge on him by attacking his children. No one believed him and my mother was outraged. She actually said quite openly:

'People always judge others by their own heinous standards.'

But my father was not in the least embarrassed and told her in his usual round terms, 'not to be a bloody fool'! It seemed he had irrefutable evidence of Mukul's ill intentions and complicity and would never forgive him for repaying his hospitality with such base treachery.

But I still thought that it was a mere ploy, paid scant attention, and I think that is why, as a last desperate measure, Father decided to marry me off and settled on Sunny, the closest he could get to Mukul in terms of intelligence, idealism and character, but with all the trappings we as a class so desperately needed to survive, thrown in. 'All this and heaven too', as far as he was concerned. But heaven perhaps was not entirely unmerciful, for I now know that despite his dubious intentions, I was given a genuine second chance of happiness with Sunny and Joy, a chance to emerge from the terrible grayness of my pointless existence, the endless cycle of envy and self-pity, into the living light of positive purpose. But if this decision did have the seal of divine approval, why did I throw it all away with both hands again, as I had done with Mukul? What drove me like a goad till I had lost them all? Can God only take you so far down the road?

When I tried to run away from the train and Sunny stopped me, it was because I had a vague idea that Mukul operated in the vicinity and that I could get away – I would somehow manage to meet up with him. It never occurred to me that he may not be alive. But Sunny made enquiries after my confession and found out that Mukul had indeed been killed in action in the drive against the nationalists. He had not been involved in any way with the abductors; Mr. Wilson had made it quite clear that Mukul's sympathies had been with Ronnie and Small and he had come to remonstrate with the perpetrators, but Father had insisted that he was playing a double game, and Mr. Wilson could not imagine that a man would lie when it came to his own children.

Sunny never told me why or how Mukul had been killed, but I found out much later, the night my father died.

I will never forget Father as he looked that night; a few days of acute physical suffering had made his handsome face gaunt, his frame sepulchral and his hands, always so strong, well-shaped and manicured, look like talons of a strange bird of prey. The one feature that was unchanged was his eyes that seemed to burn with their customary determination. But did they? When he sent for me that night and banished everyone else from the room, including the nurse, as I sat by his side and looked into the burning orbs, I was sure that something else lay behind this bravado, and I found it very difficult to believe in the evidence of my own eyes, for it looked to me very much like fear.

He took my hand in his and I felt a tremor go through his entire frame, a tremor he could not control, but what did it signify? Passion, pain, desire or the same fear I had read in his eyes? What could he be afraid of? An avowed agnostic, he did not believe in afterlife, and this life was ebbing away steadily and hardly likely to spring any surprises at this stage.

I waited a long time, and finally like someone speaking from far away, as though he were already an inhabitant of another world, his words came to me like bleak moving air whistling through bare trees in a desolate place:

'I have wronged all my children and their mother all my life, have used them as pawns to protect my miserable skin and polish my unholy image…but none more than you my dearest daughter, for while the others, even Small turned to their mother for comfort in their hour of need and learned to face tragedy with wisdom and courage, I influenced you into reacting like me. My philosophy of an eye for an eye robbed you of all chances of attaining peace and redemption. Only, you went for the wrong eye; the ones you should have gouged out with red-hot irons were mine. If you had done that, perhaps I would not be the sinner I am today, facing the fires of hell and you would not seek to make others unhappy to alleviate your own misery.'

I thought for a moment that his thoughts were rambling... that he had lost touch with reality...then it struck me that it was indeed so, for he was inhabiting a reality now that only he could sense, his eyes were fixed on visions only he could interpret. I was suddenly reminded of the doggerel that had always hung framed in his library.

'...the sharp, scarred edge of truth at last?'

But the vision was not impaired; it was preternaturally clear and brought to light a version of the fateful events that no one in the family had any idea of, and which was mainly responsible for molding me into the person I am today.

VALEDICTION: JUDGE-SPEAK

'Mukul came to our house as a spy, that much was never in doubt, but he fell under your mother's spell like everyone else and fell in love with you to boot, so his teeth were drawn. I was happy to have him around; for by intercepting his letters and setting my spies to follow him when he met his club members I knew exactly what their plans were. They actually hoped Mukul would win me over to their cause and I would pass judgments favorable to them in their acts of terrorism. Poor fools!

'However, they might never have got into trouble if they had not made common cause with the villagers over that benighted woman who climbed her husband's funeral pyre. Really, a sordid case of rape in which her husband got knifed trying to protect his wife who was too comely for her own good; if he had died the matter would have ended there, but he did not and the local police had to stop his mouth somehow for Robin's father was involved. But Wilson insisted that the case be fairly tried and a public trial be held, the British and their habeas corpus!' He said:

'"The Raj is passing through a precarious stage and we cannot risk miscarriage of justice. This case has to be carefully investigated and the man given a chance to speak."

'So we did the only thing that would turn Wilson around: evidence was planted, a bomb was recovered and it was proved beyond doubt that the target was the British magistrate, this man the culprit, and he had been injured when apprehended by loyalists who had informed the police. The case was swiftly dispatched as the proof was incontrovertible, and after that we could order his hanging without compunction. The matter would have ended there if that fool woman had not decided to be suttee and enter the flames at her husband's pyre. She was completely unafraid: her head held high, iterating till the last that she was doing this in the hope that her husband's name would be cleared and she herself, cleansed of the filth that had contaminated her body and soul, she sat on the pyre, in the lotus pose, calm and serene, while the flames licked at her greedily. A modern-day Joan of Arc, she remained upright in the fire as long as she was conscious, then fell forward and was finally reduced to ashes. The crowd went crazy and carried her remains to the Ganges, chanting anti-British slogans and the entire club contingent, including Mukul, was part of the entourage. The terrible irony was that I had created the very bogey I had avoided like poison so far, a nationalist martyr, and placed him right on my doorstep.'

His voice began to falter and he indicated that he was thirsty. I picked up the feeding cup and poured a few sips of water down his parching throat. He closed his eyes and I thought that the interview was over, but sat on quietly, in case he spoke again.

When he did speak and I almost jumped out of my skin for his voice was not of the present, but of the Judge at the time when these events had taken place, strong, authoritative and vibrant. How was this possible? Was I hallucinating or had he traveled back in time? Not only his voice, but his tone had regained its arrogance, and his words their confident harshness of yore. However, I soon understood why this transformation had taken place:

'The nationalist charade, however, had convinced no one and people were ready to deify the wretched woman and take up cudgels in her memory to get at the truth. Even Wilson was not completely satisfied and kept sniffing and one day he actually said:

'"You know Judge, this was not a purely political case, but personal vendetta dressed up to look like one; I am going to investigate some more."

'I had to do something before he stumbled on the truth and in my desperation I turned to Mukul, but found that his sympathies were entirely with the woman and that he too felt that her husband and his companions had been framed. As a matter of fact he had been planning to ask for my help in the matter! So I decided to use you, my dearest Madonna, though I was loath to do so for I knew in advance what the outcome would be.

'I spun him a masterly tale about kidnapping and trafficking in women, admitted the truth about Robin's father but painted him whiter than white as far as loyalty to the family was concerned, said he had knifed the man because he was a criminal planning a series of abductions of girls from eminent homes among whom your name was uppermost, because I was a judge who was entirely impartial and spared no one, nationalist or not. As you can see, it was a tissue of half-truths and complete role reversal, but it was a tenable story. It wasn't easy to convince Mukul though, for he had some idea of my major domo's activities and did not accept his sudden knight in shining armor image without a fight. We went up hill and down dale for three days but in the end, you tipped the balance in my favor and a plan was hatched.

'The day I took you people on that picnic I had everything planned down to the last detail, including the fan belt of the Ford, had Robin's father see through it while all of you were otherwise engaged. Don't you remember how puzzled Ali, the driver was? Kept saying all was well when we had set out for he had checked very carefully. In the end I had to shut him up quite harshly for Bobby and Ron were beginning to take his side. The plan was that Small would be abducted and recovered shortly and in the process the nationalists shown up for the scum they were. Of course the abductors were hired people playing a part and Mukul was among them, for he had promised to implement the plan without harming Small in any way. He had severe qualms about shock though, but I brushed these aside, saying children had short memories.

'Everything was thrown out of gear by two factors: Ronnie's unexpected action and the fact that some real enemies had got into the group of loyalists dressed up as nationalists, of whom Mukul said later, he had no knowledge. Ronnie played into their hands and they had no compunctions about hurting both the kids. They would have died that night if Mukul had not risked his own life to save theirs; he put the gun I had given him to use and killed three people before they backed off. He himself was severely injured and never walked straight again...that proud stance, so typical of him, was gone forever.

'But his conscience was unimpaired and he could not forgive himself for the hurt caused to Ronnie and Small.

'I have always been good at granting myself absolution

and soon managed to convince my second self the Judge that the whole thing was an unfortunate accident and the real culprit was Ronnie; by acting out of turn he had almost got himself and his sister almost killed. The Police Commissioner was more outraged by the attacks on the children than the bomb and public sympathy veered neatly to envelop me and all of you in a warm glow of sympathy. Then the photographs of the children, particularly Small, were flashed in the papers and in the flood of demand for revenge that followed, even the suttee and her courage were forgotten. The wolf pack was in action again and the hysterical baying for blood that followed even took me by surprise.

'So the case was an open and shut one and enabled me to get rid of all the trouble-makers in a veritable holocaust where no one, not even those remotely connected with the suttee or her husband, survived. Robin's father was safe and so was I, or so I thought.

'Mukul had been laid up in a private nursing home where every care was lavished on him, but he was not allowed to leave the premises. Young and strong, he healed well and within two months the doctors said he was ready to get back to his work; except for the limp and stoop he was as good as new, physically, but when I went to see him after the case I was amazed to find his face lined and drawn, dark circles under his eyes as though he had not slept nights, looking thoroughly miserable. I had taken a large sum of money with me as a contribution for his club, and as I handed it to him I promised more in future, especially if they stood by me. He thrust the money away and said angrily that his club had no right to the reward after what had happened to the children. He had seen their photographs and been unable to sleep since. Until he had visited the house, met you and begged forgiveness of the children and their mother he would know no peace. Please, could I let him come home, just once?

'Somehow your mother too had come to suspect that Mukul had been involved in this bizarre incident in some way, and was making my life miserable, wanting to meet him so that she could find out exactly why and how the whole matter had transpired. But this was obviously the one thing I could not allow. Your mother, faced with the truth, would leave me without a second thought and my precious career and image would be irretrievably ruined. We argued about this endlessly till one night, at my wits end, I struck her and told her that I would have Mukul put away for good if she did not let up, the only time in my life, but it finished her and through our remaining days we were strangers to each other, although we lived in the same house. I think you were witness to this event, and for weeks after that I could see the unasked question in all your eyes: What could I have said to silence your brave mother so completely?

'Well, now you know.'

Again he asked for water, but this time he could not swallow, and the water just dribbled down the corners of his mouth and drained away into his pillow. I was about to call the nurse when the upraised, emaciated hand stopped me once more, and the talon like index finger drove sharply into his own chest:

'I, I had Mukul killed. A group of informed policeman in native clothes sprang an ambush on him and his friends on the way back from hospital and took them completely by surprise, for I had given them the permission to visit all of you and they thought they were going home. The police had orders to shoot on sight. Even so, one man out of the three escaped and he told me later that Mukul had gone down fighting and calling out to you till the last. He had fought like a maniac and it had taken two bullets to the head and one dead policeman to finally pay his score.'

As my imagination conjured up the scene, Mukul fighting for his life on his way home due to no fault of his own, crying out to the very woman who had robbed him of life and happiness, as I watched the encounter blow by blow, wound by wound till Mukul was lying on the stones choking on his own blood, I lost my head completely. I could only see the evil, emaciated man hovering over him like a black hungry raven, a man who had sold him down the river to save his own miserable skin, and a man to whom nothing was sacrosanct. I picked up the big, five-cell torch lying on the table and was about to bring it crashing down on his skeletal face when he cried out:

'No, Madonna, no, I have too much of your blood on my hands already…no more!'

And as I watched, weapon still upraised, his eyes filled with terrible pleading, pleading for pity, pleading for forgiveness, begging for absolution…only I could absolve him partly of his great burden, allow him to face his own judge with some degree of hope, but I could not bring myself to utter empty words of comfort and turned away from him. He continued to stare at me for some more time, but I remained implacable and gradually his face changed again and the vague look returned. After a long wait I finally realized that the past had again lost meaning for him. His eyes unfocussed and began to glaze but he continued to look wonderingly at me and at the upraised torch. Finally and mercifully his eyes closed. He never spoke again.

At what stage of his life had the enormity of his own misdeeds percolated through layers of carefully created self-deception to penetrate his consciousness? Obviously a point at which no restitution had been possible; so he had no option but to lie on his bed of thorns and bleed till merciful death released him from himself. But in the end perhaps divine pity had intervened and his mind had sought refuge in oblivion. He had gone into a semi-coma and his memories had ceased to plague him.

The old bard knew it all when he said:

'...to know my deed it were best not to know myself...'

DAVE-SPEAK

I, Dave had been on tenterhooks throughout this interview, but the crash of the torch falling on the floor brought us all in a rush to the room, to find glass and metal in smithereens on the ground and Madonna sitting next to the old man as though turned to stone, completely oblivious to her surroundings and all of us. Sunny was the only person who seemed to have an inkling of what had transpired, and he urgently requested me and the nurse to give her a strong sedative. Injection administered, she was put on her bed and was lost to the world for the next eighteen hours.

When she woke up she was a different person, her eyes empty of all emotion but a rigid, meaningless smile fixed on her lips. She refused to speak of what had happened, saying she had forgotten. Sunny never left her side, ministered to her constantly, but kept Joy away from her, for the boy was afraid. Very gradually, after a whole week, she seemed to be on her way to recovering some semblance of normalcy and the terrible smile began to fade. Then the Judge passed away and the whole household immersed themselves in ensuring that the last rites were performed as ordained in the scriptures.

I thought to myself:

A spirit as unquiet as the Judge's will take some laying! He had always claimed that he was an agnostic with very strong ethics, personal and professional, and the old sinner had got away with it because no one had dared to refute him. Now his sons, no doubt thinking on my lines, spared no pains to ensure that he would get an even chance in the next world, even Ronnie, who laid no stock by ritual.

On the fourth day Madonna and Small were meant to carry out the rites for daughters, but Madonna refused to participate. Said she would sit by Small and repeat the prayers in her mind but would not offer oblations. Bobby and Ronnie were upset, but Tony and I sided with Sunny and said we should let her choose. Surprisingly, Millie and Leila too agreed with us. Joy, however, would take part along with the other grandchildren in all the rituals meant for them, Sunny had insisted on this.

All went well; Small carefully carried out the complicated rituals and repeated all the prayers, her total attention on the priest. Madonna too seemed quite absorbed, eyes closed, lips moving in silent prayer. Almost at the end, all ceremonies completed, Small obediently chanted after the priest:

> 'The progenitor is your heaven,
> Your father is your religion,
> He is worthy of worship at all times…'

This sloka brought back poignant memories of our Aunt who had always fallen back on these words at moments of conflict and crisis within the family. We all remembered her words, but the air, heavy with unexpressed emotion and unsaid words, was suddenly shattered by a peal of manic laughter from Madonna. Eyes wild, she shook Small hard by the shoulders screaming:

'How can you be such a hypocrite, you little idiot? That bastard is your heaven and your religion? I am going to kill you for telling all these lies!' And her fingers began to fasten around Small's throat.

Sunny was the first to react and he called out to me:

'Dave, get her hands before any damage is done!'

It took all our combined strength to prise her fingers open and get her away from the scene. The priest was ready to run but Small – after a couple of minutes, finger marks standing out livid on her throat – carried on as though nothing had happened, and slowly people began to breathe again. Madonna went into a stupor-like sleep in a darkened room with only Sunny in attendance and Leila made sure she never lost sight of Joy. That evening we all went to our rooms totally exhausted but with a hundred questions hammering in our brains: Why, how, wherefore?

Next morning though, at breakfast, Madonna was her normal self, sardonic and catty, but neither concerned nor repentant; she even asked Small about the marks on her throat saying:

'Been visiting your friend again, Small and did he squeeze you too hard?'

Small just looked at her for a moment and said very evenly:

'Not my friend, but another friend.'

But Madonna just laughed as though it were a huge joke!

Later Sunny told us that she had had one or two attacks of short term amnesia in the recent past and that is why he never left her alone or unattended if he could help it.

As a doctor I believed that these attacks as Sunny termed

them were attempts by Madonna's subconscious mind to erase unpleasant memories, particularly where she was to blame or was guilty of reprehensible behavior, and I was immediately struck by the dangerous possibilities of the situation. I did try to warn Sunny but he assured me that he was sure that his Madonna could never do anything morally wrong. He also made it clear that he believed Madonna had been justified in her attitude to her Father and that Small had merely been a pawn. However, I remembered the welts on Small's throat and was not convinced.

They left a week later and never paid another visit as a family.

I have often wondered since, which Madonna Sunny had in mind when he said: 'his Madonna.'

The next time Madonna came back to her father's house it was for good and neither Joy nor Sunny were with her. When questioned, she just repeated pathetically, as though programmed, that she could not remember what had happened to them.

LEILA LOOKS BACK

When Ronnie and I tied the knot, we became the cynosure of too much attention, and not all of it well-intentioned. The wedding, the entire situation was too fairytale, too perfect to be real; many of the watchers felt it was unfair that we should have it all. Our good luck was unfair and undeserved, and though both Ronnie and I did our best to live in harmony with others, the ill will, though well camouflaged, never really went away. Sounds paradoxical, but our good fortune proved to be our worst enemy. As Tony says in his sardonic way:

'Those whom the Gods damn, they make unvaryingly fortunate.'

My mother – a very strong and spiritual woman who had suffered because of the jealousy and envy of others all her life due to her own good luck – was paranoid about her children and was always marking our foreheads with kohl to keep away the evil eye. She would not allow me to gaze into a mirror and always said my nose was too long or my eyes too small, so I grew up with the conviction that I was just short of plain. But she could not stop people from talking nor could she ignore my good grades in school and college or my wonderful voice. As my teacher remarked:

'When Leila sings, a thousand violins play in accompaniment.'

A great musician, he was too old to be in love with me, but managed to be quite idiotic at times!

Then I met Ronnie, handsome, clever, good humored, and honest, rising fast in his career and my cup ran over.

But neither of us ever took anything for granted, and we worked really hard at leading good and moral lives. It was not always easy in a large joint family, and I with my very westernized upbringing did not know many of the rules. But Ronnie was a big help and I came to love every member of the family for who they were, as human beings replete with faults and virtues. This did much to not only promote understanding but facilitated communication. My parents-in-law came to love me and so did Bobby and Millie. Tony was my friend from the day I entered the family. Timmy and Sammy were like my own children and Small was my special love. And all this gave me a terrific sense of fulfillment and in order to maintain status quo I tried indefatigably to solve all family problems, to take care of everyone, to put myself last, always, on every occasion, sometimes to Ronnie's chagrin. I wonder whether he realized what I did not. That self-abnegation is the best façade for a massive ego that hides its face behind a mask of goodness? But was Ronnie too kind to warn me that altruism rarely brought its own rewards.

Whatever the case may be it is true I never really got around Madonna even though I tried so hard, or Rose for that matter after she arrived, although I was instrumental in bringing her into the family fold and had done my best to make her feel at home. Madonna never forgave me for 'usurping her place' as she said with her cryptic smile, while Rose suffered from a massive complex that I could do nothing about. And of course, Tony did not help by proclaiming as soon as she arrived:

'Try to be like Leila in every way and you will be okay. It's a tall order I know, but if you keep at it steadily you might get there some day!'

I refuted Tony vehemently but cannot deny that I felt a great sense of triumph.

It took me a long while to realize that these people would have loved me more if others had loved me less, and that some people would never love me whatever I may do. To be too greedy for love and strive for it constantly is the best way to lose it all, for it all stems from an inflated sense of self. I could not bear the thought that someone may not think well of me, wish me well, or why did I swallow Madonna's terrible lie so tamely? Why did I not take the letter to Ronnie, confront him with the accusations contained within, and give him a chance to defend himself? Ronnie, my life and soul companion, whom I trusted above all, why did I doubt his goodness? Because I wanted to believe that Madonna cared for me, was doing this to 'save me heartache later' as she said. The sheer effrontery of her design was only possible and successful because of my massive ego, which made me fall for her ploy. Also I thought, it must be the truth or would she entrust Small with the letter? In any case, would she dare to perpetrate such a monstrous falsehood about her beloved brother with the whole family around? I had no idea of the power of half-truths at that point and did not realize that she had strung together a credible scenario selected from a garbled spectrum with diabolical cunning. She had gambled brilliantly on my major weakness, my desire to be loved. Following in her father's footsteps she believed that since he had got away with it in a court of law, I, poor fool, would prove an easy victim! And she was right, damn her! Numb with shock, I failed to question her motives or wonder why she would need to resurrect a lie that had lain dormant so long without causing damage, for so many years.

Suspicion is like an army of termite, insidious, unobtrusive, its inroads are not visible till a solid portion of the human core has been eaten away, and even when discovered, it is so strongly lodged in the brain and the heart that no antidote will drive it away. I had allowed it to grow almost unchecked by failing to check with the source, Ronnie, and then it was too late: I did not even want to check or verify, so helpless was I under its murderous onslaught.

Sitting under the willow, my tears washing away the ink and turning the paper soggy, my only thought was to get rid of the horror before anyone else, particularly the children, got hold of it. So I did what Madonna had ordered:

'...burn it after you have read it, immediately!'

I set fire to it and watched it crumple, only it did not burn very well because it was too wet...and then the rain put out the fire. It did not occur to me to question why she had been so insistent. Little had she or even I thought that the very children she had been so anxious to avoid and I to protect, would tumble to the truth and open up the entire sordid business. My Sammy had found me, Sheila with her greyhound instinct had nosed around, and Timmy turned the matter into a personal battle till the truth, the 'scar-edged truth' was compelled to emerge from its dark shroud of falsehood.

I also realize now that Madonna had been working towards this scenario for some time...hints dropped that Ronnie's outstanding virtue was a façade for baser appetites...like father, like son...blood is thicker than water...he was disappointed I had not borne him a son... his secretary, attractive and intelligent, had been with him a long time...a man cannot always be held responsible for his actions for nature will take over sometime...

I took no notice and laughed off her suggestions as absurd at the time, but now appreciate that they had made an impact and been quite cumulatively subversive. I did try to question her directly, but Madonna was all wide-eyed innocence and surprise, and asked me why I was misconstruing her words deliberately. This made me feel small, suspicious and mean. But the more I despised myself for my lack of faith, the stronger grew the feeling that there was something to lose faith about, and I began to read heinous meaning into the simplest of Ronnie's words and actions. When she struck the final blow, I was more than ripe for the shaking.

Not only did she poison my mind, but Small too was taken in by her machinations for a while. But she was wiser than I and once she had tumbled to it, she gave Madonna no respite and never let me out of her sight unless my mother was there, even though Madonna never stopped taunting her as a watchdog. By doing this she prevented Madonna from victimizing me further and gave me a chance to heal. This was the flip side of the coin of love.

But all this does not exonerate me. I had committed the cardinal sin of breaking faith and deserved every bit of the suffering. People talk of Sita's sorrowing in the great epic, but does anyone consider what Ram went through in forcing her to face the fire trial, twice? We talk of Desdemona's suffering but what of Othello's agony? Ask me. To distrust someone you love with all your being is living death and the scorpions never let up. Terrible images of the flower-like Jasmine being molested by her own brother filled my mind every waking moment and ultimately became reality. And perhaps there had been other such occasions with Madonna herself, or why was she so bitter? After all, in our youth, we did not meet too many people of the opposite sex and strange feelings emerged within the family circle, so who knows where the truth lay? The questions drove me mad, and the harder poor Ronnie tried to reason with me, the more I hated and spurned him. Lost to all reason, I would not give him a chance to explain and he, without a clue to my state of mind, really thought I was losing it completely.

If Tony had not insisted on the soothsayer and the archives forced to yield their terrible secrets at the insistence of Timmy's friends, would the entire Karmic cycle have been adequate to expiate my sin? Or was all this a part of the cycle, the wheel turning inexorably 'grinding slow but exceedingly small'? The only thing I will never forgive myself for is putting Ronnie through this torture of self-reproach, horrible suspicion in the eyes of the person he loved best for a crime he was not even aware of. May the Lord forgive me, for I never will be able to do that through my entire life, try as I may.

A year later, and in a more rational frame of mind, my sense of humor restored according to Ronnie, I find it very hard to understand my own lack of realism and common sense at that point and often remember a wartime rhyme that Ronnie and I used to laugh about and the children learned from us, which in translation reads something like this:

Do re mi fa so la ti do,
The Japanese have thrown a bomb, hey ho!
Inside lies viper, cobra and krait,
The British cry 'we are so great,
Then how can this be our fate?'

It epitomizes my situation and the snakes almost got me due to my own smugness. Well, the Brits were not much better off than I was, but our children were much smarter than all of us put together! As Sammy enquired very condescendingly:

'Really, Aunt Leila, who with a grain of common sense could trust Aunt Madonna?'

Not a very flattering epitaph, yet she genuinely loved them all.

BOBBY COGITATES

Our childhood, Ronnie's and mine especially, was dogged by the Victorian doggerel that our father never got tired of repeating, 'a simple rule of thumb', he called it:

> 'Come when you are called,
> Go when you are bid,
> Shut the door behind you,
> Never be chid!'

It epitomized his faith in the system that produced it and its views on child education. He never shared our mother's opinions, which were expressed in native and time-honored rhymes. When she wanted us not to waste food because there were too many hungry people in India she would say:

> 'One who scrapes his platter clean,
> A king's son-in-law will surely be!'

Or when she wanted us to study she would exhort:

> 'One who reads and studies hard now,
> Will ride a horse-drawn carriage I vow!'

It is easy to see the difference: while the second offers positive incentives for right doing, the first merely insists on complete obedience for the avoidance of punishment, the code of which may not be challenged. It also implies complete control and ownership; children are to be molded and put to use as thought best by parents, the progeny's own desires being negligible. We speak so much today of the commoditization of women, the exploitation of children, of the unprotected poor, but has any one stopped to think of the lot of children trapped in upper class parental prisons completely hedged in by precepts set in stone, as implacable as the Ten Commandments where 'thou shall not' outnumbers 'thou shall' three to one? And the problem is that it is all so moral, so idealistic, so good, so sophisticated that the poor children never see the cracks in the monolith, 'the stone of man's good' as the poet says. They go through life believing absolutely, completely deluded, doing their best to comply, not because they have to but because they want to, and assume, erroneously, that the lawgiver lives by his own precepts. This goes on till crisis point is reached and then, crash! Every belief falls apart and they are completely shell shocked by the huge chinks in the armor of their betters, their path-lighters, and have no code of their own to fall back on.

This is what happened to me, for I always had implicit trust in my parents and took my cues from them in every walk of life. The first hint of trouble was when I found that my mother had finally given up on my Father and now lived only for her children, mainly Small and Tony. However, she refused to discuss the matter and Ronnie and I were left pretty much to our own devices. From total control to complete freedom, and I was training in Law, to be the arbiter of other people's morals, and taken it for granted that I would model myself on my Father! But as the pitfalls of the system and the essential sophistry became clear we turned steadily to our mother's home-spun, implacably moral, straight and narrow wisdom, and so avoided the pit of snakes Madonna fell into by taking Father for a model instead of Mother, Sunny or even her parents-in-law.

I also turned to Millie and became more appreciative of her acceptance of her own weaknesses and constant battles to overcome them, and she, suddenly after a shadow life of many years, turned to the sun and began to blossom. In her case, good had come out of evil, but why not for the others?

RONNIE PICKS UP THE THREAD

The British made a fine art of nepotism and their intense class consciousness found a ready echo in India with its long standing, privileged caste system. The super-imposition was seamless and erstwhile Zamindars and Brahmins quickly filled the lower echelons of officialdom. Intelligent and well educated, it did not take them long to pick up the finer points of British style administration or their language and culture. The colonial culture, a genre in itself, was created as much by the Indian Brown Sahib as his masters, and the redoubtable ICS officer, or the 'hanging judge', more British than the British, became well known prototypes.

An uncle of ours on our mother's side of the family, who occupied the position of Home Secretary on the eve of the independence, never spoke his native language except with his own mother. His children were educated in British public schools and Cambridge, and knew England better than their own country. They could not speak their native tongue at all and all Indian customs and social graces were alien to them. My aunt, charming and wise, did her best to maintain a balance and insisted on serving Indian food when we visited, but it had to be eaten maintaining the correct hierarchy of cutlery, especially when our uncle sat down to a meal with us! He was a brilliant man, but introspection had never entered or been allowed to enter his scheme of things…perhaps he could not afford the luxury?

There was also considerable confusion about the rightness of colonial rule that clouded the minds of thinking Indians. Many educated, even eminent people felt that the British had an inalienable right to rule India, since they were a superior race of kings. Maybe their white skin had some connection with this faith in their intrinsic superiority, for ever since the Aryan and Dravidian divide, the average Indian has had this fascination for fairness, as many a young bride knows to her bitter cost even today! A scholar like Bankim Chandra Chatterjee, hugely erudite, the writer of several significant, successful novels and volumes of essays, makes his Indian Robin Hood, Bhavani Pathak, philosopher and political activist, in the novel *Devi Chaudhurani*, accept British rule cheerfully in place of the current local misrule. Bhavani even went off to the penal settlement in the Andaman Islands willingly because he saw himself as a rebel against legitimate British rule. Chatterjee, who was a Deputy Collector and a staunch pillar of British administration, must have quelled his nationalist pangs as evinced in *Ananda Math* and other writings by using similar arguments. It took a Gandhi and a bunch of fearless youngsters whom the British dubbed terrorists, to put an end to these romantic notions of the rightness of British rule.

This apart, there was the question of progress; a dubious word in any context, it proved to be an anathema for the average Indian: The story of the cartridges lubricated by pig fat and Mother Earth shackled in chains by the railway line from Pune to Thane are too well known to need reiteration, and they were essentially symptomatic of the clash of cultures. But while these superstitious objections helped to forge the solidarity that led to the First Indian War of Independence in 1857, they also brought India the status of a full-fledged colony, directly under the rule of the British Crown in the person of Queen Victoria and catalyzed the process of modernization. The East India Company's rapacious policies were replaced by British Administration with its notions of fair play and justice epitomized by the game cricket and universities modeled on Oxford and Cambridge. Missionary schools inculcated Victorian values in the progeny of the elite that found ready echoes in the parents' utterances. And since these ideas sounded so plausible, the educated and political Indian was caught between the myths of Benign British Rule and the Independent Glorious India that had never been. The colonizers had caused progress to become a revolutionary process rather than evolutionary, and change that would have come gradually, had come with a rush under colonialism, destabilizing society as a whole.

The two World Wars changed things further; brought to their knees by the Huns and then beaten hollow by the Japanese, saved only by the Americans on both occasions, the supreme arrogance of the British, their confidence about being free and white and only a step down from God himself, their sense of entitlement evaporated, leaving a huge void of self-doubt that has still not been filled. Minus the empire the average British man was left without the cornerstone of his identity. The loss of the colonies, particularly 'The Jewel in the Crown', India, only added to the chaos, and this chaos was matched by the struggle of the new Indian also in search of an identity. Kipling's

'Half devil half child' wondered whether to don the top hat or the dhoti, for neither seemed to fit, and the realization that a brand new persona needed to be minted to fit the postcolonial condition is still evolving.

I, Ronnie, who was pretty much of a 'pukka sahib', more so than Bobby or Tony perhaps because of the nature of my work, faced this struggle too and was hard put to find a suitable amalgamation. It took me a long time to reconcile the Bible and the Gita, the conflicting values of our individual traditions, the 'puri sabzi' and the 'bacon and eggs'. It took me a while to realize that the time had come to put our vaunted individualism to test: to find or forge a self that was neither Indian nor Western. A self that I could be comfortable with... However, it was easier said than done.

One fact though stood out stark and clear: To get on in life, to be materially successful one had to be modern and keep pace with the western world, and we did just that. It took people of Mukul's ilk to deal the death-blow to the tottering British Empire in India by dying themselves as terrorists. But they were quickly forgotten and only trotted out as trophies on important national holidays while the rest concentrated on personal gain. The soothsayer had foreseen it all and warned us when we stood at a historical crossroads.

Not only did the colonizers pull the colonies out of their sleepy medievalism with a wrench and compel them to cope with modernity, but they also forced us to imbibe an alien set of values. In any case, a country of divided loyalties like India, particularly Indians educated by the British, found it a Herculean task to come to workable terms with this divide. The result was that their selves were split in irreconcilable ways and they found it impossible to take a holistic stand on vital issues.

This fractured identity was the last legacy of the Raj and it is no coincidence that the struggle still continues in all colonized countries and within Great Britain herself to find a tenable sense of self.

SMALL-SPEAK

I, Small, am sitting on the tree stump, Sheila's one time favorite perch, and wondering for the umpteenth time why the gap in the hedge has refused to close. Planted over again and again by the gardeners with the thorny Duranta, hardiest of deciduous bushes in India, the seedlings had withered and died in that particular spot and the gap had remained. One time they tried with oleander, slightly poisonous, but even that refused to take and the space remained conspicuous for its incongruous emptiness, as on both sides of the gap the Duranta sported its blue flowers and orange berries with gay abandon. Gulab, the head gardener, said that there was a deep well of ground termite that they could not reach and for some reason they had chosen this spot to breed. Strangely enough, they did not spread laterally but remained localized in that one area; an interesting biological puzzle.

I spoke about it to Millie and Leila the other day, sitting in Millie's studio, cups of afternoon tea in hand and Leila came up with an interesting interpretation. She said:

'That gap was meant to be a warning to us to look beyond our cocoon of comfortable security and take cognizance of what was happening down the road, the changes and their implications, which you must admit, we chose to ignore till the trouble came upon us. After all, Sheila and Sammy sat there most often and they were the quickest to understand what was happening; and Timmy hated that gap inordinately, tried very hard to get it to close by chasing the gardeners constantly. I even remember Ronnie laughing about it and saying, "It did not warrant so much worry," but Tony backed Timmy saying he did not like it either, for it was "a breach of sorts." They were troubled by the winds of change and saw the gap as a signpost long before anything actually happened... not a coincidence, surely.'

I turned to Millie and asked for her opinion, if she had one:

Millie smiled her wry smile and said cryptically

'Surely it is too late for a postmortem? What does it matter what I thought since I was not able to do anything about it? I should have, you know, as the only female antagonist that the family boasted at that point, but Madonna's gamble paid off, for she knew that I was quite ineffective in real life because all my energies went into the life I chose to create, she even told me so...And true to type, I did put my thoughts on canvas, but I never showed it to anyone or put it up for exhibition, for it hurt too much for personal reasons. But since it is only the two of you here today, maybe you would like to take a look?'

She pointed to a painting that was lying draped in one corner of the studio, which we had never noticed, and continued:

'I too had puzzled over it for many years and I tried to make sense of this oddity – for the want of a better word – but it was what Gulab had said that seemed to make the best sense, and this is what I finally came up with:

'The painting was in rich oils on canvas, executed with bold strokes of a palette knife in shades of green, yellow and brown with touches of azure; a tree, curiously shaped like a man in the twists and turns of its bifurcated bole and branches, it was holding up a bouquet of luscious leaves and flowers to the blue sky, glimpses of which could be seen through the leaves. However, on closer inspection, one could perceive patches of termite on the stout trunk and it was clear that they had made solid headway, for some of the twigs, leaves and flowers were beginning to wither in untimely haste, in contrast to the others which were healthy and untouched yet. A creeper, strongly reminiscent of a woman of sinuous grace climbing the tree, was putting out tendrils to fight the termite but without avail, for the feelers themselves withered at their malevolent touch. Termite had also eaten away patches of vegetation at the base of the tree and a once-flowering bush had been reduced to its skeletal framework, the withered blossoms hanging in tatters. Their final victim was a jasmine bush but the flowers were shaped like eyes, human eyes over which termite crawled, avidly devouring, while the copious tears that poured from them trickled into the barren ground, unheeded…'

The silence deepened with the growing gloom that seemed to come with a rush, mercifully blotting out our faces from each other's gazes. Would anything have changed if she had showed us the painting, spoken of her fears, tried to warn us? Would we have paid heed? Or would we all, including Millie, travel down the road marked out for us, by us, inexorably impelled and without an inkling of what lay beyond the next bend?

Epilogue

I, Madonna, stand today where I had stood many years ago to hear Joy calling out to me for help and then see Sunny flying past me with his new-found knowledge about me etched in stony lines across his face…and the temptation to walk in, find that patch of quicksand and end it all, is overwhelming… If Sunny and Joy are still around, may I not be able to come face to face with them, beg their forgiveness and be united with them once more, and this time for keeps? But, as I sit down under the tree where Joy and I had our last picnic, the wind singing through the tree, the whispering leaves, the rippling water all call out to me in well-remembered and beloved voices, saying:

'…It would be too easy and atonement would be incomplete…'

Sunny always said that we must give to our children what we receive from our parents, and strangely enough, both he and I did just that. But I forgot my dear mother's and Sunny's gifts of monumental patience, endless forbearance and unimaginable love, and those are debts that remain unrequited.

My mother gave me Mukul and when I lost my chance with him, she nagged my father till he approached Sunny's parents. The wonderful match was not of his making, but as usual, he took the credit and made capital out of it.

She met Sunny and his people at the Flower Show and found Sunny tying up a twig on one of her rarer potted plants, broken during travel, with infinite care. On enquiry, he is supposed to have said:

'Ma'am, do you know that broken things, if they are helped to heal, become stronger than they were before due to their determination to be whole again? But you are a gardener, and you must be aware of this from your pruning experiences?'

When she had nodded acquiescence, he had continued:

'But I wonder whether you know that this is true of animals and human beings as well?'

Again my mother had agreed and told him about Nan, our Alsatian, who had broken one of her forepaws but had determinedly won back its strength by using it constantly, even though it was painful. But about human beings, she was not so sure...

But he had insisted:

'Human beings most of all ma'am, for they do this consciously because their spirit impels them and gives them no peace till they do; believe me, I know, but only if they are given a chance...'

He had looked into her eyes intently for a moment and turned away, but my mother was convinced that he was referring to me and so left no stone unturned till she had brought us together.

And Sunny himself, how hard had he tried to initiate and nurture the healing processes, to atone? Had taken note of every pain, every desire, particularly my obsession with a child of my own, the one thing he could not give me, and tried so hard to compensate; he had given me his beloved Joy, risked the child's life to make me feel fruitful and whole. Helped me tide over every self-created debacle and kept me safe.

But neither of them had succeeded in uprooting the poison tree planted by my Father and nurtured by me, or was it the other way around? This conviction that life owed me and that my own suffering must be paid for by another's, where had that conviction come from?

'For mine own good all causes shall give way...'

A tenet picked up in the pages of a book, to be read and forgotten, but internalized so avidly by me, why? All my siblings had read the book and been repelled by the sentiment; why had I made it my own? Was it my own fatal flaw or was it because I had watched the man I almost worshipped follow this creed to the exclusion of all else throughout his life?

Love – my Mother's, Mukul's, Leila's, Sunny's and Small's – I repaid with selfishness and bitterness, thought only of my own losses and miseries, till now there is no one left who wants to be loved by me, no one who is not afraid, not even Small. I remember so vividly the incident when the children had come on their first visit to the estate and how they had almost succumbed to the same treacherous quicksand... but they had survived because of Sunny, ever vigilant, protecting not only them, but mainly me from myself, as always. In the end, he was the only one who never gave up on me...

But the debt of love must be paid and I must return to my 'Joys' of today and give them the love I failed to give 'My Joy, Sunny's Joy'. And only when the tally is done, my hair covered in frost, my face marked with lines of expiation, my body bent with the load of remorse, am I certain that Sunny and Joy themselves will show me the way to their abode of compassion, for in their own suffering they have appreciated mine.

As I turn around and walk slowly towards my adopted and last home with Josh and Bunny, Sunny's people, not mine, I look back once, and there, etched clearly against the sky are the serene faces of father and son marked only by a terrible pity as they watch me take the next bend down the road I have created for myself.

Nonda Chatterjee

About the Author

Nonda Chatterjee, a much loved and widely respected educator, was born in Calcutta in 1938 and passed away in the city of her birth on 24th October, 2012. She spent most of her long and distinguished teaching career at *The Calcutta International School* where she served both as a teacher of English and history, and as Principal. She also served as the Principal of The Cambridge School, Kolkata. In 2006 she received 'The Cambridge University Inspirational Teacher Award', a distinction granted for the first time in India. Chatterjee subsequently received The Telegraph Award for 'Lifetime Achievement as a Teacher'.

Although Chatterjee started her literary career at the age of sixty-five, she was incredibly versatile and productive. She wrote novels, short stories, and poems and translated Bengali works of literature into English and Hindi. She contributed short stories and articles to *The Statesman* and *The Sakaal Times,* among other journals and periodicals.

Her poems have been published on various platforms, including the journal, *Indian Literature*. She has to her credit a collection of short stories, *The Strawberry Patch* (Penguin, 2004), and a novel, *Half a Face* (Niyogi Books, 2010). Her graphic novel for children, *The Old Man Who Would not Listen* was published after her demise (Katha, 2013) as was her translation of Abanindranath Thakur's masterpiece, *Thumbkin* (Ponytale Books, 2013).

www.ingramcontent.com/pod-product-compliance
Lightning Source LLC
Chambersburg PA
CBHW051934240626
47153CB00005B/1481